Blood Reign

lp rothrock

Other books in this series
Reign Fall (Book 1)
Reign Storm (Book 3)

Jacket design by Rocko Bishop and Lea Rothrock
Element designs: blood by Giveaway Ongoing/KindPNG; knife found at HiClipart; stone wall by ID 158240562 Tatyana Azarova/Dreamstime.com; filigree by pikisuperstar/Freepik

ISBN: 979-8-9933184-2-4

For Kimball
With all my love

Blood Reign

Prologue

A long time ago, in an alternate timeline...

Tenn trailed along at the end of the line: the last man, the gate behind the livestock, the watching-your-backs-man. *Always available!* At least for the next half hour or so.

The line of weaving monk heads led down the steps, turning at the bottom to go through the dim cloakroom toward the light. From his vantage point on the stairs, it was all skin and robes rocking back and forth and back and forth below him. Hushed feet shuffled like leaves as they glided to the end in more ways than one.

Cool light filtered down into the great room from the full moon. Tenn watched their faces as they passed through the archway—some uncertain, some frowns, a few smiles. How would it feel to know you were about to disappear?

He was glad he wasn't going.

Servant, as leader, stood to the right of the door, greeting everyone who passed in that calm, happy-monkish way of his. He had a young face, but Tenn was sure he was eons older than he looked. Crossing in front of the smiling, nodding man, he felt a clap on the shoulder. Tenn patted the warm hand; he'd miss the guy.

As he passed through the arch, the last and least, the monks were making semi-circle rows in front of the fireplace. Tenn made his way to the other side while Servant moved to the front. Behind him, the massive stone hearth stood cold and empty, reminding Tenn that none of this was normal.

"*Pons n'i*," the young leader addressed the group as they settled. Tenn knew that meant "Brothers," but his grasp of the ancient language was flimsy, so he was glad when Servant continued in the common tongue. "If there's anything you want to say about leaving, you should say it now." His bald head nodded to emphasize his point. "Just because I tell you I've been warned about the enemy doesn't mean you have to believe it."

The group was silent, facing him. A bit eerie, Tenn thought, with their pale heads and gray robes, in this gray room washed in cool light—they looked dead. Not the best look for anyone, but then, they wouldn't look like anything in a few minutes.

"I have something to say," a voice spoke from across the room. The speaker jostled forward through the crowd and stood in front, facing Servant. He was a big man, tall. Tenn knew him only slightly—his name was Jase, one of the inventors. The inventors mostly holed up in the west wing and caused loud, questionable noises, so he didn't mingle much with them. "I would like to stay in body," the monk said. "I'd like to offer myself in service to the Royal Family."

So, the rumors were true. Somebody was staying here, on duty, helping the Royals, holding the monks' presence here and marking time until the evil reared its ugly head. That could be next week, or it could be centuries from now, in which case wouldn't the caretaker need to change out periodically? Just so it didn't look terribly suspicious?

Not his concern. Somebody needed to take the job, and Jase was a good first candidate.

"And I'd like to have permission to produce a bloodline of my own," he said.

For a few seconds no one breathed, then one guy choked on his own inhale and the violent coughing that ensued unfroze everyone. They looked around at each other: murmurs bubbled, heads shook, disapproving looks flew, and they all turned to Servant to see what he would say.

"I think that's a great idea," the young monk said, shocking everyone. "Thank you, Jase, for taking the first watch. Anything else?" He scanned the assembled. Tenn glanced around at their faces and had to bite off the laugh that nearly jumped out. All around him mouths hung open, eyes bulged, and jaws flapped without a sound.

One of them finally found his croak. "Servant…" A monk named Botharos stepped forward. "It says in our book that we are not to…breed." This time Tenn's laugh escaped, and he had to pretend to cough and clear his throat while they all looked at him. He thumped his chest with his fist, nodded and held his hand up, signaling he was all right. *Uh huh, just a little chicken bone.*

"Granted," Servant replied, "but we have to leave the book here, and someone will have to learn how to read it. The ability to do that will need to be passed down in a bloodline, and Jase would seem like a good choice."

A mumble wave swept around the room. Tenn couldn't tell whether the tone was outrage or admiration. Maybe some of both.

"Have you seen this need?" Botharos frowned.

"What I've seen is that the caretaker isn't allowed to interfere with the events of the kingdom, unless authorized to do so." Another wave, louder. "Therefore," his voice raised to be heard, "since we can't guarantee the caretaker will be able to use the book, we'll need someone who can. A bloodline would mean problem solved, and technically, the book says we are 'not to indulge our carnal desires.' As I see it, this is a completely different thing."

The leader ignored the muttered comments that followed, and turned to the fireplace behind him. Out of his belt he produced a small book, its pages cut from the pink stones the monks used for so many things. Tenn touched his pocket; apparently those stones were powerful, because his two lightning weapons, given to him as the Master Protector, were made from them, too.

A grating sound of stone on stone drew Tenn's attention to the floor. One of the carved panels of the mantel, the one on the bottom with the spiral of symbols, was turned out to reveal a hollow middle. Servant was kneeling by it; he put the book inside the hollow and turned the brick back into place. The symbols played a little tune as he pressed a pattern with his fingertips. The spiral repeated the tune, tightened a half turn, and locked the brick.

Servant turned back to the collection of monks, his expression pleasant and reassuring. "Is everyone ready?" Tenn studied the crowd, watched them shift and murmur. No, not everyone was ready; some of them gazed longingly out the windows, toward the gardens, and the mountains, and the great old forest. They had a good life here.

Slowly, though, they all moved to face the same direction, toward the path the wall of light would be coming. "Tenn?" Servant called, searching the turning bodies for his Protector, smiling when Tenn walked up to him. "It's time for you to leave us." Servant held his hand out. "Thank you for your years of service."

"It's been my honor, sir." Tenn shook his hand. "Be careful out there."

Servant laughed and patted his arm. "Same to you, my friend." He leaned close and whispered, "If I were you, I'd stay a good thirty feet away from the hole."

Of course the young seer would know he was going to the hole. And he wasn't scolding him, or talking him out of it, or reminding him of his duty to the royal family, so maybe that meant there was possibly even a pretty sizable chance of success. Instead of none. He didn't want to be stupid, but if there was any chance at all he could nip the evil invader problem in the bud, well, that was worth trying for.

Tenn clasped Servant's arm and didn't answer. Instead, he met Jase at the front of the group and bowed to the departing monks in farewell. Kind of sad, now that it was right down to it. Okay, it was really sad. He searched for the faces he knew best: the round-cheeked Chares, who liked to cook and made the best meat pies; Phenlo and Barc, the comedians; Harbin, always so generous with his healing arts. He'd miss them. He'd miss all of them, and the world would too, even if it didn't know it yet.

When he turned to go, he smacked his face into Jase's chest. The big monk looked down at him, eyes laughing, and he raised the eyebrow the others couldn't see. *So, this is the guy starting a bloodline.* Tenn suppressed a grin and waved the monk ahead, following the maverick progenitor down the short back hall and out through the kitchen.

Outside, the two men didn't look at each other when the bright light flared behind them for a few moments. They kept their eyes on their shadow selves, sliding across the uneven ground until the light faded and they disappeared with it.

The moment felt huge, like the whole world had moved through a doorway, and the door closed behind it. And only the two of them knew.

At the edge of the forest, Jase stopped him. The tall monk set his bag down and turned to face Tenn. "Keep the contact point inside the hole, *not* at the edges. If you hit the edge, it could make the hole bigger. When you use the energy weapons, the quality of your source energy matters. Courage and determination are good. Panic and terror are bad. The first should repel whatever's in there, the second will feed it."

Tenn frowned. "Oh good, I was afraid this might be hard."

"Are you taking anyone with you?"

"No, I've already released the others from their duty. I didn't think there would be strength in numbers." More like multiplying the risk.

Jase squinted at him for a long few moments. "I could sure use you at the palace," he said. Tenn knew he wanted him to go with him, protect the royal bloodline and all that. Start one of his own, maybe?

"I wish I could, big guy. I'd love to come with you, and I know Servant wants me to, but the possibility of stopping a maniacally evil second-dimension shitbag from sucking the life out of our world is too tempting. Even if I fail miserably, I have to try." *Try* being the operative word. He wished he had a better plan, but it wouldn't be the first time he put his instincts to the test…and actually they were pretty good.

Jase was still squinting. What more could Tenn say? "But I tell you what, if I survive, I'll be there." He tried to sound reassuring, but he had no idea what he was going up against, and a vague promise was the best he could do. Jase thought a second, nodded, and the two men clasped hands and parted to go their separate ways.

Tuesday

The present

Chapter T.1

Heart pounding, Thorn peeked around the corner of the building and checked the street for the night patrol. They were off schedule. Lollygagging, his father would have said. The drainage grate had slipped out of Thorn's fingers, clanged into place, and the guards had seen him scurry into the dark alley. He'd hidden in a pile of knocked-over trash bins and old food containers, trying not to breathe. Lucky for him, coming after him was too much trouble, and they'd dismissed him as being a cat.

The street was clear now, though, so he tucked his bundle under his left elbow and stepped out onto the cobblestones. A cold wind funneled between the buildings, whipping his cloak open and freezing his face inside his hood. He clutched at the cloak's edges and pulled the heavy wool back around him as he turned and hurried toward the plaza.

A block ahead, the ever-changing lights of the holo-ads threw patches of color onto the buildings framing the town center. The effect was garish on the stately brick, and Thorn felt sorry for them, even if they were just buildings. They were *old* buildings, and their pull-shade windows made them look tired.

He knew how they felt.

As Thorn neared the big open space, raucous laughter slapped the air and voices raised. Ducking left, he put his back to the rough brick, and edged forward just enough to peek. The flashing light from a beer commercial showed the patrol sitting on the cover of the old well, smoking and talking.

"I don't care what he says." The tip of a cigarette glowed for a few seconds, and a quick suck of air followed. "We ain't gotta do no

"

cleaning for no other army." Exhale. "They can clean their own shitty stuff."

"Right, and you gonna tell him that?"

"I will if he asks me!" (*general laughter and taunting*)

"Like the Overlord's gonna talk to some shit-for-brains pee-on in a patrol!"

"Ask him for his opinion on work detail." (*more laughter, with derision*)

Thorn eased back along the wall, into the deeper shadow. He'd have to wait until they left, but it wouldn't be long. At least Dagge had them on a regular schedule these days. A year ago, the rounds were random, and soldiers caught a lot of people committing all the new crimes, like trying to leave the country. But after thinning so much of the population, the Overlord got lazy, and patrols settled into a routine.

In recent months, the only law-breaking had been the increasing acts of sabotage and civil disobedience. So far, they were just his own, but someday it was bound to catch on. Did Dagge even know about his one-man rebellion? Well, if he didn't, he would after tonight. Thorn patted his bundle affectionately and pulled out his stopclock. It generally took twelve minutes for the soldiers to make one round, but they were taking too much time here, so they'd probably speed up once they left. Ugh, they were cutting into his window.

In a couple of minutes, the sound for the holo-ads would come back on. Dagge had insisted on night silence as one of the concessions the nobles had had to make to put their projectors up. Now, even with the nobles gone, the ads were still playing—the same ads for the same products. Still, more than once Thorn had wished he could turn the sound on. His work would be a lot easier with more obnoxious babble to cover his noise.

The voices in the plaza began to fade, echoing off the buildings on the other side as the men continued on their patrol. Thorn hurried to the open space, glancing left and right for anything unexpected, and like clockwork, the overexcited voice above trumpeted the virtues of Great Hand tonker paper—the ad that pissed his wife off the most.

It was perfect for the moment, though, and John Treslo hoisted the bundle he carried up into his hands and ran to the edge of the well. The well wall was three feet high, so he set his bundle on the cover and rolled his body over next to it. Eyes sharp, he unwrapped the bundle, pulled Joey's pipe flute out of his pocket, adjusted its configuration, and got ready to play.

No shouts, no running, no shots. Good.

Chapter T.2

Under Hellen's feet, the crunch crunch of the snow seemed loud in the predawn hush. Nothing she could do about it. She walked as softly and carefully as humanly possible across the unpredictable ground. At least the big fat flakes weren't falling anymore, and the white brightened the forest floor enough so the moon could help her see. *Which is fabulous*, Hellen thought, *because a bulb torch would be suicide.*

This morning's errand had her taking the last bundle of fire rods to the rock giants so she wouldn't have to do everything on Saturday. Hopefully, they wouldn't figure out some way to light them and have their own little show before then. She never knew with these guys. If they were any indication, the twelfth dimension had to be the comedy dimension. *Welcome, ladies and sediment!*

She shook her head to stop the endless broadcast. The circle wasn't far now, and she needed to pay attention. No room in her world to take safety for granted anymore.

Hellen gathered her dark gray cloak into a slim casing and walked quickly through the trees, dissolving into the shadows, her senses on high alert. This close to the border, she might run into one of Dagge's patrols, or even a group of Pulari's men, and they could certainly kill her before the forest got them.

The monks never said this would be easy. In fact, whenever she ran into one of their glowy selves in the forest, they always seemed sort of…overly sympathetic. It made her wonder how much worse things were going to get. They weren't telling her, either, no matter how much she asked.

As she got closer, the trees thinned out a bit, and the big rocks came into view. An open stretch buffered their circle from the rest of the forest, leaving their hulking backs looming in the moonlight, all hard granite and black shadows. Hellen noted the irony every time she saw them—they should've been made of chewing gum or pretzels.

At the edge of the clearing, she scanned the area for movement or glints of gunmetal before she had to make the run. Night glasses would be really handy, but she hadn't been able to get any yet. She and John had nicked a few things here and there, but it was only thanks to Diit still living in the palace that she had managed to get a gun and a decent uniform.

Deciding she was alone, Hellen ran across the small open space to the edge of the rock circle and ducked into a crevice. No shots, no arrows, no shouting or running. Relieved, she squeezed her way between two of the giants' big butts.

Inside the circle, she dropped the bundle of fire rods off her back and threaded her way around the boulder knees and feet, being careful not to kick any rock toes. (She did that once and never heard the end of it. Flathead still gave her grief.) Nine strides to the middle of the space, and she stood at the edge of the small pool and waited for the comedians to show up.

It wasn't long. She spun in a slow circle to watch for signs of life. The boulders around her rose eighteen feet or more, so it was hard to see heads, but they were up there, she knew. Just hanging around waiting to wake up and harass her. Finally, she saw a face had moved forward and was gazing down.

"It's the human," it announced in a voice like infinite sand.

"Which human?" another one quipped drily. "We've been getting so many lately."

Hellen figured he wasn't kidding. She shifted her eyes to watch the big guy come to life, which he did, stretching and rolling his parts in a darn good impersonation of a body. Big arms separated from his sides and reached into the air, his lumpy legs straightened in front of him and he wiggled his toes. Basically, he was a bunch of rocks held together by an invisible force—a twelfth-dimensional...something.

A group of them, in fact, who she guessed had nothing better to do than hang out in rocks on the 3D side of the tracks. They probably felt really superior here, but back home in the 12D, they were the guys who sat around and drank beer and watched sports. If they had that sort of thing there.

Kidding aside, though, she knew what they were doing here, in this forest, and it wasn't because one of them caused a nuclear meltdown in their dimension and they all came here to hide, like Flathead said. The monks told her and John the real reason when the two of them first found the monastery all those eighteen months ago, and the truth was a lot scarier than Flathead's story.

Somewhere in this circle there was a hole in the air, a tear, ripped by a very dark being from the second dimension. Said dark being apparently had a voracious appetite. It wanted to feed on this world. Energy cubed. A superpowered high for the depth-impaired. Fun, fun, fun.

Problem was, it couldn't survive here in its 2D form, it had to have a host body. The first attempt at getting one failed, and that was when the monks recruited the rock giants to guard the passage. Eventually the entity gave up waiting, choosing instead to be born in a 3D body to get what it wanted. Someday it would show up in Great Hand, the monks said, because there was some kind of energy fulcrum here. Oh boy.

In the meantime, any 2D entity with sufficient power could get out through this handy hole, provided it could grab a host. And not only that, the hole itself was dangerous, so the threat was never-ending.

Why the monks chose a bunch of jokers for an important job like guarding a dimensional tear she would never know, but she had to admit that even with all their b.s. they were reliable. As many times as she'd been here, she never once saw the hole, and when she asked they'd feigned ignorance. It reassured her to know that as long as the rock giants contained the tear, nothing could get through.

And when an enemy invaded the forest, they took care of it. In spite of what the rocks said—that they were planning an invasion, or harvesting slaves, or they were really trolls from the seventh level of hell—as far as removing threats went, she had to be thankful for them. Maybe they were honestly good guys.

"Have you had a lot of visitors?" she asked.

More boulders flew around as the rest of the giants repositioned themselves. A low, gravelly answer drifted her way. "More from the other side of the river, Pulari's men," Browbone rumbled, his rock ledge lowering on his face. He was the serious one, and Hellen took him seriously.

"Any threats?"

"Definitely," Duncecap said, "they're giving me indigestion."

Hellen wasn't entirely sure he was joking. She didn't know exactly what happened to the humans who disappeared here; maybe snacks were the reward for guard duty. Maybe the rockheads genuinely liked this place because they thought it was a good vacation destination, what with all the yummy food and entertainment, and they spent their time just hanging around the 12D door waiting for some of it to show up.

"We're grateful for the protection," she said.

"Who says we're protecting you?" Flathead shot back. "Personally, I'm here for the climate."

"I like the view."

"I'm looking for a wife. Are you available?" Egghead snickered, and the group chuckled like a small avalanche. Jerks.

Okay, fine, they didn't have to tell her their secrets, but she did have another sort of question. "Has Dagge stopped patrols then?" Patrols never made it back to the palace, according to Diit, but that didn't mean the boss wouldn't keep trying. And one of these days, a patrol might not find the rock giants, and find the monastery, and that would be the end of the Resistance.

"What, are we mind readers now?"

"How are we supposed to know what old sick-and-twisted's planning?"

"That's *Mr*. Old Sick-and-Twisted to you."

"Ah, eat this, *Mr.* bird poop." Flakygut patted the general area of his rump.

"You'd know all about bird poop, except you can't see the top of your head."

"I wouldn't be talking with what you got running down your chin!"

"Guys, I have indigestion already, okay?"

Hellen rolled her eyes; wasn't the twelfth dimension supposed to be more advanced or something? If these guys were what it was like, she hoped she never went there. "oKAY," she interrupted the clever repartee, "can you at least tell me if it's been a while since you've seen one?"

"It's been a while," Browbone said. "Hard to say how long."

"Could be another one any day."

"I don't really want to eat another one."

"Shut up, idiot," Browbone raised his enormous fist, and Duncecap gave a short laugh.

"What, you don't want the little lady to know what really goes on?"

Browbone ignored him and turned back to Hellen. "We'll keep an eye out, okay? Maybe a couple of us can do a little patrolling of our own.

"You can do that?" Hellen was flummoxed. "You can walk around by yourselves?"

"We have a certain amount of energy we bring with us." Egghead sounded very eggheadish. "We just have to be careful not to run out."

"What would happen?"

"We'd be rock here forever."

There was an uncharacteristic moment of silence, during which she guessed not one of them could think of a smart remark. But it only lasted a moment.

"I hope I'm sitting down."

"Aw, gee, what are the chances of that? Have you even been up in the last year and a half?"

"I don't want to be sitting down. I think with my last vibration I'm going to throw myself out of the forest, so the humans can all look at the mysterious new boulders and wonder where they came from."

"Hey, I like that idea. I'll go you one better. What say a couple of us make a formation on the open land? That'll really mess with their heads!"

Hellen rolled her eyes again and walked out of the circle, ignoring the catcalls behind her. It would be so much easier if she had a regular army.

Chapter T.3

Dagge leaned against the balcony and opened his arms and lungs to the cold gusts of air parrying around the castle. He breathed them in and whooshed them out, and when they snipped at his hair and bit his cheekbones, it was the most alive he'd felt in days. Kind of pathetic, really. His life was way too soft.

He opened his eyes and gazed into the blackness across the meadow for some hint of light in the creepy old forest, some mysterious thing he could maybe jump on his horse and ride down, or at least try to. Like in the old days, when he first had to get past the fear and act like he belonged on the throne.

Those were hard days, full of lots of new things, and many of them, like bringing the nobles around, were more satisfying than the trips into the forest. But the forest chases, even though they were always a breathless fail, were more and more fun every trip. Sadly, there hadn't been lights over there for a long time; not since the first couple of months.

So much for the decaying gas theory. And the poacher theory. His own theory was far more sinister, and if the disappearance of border patrols was any indication, it was a lot closer to being right. Screw the skeptics.

Having enough of the cold, he turned and went back into the sitting room. Home sweet home. It was his now, with his own odd assortment of stuff on the shelves, and the furniture where he wanted it, plus the addition of a few new items he liked from around the palace: a warrior statue from the museum, a giant gilded vase, an ornate mirror, among other things. But even without a lot of the books, and the cheesy kid art, and the tall man at the desk, it was still that old room, and that was the best part. Possessing that piece of space somehow made him feel stronger, like he'd ripped out Ol' Kingy's heart and eaten it whole.

Past the two big columns, and the sofa, Dagge made his way to the desk and pulled the chair out. Sitting on the hard cushion, he yanked open the deep drawer and lifted out the shiny dish and small dome of his harkener. He'd caught more than one traitor whispering inside these walls. A little death taught them he was eavesdropping, though, so he guessed if there were any balls left, they were using sign language or something.

However, it was best to keep tabs.

Dagge trained the receiver in a hundred-and-eighty-degree sweep across the palace. Nothing. Same old same old. Disappointed, he laid the pieces on the desk, leaned back in the chair and put his feet up. Good to know that he was in control, anyway.

The nobles' deaths had been nearly as satisfying as the King's. At first the arrogant prissy-men thought they'd stand up to him, which was actually kind of comical, but they learned pretty quick. Death's a great teacher, especially when it involves heirs, and Dagge told them he'd like to spare some of their whining brats, but he didn't mean it. So when some of the rich puke-buckets were too slow to swear him allegiance, he had to cut right to the heart of it and eliminate the bloodline. As a consequence, in the process of establishing his rule, Dagge acquired a lot of property real fast. And when he had more property than any of the rest of them, he decided the title of Overlord was fitting: better than Lord, better than King, better than anything. Wouldn't it be nice if he could rub that asshole Camberton's face in it?

Then the plots against him started, starring the prissy-men who were too chicken to defy him openly, and too bad for them they didn't know who they were dealing with, because a lot of people died again, and some of them were probably innocent.

He thought about it sometimes, and it unsettled him. Not because he slaughtered so many, no, that was easy; he worried because every one of his enemies' deaths fed his appetite instead of sating it, fed some beast that grew until what was left of Tomius Dagge—the boy he was, and the lover and the man—was like a ghost in there, intact but pale, and not very bothersome.

Still felt him, though, when he thought of Hellen. He never said it out loud, but he was convinced she survived the explosion in the stable. The princess almost certainly died. He saw her, right there, smack dab in front of the barrel before it exploded, and who could survive that? If she wasn't dead, she was so destroyed she was as good as, so he declared her dead. Better for him that way.

But Hellen was a different matter. She wasn't right there, so she had to be farther away, more protected, and they would have found her remains if she'd died. Only some of the horses died, and she had just as good a chance as they did, if they were blocking her.

So even though he officially declared her dead, he was happy to believe she lived, even if she was trying to mount some ridiculous rebellion. It would be easy to forgive her taking on this "Thorn" persona and bulldogging these clever little missions, because she did have a vendetta, and the gifts to pursue it. Really, he wouldn't have expected any less.

Still, he was going to have to stop her. Oppression didn't work so well when some smartass was pulling pranks and making you look ridiculous. The crackdown in the mines hadn't stopped it, which he thought it would, or the increased troops, or the strict curfew. In fact, it was increasing and in danger of becoming a serious player in this situation. If it spread, it could infect the town like a virus.

When he got her, and he would, there'd have to be some kind of punishment...just nothing damaging. After all, defying curfew and pulling off minor acts of civil disobedience wasn't necessarily a death sentence. Not for her.

What was the point of all the insubordination anyway? If she thought she could pull people out of their fear, she was going to be disappointed. He'd made sure of that. It only took a couple of weeks, then the growing numbers of staked bodies around the well had done their job, and he could feel the fear in the very air. Now all that was left was a quiet, uncomplaining work force for the mine, walking with eyes down and not a foot out of place. Did she think she could stir the livestock into an army?

Dagge yanked his feet off the desk and leaned up to examine the map of the kingdom mounted on the wall over it. Clustered in the town proper, the "Thorn" incidents were marked with little pink flags—pink partly for her, and partly because red would give it too much importance. The idea was to see if the activity had a pattern, because if he could anticipate her, he could catch her, but after studying the map exhaustively, there didn't seem to be one.

Well, if he couldn't anticipate her, maybe he could hear her. He grabbed the two halves of the harkener and tucked them under his arm. With one mighty thrust, he propelled himself out of the chair, swept his cloak up off the sofa and strode out the door.

Time to go for a ride.

Chapter T.4

Screams floated up to her, echoing through the doorway and up the hall . . . . . . long, desperate fingers of them, high and breathless and inhuman with pain. They stopped, trailed off…a murmuring of voices, but she couldn't hear what they were saying. Two voices, something stolen. Then the screams started again.

The dungeon door was open, but she couldn't bring herself to go through. Whatever was below, she didn't want to see. But the fingers had their own plans, they wanted her, they insisted, they wrapped around her throat and pulled.

One by one she eased down the stone steps, eyes transfixed by the man hanging suspended in the air high above the dirt floor. His hands were tied together over his head, attached to a rope that came down from a pulley in the ceiling. The rest of his body dangled, cross-hatched with cuts, painted in gruesome colors of black and blood and purple bruises.

She couldn't see his face. His body swung and turned from his struggles to get away, he threw his head back and sucked in long, ragged breaths, coughing them out again feebly. Smoke was rising off his burned body. A grey ponytail hung down his back.

Stopped on the stair, she stood level with John Treslo, who hung maybe thirty feet away from her. But she couldn't help him. She couldn't do anything, because when she turned to look for the torturer, her whole world was suddenly the black dragon crouching at the end of the stairs.

Its head weaved and bobbed, hypnotizing. Its tail thrashed in small whips across its hindquarters. Scales glistened over taut muscles, and the flare of horns around its head and jaws were ferocious. It opened its mouth and hissed, and John jerked and kicked before the stream of flame hit him.

She screamed, stopping the flames and drawing the dragon's attention to her. He turned his big head and narrowed his eyes, and his look was like an ice pick, right into her, piercing her with a cold dread. Horrified, she watched his hissing mouth open in slow motion, and she couldn't move, couldn't run, she could only watch in horror as the fire came for her.

Adia struggled up to consciousness, fighting for the surface, arms flailing and legs kicking, finally coming awake when she pitched off the bed and hit the floor behind her. *Ow*. Her hip was still tender from the last time. She had to stop doing this. Why couldn't she have nightmares like normal people, and wake up screaming?

Still, she'd rather be on the hard floor with a bruised ass than in that dungeon.

Exhausted and out of breath, she dragged her coping skills out, checked her surroundings, and discovered she was by the wall at the head of the bed, on the left side. The brazier was over here, she could feel the bare warmth of it on her face.

Reaching up with both hands, she pulled herself off the cold floor and sat on the edge of the bed…if you could call a packet of straw on a stone block a bed. From the depths of her mind, she could hear Hellen's voice chastising her, and she knew it was pointless to argue. *Okay, it's a mattress, and a mattress makes a bed.*

She hated it when days started like this—all cold, and hard, and rude. Her real bed floated in her mind like a fantasy, with its soft green silk and fluffy pillows. The universe had been painted on her ceiling, and she used to gaze up at it and imagine traveling through the stars.

But she couldn't think about that. Even the simple memories were off limits these days—food, hot showers, infinite tonker paper.

Her covers must have fallen to the floor somewhere—she'd have to search for them, but she wanted to think about the dream first. There wasn't any reason she should be dreaming about John Treslo, she hadn't seen him in months. (*Seen him. Ho ho ho.*) The last time was when Hellen was making her learn the layout of the monastery, and she had just barked her shin on the corner of the bench in the great room downstairs. John, funny guy that he was, said he didn't know princesses knew words like that. The stream she let loose then probably curled his hair. Too bad she couldn't see it.

But the dream definitely wasn't funny. John's screams still echoed in her mind, wrenching her heart. His suffering was very real. It could happen, she knew, he could be tortured if he was caught. No, strike that—he would definitely be tortured if he was caught. You don't cause as much trouble as John Treslo had and get off with something as easy as death.

Was the dragon Dagge? The most likely answer for a true dream, but these days she always had to take into account the whole fire thing, so it might just be one of those clever ways the brain makes you live stuff over and over. Thanks so much.

Where was Hellen? It was cold, the brazier was pretty much out, and she hadn't quite graduated to lighting fires. "Hellen!" she called and waited for an answer. Sometimes Ms. Self-Appointed Coach liked to make Adia wait, no doubt hoping she'd get tired of it and do whatever it was herself. Maybe it would get her attention if Adia set the mattress on fire, but then Hellen would probably just make her sleep on it until she had time to make another.

Not that Adia could blame her. Thankless job, handmaid to a ghost. Can't exactly ask someone to babysit.

It was creepy, but sometimes she wondered if she was really dead. She might as well be, right? Almost no one knew she existed. And by the way, why should she be glad she survived again? Because of all the great life she had now?

Self-loathing licked her insides. She should have saved her father. Maybe if she had run screaming into his room, leapt onto the bed, and tackled Dagge off of it, her dad would have been able to get up, the servants would have come running, and none of the rest of the bullshit would have happened.

Her throat closed on her for a moment, and she held her breath until she could swallow through it. Down it went, again, the turgid grief and rage that sickened her. She wanted to throw things, but better not to do that, either. It sucked having to clean it up, because Hellen wasn't doing that anymore.

So she breathed instead. And she'd wait for Hellen. Again. Just like she'd done ever since the first time she woke up in this hells hole.

She'd had no clue where she was, or what happened, or why she felt so heavy, like there was a lead blanket on her even though the sheet only came up to her hips. She found out later Diit was bringing in honey, and Hellen was pouring it on her, and it was so sticky, and got everywhere, that Hellen had to keep buckets of water in the room just to contain it.

And the flies came from miles around, buzzing, crawling all over her, getting stuck and biting. Yeah, it was a horror, but even that wasn't as bad as the pain. Diit brought all the pain relievers he could get, but it didn't come close. During the worst, when her tears soaked the pillow, he and Hellen would carry her out to the waterfall and put her in the pool. That was the best. Then it got cold, and she healed, and now Hellen was too busy to take her.

Okay, so it was a hassle for Hellen to have to do so much for her, and maybe she was acting spoiled, but the woman ought to try getting burned blind.

Chapter T.5

The blue balloon looked a little odd floating upside down, but if someone saw it, Thorn doubted they'd be able to put a finger on why. Anyway, the hope was to get the blasted thing up atop the granite slab before anyone else could even get a glimpse. Forty-eight monks would sure help, too bad those guys weren't still around.

Tricky as it was, he did his best to maintain the music even with needing to breathe. He'd made a little balloon bladder, but it leaked, and between the yammering ads and him trying not to be too loud, it was a miracle the thing floated at all. But bless the colossal irritations blaring in the sky. Those commercials had masked more than one little excursion in town.

The balloon rose unsteadily up the dark face of the monolith, obscuring the new Patriotic Laws one after another until it reached the top and settled on the flat. Lying on his back at the base, Thorn pocketed the pipe flute and smiled. Easy to guess what would happen when the balloon was spotted.

In the next lull between commercials, there came a faint noise like the squeak of leather followed by the scrape of boot on stone. Thorn's senses pricked and his head came up. He stopped breathing, slowed his heartbeat and became night—that was the theory anyway, and why couldn't Hellen tell him something normal? Damn. Nothing happened but the next ad, for *Halabate! One pill a day gets rid of bad breath forever!*

Getting caught would mean torture, torture, and death.

Better gone than dead, so he grabbed up the bundle fabric, rolled nimbly off the well, and squatted in the shifting shadows beside it. The sound wasn't a patrol, they made noise, but Dagge had spies, too. If someone was watching, Thorn would have to try and lose them in the buildings. Most of the shops were empty, and there were ways to get around.

At least that's what he told his pounding heart as he vaulted out of the shadows and toward the cover cast by the south side trees. His plan was to veer around the buildings on the west and cut through the alleys. He knew how to move; Hellen had taught him a few things about getting around on the run, in the dark.

The biggest problem was that he didn't know his enemy. Had to assume it was hostile. Rounding the first tree, he stopped and listened for a moment. No running feet, no calls or whistles. Maybe they hadn't seen him yet. He dashed through the next few trees on his way to the corner of the old print shop, where he stopped and listened again. Still nothing.

At the back end of the building, he cut right, into the alleyway behind. Stop. Listen. Nothing. Now he felt a little silly. He glanced down the long stone passageway, but couldn't see around the convex curve. High risk. His other choices were to continue down the open road, or maybe he could *dash across the big empty field toward the palace*, his inner sarcastic-self suggested. Better to risk the alley. He turned north at a light quick pace.

No sound but his own feet. Before he came out on the next block, he slowed, checked the road, saw it was empty, slipped left around the corner…and came face to face with a horse.

The horse jerked its head back, but didn't make a sound. Thorn knew immediately whose horse it was. His heart jolted into his throat, and he scrambled for the relative cover of the alley behind.

Where was Dagge? Holy crap, he knew Thorn was out here. No, he knew someone was out here, but he didn't know who. *Pull yourself together, John.* It could be anyone in a cloak…floating a balloon up to the top of the Patriotic Laws. *Yeah, anyone.*

Thorn hustled back through the alley, around the curve, and realized he'd been trapped. The other end teased him when it came into sight, pretending to be open and safe, but how likely was that, really? Of course Dagge would be at this end—he put the horse at the other end to scare Thorn and make him come back here. John kicked himself. The only chance he had was to turn around.

John stopped, thinking he should turn around, but Dagge would've known Thorn would do this, second guess, and he was probably waiting for him at the other end now, standing across from his quietly smirking horse.

Maybe he was overthinking this, but how was he supposed to know which it was?

His best chance would be to wait until he heard footsteps coming after him, then he'd know which way to run.

It wasn't five seconds before a quiet scraping sound gave away the feet on the gravel. Coming from the horse end, he knew it. He slipped quietly back to the first entrance, stretching his long legs to get the most of it, and it wasn't until he was close that he saw the shadow move at the opening.

He froze, not sure what to do. He'd made a serious mistake; it never occurred to him that Dagge might not be alone.

His brain shifted into a lower gear. What would Hellen do? She'd have her knife out already, he knew that.

Screw it. If he was fast enough, he wouldn't have to fight. But he wouldn't want to try to outrun a horse, so John was just about to make a run for the south end (maybe he could lose himself in the forest) when the ground opened up under him and he dropped twelve feet of cardiac arrest. His knees buckled under him when he hit, and he rolled off to the side of a pile of... old bedsheets or something. It was dark, but up the way he just came he could hear the smooth heavy slide of the trapdoor brace.

A hand pressed itself over his mouth, gentle but firm, and John found himself nodding, *Yes, of course we need to be quiet.* The hand lifted off his mouth and pressed on his shoulder, *Stay still.* Above his head, a faint pock pock of running feet waved in from the left and faded out to the right.

Silence. They waited a full minute, listening, while John tried very hard not to breathe loudly. Finally, someone turned a light on.

Beau Hodges, the blacksmith, stood above him, smiling, taking off a pair of night glasses. It was his hardworking hand that had been over John's mouth. Next to him, one of the merchants, a woodcarver he thought, and beside him Chief Taymer with the lamp. Around and behind him a woman climbed down out of the chute. He'd seen her before. She was the Plant Lady. Roberta quoted her, usually after buying some exotic specimen to put in the yard.

Chief had his finger to his lips, nodding, then he pointed up to the alley, cupped the hand behind his ear, and waved the other hand in front of him like he was holding something.

Dagge had a listening device. That was news to John.

A faraway catcall drew everyone's eye to the high south window, or at least to the black screen that covered it. Another catcall, gleeful, answered it from a different direction. John looked around the group, and a light went on for him. *They're luring him away. They're organized!*

Suddenly, they were all in motion. Beau was pulling him up with his strong arms, the rest were hustling across the basement, and Chief was holding a lamp up and waggling his fingers at the loiterers, telling them to hurry. Beau jerked a bulb torch off his belt and lighted the ground ahead for John. They followed Chief, jogging through old shelves and dusty junk, through a wall into another basement, through some more junk, down a narrow tunnel, through another wall, and this went on until in one of the basements, a young man came running up out of the shadows to join them.

"He's on his way back to the palace." The young man stopped the Chief and leaned over on his knees to catch his breath, grinning when he looked up. "Firio's whistle's gotten good enough to fool the horse—she followed him north, and he and Dagge had a whistle war until you guys could get away. Last I saw Dagge, he'd gotten the horse and they were clomping through the buildings, headed south."

Two more trickled in out of the shadows—one breathing hard, and restless, and the other, a very slight, pale woman who said, "He's got her at full run to the palace now. Off road, like he likes."

John put his hands on his hips and grinned around. Looking at Chief, he imitated the listening moves from earlier and asked, "What's this?"

Chief said, "It's a harkener. He can hear us if he's fairly close. Which he reportedly is not at the moment." Never losing that sharp twinkle in his eye, he held his hand out to John. "Hello, John Treslo, it's mighty good to see you."

John took the hand and exhaled. "Not half as good as it is to see you, I can promise." The little group huddled in the dim light, high on the night's rescue, and John would have liked nothing better than to ask a million pertinent questions, but they should probably wait.

"Time for the long stuff later. We'll have a head-to-head with everybody." Chief held his hand up for attention, and spoke to the group at large. "For now, let's get Thorn to NHQ. It's almost dawn, and whatever happens with that balloon will get things jumping. Right now, we need watchers. Just in case The Boy comes back mad. Volunteers?" The smaller guy—wiry, with jet black hair—held his hand up…and the pale lady, flashing her palm in the shadows. The two of them went separate ways back into the dark. Chief turned to John. "You're with me, let's go."

Chapter T.6

Dagge stormed through the sitting room door like a man prepared to take the whole room apart with his teeth. Furious, disappointed, humiliated, yes, and as he yanked his riding gloves off his fingers, he fumed over what to do about it.

He almost had her. She stopped playing just as he was getting off his horse, and she must have heard him because she wasn't there when he made the plaza. He guessed she'd go west, away from the homes, and down to the second alley, where the sightline went all the way through. But she took the first alley, he realized, and when he went back, thanks to his horse she was already going back the way she came. He started to follow, but he was too late, and lost her.

She was apparently not working alone.

With one hand he unhooked his cloak, whipped it off in a single quick motion and flung it onto the desk beside the gloves. Then he pulled out the chair, slammed his butt down in it and practically tumped over backwards to get his feet up on the desk. *Not funny,* he growled in his head. *None of this is funny at all.* He ground the heels of his hands into his eyes, trying to rub the last hour out.

The catcall surprised him. Then the answering one from the north just pissed him off, and he decided to take that arrogant shit-city bet. But the rabbit he followed was in excellent shape, and they called his horse away before he could get back to her, so Dagge lost his second target that evening.

He knew his life was too soft.

Chapter T.7

North headquarters amounted to an empty basement on the very edge of town where the private homes started. It had been a men's and women's accessories shop before Dagge closed all the unnecessary businesses and put people to work in the mine. John remembered the building; it was unassuming and in a mediocre location—bad for a business but perfect for the kinds of things that don't want attention.

After he passed through the door-hole in the last wall, he settled into a no-frills chair just like everybody else in the room. "Thorn" took the opportunity to size up the group at a glance. In the stark light from the bare overhead bulb, they looked like a battle-hardened special ops unit. *How do people get like that?* John leaned forward, elbows on knees, and said, "How many of you are there?"

"About thirty," Chief Taymer answered. "We five, plus Ciara and Firio are the wee morning shift." He pointed: "Beau, Cary, Lan, and Zola." John marveled at the assorted rebels: some were young, some older, all wearing black and carrying various knives and whatnot. Chief was the oldest, but Beau was also graying. Still muscled and tough-looking, though. Firio wasn't exactly young, either. John recalled him from the old days, now that he heard his name. He was an electrician. Handy.

"And you're 'Thorn.'" This observation came from Beau the Blacksmith, and every eye turned expectantly toward John.

Should he admit it? It wouldn't be good for everyone to know, but it might be good for these people to know. After agonizing for a few seconds, he owned up. "Yes, it's me...for what it's worth. I don't have near the thing going that you guys have. I mean, you look like a special ops unit."

"We're not," Chief answered, but Beau and Lan laughed heartily and clapped each other's hands.

Chief took a second to wait out the general mirth. "But you're doing the most important thing, Thorn. You're communicating with people, telling everyone that something can be done, and the situation isn't hopeless. We've been concentrating so hard on creating our own survival, that we weren't thinking about how to end the problem. By defying Dagge openly, you take us closer to a resolution."

"It looks to me like I'm making it worse. Every time Thorn does something, Dagge cracks down somewhere." John had to stand up and move. He paced a few steps and turned back. "I don't want to make things worse if it's not making things better."

"It's making things better more than you know," Zola said. "People love what you're doing, it encourages them. There are a few who'd rather lie down and take it, so they can have their comforts. But most of them wish they had the courage to do what you do. They come into the shop all excited when Thorn's done his latest thing."

"I agree," Beau said, "and I'll go a step further: I think a lot of people would join a rebellion, and there's a real chance we could get this kingdom back."

In the silence that descended John sat down again. The first law on the monolith, the hardest thing he had ever had to carve into stone was "Obey or die." Dagge had lived that, every minute of every hour of every day of the last year and a half. It wasn't any wonder some people would rather keep their heads down.

John was the first to answer. "I don't know how to do that." His eyes traveled around the circle. "Does anyone here know how to start a rebellion?"

No one answered. Right.

"Well, we'd have to communicate, wouldn't we?" Cary stood up, eyes sparking. "Thorn, I'm Cary Roades." He crossed the circle to shake John's hand. "I'm a great admirer."

Chief Taymer said, "Cary is one of our rabbits, Thorn. In his past life he was the print manager at the Books n All. Now he's found his true calling." The others laughed and Cary sat back in the circle to say what he was going to say.

"Since Dagge has the ethernet monitored, and the media controlled, there isn't much available in the way of mass communication." Cary nodded and gestured at the murmurs and grumbles. "If communication is the key—which it is—let's print. There's a press in the basement of the old print shop on the plaza. Just one more tiny tunnel."

John wondered he hadn't thought of it before. He could remember when that old press was actually being used. He saw it through the window when he was a kid, but they took it away when energy-sensitive paper was invented. Of course they would keep it, it was very cool, not to mention a valuable antique someday.

"That's a great idea, Cary." John felt his heart start to pump. "We can ... print flyers at first, and put them around. Anywhere. Everywhere. And we can use code so the goons can't read them."

"I can carve new blocks with whatever you want," Lan said.

"We could make it up," Cary said. "We could assign the symbols a letter value—"

"Or an idea value," John added. "Like a bat could represent midnight. A flower could mean a meeting. Start small."

"We can draw their attention with confusing phrases. Put cryptic words front and center in big type, and Dagge may spend all his time trying to decipher those," Zola said, grinning.

"I can make the code blocks look decorative. Vines, maybe. Flowers, animals, leaves…we can use them as a border, but they'll mean something."

"The most important thing at this point is to let people know we're here. Thorn isn't alone." Chief stood. "Let's save the rest of this for the meeting with everyone. I'm sure our resident pain-in-Dagge's-ass would like to get home. I need one person who wants to help me get him there." Cary's hand shot up.

John never imagined he'd be in this position, even as Thorn. How to Start a Rebellion 101. There were so many things to think of.

And so many possibilities. "Maybe we could use homing pigeons, too."
He beamed at everyone, all standing now, and the special ops unit
squinted at each other, like they were wondering for all the world how
old Thorn made it this far.

Chapter T.8

Hellen pushed the heavy door open and walked tiredly inside the monastery, where the dark was safe and she could relax a little. The temperature had dipped nearer the mountains, freezing her hands and face and toes, making her want a fire really badly. First things first, though...she removed her cloak and drifted left to the foyer's makeshift dressing area.

Hard as it was, she suppressed the urge to shout *Honey I'm home*! Adia wouldn't appreciate the humor of it if she was asleep, and she wouldn't appreciate it if she was awake, either. The girl was a little hard to please these days. Hellen shook her head and took off her army uniform.

Belt, boots, pants with a million pockets, vest, shirt, oh yeah cap. Hellen was standing by the costume chest in her undershirt and boxers when Adia scared the living daylights out of her. "Where have you been?" the whiny voice insisted. "You know I worry when you're not here. What if something happened?"

Hellen grabbed her robe and turned to face the music. Framed by the archway to the great room, standing in her robe and socks, Adia appeared tiny—as thin and frail as spun glass. Her shoulder-length dark hair stuck out in all directions, and her robe hung on her like she was wearing a parachute. The rising sun through the east windows cast a soft sidelight on her face, and she looked so miserable Hellen didn't have the heart to be annoyed. But she did wish there were two Hellens, or fifteen.

"I had to go to the rock giants, and when you're sleeping is the best time to do that." She wrapped her arms around the distressed girl and squeezed her back to life. "What are you doing awake, anyway?

You should be upstairs in the bed, loving that cushy mattress I made for you."

"Well, I was loving it until I fell off of it onto the floor."

Hellen unwrapped her and looked at her dejected face. The scars had healed, but still looked angry, and Adia said they hurt sometimes. If you looked at her from the right, she looked the same as ever; on the left side, though, a permanent, uneven flame licked up her neck, skirted her mouth, reached across her cheek to her nose, and up over her eye. Hellen was glad the girl would never see it, because it looked like the fire that made it was still there.

Right now, though, she was ready to get to bed herself, so she bent her considerable skills to pointing Adia in the same direction. "How about we heat up some of that fresh milk and let it knock us out?"

"Okay."

Whew, easier than she expected. Hellen took the girl's hand, hooked it on her arm, and led her through the great room into the kitchen. At the risk of getting her worked up, because she knew Adia would want to talk if she had one, she asked, "Did you have a bad dream?" A few seconds of silence pulled her head around. Adia was walking like she hadn't heard her. "I said did—"

"Oh, I heard, I just haven't decided what to say."

Odd. By Hellen's own accounts, that was a pretty simple question. Or maybe she didn't have a dream. Maybe something happened. That being Hellen's worst nightmare, she turned to face Adia so she could read her. "Did something happen?"

"No, nothing happened." Adia's voice got that petulant lilt, so Hellen turned back toward the kitchen and pulled her along again. The lilt followed her. "You worry so much, I'm not a total idiot, you know."

"I never said or thought you were an idiot," Hellen replied. "A little unmotivated, perhaps, given the absolute refusal to do pushups and situps." Adia surprised her by bursting into tears. She pulled her hand out of the crook of Hellen's arm and stood there crying. Hellen turned around to her, put her hands on Adia's arms and peered in her face.

"What is it, Adia?" She pulled Adia's chin up, but just as fast it was jerked away.

"Don't look at me! I'm tired of you looking at me!" She backed off a couple of steps and spread her hands over her face, then she turned around and stumbled back into the great room.

Hellen watched her, fascinated. When the distraught girl realized what she'd done— moved without counting or paying attention—she went on alert to get her bearings. She half turned back, retraced her steps in her mind and estimated where she was, then she took a couple of hesitant steps toward the nearest piece of furniture, in this case a sofa.

This was big. She didn't panic, she didn't run into anything in a wild rush for the familiar, and she didn't demand that Hellen help her. Hellen couldn't have been more proud of her if she had flown to the moon. When her hand touched the back of the couch, she grabbed the wood frame and pulled herself to it. "You have no idea what it's like. You look at my face to see what I'm thinking, or feeling. It's all there." She pointed at her smooth cheek. "But I can't look at yours. All I get is silence when you don't want to say."

It stunned Hellen; she never realized what her lack of commentary meant for Adia. She'd have to talk more, starting with now. "I'm so proud of you, I . . . I don't have words to describe it. Do you realize that you handled that beautifully? You knew where you were, didn't you?"

After a moment, Adia smiled hesitantly, and even laughed a little. "You know, I did. And a little while ago, I knocked the spoons over on the table, and I found every single one of them, including the four that landed on the floor." She tapped the side of her head with her finger. "I knew that because I could hear them, and I knew it was four. It was kind of weird."

Admittedly, these were minor things, but they were progress. Hellen watched the smiling Queen walk cautiously toward her, counting her steps, following the direction of her voice. Another crisis averted. Too bad it didn't always end so well.

"Shall I let you show off?" Hellen asked her when she reached the short hallway. That made Adia snort and she walked carefully around Hellen to the doorway that let into the kitchen. Hellen followed her. It was warmer there, the stove was good about keeping its fire and the ceilings weren't so high, so as cozy went, it was the best the old monastery had to offer.

Adia found her seat at the stone table and waited while Hellen went to bang around at the complicated cooking fireplace. If she'd had a dream, it would come easier now, and thank One that burdens divide with the sharing. The nightmares weren't always the same, but the fire dreams upset her the most. Who could blame her? The months of recovery, the excruciating pain, the loss of almost everything that meant anything to her.

"I think John Treslo's in danger of getting caught," Adia said.

Hellen felt like she'd been punched in the stomach. She whirled around, forgetting her new resolve to speak, and looked wide-eyed at the last Beldenet.

"Dagge's going to catch him if he keeps doing what he's doing. And it won't be pretty." Her face got all miserable again, and Hellen thought it was no wonder she had hair-trigger emotions.

"Oh, Adia…" Hellen forgot the milk and sat at the table across from the younger woman. "It could just be a dream. Was there fire?"

"Yes, he was a dragon." She spoke like she was in a trance, her voice quiet with remembering.

"John was a dragon?"

"No, Dagge was a dragon. I'm certain it was him. The look on his face…cunning, and gleeful to be doling out misery."

That would be Dagge, all right. Hellen reached across the table to take Adia's hand, and remembered she was supposed to talk. "John was there?"

"Yes, the dragon was cooking him."

"Oh," she blurted. That was worse than she expected. Not a good recipe for upcoming sleep. "Given the dragon and the fire, I'm going to take the position that it was just a dream." She spoke over

Adia's objections, "I would suggest that you do the same. But..." she said, and waited for Adia to close her mouth. "I will tell John he needs to be extra careful, all right?" At the stubborn silence she added, "What are we gonna do, say 'John, you're gonna die' when it could very well be just a dream?" This made Adia rethink, and her head shook reluctantly.

Hellen got up to get the milk bottle from the melted ice in the sink. *Besides, Thorn can't stop now, we need him.*

She didn't say it, but she thought it.

Chapter T.9

General Wharton crossed the barracks field sipping his morning coffee. His feet cracked the light snow on the ground and his breath came out in great clouds, visible in the floodlights they'd mounted on the high palace wall. Floodlights came on at six sharp, summer and winter, and every bucket-head in this army better be ready for anything by half past.

To his left was the usual bustle in and around the tents, which he monitored in a perfunctory way. The newest arrivals were always scattered around so the oldsters could keep them in line. No one wanted cut rations, or extra work detail, or a grim drawn-out death.

To his right, the palace. Guard detail at every door, and no disturbance there either. It was looking like a good day.

Most days were good. It took a while, but what started out as a sloppy collection of so-called mercenaries had evolved into a pretty decent army. A lot of the guys the King fired came back, and they lorded it over the others like senior officers. Wharton actually made some of them officers, they did it so well.

The thing was...the thing that occupied his mind this fine morning was that Overlord Dagge had a big shindig coming in just a few days, and the General wasn't sure the discipline would hold up when presented with temptations like serving-girls and fights with visiting soldiers. He'd dismiss it as not-worth-stressing-over, except the Overlord told him that he must make sure the ambience was relaxed and happy.

Yes, he really said that.

Wharton could hand-pick the hundred on duty and confine the rest to quarters. Or another option would be to let some go on leave, but he didn't think that was a good idea. With this many power-loving pinheads in one place, he half-expected a coup of some sort. They'd all have soldiers with them, and if something happened at the banquet, he'd need a sizable army outside to take out any support personnel.

The visitors' tents would be in the big field on the east side. The royals, presidents, etc., would stay in the palace, under heavy guard, of course, and add that to his full plate of woes. Kings and such were likely to put any kind of specialist in an entourage—hide 'em right out in the open, looking all unsuspicious, then they turn out to be deadly. Nothing he could do about that, but he could put an intimidating force in the palace; he had enough good soldiers here to impress the royals and their guards alike. A few troublemakers could almost certainly be contained by his best men.

Fortunately, they'd only be here two nights, which would be plenty for everyone, he was sure. Truth be told, he was surprised anybody accepted the invitation. They were probably all afraid to get on the Overlord's bad side. And they'd be right, but why did Overlord want to buddy up to a bunch of spoiled hand-wavers who despised him? Why do that?

Not his business. He checked his thought process, stopped walking and ran his eyes over the barracks and tents and soldiers. Time to focus on the day at hand.

"ReeePORT!" he shouted in his deep spreading general voice. His officers took up the call and repeated it until the men stopped eating, cleaning up, talking, shitting, whatever they were doing and hustled to attention in front of him. Row upon row of ham-fisted obedience. Wharton smiled.

Word had spread when Dagge took this kingdom, and it must still be spreading. They were adding every day. Outgrew the barracks more than a year ago and had to set up permanent tents, which were the subject of this fine morning's assignment.

Oh, he loved his job.

"General! General!" A tiny faraway voice trickled to him from the front of the palace. Wharton turned to see who-what-why it was, and across the front lawn, a soldier was running straight toward him at full speed. He was fully armed, so he must be on patrol, and without needing to think, the General was on the move.

"Rapp! Tapowski! Twenty men with guns!" he shouted, pulling his pistol while he ran. Behind him, his officers shouted instructions. Ahead of him, the soldier turned and took off back the way he came, headed straight for the heart of town.

Chapter T.10

Heavenly smells of bacon wafted to Roberta's nose, even buried as it was in the mountain of blankets covering the bed. What time was it? She pushed herself up into the cold to grab the clock. 6:30. Who was cooking at 6:30?

The mountain of John didn't move. She checked to make sure he was breathing—he was—and slid gently out of the bed so not to wake him. He'd been up all night again, and she wanted to let him sleep as long as he could before he had to go to work.

Robe, socks, slippers later, she padded out the door and through the entryway. There were no other sounds in the house, just the frying, and, oh wait ...the coffee maker. Excellent. Maybe the house elves had finally put her on their list.

As she neared the doorway to the den, she could see the tall back and dark blonde hair of their middle son, David. He would be the only one to get up and cook. The other two boys were a lot more likely to come wake her up before they'd get in the kitchen.

"David, what are you doing up?" she whisper-voiced as she crossed the linoleum line into the kitchen. He turned around and plastered a smile on his face, but it didn't fool his mother. The mashed-up hair and giant eye-bags gave him away.

"I couldn't sleep."

"What, all night? You look terrible, go sit down and I'll do this." Taking the spatula from him, she shoved him gently toward the table and assessed the food; it'd be okay for a few minutes if she turned the fire down some. Mission accomplished, she grabbed a cup out of the cabinet to pour herself some coffee. "Want some coffee?"

"Boy, do I." The muffled answer came from the depths of David's arms folded on the table.

Roberta poured them each a cup, sat across from him and waited for her son to emerge. Ten seconds or so later, David sat up and accepted the hot mug. "Mom, Robert's driving me crazy."

"What else is new?"

"I'm serious." His voice got an urgent tone.

"David, you've known Robert for nineteen years. You know what he's like. What's different now?"

"Now he works in the palace." David held her gaze with unspoken meaning.

"Yes, I know that." The mother took a sip of her coffee.

David's voice dropped to barely a whisper, and he leaned in. "He thinks he's on the fast track to power now." His hands curled into claws, like they were around...say... his brother's neck. "He keeps telling us how he'll convince Dagge to show mercy on us when we're brought in for treason."

"Treason?" Roberta's alarm bells sounded.

"He says we're in violation of the law when we say bad things about him."

"About Robert?"

"No, about Dagge."

"Let me get this straight. You say bad things about Dagge, and Robert tells you he'll stand up for you when you're brought in for treason."

"Yeah."

"Well, you should be thankful. Dagge could kill him, too."

"Mom! I'm not joking!"

"David..." She stretched her hand across the table and laid it on his. "It seems to me the solution is simple. Don't talk bad about Dagge in front of him."

"You don't get it." He exhaled like a 400-pound man just sat on him.

Roberta got up to tend the food. "Maybe I don't, or maybe... maybe you're just tired of him. But it's not his fault he got stuck here, and he's probably as miserable as you are."

"That's just it, though. He's not miserable, he's walking around with stars in his eyes because he thinks Dagge is the most brilliant, amazing leader the world has ever seen."

"He said that?"

"Along with a lot of other bizarre adjectives!" David got a handle on his volume and continued, "I'm seriously disturbed, Mom."

Roberta frowned and let the quiet sit while she finished taking up the bacon. She set the plate on the counter and covered it with a towel so it wouldn't get cold, then she went back and sat down with David again. "Are you sure he's not just pulling your leg?"

David scowled. "He doesn't have that much of a sense of humor."

That was true. Just like the rest of what David was saying. When Robert took that second assistant's job, he wanted it so bad, and she was afraid it would be right up his alley. Still, she had to pull for the best in him, and she told herself it would be educational for him to have a such clear, unobstructed view of the dynamic Master of Darkness.

Unfortunately, it appeared to have the wrong effect. Since his employment, he'd been to every execution, every offensive ceremony, every everything. Almost like he was love-smitten, One help them.

"Okay, I'll have a talk with him," she answered, and when David started to protest, she overrode. "I won't tell him you said anything. I won't mention treason, or brothers, or David, so quit worrying. I'm pretty smart, you know…Professor Treslo?…PhD in Humanities? I think I can manage this without incriminating anyone."

David sank; he dropped his head back onto his arms, his whole body collapsed against the table. He was clearly relieved his Mom was going to charge in on her white horse. Very different from his usual "I can do it" attitude. Her heart constricted, maybe Robert was worse than she thought.

Chapter T.11

Perched on top of the black granite slab, the balloon nodded in the breeze, a pointed head staring down at them. Wharton could practically hear the laughing. On each side, in brown marker, the "Thorn" symbol dressed it like ears. A laughing, nodding elf balloon.

One of the patrol soldiers had a powerful bulb torch trained on it when they got there. It hadn't moved, they said, and he wondered if they expected it to dive off.

"Has the area been searched?"

"Yes, sir. Immediately, sir. No sign of anyone."

Wharton put away his gun, borrowed the bulb torch and walked around the well slowly. He studied the balloon, but he also examined the ground, and the well, and the granite. On the south side there were running footprints, heading away from the well, and now trampled over by every soldier currently in Victory Plaza.

"Cordon this area off immediately!" he shouted. "A four-block radius! Rapp! Call for thirty more! I want every street from here to the outer wheel. Standard A, B, C company drill!" He gestured to the soldier who had the bulb torch to meet him on the east side of the well. Young and eager to please, he tiptoed all the way over, trying not to mess anything up.

"Yes, sir?" he asked when he made it.

"Who was on duty last night, private?"

"Sir, our group went on at midnight thirty. Before us was . . ."

"I don't care who was before you. What I care about is why did no one see who did this?"

The young soldier was speechless, then stammered a nothing reply. "Sir, we...we just weren't here, sir. We...were probably over...on the west or something."

Wharton weighed the advantage of making the young man pee his pants, but he decided there wasn't any. Overlord would probably execute him, and it wasn't the kid's fault, patrols couldn't be everywhere at once. They needed to change up the schedule.

This Thorn stuff was really pissing Dagge off. After losing a few decent soldiers to his wrath, Wharton started taking the heat himself. He didn't think Dagge would execute him, but never say never, right?

Later he'd come back out here and examine the scene. Right now, he had a report to make.

Chapter T.12

Morning sun was glinting off the snow by the time Dagge made it out to the plaza. He stood in the road, facing the old well and the black granite monolith erected on top of it. Empty windows surrounded him, staring like vacant, accusing eyes.

The balloon rocked back and forth on top of the Patriotic Laws like a head making complete fun of him. Balloony the PinHead, ho ho ho aren't you funny? Dagge wanted to climb that stone and crush that head with his bare hands.

"What if it has explosives in it?" That was Wharton, always the strategical thinker. Or maybe he was just paranoid.

"What if it has something in it like puke or crap?" This from some kid who was in the on-duty patrol.

"Shut up, private," Wharton barked. "If we want your opinion, we'll shoot ourselves."

That made Dagge want to laugh, and he had to fight the hysteria that rose up in him. It expanded and caught in his chest until he needed to cough, but he couldn't suck the air in so he cleared his throat instead. That expelled it, and a ragged breath later he agreed. "Yes, there might be anything in it."

To get the full picture, he walked around the well and glared at the balloon from all angles. Nice ears. The head nodded and laughed. Balloony the PinHead. Quick, somebody take a picture.

Focus, you idiot. Dagge beat his distracted mind into submission and sent it over all the possible traps.

There could be something in it. It could be attached to something. Something that would move, or spill, or fall, or rise for that matter. Damn fools. He walked to the nearest soldier, grabbed the guy's rifle, put it up to his cheek, and looked through the scope. No wires that he could see, no moveable parts.

All right then, I'll take care of this the efficient way. He placed his finger on the tripper and squeezed off a perfect shot. The balloon vanished into rubber shrapnel, and a spew of thick white paint splatted the top two feet of stone, like some giant bird had taken a shit.

Dagge's brain went apoplectic. Blood rushed up his neck, pounded in his ears and tried to blow off the top of his head. He wanted to crush that granite into dust with his bare hands, to suddenly be fifty feet tall and destroy everything. He was very near exploding when he saw something move in a second-floor window on the east side. A pale flash. Where was it? Which window? That window? When he drilled it with his throbbing eyes, he saw nothing.

All right, then, if she wanted to watch, he'd give her something to watch.

He turned and shot the patrol that was on duty when it happened. *Bam bam bam*, three were dead. The fourth ran, but once he got clear of the crowd, before the kid could disappear into the old buildings, Dagge got him, too. *Bam.*

He was far too good a marksman not to enjoy a little chase.

Satisfied with that, he turned to check the windows. Nothing. Yeah well, she saw…and he'd have to hurry to catch her.

"Wharton, take two men and search that building," he said, pointing. "If you find anyone, bring them to me unharmed." He shoved the assault rifle at some soldier's chest as he turned and stormed out of the plaza. "And clean that mess up!"

Chapter T.13

Hellen jerked her head back out of the window when Dagge saw her. She'd made the mistake of craning her neck, and she went out too far, and there couldn't be much doubt he knew someone was there. Time to exit, stage left.

Across the floor, down the stairs she ran, keeping time with the mindless, peppy music of the holo-ad in the background. "Here's a wipe! Sani-wipe!" Hellen shoved the inanity out of her mind and replaced it with *Who's my enemy?* Ten to one it would be Wharton. She remembered him from the old days. He had skills.

Gunshots sent her crouching, arms over her head like that would do any good. Three quick shots, she leapt to the bottom of the stairs and plastered herself against the wall. In the gloom she listened, listened, running feet fading away, then *blam!* No more running feet.

She had to go, she had to GO! Hellen forced her legs to get her down the back hallway to the door.

The alley was still clear, but it wouldn't be for long. The sun shone over the treetops in the east now, and it would only get worse, so she needed to become invisible. She whipped off her black wool cloak, turned it over to the brick-brown lining and put her hood up. Disguised as an innocent villager, she cut through the narrow walkways between buildings, trying to keep off the snow so her footprints wouldn't scream *she went this way!*

John's house would be her best bet, easy as long as the boys weren't up and didn't see her. Roberta had to be told about her pretty early on after the King's murder, after the explosion in the stable made everyone else think she and Adia were dead. Isolated and alone at the monastery, they had nothing—no food, no clothes, no supplies at all, and Adia was so desperately hurt Hellen couldn't leave her. Diit got a message to John, and John took items from his house to donate to the cause until one day Roberta wouldn't let him leave with a box of food until he told her what he was doing.

He'd told her about Hellen, but not about Adia; she and John agreed that everyone should think Adia was dead, and that meant Roberta, too. Thank One she wanted to help, and it was lucky for both exiles, because clothes and linens and more blankets and the kinds of things men wouldn't think about started showing up in the care packages. Hellen was so grateful, and it was better that Adia's clothes were too big, because once she could wear them, they were easier on her skin for it.

All of this to say, she didn't think Roberta would have a heart attack if she showed up on her doorstep. They'd met several times over the years, and the only hitch was that since her death, she'd dyed her hair, and this morning she'd smeared darker makeup on her skin (thanks to Diit, who had agreed she couldn't run around town as her dead self).

When she reached the residential area, she turned east and dissolved into the landscaping—bush to tree, yard to yard, constantly checking behind her until she got far enough away to feel safe. All that sneaking around outside the palace she used to do, on the nights she met Dagge, was really paying off, yes sir.

At the next road she turned left. John lived five streets up and a few houses over, and she hoped she could remember which one. She'd only been here once, at night, in a carriage with John and the King, but she felt pretty sure she knew what the house looked like. The only question was how many of the other houses were at all like it.

The morning light was getting bright now, the weak winter sun shining over the trees and laying a sheen on everything. She moved to the sidewalk to appear less alarming, but kept the hood up. People had awoken in their houses, lights were on and curtains were opening. Hellen hugged her cloak close to her body to keep it from billowing and drawing attention.

When she got to the next street, she looked back and saw a soldier running from house to house, peering at porches, checking down walkways, behind bushes. Turning, she escaped up a side street at a brisk walk. Once she got blocked from view, she ran like crazy, weaving through back streets and alleys until she thought she might come out where she needed to, and sure enough there it was. John's house.

Lights on in the kitchen, none upstairs. Hellen kept her head down and hurried up the driveway. The kitchen door would probably be best, but she might ought to look in the window first. She rounded the back corner of the house, stood on her tiptoes and tried to see in. No one at the sink, no one at the table that she could see. Good.

She stepped lightly back around the corner and snuck up on the door. Since Thorn was busy last night, John was probably still asleep. Boys too, she wagered: winter holiday for Joey, unemployment for David, Robert doesn't have to be at the palace for an hour and a half yet, if her watch hadn't stopped. All in all, a better-than-decent chance she could slip in without setting off a testosterone alarm.

The knob was unlocked; she turned it quietly and pushed the door in. There, so close the door hit the hand reaching out for the knob, was Robert.

Chapter T.14

Dagge watched the hooded figure hurry across the street to the house. John Treslo's house. Lately he was getting some red flags about the honorable architect, and this morning he had a hunch there might be a connection. This wasn't Treslo, though. Too small and quick.

Why would Hellen be going to John Treslo's house?

He tossed his chewed toothpick down into somebody's grass and swung himself back up onto his horse. Retribution, yes, but not today. He needed Treslo to finish his wall first, then he'd take care of him. And Hellen...let her think she got away. He had plans for her, too. Dagge slowly turned his mare back around to go call off his dogs.

Chapter T.15

"What the hell are you doing sneaking into our house?" Robert grabbed her wrist in a surprise move, and pulled her into the kitchen.

Hellen was so shocked she couldn't say anything for a few seconds, during which Robert yanked her hood down and called up the hall, "Mom! Somebody tried to sneak into our house!" He turned his attention back to her, examined her dark hair and skin, and she hoped upon hope she'd done a good job with the makeup, and that her blond roots weren't showing.

He was very tall, and she had to lean her head back to look at him, but she kept her eyes veiled as much as possible in case he could tell she was wearing dark eye-lenses. His big hand held hers up higher than her shoulder, and the flesh was turning pale from the choke hold he had on her wrist.

Soon she found her wits and her voice. "Sir, I my name Junika, and I am so apologize," she stammered with a Tirlan-ish accent, she hoped. Maybe he wouldn't know the difference. "I must come here with mistake. I am to work some house, I thought this house." Robert was totally unconvinced.

"More like you "am to steal" in whatever house you could get in, don't try to pull one over on me." He wrenched her arm to remind her who was in charge.

"Ow!" she yapped.

"Robert! What are you doing?" Roberta swept in from the hall, grabbed their hands and pried open Robert's fingers. Hellen got a probing look to go with her wrenched arm, then an incredulous raised eyebrow, and finally a half-amused scowl directed at Robert. "This is not necessary. I appreciate that you're protecting the house, but this is obviously just someone who's lost," she said, freeing Hellen from his iron grip. "Really, does she look like a threat?"

"You can't always tell by looking, Mother." Robert thrust his bottom jaw up, still pinning Hellen with that dead flat gaze.

"Is all right, ma'am, all to me fault. Just accident be in wrong house. I go now, find right house." She gave a self-deprecating laugh and turned back to the door, confident Roberta would pick up the frayed storyline.

"Robert, please go find the goat cheese in the back yard cooler. I'm going to see if I can help this woman find the people she's looking for." She ushered Hellen back out the side door and into the shadows of the neighbor's walkway. They didn't talk until they heard the back door close again, and then they looked around the neighborhood, up and down the street, gesturing and appearing to all the world, or at least to the young man spying through the window, to discuss the neighbors and their various cleaning needs.

"I just needed somewhere to hide," Hellen said. "I think I was seen this morning, by Dagge." It was hard to juggle what she could say and what she couldn't. Roberta knew about her, but she didn't know John was Thorn, so it seemed best to just avoid talking about what he did.

"I know John is Thorn."

Crap. Everything was going wrong this morning. How to respond? To admit, or not to admit, that was the question. No, there's no question, she couldn't do the admitting to the wife for him, that was his job. Better to just plead ignorant. "I don't know what you're talking about," she said, trying to ignore the rolling wife-eyes, and rushing over Roberta's sarcastic remark. "And if I di-id, I couldn't say anything. That's between you and him."

"Fine, but I'm pissed off. Not at you," the long-suffering wife complained, "you are fabulous, but he's on my kick list." A distant whistle stopped all conversation. Dagge's whistle, still south, but in the neighborhoods. Time to get inside in spite of Robert.

He was still standing in the kitchen when they hahaha'd their way in. Roberta had her story ready, and in a brilliant maneuver, went immediately on the offensive. "What are you doing still standing here? I told you I'd take care of this. The poor woman's hungry; she's going to have to go home to find out where she's supposed to be, and I'm going to feed her first. Did you bring in that goat cheese?"

"Yes, it's on the counter."

"Then would you please bring in some firewood?" Roberta sat Hellen down at the table and bustled into action to get her some food. Robert looked consternated.

Hellen wanted to laugh, so bad. Moms do know their children, don't they? Apparently asking for firewood was the quickest way to get Robert out of the house, because he lifted his coat off the back of the chair opposite her and said sharply, "I can't, I promised I would file the requisition orders today, and this is the best time to do it." He ignored Hellen the entire way out the back door, and she resisted the impulse to pat his arm as he walked by.

Whew, that was close. She got up and joined Roberta at the stove when Robert's footsteps faded away. "What about David and Joey?" she whispered, not looking forward to a repeat performance.

"They should sleep a while longer. Joey will probably be up first, and David just went back to bed." Roberta's keen eyes sparkled at her. "Don't tell me you don't think you can sell this." She waved her hand to indicate Hellen's disguise.

"I haven't had to actually talk before. It was a little scary, I admit. I have no idea what that accent was, probably nothing remotely real."

"You did fine, because with Robert, you'd know if you didn't."

That was reassuring. Hellen did resolve, however, to practice talking with accents. Adia would be an excellent captive audience, poor girl.

"Hellen," Roberta began as she sliced bread, fetched eggs from the fridge, and cut off thick slabs of cheese, "you must have come into town for a reason." Roberta finished what she was doing, wiped her hands on her apron, and pulled the foreigner to the table. "And it seems like there's a good chance your reason got waylaid by whatever those gunshots were about in the plaza. Am I right?"

"You know…" Hellen responded, gearing up to dodge one or more questions.

"Is there something I can do to help?" Roberta asked.

That put the brakes on her deflector shield. Could she help? Maybe she could. She wasn't wanted by the authorities yet, so she could move through town without attracting suspicion. "Well, you could go get Beau Hodges and bring him here."

"Done." Roberta pushed herself up from the table and took off her apron.

She hadn't expected Roberta to agree so fast. It was a fairly long walk from here, and pretty cold, to boot. "Seriously?" Hellen followed her to the sink.

"I can't wait to get out of here." Roberta reached around her and turned on the hot water to wash her hands. "You can finish cooking?"

"Sure…" Hellen eyed the food warily. Her cooking skills pretty much stopped at roasting something over a fire.

Roberta noticed her hesitate. "Don't worry, it's pretty self-explanatory. Crack some eggs, let them fry until they're done." With a pat on the shoulder, she was gone.

"I think I can handle that." Hellen took her cloak off and laid it over a chair, then she stepped up to the stove and fiddled with everything. She was just peeking under the towel laid over a plate of bacon when a voice startled her.

"Who the heck are you? Are you supposed to be here?"

She whirled around in the middle of her heart attack and came face to face with another son.

"I am was Junika." She smiled stupidly and ran through her brain files on this son, almost certainly David. Nineteen, give or take? Bored, stressed ... very smart. Like really very smart. *Hm, I should probably just get out of here somehow.* "I am was help by...um, lady? There is food, I cook for help."

David was squinting at her. Maybe this wasn't going so well.

"David! I thought you were asleep." Roberta to the rescue again. She came in from the hall carrying her coat, and swung it onto her shoulders as she walked into the kitchen. "I want you to run an errand for me."

"Now?"

"Yes, now, when do you think? I want you to run to Brander's Farm and get milk."

"Where are *you* going? Who is this? It's not even 8 am, are you trying to get rid of me?"

Roberta speared him with a look like only a mother could do. "None of your business, her name is Junika, and I'm trying to get some milk, now stop asking questions and get a move on."

David gave Junika a slow, baffled stare, which he turned on his mom, then he rotated slowly and threw his hands in the air as he walked toward the doorway. They could hear him grousing to himself, "Did I deserve that? I don't think I deserved that. All I did was challenge a possible burglar. Is that wrong? I don't think that's wrong," and he disappeared into the gloom.

"I'll stay until he leaves," Roberta whispered as she passed Hellen on her way to the stove to check the food. Hellen followed her because the bacon smelled so good over there, and it had been a long time since she'd had it. She wanted to look at it.

The two women were huddled over the stove, cracking and flipping eggs, when a big voice croaked out at them from the well-worn doorway. "What's going on out here? It sounds like a train station."

"I'm sorry, honey." Roberta crossed to John and cupped her palm on his cheek. "I promise we'll be better. What time is it? You still have an hour before you have go, why don't you go back to bed for a bit?"

"Who's that?" John's eyes were fixed on Junika.

"My call am is Junika." Hellen walked over, eyes sparkling. John watched her approach him with a completely confused expression, until he finally recognized her after she stood there in front of him and looked right at him for a few seconds. He let out a hearty laugh. "Hey! That's really excellent. I especially like the unibrow, it makes you look a lot different."

"Yeah, it's better than just the hair, isn't it? Now even someone who knows me wouldn't recognize me easily." She chuckled and held up a finger. "Now watch this." She turned around, bent over a little, and hobbled a few steps like a much older woman.

"You look like a witch."

Hellen stood up and faced him, indignant. "A witch!" Then she thought about it for a second. "Really? That's pretty good."

"Exactly!" John exclaimed with a big smile.

"Okay, you guys have fun, I have to go." Roberta kissed John's cheek and grabbed her satchel off the chair.

"Where are you going?" John asked.

"She's going to get Beau Hodges so I can meet with him." Hellen closed the distance and spoke softly, "It's time for my friends to know I'm alive, because we're going to need their help." Too late, Hellen realized she said more than she should have.

John paused, then abruptly turned to Roberta. "Honey, would you get my robe and slippers for me?" One of her eyebrows went up and she twisted her mouth into an expression that said *I can't believe you're such a blockhead.* "Please?" he said in his sweetest voice.

Head shaking in disbelief, she turned toward the hall and threw up her hands in a perfect imitation of David. "Did I deserve that? I don't think I deserved that." It plucked Hellen's hilarity string, and she had to slap a hand over her mouth to keep the eruption down.

Goodness, she was ready to deal Roberta in. The woman was smart, efficient, capable and funny, and how often do you get that? She could be such an asset. John, however, was immovable on the subject; he had his reasons for keeping her out, and Hellen had to respect the family.

Not that she thought Roberta would let it go.

Chapter T.16

Once Roberta was out of the room, Hellen got pulled over to the table by a big meaty hand on her elbow. John's voice was as excited as a whisper could get. "I just left Beau Hodges and a bunch of other people a couple of hours ago. They've done the most amazing things! They connected a lot of the basements in town and made a tunnel system. They have supplies down there you wouldn't believe. Everything. They have a spy system, and three patrol shifts every night. They know what's going on everywhere!"

Hellen stood speechless while she worked to process what John said. Her friends made tunnels under the town, and they stocked supplies, just like Adia told them before everything fell apart. Of course Beau Hodges would do that, he would be the one, wouldn't he? And it wasn't just him. She gasped when she realized what this meant. "John," she whispered breathlessly, "We have people!" She leaned in closer. "We have other people, with brains and skills and guts!" She was deathly serious, but she felt elated, and proud, which seemed ridiculous since she didn't have anything to do with it. "Who is it besides Beau?"

"Chief Taymer is the leader, then the younger woodcarver, the plant lady, an electrician, Beau Hodges, a couple more. Only seven of them were there, but they have about thirty people. And get this…" He leaned in over the table. "They have a printing press. We're going to make flyers—"

"Here comes the wife!" a voice called from the foyer. "Here she comes, getting closer! Oh! Are those little whisperings I hear?"

Roberta swept through the door into the living area, draped with John's robe and waving his slippers in the air in an absurd dance. Hellen bit her cheek, but laughed anyway—John was never going to live this down. Still smiling, she got up to sneak a bacon.

David showed up while John was putting on the robe. He was washed, dressed, and coated in resignation. "Okay, what do you want me to get?"

"Get what?" John bent over to put on his slippers.

"Milk," Roberta said. "Two gallons, with the cream. We're going to learn how to make butter."

"Seriously?" David was incredulous, and slumped like a two-year-old.

"Are you whining?" His mother glared at him. "Straighten up or I'll buy a cow and you can milk it, too."

"Ugh!" was David's eloquent reply.

"What's going on out here?" Joey's voice piled on as he entered the room.

"Hi, honey." His mother kissed his cheek on her way out past him.

"WAIT!" John called after, poised to get up and chase her down if he had to. She turned and stuck her head back into the room.

"What?"

Don't bother going to the blacksmith's," he told her. "He's not going to be open this morning."

"Really?" Roberta asked curiously. She thought about it for a second, then her body joined her head from the depths of the doorway, where they leaned an arm against the corner and looked solemnly into the room. But she didn't ask why, Hellen noticed.

"Yes." John nodded. "Hey, is that bacon I smell? Anybody want toast?" He jumped up, grabbed the bread, and dropped a couple of pieces in the toaster. "I need some coffee, anybody else want coffee?"

"I want coffee," Joey mumbled.

"No," his parents said together.

"Krikey!" Joey held his hands up in defense. "Who's that?" He changed the subject deftly, pointing his finger at Junika.

"Junika," the triple-threat answer.

"And don't ask any more than that," David continued, not really disguising his grumble as a warning.

"Okay," Joey answered, happy to be agreeable.

Roberta gave in. "Well, if that's the size of it." She shook off her coat and laid it over the back of the couch. "Boys, milk." She pointed her finger at them.

"What?" This whine came from Joey.

"And eggs," the Mom overrode, picking money out of her wallet. "Three dozen, go!"

"I'm not even dressed!"

"You're dressed enough, grab your coat and boots on the way out."

"Come on, Joey." David shouldered the responsible older brother garb and pulled Joey away toward the coat rack.

"What are you getting?" Roberta called.

"Two gallons of milk and three dozen eggs!" he yelled back.

"With the cream!"

"With the cream!" sounded decidedly irritated, then all they could hear was the murmur of barely audible grumbling, and the opening and closing of the door. Roberta waved at them as they left, still standing in the living area where she could see the front door. When they were gone, she joined Hellen and John at the table.

"Okay, look," she started right away, her eyes on John. "Are we really going to keep doing this? You honestly think that keeping me in the dark is going to save me if something goes wrong? Dagge would kill all of us just for spite." John gaped at her, horrified speechless, and Hellen watched them without saying a thing. She knew which side she rooted for.

"John, I know you're Thorn. And I know you and Hellen are working together to try and save the kingdom. I want in."

"No, Roberta, you really don't."

"John Treslo, are you saying I don't know my own mind?"

"No! It's not that. I know you know your own mind...you know my mind, and everyone else's mind in this house, and that's the thing—we have kids, Roberta, they need their Mom."

"They need their Dad, too, John. And while we're at it, they need their freedom, wouldn't you say? They need an education, and they sure can't get much of that, can they? With the university closed, and visas canceled. Well, an ignorant population is much easier to control, isn't it? The public schools will be next, you mark my words!"

"That doesn't change the fact that if something happens to me, David and Joey will still need you. They need a parent, and I can only do what I have to do if I know you've got this at home."

"I can't sit here and do nothing." Roberta eyes bored into him. "David and Joey are nearly grown, and what kind of futures are they going to have if we don't fix this? Working in the mine? I would rather they grow up without me, and know that I cared enough about their lives to die fighting." She peppered the table with the tip of her forefinger. "That's the kind of Mom I want to be. I want to fight for their future!"

John sat speechless again. Hellen watched him because who could argue with that?

"Roberta..."

"This better not be another no, John, or I'm moving to the monastery with Hellen. You can stay here and be the parent, and I'll be the revolutionary."

Hellen wanted to laugh again. Or was it lunacy? Hard to tell.

He gave in. It was bound to happen, Hellen knew. After staring at Roberta for a long thirty seconds, he shook his head, sighed, and his chin dropped to his chest. When he raised his gaze again, he looked at her with such love, and faith, that it made Hellen's heart hurt. With a worried smile, he took his wife's hand, kissed it, and said to both of them, "All right, we've got plans to make."

Chapter T.17

Adia lay on her luxurious mattress and stretched in the morning sun shining through her window. Well, probably not too early morning, but still morning, judging by the fact that there was any warm patch at all. By midday, the sun would be over the roof, and even if she had cut it close and the patch was crowding the wall, it still counted as morning.

To her surprise, she'd slept pretty well, even after the nightmare thing and the talk with Hellen. Speaking of which, it was awfully quiet now. Hellen would've had her up before this if she was here—she'd be making lots of noise in the kitchen or something else really subtle.

Do I always think in sarcasm?

She flicked the annoying voice out of her head because she could think in sarcasm if she wanted to.

Isn't that a bad attitude?

Shut up!

Flinging the covers off, she swung her feet out of her warm bed onto the cold stone. Yikes, she hated this about the monastery. Tapping her toes every few inches, she felt around for her slippers, which she had apparently knocked away sometime during her trip to the floor, or on the floor, or whatever. Naturally she didn't remember to locate them while she was down there, so they weren't in their usual place this morning.

Not too far away, her toes brushed the hard edge of a rubber sole. Thank goodness. She could just slip her foot in if she pushed her butt up off the mattress and reached. It took a couple of kicks, but she got it on and stood to find the other one. She found the robe on her bed, put it on, tap tap tap with her bare toes, where the hell was that other slipper? Found it, shoved her foot in, turned to get her bearings.

"Well!" Hellen's voice made her jump. "That was very well done. Not too much cold stone."

Adia could hear the smile on her face. She smiled herself and laughed lightly, reached her left hand out to the wall to check her orientation. Satisfied, she took the few carefully confident steps to her coach. "You didn't drink your milk."

"No, I did not."

"Why didn't you wake me when you got back?"

"I figured you needed it." Hellen pulled Adia's hand through her arm and they walked together out the doorway. Right turn down the hall, thirty paces, left down the stairs, eighteen of those, and into the kitchen. In the meantime, they talked.

"I saw John Treslo this morning."

"Is he okay?" A picture of roasted John flashed through Adia's mind.

"He's fine," Hellen rushed to assure her, "but Thorn was active last night."

"Did you tell him he needs to be careful?"

"I did, but there's stuff you should know. Big stuff, and I want us to sit down before I tell you."

Adia did not like the sound of that, except that Hellen's voice was happy. Could there really be news so happy that she would need to sit down? Hard to imagine.

Once she was comfy on the stone bench alongside the stone table, Hellen sat next to her and faced her. "Our merchant friends...remember them?"

"Of course."

"They've dug tunnels connecting basements on the entire west side and some of the north. They've organized their own resistance. Six of them rescued John last night—he was almost caught by Dagge."

Adia felt like her entire brain went *poof!* and disappeared. Her heart skittered. She sat open-mouthed for a minute until she realized she'd gotten very dry. "Could I have some water?"

Hellen's energy disappeared, made some noise behind her, and reappeared with a cup of cold water, which she pressed into Adia's hand. Adia drank like she'd been in the desert for a week, and put the cup down empty.

"Would you like some more?"

"No, I'm fine, thank you" Brain functional again, she considered what Hellen told her. "That's incredible," she finally said.

"Yes, it is!" Hellen leaned in and whispered conspiratorially, "Adia, I think we can do this. I think we can take this kingdom back."

Adia fixed her with her sightless eyes. "Hellen, how can a handful of people with few weapons and no experience defeat an entire army and the murderous psychopath who pays them?" Hellen's silence was loud in the room, and she sat very still.

"I don't know how we can do it," she answered, "but I know we have to try."

"You'll all get yourselves killed," Adia said, louder than she meant to. She hated that her lifeline, the person she absolutely had to have, thought she should be able to go out and run dangerous little missions. What good did it do to check in with the rock giants? To keep tabs on Dagge's and Pulari's patrols? It wasn't like she could stop them if they got near the monastery.

Adia shuddered. The one thing that terrified her the most was losing Hellen. She didn't think she could survive that.

"Adia, we can't just let your kingdom go. It's your kingdom now, we have to fight for it."

"*How am I going to fight for it?*" Adia yelled at her, starting to get up, but deciding against it. "I'm trapped in this empty, black world, in this horrid body—you have no idea what it's like!" Her hands clutched her stomach, wishing she could tear the damaged skin away. "I can't stand it!"

She could feel herself unraveling and didn't know what to do; she'd had too many bad scrapes and bruises to want to navigate the monastery while she was upset. Her hands flew to her face and covered it, like they had since she was a child and she didn't want to see or be seen. Her shoulders slumped, and she leaned over the table and cradled her head in her hands.

Her voice was small when she spoke. "I can't be the queen now. I don't have it in me anymore, why can't you understand that?"

****

Hellen saw that Adia was right, it was a real advantage to be able to look at a face. Same with a body. Adia's had misery written all over it. Hellen stayed quiet, letting the moment cool off, then she reached out and touched Adia's leg to see how she'd react. She didn't jerk away, or get up, or push her hand away, so the mother-substitute scooted closer and put her arms around the shaking girl. Adia sank into her, and Hellen understood that she was torn apart with fear, and grief, and all the things she couldn't control.

Chapter T.18

It gratified Dagge to see so many servants running around the palace. Maids scurried everywhere, deliveries arrived for the banquet, servants hauled armloads of Winter Festival decorations (lots of spiky stuff, because it amused him). The whole thing was rather exciting, really. All the bustle had a party feel to it, and he decided it was almost enough to cheer him up.

In spite of the danger of being pleased, he strolled along the second-floor balcony overhanging the main entry. The enormous room was transforming before his eyes into a winter holiday fantasy. Doors, walls, pillars, and balconies were all lush with festoons of evergreen branches, and long ropes of fresh, fragrant garland sparkled with little white lights. Gleaming ornaments dotted the spaces in the greenery, gold-ribbon and wine-red bows hung artfully around, and the smell of cinnamon spiced the air. Dagge smiled. Not too shabby for new money, right?

It comforted him to see this evidence of his mastery. Particularly after the fiasco in the plaza this morning. After that special event, he really wanted to kill someone. Oh yeah, he did kill someone—at least there was that.

What he had to do was lure the rebels out. "Thorn," he said out loud without meaning to, and a couple of maids vacuuming the drapes turned their heads, but only for a second. He kept walking and didn't acknowledge them. *It's a stupid name.*

And John Treslo. What to do about him? Dagge generally made a point of treating his good people well, and the architect did good work, was always polite, and didn't act superior like the nobles did. It was only lately that he got those warning feelings about him. Never had anything to pin that on, though.

Lure them out, yes. Whatever they thought they were going to do, tempt them to do it. Better sooner than later.

He arrived at his sitting room (*war room* he corrected automatically), to find Wharton there waiting for him. Diit was there also, guarding the place, Dagge supposed. With an impatient hand he waved the servant away, and the young man and his ridiculous white wig disappeared down the servants' hall.

"General," Dagge greeted his pet, "please, have a seat." They made themselves comfortable in the cozy chairs now pushed in front of the fireplace. A snappy fire was burning, and Dagge felt every inch the commander-in-chief.

"The Thorn incident this morning was unfortunate. I hope your men have cleaned up the mess by now."

"It's better than it was, sir." Wharton had stopped giving negative answers, Dagge noticed. At some point he learned that negative answers were bad for everyone.

"It was oil paint, wasn't it?"

"Once they figured it out, sir, it went easier."

"I'm sure." Dagge was smoothly polite. He paused for a moment to figure out how to say what he wanted. "It goes without saying that Thorn must be caught."

"Absolutely, sir. No question about it. Shall I increase patrols?"

"No, Wharton, I don't think so." Dagge shifted in his seat, crossed a leg over, raised his arms and leaned his head back into his hands. He could see the puzzled look on Wharton's face, and it pumped him—he loved being so good at this. "We're going to try something different this time. We're going to bring Thorn to us."

Chapter T.19

Lunch break for John and his crew was a raw, cold affair. Every time they'd brought in another brazier, Dagge would claim it for the army. One was all they got. All the rock layers, the mortar men, the mixers and haulers, had to wait their turn around the brazier for hot food. In the meantime, they had only warm coffee to try and thaw their fingers by. Honestly, John was glad this job was almost over, even if finishing the wall did mean total captivity.

Or near-total captivity, at least. As much as he hated the job, he was glad it fell to him, because he was able to scatter six secret exits along the length of the wall—under, over, and through. However, the main entrance was over here, and it would get a lot of traffic, so this section was pure wall.

With rock coming from the mine, the construction of a perimeter wall should have gone pretty quickly at only eighteen feet high and six feet thick, but truthfully, John was delaying it as much as possible, for the sake of the intrepid, and for general morale. Life was bad enough already without taking away the last view of freedom.

John was tired, he just wanted to be home in bed, but there were many hours yet left in the day. Consequently, he did less lifting and more running around than usual, since he didn't want to collapse in the hard dirt. Never an advantage in that.

At least the rest of the hours were going to be sunny. That was his happy thought, and he was sticking with it. Screw the bitter wind coming down from the mountains, at least his people were partly blocked by a couple of trees.

A commotion to the right drew his attention: Dagge was trudging through the site at the front of a small contingent—straight toward him, eyes fixed on him, no getting away for John. Oh, great, he always loved these little visits.

Couldn't he ever walk over here by himself? Do powerful men always have all those barnacles around them? The Group made John feel like he was on trial, or at least in trouble. Hopefully not either of those today.

John threw his cold coffee out on the ground and waited for Dagge to arrive. "Mr. Treslo," he called as he got near, "a word, please."

"Certainly, sir." John moseyed toward him... not anxious, see?

Dagge stopped where he was when John started toward him. He waited and watched John move, which made John very uncomfortable. *How much did he actually see me last night? Any?* He didn't think so, but couldn't be sure.

Once he reached Dagge, John stood right in front of him, monumental controls over his aching-to-race heart, face carefully pleasant when Dagge spoke. "As I'm sure you know, Mr. Treslo, there are several royals visiting this weekend for my first annual Winter Festival Banquet." He smiled like he couldn't be happier, the perfect host. "I expect the caravans to begin arriving on Friday, and I'd like to make sure the wall is finished by then, so there isn't an ugly eyesore to ruin the landscape."

The irony was staggering, but clearly lost on Dagge. It took every bit of social skill John had left to reply, "Sir, I'm certain we can make that deadline, but I think you should understand that the mortar will not be sufficiently set to endure any kind of assault."

"Of course I understand that, Treslo," Dagge replied, "but I doubt our guests would have any reason to assault it, and I'm certainly not planning to. Do you know something I don't know?"

What a question. The fact that Dagge asked it would be funny if it wasn't so terrifying. "Me?" John joked, "I don't have time to know anything. I eat, sleep, and breathe this wall."

"Sir," Dagge said.

John blanched, swallowed, and bowed; people had been killed for that. *Unless he likes you.* John had gotten away with forgetting it many times, which a person could if they were in Dagge's good graces, but pointing it out this time meant it mattered now...which was very, very bad. "Sir," John repeated as pleasant as could be.

Satisfied smirk in place, Overlord turned his gaze to the wall. "Mr. Treslo, I'd like you to attend the banquet on Saturday." John froze, while Dagge continued, "I think an intelligent wit like yours would represent Great Hand well, don't you?"

"Well, thank you sir, but--"

"That wasn't a request." He probed John with his eyes for a long five seconds, turned to leave, then added, "Bring your wife, too, if she likes."

Dagge smiled that crocodile smile of his, turning John sick to his bones.

Chapter T.20

Hellen had her hunter hat on, traipsing through the forest, quietly looking for something to kill and eat. Life in the raw. Pretty soon she wouldn't even have to cook it.

She was glad she had skills—thanks to the ancestors, no doubt. Strange that she came from a long line of Protectors, but it felt right and suited her just fine. Near-starvation had taught her that protector skills were handy and multi-purpose; right now, they were tuned in for targeting. *Not just for death threats anymore*!

The ground was rocky at the bottom of the mountains, so it was hard to walk and not much game. She might have to move north. Hellen's stomach was hoping for a good-sized rabbit, the plus being she could add to the rabbit-skin blanket she was making for Adia. Two rabbits would be even better, she decided. But rabbits burrow, so yeah, time to trek for the woods.

"Human." A familiar gravelly voice surprised the piss out of her. It came from above her head, and she craned her neck to look. Eighteen feet up, at the top of the cliff, a big square rock gazed down at her. Two arms reached up, took the head off the shoulders, and brought it down to her eye level. It was Browbone.

"Wow, what are you doing here?" Hellen said, brilliantly spy-like.

He looked around, turning his head with his hands a bit to get a wider view. Apparently, all was clear, because his face came back around and spoke as low as a boulder can. "You know the dimensional hole we protect?"

"What?! Fifty times I've tried to bring this up with you guys, but you always act like you have no idea what I'm talking about."

Hellen nodded and pointed her finger at him. "They don't know you're here, do they?"

Browbone's big head chuckled mirthlessly. "That's very clever of you, but alas not true. We have a problem, and we all felt it was necessary to speak to you about it, for your own safety." He cleared his throat, even though he didn't have one. "You've never seen the tear because it's hidden inside one of us at all times. The slow vibration of the rock contains it, but the tear bleeds second-dimensional energy, and disrupts the energy patterns of whoever contains it. Over time, it becomes increasingly uncomfortable and we have to switch with the next of us.

"What I need to tell you is that the tear is increasing its energy output rapidly now. Too much negative energy is building up. So much so that Duncecap's having a hard time with it, and he's not sure he can take it if it gets any worse.

Well, that didn't sound good. "Why is it increasing so fast?" Hellen asked.

"Our mandate to protect the forest has meant the...elimination of a growing number of threats." He paused, then shook his head with his hands. "Frankly, up to now, if Dagge sent a patrol, or a recon group came from Pulari, we'd back off the hole, the flashing lights would draw them like flies, and they'd get sucked in. Recently the monks learned that the entity who made the tear, and came here, left others there to wait for him. They're feeding on the energy that goes into the hole, and so many have gone through lately that they're bursting with it."

Hellen blanked. This was way beyond her surreality quotient. So basically, the tear was a wormhole to the main course platter at a feeding frenzy. Her mind pictured big fat slobbering monsters devouring arms and legs and heads. Yeah, so it probably looked different in 2D, but did all those soldiers deserve that? She didn't know. Except to say it was either them or Adia.

"If the energy hits a certain level, the tear could explode and suck all of us into the rift."

"Who's all of us? Like, the whole world?"

"I don't think so."

Gee, that was reassuring. "Will the energy fade if it's not fed for a while?"

"It will take some months in your time to dissipate, but it will eventually, I think."

"Are you going to leave it unguarded?" That would be very bad news.

Browbone's ledge went down on one side. "We'll cover it with our rock bodies, but our energies won't be in them. Unfortunately, that will leave you vulnerable to both Dagge's and Pulari's soldiers."

"And we hope the tear doesn't explode, and suck everything in…say, in the immediate area…into the second dimension, because then the hole will be exposed, and there's no telling what could happen."

"That's the idea."

Devastating news. The rock giants made her life possible. She didn't worry about leaving Adia because she knew the patrols would be taken care of. What was she going to do now?

"Is there anything else you need to tell me?" She could barely keep her voice from whining, really not wanting more icing for the bad news cake.

"Just that Servant says you should look into the past for answers." His head shrugged the best it could without shoulders.

Sometimes the monks were infuriating.

Hellen hadn't been this dejected since the early post-palace days. All this time, she'd taken for granted that the forest would be safe. Now nothing would be the same with the rock giants gone.

Then she had an idea. "If you leave," she heaved out, "can you come back?"

"Yes, certainly, as soon as the energy is tolerable. We can sometimes take other forms, too, and we can be here without form, but you can't see or hear us that way."

"And if we could neutralize the tear, or bleed some of its energy, you guys would be all right, like before?"

"Yes, I don't see why not, but you must be aware that if any of you gets too close to the hole, it will suck you in and kill you. Do you understand that?"

"Yeah, I get the whole 'it eats people' thing. How far away?"

"Servant said thirty feet, but it could need more if the energy is strong."

"Did he say anything else?"

"No."

"Sure? Okay, let's recap. The hole is getting more dangerous, could create a massive wormhole to another dimension if any more people get sucked into it, and there are bad guys on the other side just waiting for that to happen. Number two, you rock elementals have to abandon guard duty or face death, so you're going back to the twelfth dimension, where you came from, and we'll have no protection except your lifeless structures in some kind of water ballet dome configuration. Does that about cover it?"

"What's water ballet?"

"Forget I said that. I know it's not your fault, I'm sorry. It's just that everything seems to be happening at once, and I'm a little…edgy," she huffed out in a sigh.

"'Look to the past,' he said. "I'm sorry it's not more, but you know how they are." Browbone lifted his head back onto his shoulders, settled it comfortably and looked down again.

Hellen turned up to face him, and backed away some so it wouldn't kill her neck. "Yeah, I know. No interference unless authorized." With monumental effort, she managed a weak smile. "You were always the best, you know, thanks for really helping me."

"You're welcome," he answered, giving her a nod. "I'll probably see you again sometime. If…you know."

"If we don't all die, and the planet doesn't get sucked into a wormhole?"

"Pretty much that, yeah," he acknowledged, a little embarrassed. "Anyhoo, I've got to get going…" He leaned away from her.

Anyhoo? Hellen laughed to herself, tickled that this enormous rock would have it in him to say that. Browbone was a lot cuter out here on his own. She realized she truly did want to see him again.

"See you around, big guy, never you doubt it." She patted his hand and turned away to finish her hunt.

Chapter T.21

From her position in front of the big fireplace, on a stool, Adia could tell by the fading heat that the fire would need feeding soon. She always put if off as long as possible—*seeing as how I have this fire-aversion thing*—but she would do it, because not having a fire at all was worse. Hellen had everything right there for her: wood, a poker, bellows, some giant tongs. She also had a shovel and pail, but so far Adia had never used them.

Her fingers ran lightly over the carved stone panels that lined the outer edge of the opening. Hellen said they were monks, doing things like praying, working in the garden, lifting one of them on a net of sound. She had said that last bit so casually, Adia almost missed its significance. After a confused few seconds, she made Hellen tell her what that meant. "Just what it says," she said.

Even the full story didn't shed much light for her. The carving showed monks singing and playing horns, and the sound waves wove together to make a net-like thing. Another monk was lying on the net, being lifted into the air. At the time, her comment to Hellen was something like he was probably "Lifted to Heaven by Celestial Music." Hellen had said "Right! Except John told me he read that they could make boulders fly by using sound, and that was before we even saw this."

No doubt the monks knew a lot of things, and had skills that went unmatched even in this day and age. They designed and built the palace out of gigantic blocks of stone centuries ago. It had an incredible plumbing system, and secret passages with massive stone doors that opened like they didn't weigh anything. The monastery had plumbing, too (thank One), and it was pretty well heated throughout by this fireplace—some kind of duct system branched out from the chimney, John said.

Then there was the space mural on the monastery wall, with planets and a nebula they shouldn't have known existed all those centuries ago. Adia had spent many hours feeling the different textures and shapes she could reach, after Hellen had described the whole picture to her that first day they'd ventured outside. Clearly, the monks weren't just some local religious order, and that knowledge made her much more aware of what was possible.

Maybe the net of sound wasn't figurative. Sound was energy, so why not? And if she drove herself crazy trying to figure it out, no big loss. With all the solitude she was getting, at least it was something for her brain to do.

And she needed something. She'd spent countless hours combing empty rooms, feeling the walls and floors foot by foot for possible tunnel entrances. Would she tell Hellen what she'd been doing? Only if she found a seam. But not until then, because she also spent time raising and lowering the dumbwaiter, and listening at the bank of pipe ends connecting every room to the kitchen. Logic said if she wasn't mental yet, it was only a matter of time.

In the interim, while she was still sane, she ran her hands over all the panels, seeing if she could get a feel for something. Anything. Over and over until she knew them by heart, how many, in what order. She noted the musical instruments, the apples in the trees, the different-styled sandals the monks wore.

The spiral stone at the bottom left was immensely intriguing. Hellen had told her the spiral spun and played music when the monks unlocked the stone to get the book for John. How was that even possible? But it happened, so it must be. As possible as their little trip into the infinite dimension, courtesy of the monks, and that happened, too. Unreal.

Swimming heads and fires do not mix, so Adia got up for a minute to cool down. Three steps to the couch, handmade by Diit and brought here as raw materials. Sitting for a moment, she ran her palms over the soft fabric next to her. He even sewed the cushions, stuffed them with cotton and oiled the wood. Adia wondered if Hilman could have done all that. Yes, of course he could. Hilman was the most amazing person she had ever known—the best king's valet and almost-grandpa that ever existed. When she thought of him, how he died, all her dormant rage leapt up and incinerated her.

She hated Dagge. She wanted him to die, she wanted to kill him herself, and feel the life go out of him. She wanted to gouge his eyes out, and rip out his tongue, and slit his neck and feel the hot blood wash her hands slick. She hated him; it was a red-hot poker in her heart, and it never went away.

The pounding in her head was deafening. *Okay,* she forced herself to breathe, *time to change tacks.* Having a stroke would not help her situation. By golly, she should stoke the fire instead. Her useless anger drained to the bottom, replaced by useless dread. With dead-weight legs she hoisted herself up and over to the fireplace. It was nearly too late, the fire was so low she was going to have to work really hard to revive it, and she hated that. Much smarter to brave the bigger fire and just have to throw on a log. You'd think she'd learn.

But here she was again, sticking her hands in there, trying to determine where she should pump the bellows. Her hands were her favorite bits of as-yet unburned skin, wasn't it stupid to stick them this close to fire? Adia suppressed her instinct to jerk back. She was careful, she was always careful.

But fire was not.

She was on her knees pumping the bellows when she thought she heard a sound from the front. Hellen usually came in the front, but had drilled into Adia's head that it could be anyone, so Adia knelt very still, waiting. Hellen's voice echoed in from the foyer, "Honey, I'm home!"

Such a cut-up.

"Did you get food? I'm starving!" Adia called back, then resumed pumping oomph into the warm embers.

"Only two rabbits," Hellen announced proudly as she came into the room, still wearing her hunting gear—Adia could hear the heavy fabric and the dangling canteen. That meant she was going to clean them at the sink, which was okay since John had figured out the water supply some time back.

"Two rabbits!" Adia was excited, she didn't often get enough to eat, so she was looking forward to devouring a whole one herself.

"One for now, one to save." Hellen must have read the greed in her face as she passed through on her way to the kitchen. Only half a rabbit then. Save the skin, bury the head and feet. She pictured a naked, gutless little torso, short legs frozen in mid-run, a stick through its middle, roasting slowly as it turned and turned above the flames.

Yikes. Maybe there were some wild onions left, or potatoes, and Hellen was going make a stew.

Her stomach growled and suddenly the fire whooshed into life. It was very satisfying. She piled on another log and waited to make sure it would catch. Adia Beldenet, keeper of the fire. Did it get any more basic? She felt like she was on an endless survivalist camping trip, only with running water.

When she could hear that the log had caught, Adia crawled to the elk rug behind her and stretched out on it. Hellen wouldn't take long skinning two rabbits, and Adia had to have a topic ready, a question to ask her about something to divert her attention so she wouldn't bring up the whole Resistance thing again.

Stupid, impossible idea. A Resistance without weapons, without trained fighters, and without a clue, for One's sake. How could a bunch of wannabes outsmart and outmaneuver the High Wizard of Wacko himself? The woman needed to face the fact that their lives had changed, and all the clever protests in the world weren't going to get Great Hand back. They were way past that now.

So what could she ask about? Hunting...too short. Her trip here with John? Too close to Resistance. Her past? Anything but her relationship with Tomius Dagge, because the only time Adia asked about that, Hellen got stoney and said she didn't want to talk about it.

Then she got grouchy and wouldn't talk about anything, she had to go scrub the kitchen floor or something instead. Adia had backed off that topic, even though given the outcome, she really wanted to know.

****

Freshly skinned and spitted rabbits in hand, Hellen decided to cook them in the living room since Adia had the fire going already. It would be nice for them to sit on something more cushy than stone. They had a lot to talk about.

"I know you're trying to think of some way to distract me." Hellen called ahead out of the kitchen and down the hall. "But you can forget it, because there are things I need to tell you." She looked down at Adia's gape-mouthed face and knew she'd nailed it. Maybe the girl would listen if Hellen didn't bring up "queen" or "royal" or anything like that.

Adia kept quiet while Hellen set the rabbits over the flames. A little pokering, arranging and another small log, then it was time for the news.

She joined Adia on the rug, remembering the horrors of last winter when she and Diit made it. Every single thing was hard then, no joke—Adia's healing process, finding food, making this place liveable. It was so cold here she never could get warm, and the fires didn't seem to make much difference. Sometime later John discovered the duct system was shut off. He opened it up and fixed it so that only the rooms they used were heated. Diit also brought a couple of braziers for the bedrooms, and that was better, too.

Cold was better than hot for Adia, though. It got hot in those first days, when she was still largely unconscious, thank One. Between the heat, the honey, and the flies…what a mess.

But that was then, and this was ... what? *The moment I have to tell Adia that I'm going to a real meeting of the Resistance tonight, and we're going to print and distribute flyers, and in spite of her lack of faith, we are going to take the kingdom back, and she's going to have to be queen.*

Ha ha ha, no telling what would happen after that.

****

Adia sat unmoving after Hellen's little speech. She had told Hellen she would just listen, and not interrupt. Her jaw clenched of its own accord. Her heart was terrified, her mind furious. More than anything she wanted to pitch a fit like a two-year-old and hit Hellen with pummeling fists.

But she didn't. She sat there until a long silence indicated that Hellen had finished talking. Had she asked a question? Adia didn't know. Hellen was going to be annoyed that she wasn't listening.

"You didn't hear me, did you?"

Better to just admit it. "No."

Hellen breathed a deep, slow sigh. "I said my code name is Tallulah."

It took Adia a few seconds to process that, then her intelligent response was, "You have a code name?"

"I do," Hellen answered rather gleefully. "Because my comings and goings must be top secret."

Adia could hear the smile in her voice, it confused and enraged her.

"Hellen! How can you DO THIS TO ME?" She leaned forward, hoping she was in her face. She wanted to hurt her, like she'd been hurt, abandoned by everyone she loved. How could Hellen do that? How could she want to leave her?

Overcome, she slapped her hands over her own face and let it out—all the fury, all the fear crying aloud in one long agony, straight up from her gut, through her throat and out her mouth to fill the big space like nothing had before. At the end of it, sobs, and more shouting, "You LOVE this…this SUICIDE GAME! You're going to leave me here, alone, and I CAN'T SURVIVE WITHOUT YOU!"

****

Hellen felt like the wind had been knocked out of her. Anger she expected, but nothing like this. Adia shook and seemed to expand in a paroxysm of emotion, her fury lashed the air like she was a tiny hurricane, trying to destroy everything in her path. Against a wall of screaming wails, Hellen tried to make herself heard. "Adia, Diit will always take care of you, you know that! If something happens to me, he will leave the palace and come here! He would be here now if I didn't keep telling him we need him there!"

It didn't seem to help. Adia was beyond talking, or listening; she rocked back and forth, brought her hands up and pounded her fists on the sides of her head, and Hellen had to grab her arms and pull them down. They struggled, Adia didn't want Hellen to touch her, and fought to get away, but Hellen was bigger and much stronger, and she pulled Adia to her and made her sit in the crook of her body. She put her arms around the hysterical girl and held her, and held her, until at last she gave up fighting, and sad, gentle sobs settled into her as her body relaxed.

Hellen's heart ached. What she would give to set the clock back, return everything to the way it was, and not have to live any of this. The King would still be alive, and they'd be living in the palace, and she'd know better than to start anything with Tomius Dagge because all those lessons would go back with her. She'd know Adia was right, that they needed to get rid of him right away, before he got ideas about taking the kingdom, the carapaz, and every scrap of everything for himself.

But that wasn't going to happen, and they had to deal with what was at hand. If the two of them could survive an assassination attempt, an explosion, a long trek through pouring rain in the dark through the woods, acute burns, primitive living conditions, hunger, cold and want, they could manage a minor meltdown. If Hellen had to be mother, father, provider, protector, servant and cheerleader, she could do that, too. Tack on covert operative and resistance fighter, and it was all in a day's work.

Because survival aside, the most pressing concern facing all of them consisted of figuring out how to take back a kingdom. A seemingly impossible task which none of them had ever done, and the person most able to help her was crying in her arms.

Chapter T.22

The bustle in the castle had thinned out by late afternoon. Restless as usual, Dagge prowled the halls at a quick pace He liked to keep an eye on things, and he'd found roaming around the palace to be the best way to work off the nervous energy. At the moment, an absence of maids with cloths and buckets told him the cleaning had been finished, and Dagge was on his way to the main entrance to check the decorating.

A single footman rounded the far corner with a pair of gold candles, and when he saw who was coming, ducked through a panel at the end of the hall, leaving Dagge alone again. All the servants avoided him if they could. Quite tiresome, really. At first, he liked the fear and the cowering, but now it irritated him—nobody had any gumption anymore. As a result, he'd started staying up at night and sleeping later in the day just to avoid the staff. Part of him would've liked to move back into his old quarters on the west side, with his tiny stove and favorite blue cup, but that wouldn't be very Overlord-like, now would it?

And he did enjoy the palace lifestyle. Beautiful things, fabulous food, servants tending to his every whim even if they were asleep at three o'clock in the morning when he rang the bell. What's not to like? And if it might be possible that Mr. Overlord was getting a wee bit spoiled and losing his edge, it was no big deal, he could get edge back easy.

Out of curiosity, he stopped, pulled back a tapestry and swiped a finger across a piece of moulding behind it. Clean. At least he wouldn't have to kill the upstairs maids.

Ha ha, he was joking, of course. Maids were hardworking, pleasant people, and some of them had nice figures, too. No need to kill them, a good beating was enough.

Still joking. Sometimes he wondered about his brain, though. These thoughts were constantly lurking just under his surface thoughts, waiting for a chance to jump out, all big sharp teeth and maniacal laughter. It was disturbing; he didn't think he used to be like this.

Ah well, success changes a person, doesn't it? Power, riches... he could laugh any way he wanted to.

Dagge exited the royal chambers hall into the big front foyer. Servants had finished the lower floor and moved upstairs. Several walked long planks that were stretched from balcony to balcony, and with poles they attached artful gold streamers of shooting stars to the high ceiling. Filled with tiny lights, the stars dangled down to the ceiling level of the first floor and twinkled. Other servants hung decorations around the big pillars that punctuated the upstairs banister, and a number of others plastered the big ballroom doors and the balcony itself with garland, pine boughs, holly, balls, baubles, blah blah blah blah blah.

Looking good, though. Rich. Yep, all the snot-nose royals oughta be plenty impressed.

He kept walking. Past the massive pillars, across the balcony in front of the closed ballroom doors. No point decorating inside the ballroom, there wasn't going to be any dancing that night, he was pretty sure.

With a little chuckle to himself, he ran lightly down the wide, curved stairs. At the bottom he jogged over to get a look from the main entrance, which is what his guests would see first. Pretty magical, if he did say so himself. He glanced around for some appreciation, a little pat on the back, or a smile, or a nod for crying out loud, but no one met his eye or acknowledged him in any way. Fine, he didn't need their stinking approval. He saluted the soldiers hanging around at attention, then proceeded around the public bathrooms to the hall that would take him to the Official Dining Room.

All the prep for the banquet was coming along nicely. The menu was finalized long ago, the wine and special liqueurs delivered, the invitations sent and replies received. Winter Festival was the perfect time for his society debut party, he'd decided. What better way to meet the neighbors and make a good impression?

Frankly, he was surprised they all agreed so easily. That was real power, he congratulated himself. Oh, it was only because of the carapaz, he knew, and probably a sizable degree of curiosity, but still, you knew you'd arrived when everyone wanted an invitation to your party. It made him feel darn good about him.

On the left, past the ballroom, the doors to the dining room were open and the lights were on, so either someone was in there, or they'd forgotten to switch back to energy-sensitive mode. He was in an expansive mood, so instead of scaring the crap out of someone, he spoke when he went in. "Hello?"

In here the decorations were finished; the walls, the mantel, the doors, all were richly hung and adorned. A subtle smell of cinnamon hung in the air, the table waited to be set, the buffets to be loaded with drinks and treats of all kinds. Everything looked perfect, except for the pale young man gangling over the table, looking a bit like a giraffe in a pen.

"What are you doing in here?" Dagge wasn't one to waste breath on pleasantries with an employee.

"Uh," he stammered, "I was just, uh...."

"Don't be stupid, out with it, boy." Dagge closed the gap between them slowly, never taking his eyes off the guy. He recognized the fellow, remembered hiring him, some second assistant or something... son of John Treslo, wasn't he? Odd that he should be in here, or perhaps it wasn't.

"Overlord, sir." Robert finally found his voice. "I was just admiring your choice of décor." He indicated the beautifully festooned room. Dagge looked skeptically at him, waiting him out to see how much he'd reveal.

"I remember my father saying the palace was really beautiful, but I never got to come here myself." He cleared his throat. "Except for the one time, with the school. All the kids get... got to do that." He corrected himself, fumbling awkwardly, and Dagge's read on him said there wasn't any more to his being here than what he claimed. If there was, he'd be doing better.

He changed his expression, and smiled a fake, bright smile. "Well, Roger, is it? Are you satisfied, then? Because I'd hate for you to be blamed if anything went missing." He put his hand on the young man's shoulder and steered him toward the door.

"It's Robert, sir." Dagge looked at him like he was truly a small mammal, but it was wasted on him. He turned his gaze around the room with enthusiasm. "It all looks great. If I may say so, sir, I think this banquet will be a night for the history books."

What a dork, but he was righter than he knew.

It was going to change everything.

Chapter T.23

John was glad to head home when dinner time finally rolled around. Work on the wall was going quickly, so no one had to second shift, and they were all happy to bust their butts to make it that way. Two and half more days and the job would be done.

How could he be glad about that?

A little snow flew in with him when he opened the front door. It had just started flurrying since it got dark, and the wind sent tiny flakes everywhere: into his eyes, up his nose...he was happy he'd worn his heavy coat. Once inside, all the little white flecks clinging to him were melted by the time he reached the coat hooks in the foyer.

Familiar voices joked around in the kitchen, soft then loud. David was teasing his mother about something, then Joey joined in. They all laughed. Man, he loved his family. It was so good to be home.

Boots came off, coat came off, they landed in their rightful places and John trotted around the stairs and into the living area. "Hey, what's the day, Treslos?" He greeted them like he used to do when the boys were little, when he'd come home from work and let them all pile on him in the den floor.

What he didn't anticipate was how much that was like ringing the bell for those salivating dogs. The boys jumped up immediately and tackled the unsuspecting father, then piled on him just like in the old days. He'd have protested if he could breathe.

"Wait a minute! Wait a minute!" He laughed, pushing them off, sitting up and trying to catch his breath. But that was only temporary, because Joey reared up and took him down again, and this time John had to teach him a lesson. Fortunately, he was still bigger than they were, and in good shape now, so he had a fighting chance. He wrapped his big arms around both of them, and pulled them together and lay on them, and that was all it took. They started groaning and coughing and Roberta had to intervene and save their lives.

"All right, you miscreants, let's show some respect for the older, still better man. When he deigns to release you, go wash up for dinner." John got up and pounded them with his open hands, in a guy way of saying "Happy to beat you." Then he stood up and sauntered to the kitchen, all studly for his wife, who smiled flirtatiously as she watched him get near. They still had it for each other.

Boys disappeared into the guest bathroom and John kissed his wife hello. "Why Mrs. Treslo, you're looking quite lovely this evening," he whispered to her smiling face. She chuckled deep in her throat and put her arms around his big, strong body, turning her face up to meet his kiss.

The boys were back way too soon. They poured around the end of the counter like a flood, which seemed impossible, because weren't they just two boys? Anyway, they filled the room and John and Roberta both had to stiff-arm them just to keep them out of their space. Couldn't they see they were busy?

"Guys, come on, it's time to eat," David reminded them. "You sent us to wash our hands, remember?" Still they lingered, until the boys got the hint and went to help themselves.

"Gosh, you smell good," he breathed in her hair, and Roberta laughed.

"Are you sure you're not smelling lasagna?" she said, and they got tickled and started whispering very quietly.

"*Guys*," complained an insistent teenage voice.

"Hey, you'll be lucky to have this much fun when you're our age," the Father retorted. "We don't have to pay attention to them." He slowly shook his head to his wife, and pulled her close again, making Roberta squeal a little.

The two boys made horrified noises, which really cracked the parents up, laughing and hanging on to each other, but eventually they agreed to stop the torment and went about dinner. Once they were all at the table, the topic of Robert came up.

David started it: "I guess Robert won't be coming home for dinner, then?"

"Apparently not, since we're having it, and he's not here," Roberta didn't sound particularly repentant.

"Has anyone heard from him?" John stuck a forkful of lasagna into his mouth.

"Yeah, he visaphoned," Joey mumbled around his fourth and fifth bites.

"Why didn't you say so?" David paused in his careful cutting of bite-sized pieces, and fixed his younger brother with a glare.

"Nobody asked me," Joey said defensively, stuffing another bite in.

"Joey, slow down," his mom scolded, "it's not going anywhere." Joey tossed his head impatiently, which was a big surprise, of course. John picked up the ball:

"What's he doing? Working late?"

Joey chewed before he answered, making them all wait for it. "Yeah," he nodded in the affirmative and took another bite. Boys.

"He sure works late a lot," John observed. "Anyone know what he's doing?"

"He's a little evasive," Roberta said, frowning.

John hated to hear that. Robert didn't like to lie outright, but he did like to hide things from people. That didn't necessarily mean the thing was bad, but there was a good chance it was bad, so secrecy always stood as a cause for concern. They ate in silence for a few moments, then David spoke up again:

"Is anyone going to press it?"

"Really, David?" Roberta looked skeptically at him. "Do you think that would be productive?"

"I think the time has come to take sides," David answered, "and that means Robert, too."

The parents stopped in mid-motion, the same dread freezing both of them, John was sure. "What do you mean 'take sides?'" he asked.

David looked at them like they came from another planet. "The *Resistance*! You can't tell me you don't think it's happening!" His eyes shone with fire. John got goosebumps; this was just the kind of people they needed, but *not* his child.

"What resistance?" he scoffed. "It's one guy with a death wish."

"DAD! How can you say that?" David's fork clattered onto his plate. "Thorn's a hero! He's just what this scared little kingdom needs! Someone with the courage to defy Dagge, and say 'You cannot own me. You cannot ever completely shut me down, because I will find a way.'" With a frustrated sigh, he picked up his fork again. "Someday Dagge will be wishing he had killed him sooner."

Wow, this is a mixed bag. John struggled to swallow his bite. On the one hand, he exulted that his son admired him and believed in him, even if he didn't know it was him. On the other hand, *"killed him sooner?"* John was a little choked, so he couldn't talk, but Roberta jumped in and saved the day:

"David, honestly. Eat your lasagna."

Chapter T.24

The meeting was supposed to start at midnight, and Hellen's glow-dial watch said 11:32 so she had plenty of time. John had told her he would wait for her in the drainage ditch—he liked getting around town via the underground drainage system, but Hellen never used it. Small spaces made her a little squitchy, and when you had to come up, which you always did, you couldn't be sure who was watching. This time, though, there were Resistance tunnels at the other end, and the plan was to meet Chief where the two systems intersected on the west side of town.

Flurries of snow earlier had left another light layer of white to reflect the moon, so even though visibility hadn't been good, it was doable. As she approached the wall, she got careful and quiet. About twenty strides shy, she hid behind a tree to look and listen. A single brazier burned at the unfinished end of the wall a fair distance away. Several uniformed guards stood around it, guns hanging on their backs, hands out to the fire. Most of the goons were blissfully unobservant, but it wouldn't be wise to underestimate the danger. Sometimes one or more of a patrol would investigate something outside the wall—like a tree to pee on, maybe, but still. Better quiet than sorry.

But no one was coming, and she crossed the last stretch, thankful again to have the soldier's uniform, just in case someone looked. It was big, and she had to hem the pants some, but Diit brought a pair of boots that were close to her size, and since soldiers weren't restricted to town, the whole outfit made getting around outside the wall a lot easier. Diit had snagged a gun, too, but the laser didn't work anymore, and she hadn't remembered to ask John to fix it. Like he ever had time, anyway. As busy as *he* was, it was easier to just stay unseen.

Before beginning the climb, Hellen slung the rifle over her shoulder and tucked it behind the ammo belt across her back. Running both hands over the stones, she located the first hidden pocket in the rock and started up. Hellen hated this wall, as it represented everything wrong with Tomius Dagge, but every time she reached the top, it felt like a victory over him. Also every time, she used that feeling to throw another shovelful of dirt onto the memory of sharing his bed.

Handhold by footrest she scaled her way up, reaching, pulling, never having to search too hard for her next grip because somehow John had managed to put them all right where she needed them. At the top, she heaved herself onto the flat rock and scooted to the other side so she could peer between tree branches at more tree branches. Faith carried her a lot these days, and grabbing the handhold on the top, she swung a leg down.

Moving quickly, she lowered herself as quietly as possible, dropping the last couple of feet and melding into the rock behind to listen: no shouts, no running, or clanking. Leaning out, she craned her neck to check for the guards at the gap; the ditch wasn't far away, but it was a fairly open stretch between here and there, and if any of them were facing this way, the dash over the white snow would be plenty risky.

None of them were, though, and she sprinted to the edge of the ditch and down the stone-paved side, half climbing and half sliding over the uneven surface. John was waiting at the bottom, took off toward the culverts, and she followed. They crouched and ran on tiptoe, feet tapping lightly on the snow, to the man-sized holes yawning like big mouths not far away.

A few feet into the left maw, John pulled out a bulb torch and flicked it on, so Hellen did the same. Luckily there hadn't been any rain for a while, so the passage was dry, and the only stuff they had to walk through was an astonishing variety of litter washed down from the streets. All the way through the old drainage shafts, the only thing Hellen could think about was flash flood. It seemed like a long trip.

Once they got to the inner half-wheel that ran around the plaza, John turned them right and pulled out a walk n talk. Voices stopped him. He doused his light, Hellen doused hers, and they pressed themselves against the wall under a grate. Light from the holo-ads cast a vague, moving shadow on the wall opposite. A group of soldiers stood in the street above, and one of them was saying, "...I got three-day leave startin Monday, and I'm gettin flat-on-my-face drunk." As he spoke, his voice got louder, footsteps rasped on the gritty street, and a cigarette butt came flying into the dark from above their heads.

"Just don't end up in the stocks like you did last time," another voice answered him. "Two days, sick as dog, puke all down your front, it was disgusting."

"Ah, served him right, picking that fight with Bagby."

"Choke on this, drippy." A soldier's shadow squatted down and he shined his bulb torch into the drain. Hellen watched it wave back and forth in front of them, lingering on the smashed remnants of a cuckoo clock inches from their feet. "I hear there's a new place up by the train station, anyone want to check it out?" He stood up again.

"Yeah, I'll go. I hear they got dancers in cages. I could see me some a that!" Laughing agreement as the shadow turned and faded, and the voices drifted away.

John reached over and yanked Hellen's sleeve. Minus their torchlight, they kept going.

Chapter T.25

Hellen wanted to laugh when she saw Chief Taymer waiting at the opening of the hand-hewn tunnel. Relief, she supposed—no more having to do nearly everything solo. Standing with his lamp, he was a light at the end of the tunnel, literally and figuratively. As they got near, he saw her, and his mouth dropped open in shock.

"Hello, Chief."

"Hellen Parker?" His whisper was incredulous.

"Yeah, Chief, it's me," she said, ridiculously glad to see him. Doubly so when he reached for her arm and pulled her into a bear hug. Other people appeared behind him; she searched the assembled group for familiar faces, but she only recognized Zola, the nursery owner with the brass tongue.

"Hellen, you're supposed to be dead." Zola reached for her turn to hug. "I am so glad to see you."

"No more than I am." Hellen laughed, looked around the group, and pulled back to look Zola in the face. "I'm so happy to be with you guys, I can't tell you."

Chief smiled at her and patted her arm. "Listen, time for this back at HQ." He looked at John, who stood behind Hellen. "Any more surprises up your sleeve, John? Are you gonna turn into a bat or something?" Chief teased as he ushered the group through the basement and into the maze of connecting tunnels.

****

John chuckled to himself and wondered if he should confess some of the other secrets he was carting around. *Well now that you mention it, Chief, I've been reading a crystal book by putting it under*

Best to just let that rest for now.

A long, twisty hike took them to HQ, which was the big room under Beau Hodges' smithy. On the way, they passed through stacks and stacks of supplies in basements, part of the underground plumbing system, and three groups of people who were waiting for Thorn. John shook a lot of hands, but when the folks saw Hellen, too, some of them cried.

The last two were Vartile Sha, the soapmistress, and her husband Luhe. "I can't believe you're alive." The tall woman hugged Hellen like she'd never let her go. It kept going on so long John thought Chief would surely get them moving again, but the man just stood there and smiled, completely unlike the cow pony he was before.

John thought that curious, and for the first time he realized what Hellen being alive would mean to people. Besides the fact that they loved her, and were glad she didn't die, her very existence meant that Dagge hadn't won. He wasn't as all-powerful as he seemed. And that meant there was hope.

Imagine what they'd do when they found out Adia was alive.

Just before they passed from the last tunnel into HQ, Hellen stopped abruptly in front of John and turned around, making him run into her. She pushed him back, shined her bulb torch up onto her face and appeared demented. "John, we have to tell them."

Having brought up the rear of the procession, John, Hellen, and Chief stood crowded together in the narrow tunnel with Chief shifting his eyes back and forth between the other two. They came to rest on John, who wished Hellen hadn't brought this up. "We have other things to talk about first," he said, trying to put her off until they could discuss this.

"Tell us what?" Chief wasn't about to let it go that easy.

"About the plan for Saturday." John nailed Hellen's mouth shut with his eyes and glanced at Chief. "You know, the sign in the forest? I told you."

"I've been thinking about that." Chief herded them forward, following everyone else into the main room of HQ. Other people were already there, at workstations on the left, or picking things off shelves that covered the entire right wall. John recognized the undertaker, and the lady who owned the candle shop.

But Chief kept talking. "We have ten capable operatives, and four highly skilled ones. Maybe there's something else that can be done," he said, voice loaded with suggestion. "We can talk about it while we print. Two hundred copies of a flyer will take a little while." He gestured to the printer, which took up most of the right side of the room. "Do you have a good design?"

"I think it's brilliant." John pulled the piece of paper out of his pocket. "Roberta did it, said she wanted to find a symbolism that most of the villagers would understand, but the guards wouldn't. Look at this." John held the paper down in front of them, and on it were two bars of written music. No words, just the notes.

Fifteen people crowded around them and looked down at the paper. "What's the song?" Hellen was the first to ask.

"See if you can figure it out," John said. They'd all been taught in fifth grade to read music, but whether a given person remembered was variable. A number of people began sounding it out until one person, Lan the woodcarver, caught the tune and started singing,

"…da dada dum…Win the fight, and you'll be free...." He held the last note amid excited murmuring and the start of another verse by Firio, who had a surprisingly nice baritone:

"When times are vile,

And fear is nigh,

There's always light

From up on high,

And never think

That all is done

For faith and courage

Are from the One."

The old hymn got a smattering of applause, and they all wanted to look at the paper again.

"It's the last two bars of the chorus," Lan explained, and sounded it out for everyone. "Without the fight, life cannot be, Win the fight and you'll be free."

"It's perfect." Hellen nodded. "Roberta needs a medal." She smiled and nodded until she stopped and frowned. "Where's the Thorn symbol?"

"She asked me to put it on, but I wanted to talk to the rest of you about that." He gazed around at the expectant faces. "It's not just Thorn anymore," he said, "it's all of us. I think if we want people to join us and really do something, we need to let them know that we're a... a thing ... a team ..." He grinned. "A bona fide force to be reckoned with."

****

"We need to tell them," Hellen blurted out, apparently ruining John's mood because he turned and glared at her.

"Tell us what?" Zola asked, which meant of course that Hellen had to answer.

"Adia's alive," she blurted again. John's head started shaking and he sputtered.

"Hellen!" he scolded, but that was it. Too late now, anyway.

"It's time, John." She gave it right back, ready for all the waiting, and the hardship, and the isolation of the last year and a half to be at an end. "Time to come together and agree on what we're fighting for. I don't know about you, but I'm fighting to put our Queen back on the throne." Adia couldn't say no if the people asked for her, and they couldn't ask if they didn't know she had survived.

Unfortunately, the comatose faces around her weren't encouraging. Maybe John was right. Mouths were literally hanging open, and the moment stre-e-etched out like slow motion . , . no one could seem to snap back. Hellen started to think maybe they were going to need some heart paddles, but she didn't have any, so instead she plowed on into the story with the hope it would revive them. "She was terribly burned in the explosion. Her horse reared, she was dumped, there was fertilizer from the barrel, which was crushed by the flaming tree. Terrible lightning storm? Does any of this sound familiar?"

Everyone was silent, looking at her.

"She was blown to the other side of the stable when the barrel exploded—to the part of the back wall that wasn't obliterated. After I found her, I looked for Hilman, and he was . . . he was killed by two of the soldiers." She shook her head, not wanting to say he was repeatedly gored with a hayfork. "Dagge was there." She nodded vehemently (*he always claimed he wasn't, the liar*). "And he was trying to get to us, but the roof kept caving in, and he couldn't get past it. I picked Adia up, over my shoulders, and took her out the back."

She clenched her jaw and swallowed, remembering. "It was raining so hard, I could barely see, and it took so long to get to the trees, I just knew Dagge was going to appear out of the rain and catch us. But by some miracle he didn't."

"Where did you go?" Vartile asked her.

"To the old monastery in the forest. It really exists. John and I found it right before the King was killed. Lucky for Adia and me." She smiled wanly. "At least it was something. It kept the rain and sun off, and we could have fires in the winter and stay relatively warm. It wasn't the palace, but John helped us, and Adia's valet, who still works up there." She inclined her head to the castle.

Every eye was on her, not a sound could be heard. "You know, carrying Adia to the monastery in the rain, in the dark was the hardest thing I had ever done up to that point in my life. But it was nothing compared to the next eight months. Her burns were terrible. Diit brought honey and we poured it on her. Half her face and her torso were burned—straw stuck to her and made it worse. Her hair was nearly gone. It could have been worse, but it was bad enough. She was unconscious for a long time, then when she started waking, she was wracked with pain, miserable from flies, and nothing to do all day but lie there."

Should she tell them about the pleas for death? About the hateful, angry rants that Hellen just walked away from? *Nah.*

"She's blind now. Scarred on her torso, chest, and face. Her hair did grow back, though," she added, unwilling to end it on such a negative note. "And she's alive, and she's got the best brain for this sort of thing that I know of. I need you all to help me get her to join us."

"She doesn't want to?" Vartile asked.

"She doesn't believe she can do it." Hellen rested her hands on her hips and let the worry show on her face.

"We'll get her to join us," a young man said, and it took Hellen a moment to recognize him as the print manager from the Books n All. "We'll make ourselves irresistible," he added, and smiled.

"Is 'irresistible resistance' a contradiction in terms?" Luhe quipped.

"I'm not sure 'irresistible' is a word that could ever apply to me," the undertaker said in a monotone.

"Oh, Cary will take the job," Zola teased. "He's been mooning after her since she got home and he saw her at the train station. What about it, Cary?"

He laughed right along with the rest of them. "I guarantee you I can make myself irresistible," he said. "Just give me a chance." With a wink, he took the paper from John and headed over to the press to get it started.

Wednesday

Chapter W.1

Dagge toweled the water off his hair in front of the bathroom mirror. Every inch of his scalp tousled, ears dried, he came up shaking his head like a dog. Checking his reflection, he noted it was time for a haircut. Hellen liked his hair short, and it wouldn't hurt to look his best when he caught her.

He hung the towel on the rack and stepped closer to the mirror. Good light here in the Royal Suite bathroom—not from the overhead, so it was minus the usual haggard effect. No, somehow the light from the skylights was reflected to this spot, and it gave a good natural color, even if it did show every wrinkle.

Wrinkles, gray hairs and the weird gray patch on his cheek. He leaned forward to look at the square-ish spot growing on his jaw, nearly coat button-sized now. At this rate it'd take over his face within two years. A finger reached up and rubbed it. Was it a little numb? Maybe. Probably should have it checked out, but truth be told, he wasn't sure it really existed. No one ever said anything about it, and as far as he could tell they hadn't noticed it. No averted eyes—well, except for the usual—and no horrified stares. But he couldn't be sure anyone would say anything if they did notice it; that was one of the side effects of being the tyrant.

A knock on one of the suite doors jerked his attention. He stepped over to the open bathroom door and stuck his head out. "Yes?" he bellowed.

The servants' entrance door opened and the valet stuck his head in. "Sir, General Wharton is waiting in the War Room, as you requested." *Stupid valet, an Overlord doesn't request, he orders.*

"Fine, that will be all." He dismissed the servant and went back to the sink to comb his hair. When he glanced in the mirror as he walked up, a glowing pink light flashed in one eye then the other, sweeping across the blue like a person passes in front of a window. *What the hell?* He jumped back and stared at his wide-eyed reflection. Normal. Must have been a... trick of the light or something. He ran the comb quickly through his hair and got out of the bathroom.

Dagge dressed quickly and crossed the short hall to his sitting room. Wharton was there, standing and looking around, and Dagge walked right over to him and got so close Wharton's head backed up to keep him in focus. The General looked surprised, but showed no signs that anything was shocking, so everything must be all right.

"General, there's something I want to discuss with you." Dagge turned toward the chairs in front of the fire. "Please, sit," he said over his shoulder and settled himself into the chair that faced the door. Wharton followed and lowered himself into the chair opposite, looking very out of place as always in the soft cushions and luxurious fabric.

"I have reason to believe that Pulari plans to stage some kind of coup with his army while he's here this weekend." Wharton's face gave away a slight surprise, and Dagge held up his hand to forestall any commentary. "My spies have reported that the army is collecting in the forest on his side of the border, and that would only be strategically advantageous for an attack here. My thinking is that Pulari wants to seize the advantage while my attention is elsewhere, like hosting a party, for example." Dagge shrugged admiringly. "Not that I blame him."

Wharton opened his mouth to speak, but Dagge stopped him again. "However, I don't want to cancel the party, so we must find a way to thwart his plan, and hopefully humiliate him while he's here. Wouldn't that be fun?" He meant to laugh lightly, and conspiratorially, but it came out a high-pitched giggle and Wharton did wince a little then.

"Sir, may I speak?"

"Yes, of course, General."

"I've also heard that the army is in the forest, but the word is that it's a training exercise, they're using blanks."

"And you believe that?"

"We have a contact in the army, sir."

"And what if that contact was told he could have carapaz out the wazoo if he gave you false information?" Wharton was silent. "Greed makes unreliable bedfellows, General, do you admit that's a possibility?"

"Yes, sir, I do."

"Fine, then. No hard feelings." He tried to smile reassuringly, but couldn't be sure what actually read on his face, so he rushed to continue. "What I want to do is send our own troops to the border, and I want them to be there when the caravans arrive on Friday. I want Pulari to know there's no way an invasion will succeed."

"What about the mine, sir? Shall I double the guard, or put all available men on the border?"

"Put them all on the border, then they can't get to the mine." Dagge had to stand up— his body had gotten fidgety with excitement and needed to pace. He missed being in the field, and found it hard to hand all the good stuff over to someone else. Except for the part where he didn't have to risk getting killed; that made it better, because honestly, he wasn't sure he could pull off the skills anymore. Too soft, too soft.

Wharton stood up, too. "All right, sir, the men will be deployed tomorrow. Along the border and into the forest." He paused slightly, like people always did when they mentioned going into the forest. "Is there anything else?"

Dagge had moved over by the desk, and caught his reflection in the big mirror he'd hung beside the map. Eyes still normal. He turned back to Wharton. "Leave a contingent here at the palace, of course. Our best-looking, most professional men. Everything must proclaim our superiority to the other leaders. Do we agree?"

"Certainly, sir." Wharton bowed and made his way toward the door.

"General…" Dagge stopped pacing and faced him. "Is there any new information on Thorn?"

Wharton pulled up like a horse and turned to him. "Sir, there are some paper signs posted in various places around town, but they don't carry the Thorn signature, so we can't be sure who put them up."

Words fled, leaving Dagge stranded for a long few seconds. If it wasn't Thorn, then it was somebody else, and what did that mean? Nothing good. "What do the signs say?"

"I'm not sure, sir. It's two bars of music, and while we can hum the tune, it doesn't mean anything."

"It means something to somebody," Dagge pointed out, then took the only tack he could think of. "And when were you planning to tell me this, Wharton?" Wharton blanched, like Dagge knew he would. He'd never kill the man, he was too valuable...but he might hurt him.

"I'm sorry, sir, I intended to tell you, but I was surprised about the planned invasion. I see I put too much trust in my source, and it won't happen again."

"I dare say." Dagge smoothly wielded the upper hand. "I'm sure you'll take appropriate action." He let that hang in the air a few seconds, then continued, "We'll say no more of it, but do find out what that song is." Pinning the General with his eyes, he turned him right there into a giant wiggling bug: a shiny spiny black beetle squirming on a pin in front of him.

WHAT THE HELL, he snapped out of it. That was odd, he liked Wharton.

Dagge turned away and walked to the back of the desk, careful not to look in the mirror. "Ask around... the servants, the delivery drivers, whoever." He waved his hand in dismissal. "Somebody knows."

Chapter W.2

It felt way too early to Hellen for Diit to be shaking her awake. She hadn't gotten home until nearly dawn, on top of too little sleep the night before, and didn't appreciate his insistent rudeness now. "What?" she demanded.

"Miss Hellen, I have to tell you something." He stood by the bed, bent over to her, his voice low and face concerned.

"Can't it wait, Diit?" Hellen sat up cranky. "What time is it?"

"It's nearly nine," he said. "I know you were up late, and I'm sorry, really, but I overheard Dagge talking to General Wharton this morning, and I thought it was information you needed to know."

Hellen groaned. This didn't sound good at all. "What is it?"

"They're deploying troops to the border to fend off an invasion they think King Pulari may try to mount while he's here. There will be soldiers in the forest starting tomorrow." Hellen sat there with her mouth open, trying to process all the ramifications of what Diit was saying. "Fortunately, they should be far enough away from the monastery, but it will certainly interfere with any traveling, and with the plans you have for Saturday night."

It was too much to figure out in her pajamas. "Let me get dressed and I'll meet you downstairs." She threw the covers off and for the millionth time hated the cold draftiness of the old monastery. "Will you start a fire?" she asked his back, which was receding quickly toward the door.

He stopped and turned, a little smile on his thin face. "It's already done." He bowed slightly and his eyes twinkled, then he turned again and went on out through the curtain.

They were so lucky to have him, even if he was only part-time. Someday it would be full-time, and that would be even better.

Out of bed, Hellen hopped across the frigid stone, keeping her feet on the rugs as best she could. Her room didn't have as many as Adia's did, but it wasn't so easy for Adia to jump. Overall, she was happy to do it, except maybe when she felt this tired, and couldn't be happy about anything. Looked like it was going to be one of those days.

Fifteen minutes later, she had washed and dressed, and sat downstairs in the kitchen with Diit. They didn't stand on formalities here. Diit sat at the table with them, though he did address Adia as "Your Highness," which Adia had said kind of irritated her and kind of pleased her at the same time. Anyway, he wouldn't stop doing it, so she had to get used to it. *Too bad.*

At the moment, though, it was just Hellen and Diit, and the news piled crap on top of crap. "The rock giants are leaving, too." How could this possibly be happening all at the same time? "We depended on them to keep the forest safe. Once the soldiers know they can survive coming in here, they'll be swarming like termites. But how can we move?"

Her heart sank like fifteen stone. Something had to change. They had to keep the soldiers out of the forest, because there wasn't going to be any way to save it, or save themselves, if they didn't.

"I'll have to go back to the rock giants," she said. "I'll have to get one or more of them to stay, to switch with Duncecap for a while. Just long enough to…get the kingdom back, I suppose." She sighed. "That could be a long time, though." She looked up at the young man listening across the table. "But what else can I do?"

"You can get the kingdom back yourself."

Shocked, Hellen had to wait a second for words to reenter her brain. "How?"

"Who's the biggest problem?"

"Dagge."

"Where is he?"

"In the palace."

He didn't say a thing after that, and sat there looking at her until she got it.

"I need to get into the palace," she whispered, "and kill Dagge."

"You are the Protector," Diit said softly, nodding his head.

"And he's probably the evil entity." No comment from Diit, but she and Adia and John had talked about it, and they all suspected it. Dagge fit the profile completely…seizing the kingdom, all-consuming greed, relentless evil. Him to a T.

But before she could stop them, memories of him floated into her mind: his eyes, his smile, his body…she shoved them back angrily and replaced them with the image of entire families hanging staked around the well in the plaza. Only something monstrously vile could have done that. It made her even sicker to think she'd slept with it.

Eliminating him was the answer, of course. Hard to believe she hadn't thought of sneaking in and killing him before. All this time, the palace had seemed impregnable to her, a wasp nest she didn't want to mess with. But it wasn't impregnable. Far less to her than it was to Dagge that murderous night, because she knew secret passages, and hidden doors and servants' halls. With Diit's help, she could do it.

"Diit, you have to help me." Her heart burned with an intensity it didn't have before, warming her to her very soul. "Tonight, before the soldiers deploy tomorrow." She paused, thinking. "I have to make arrangements for Adia, just in case something happens to me...and you. I should go into town now." Hellen gathered her cup and plate up and took them to the sink, still talking. "That way I can rest this afternoon. I want to be in good shape tonight, not tired." She came back to the table and met Diit's clear eyes. "Meet me at the atrium secret door about thirty minutes after his light goes out." Her voice had dropped unconsciously into a whisper, which Adia interrupted.

"What are you two whispering about? I can hear you, you know."

Hellen whirled around and faced the back stairway; Adia stood there wrapped in a blanket, her sightless eyes fixed somewhere above their heads, a not-very-happy look on her face. Diit jumped up immediately and went to offer her his arm.

"We were talking about the secret passages in the palace, Your Highness. You remember them, don't you?"

"Yes, of course, Diit, I lost my sight, not my mind."

"Quite right, ma'am," he agreed, patting her hand on his arm. He led her over to the table and sat her down where Hellen had been sitting, and Hellen came around behind her and sat straddling the bench farther down.

"So you're going into town now?" Adia half-turned to Hellen when she had settled.

"Yes, I thought I'd do that now and rest some more later, if you can do without me."

Adia's silence wasn't stony as much as it was prickly, or spiky, or even loaded with explosives. "But that's just it, isn't it Hellen? I can't do without you, even though you seem to think I can. What am I supposed to say? Of course you can go out and leave me here alone again. Of course you can stay out all night long doing One knows what, risking your life, and my life in the bargain. Anything you want, Hellen, because why should you be saddled with my useless carcass?" She stood up and yanked the blanket tight around her. "I'm going back to bed."

"Your Highness…" Diit stopped her in his gentle way. "I've brought you something from the palace." A sizable bundle appeared from under his coat and he pressed it into her hand. She felt of it awkwardly and sat down again, laying the bundle on the table in front of her. Hellen reached for Diit's hand and squeezed it, thanking him with her eyes.

Adia's hands ran over the bundle, searching for the means to unwrap it. Hellen resisted the impulse to help her, the girl needed to do these things for herself. Six months had seen some big changes—Adia could get around the monastery by herself, she could find food and water and stoke a fire, but she still had a long way to go before she'd be self-sufficient.

Guilt chewed at Hellen like an ulcer. It tore her up that Adia got that angry and hurt over her leaving. Yes, Adia was her charge, her responsibility, but so was the royal bloodline, and she couldn't let Adia abandon it out of self-pity, or despair, or anything else. They both had a responsibility, even if Adia didn't accept it and it was left up to Hellen to do it for both of them.

Adia pulled the end free and unwrapped a long sweater from around a hat, a pair of gloves, some socks and a furry pink orangutan. "Pinky!" she said, delighted. "It is him, isn't it?"

"Yes, it's him," Hellen confirmed, pulling the long arms up over his head and stroking the faded eyes. Quiet, smiling, Adia explored him with her fingers: his eyes, his mouth, his ears and arms and big pink belly. Some potent memories came with him, Hellen knew. Pinky was the one Adia always asked for when she'd had a bad day. She'd say she needed the hugging arms, and she'd wrap them around her neck and bury her face in him to go to sleep. Hellen wondered if Diit knew that— but how could he? How could he know what a perfect gift this was?

All the stress of the soldiers coming, and the rock giants leaving, and the whole crazy mess swooped down on Hellen and she felt a part of her heart give way. It broke off and floated through her chest, letting the hot fear leak, and she wanted nothing more than to grab up the orangutan's arms and wrap them around her neck and put her head down and cry.

But she didn't, and when she looked up, Diit was gazing at her with his brow furrowed. She sighed involuntarily, drawing Adia's attention, but she waved to Diit that she was okay. "Diit, you did it again," she said, covering. "This is perfect, isn't it, Adia?"

Adia nodded, and Hellen realized she couldn't speak. Her heart went out to the poor girl, who had so little left, and who suffered hardships even Hellen couldn't understand. It made her feel doubly cruel.

Maybe it was time for Diit to leave the palace. Adia needed him, and wasn't that what he was here for? Of course, after tonight everything could be different. They could be in the palace again. Or she herself could be dead and Adia would be screwed even worse.

Time to get up and stop thinking.

Chapter W.3

As a mother, Roberta didn't feel the least bit bad about making her sons work outside in the winter. As dramatic as Joey tried to make it sound, she hadn't killed him with it yet. She did, however, occasionally indulge in daydream scenarios of defending herself in court: "Honestly, your Honor, he was out there less than an hour, and I *told* him to put a hat and gloves on." Would it wash?

They needed firewood, so there was no help for it. "Go out and chop some." She finally had to put her foot down. "Right now!"

It didn't have anything to do with the fact that she really needed them out of her hair for a minute. Winter togetherness could be a bit overdone. No wonder people looked forward to spring.

John was still in bed. He got in very late, and there was only so much time-stretching she could do before he absolutely had to get up to go to work. But she was doing it, stretching the stretched, and she had about one minute to go before the meanness had to be done.

"Why didn't you wake me?" John's bleary voice interrupted her inner monologue. She turned from the dishes in the sink and dried her hands on her apron, drawn to the big sleepy kid standing in the entrance to the foyer.

"I was about to," she soothed, turning him back toward the bedroom. "It's time for you to hop in the shower and get ready for work. I'll have some coffee and breakfast waiting for you, but you have to hurry." She shoved him gently and made sure he was locomoting in the right direction, then she turned back toward the kitchen.

She pulled the eggs out of the fridge and turned on the stove, cut two slices of bread and stuck them in the toaster, then she pulled out the cheese and the jelly and the peanut butter, because she didn't know what he'd want. Then she checked the boys out the window—they were fine, sullen but working, so she hustled over to her office door and slipped through it.

Roberta hurried to her desk and rifled through the drawers. *Where did I put that?* It always seemed like such a good, logical idea when you hid something somewhere. *But it almost never is,* she scolded herself and slammed another drawer closed. This was taking too long, why didn't she think of this last night?

Finally, she yanked out the big bottom drawer and dug through a random assortment of tools, old classroom supplies, and everything else she didn't know what to do with. Well, it was in there, which was very logical.

The tiny bugging device tumbled out of its box into her hand. She'd gotten it years ago from a professor friend who eavesdropped on public places as a hobby. The guy was a little weird, but it did make sense to Roberta that a bugging device could be useful, so she asked him to get her one. She always imagined using it on one of the boys if the need arose, not so much her husband.

"Testing, testing." She checked the receiver…perfect. Palming the little black disc, she closed the heavy drawer and tiptoed to the double hall doors. Her plan was to put it in his coat, which he would wear all day, and she could know he was safe. He'd wig out if he knew she had it on him, hence the sneaking.

When she opened the door, he was standing there. "What are you doing?" he asked, much more alert. "I looked in the kitchen and you weren't there."

"Did you take a shower?" She slid the disc into her apron pocket and put her arm around him, guiding him toward the kitchen.

"No, I just freshened, I had a shower last night when I came in." He smiled at her and put his arm around her shoulders. "What were you doing?"

"Oh, just looking for something," she hedged, "from my old college professor days."

"Ah, the old days," he joked with her. "Can you still remember that stuff?"

"Barely." She laughed. "Truthfully, I'm not even sure I really had old days."

"That's pitiful," he teased her gently. "You could try asking me, I might remember."

"Oh, right, you can't even remember to hang up your coat."

"Well, it's harder to remember stuff from two minutes ago."

The back door burst open in front of them and two snow-dusted boys entered with armloads of firewood. Roberta took one look at them and said, "Please tell me you have chopped more wood than that, and it's piled up by the door waiting it's turn to come in." The two boys stopped in their tracks for a moment, then turned grudgingly and went back outside, grumping and growling and tsking their tongues.

John squeezed her. "Ahh, what a convenience it is to have children old enough to do manual labor."

"You can say that again," Roberta agreed. "Worth every crack of the whip." They laughed to each other and the good wife pulled the good husband into the kitchen to feed him.

****

Thirty minutes after his breakfast with Roberta, John was sipping hot coffee while he surveyed the work that had been done in the last hour and a half. All good. His second-in-command was a stonemason who had worked with him for years and knew what to do. Rack was a really smart guy, so much so he never asked John why he was late, and John was pretty sure Rack knew what he was doing from the very first Thorn outing.

Better not to ask, after all. If he didn't know, he didn't have to lie. Bad enough keeping the secrets of all the ways over and through the wall, which he did know about because he had to, there was no getting around it. One of the other guys also sort of knew, though he never asked about it, and he could probably fake not knowing since he didn't *know*. You know?

John ran his hand over his face and tried to wipe off the stupid wordplay. His brain picked the worst times for the dumbest remarks. With a wave he caught Rack's eye and gestured him over to the edge of the work area, pretending to need to tell him something. When they were decently out of earshot, he stopped the other man and they stood side by side, facing away from the work area.

"Was there anything unusual being talked about this morning? By the men? You know, something in the town? That happened?"

"No," Rack answered, "not anything unusual." They faced the same direction so John couldn't see his face very well, but the half-a-smile John could see told him Rack was enjoying himself. A glance turned into a double take and he said, "Do you mean something in the town? Unusual?"

"Yeah." John tried to be nonchalant.

"No," Rack said again, "not unusual."

That Rack, what a card. Something was coming, so John waited. Rack cleared his throat and put his hands on his hips, turning his body to survey his surroundings, then a quiet hum began, with no change in his expression. It was the chorus to "We Are Free," and John knew at the first note that the message was good, it would fly, that the people would get it, and if they knew the words at all they'd sing them, and they'd teach others, and the song would have a new meaning for everyone who needed it.

Elated, John raised his face to the sky, to the snow that drifted down in no hurry. For the first time he thought they might actually be able to defeat Dagge, tear him down, usurp the usurper. Murder the murderer. The depth of his anger surprised him, biting him all of a sudden right in the gut.

Rack pounded him on the back and asked him if he was okay. "Yeah, yeah," John said from a bent-over position. His head was swimming. Ugh, he needed some sleep.

Not to be had today, however. When he stood up, the first thing he saw was General Wharton coming straight for him.

Chapter W.4

Hellen had on her Junika personality when she walked into the smithy's to see Beau Hodges. She didn't know if he'd be there since he had a couple of guys who worked for him and they might be covering for his late night, but if he wasn't, maybe she could find a way to sneak down into the HQ and leave a note.

The holding stalls were to her immediate right, so she pretended to be looking at the horses while she worked her way down the side in the direction of the office.

"Can I help you?" A young masculine voice made her jump. What to do now?

"Oh, hollo," she totally faked. "Can I help you?"

The good-looking young man in front of her laughed a little and said, "That's what I just said." Then there was significant pause while he waited for Junika to say something.

Oops. "O-o-oh, you ask me..." and she laughed like that was the funniest thing ever. The frown on the young man's face eventually got her to stop, then she was stuck. Why hadn't she rehearsed for this on her way over? "I am having, um...foot? Yes?" The young man nodded helpfully. "With my horse, or ... mule? Yes? Mule?"

"Yes, whichever. Did you bring him with you?"

"No..." Hellen's mind searched frantically for a good reason. "I leave him . . .." and her finger made circles in the air, more or less pointing behind her. This had to stop; she let her arm drop and held her hand up in front of her, palm out. "Is the Mr. Hodges here?"

"Sure, he's in the office, just that way." The young man kind of smirked at her, and she wondered if he thought she was a girlfriend. Well, that was one way to handle it. Junika swung her hips a little on the way down the wall, just for grins.

Beau sat behind his desk, looking more like a zombie than usual. "Beau!" she hiss-whispered, closing the door behind her.

He looked up with a confused expression. "Can I help you?"

Oh, right. "Beau, it's me." Hellen rushed to the front of the desk and bent down to eye level. "It's Hellen," she mouthed, pointing at herself.

Understanding dawned on his face, spread like his smile. "What can I do for you, miss?" he asked, indicating a chair.

Junika sat herself on the very edge of the cushion and leaned over the desk as far as she could. "I have some news," she barely whispered. "Maybe we should go downstairs." His expression changed, he picked up the concern in her voice, nodded and stood up. Then he walked around the end of the desk to the office door, which he opened and stuck his head through. "Zach! I'm going to be on the visaphone for a few minutes, do me a favor and keep anyone from coming in!"

"Oka-ay," came the faint reply. Beau closed the door again, went to the opposite wall, pressed the button that opened the hidden door, and motioned for Hellen. They ducked in, went down the steps, and the piece of wall closed behind them.

Ten minutes later, the rebel blacksmith was up to speed, and had promised her that Adia would be taken care of no matter what. Once he said it, she knew it to be true, and that took some of the crushing stress off. Not that she didn't have enough other stuff to worry about.

"If I succeed, and Dagge is dead by morning, we may still have to contend with the army, although Wharton never struck me as the kind of guy who wanted to be king."

"Someone will," Beau mumbled. "Someone always does."

"Pulari, maybe," Hellen agreed. "But maybe he'll turn back when he finds out Adia's alive." She smiled. "The Beldenets creep him out, they have *powers*."

Beau grinned, but it was fleeting. "What if you don't succeed?"

Hellen paused, then said, "If I die, someone will have to get Adia out of the forest—her valet, Diit, will help you. After that, the rest is up to you. If I don't die, I'll get Adia out of the forest, and I'd like to come here, or somewhere down here."

"That's a great idea," Beau said. "We can bring her here either way. You guys don't have to live way the hell out there! Vartile and Luhe's basement is right down that tunnel, they would love to have you, and we can set you guys up with beds and everything. It's not the palace, but I bet it's warmer than the monastery, and there'd be people to help. She'd have company all day if she wanted. It'd be better for both of you."

It was a tempting offer, and Hellen was grateful, but she'd have to think about it. Adia was just coming around to the practice of self-sufficiency, and as hard as it was, it was what she needed. If she had people around she could ask to do things for her, she wouldn't be as likely to do them for herself.

Deeply difficult choice, but she could wait to make it. Right now, gee, assassination was at the top of her list. "Don't mention that to anyone else yet, okay? I need to think about it. It may all be taken out of our hands anyway, so first things first." She stood up. "Spread the word about the troop deployment, will you? Maybe someone will come up with a good idea, just in case I fail."

"Would you like some help?" he asked for the second time.

"No, Beau, but I appreciate the offer...you have no idea how much. I just think it would be better if I was solo."

He shook his head, distressed. "All right, it's your party. I'm pretty sure I could help, though."

"I'm very sure you could." Hellen patted his shoulder. "But I'm trusting you to have my back with everything else."

"I'll do it." He stood, too. For a couple of long moments, he looked down at her, then he wrapped his big arms around her and hugged her close. It felt amazing.

Chapter W.5

Roberta sat on the edge of her office desk and listened, stricken, to the little scene taking place in the palace. John was talking:

"No, sir, I don't know what that tune is. It sort of sounds familiar, but truthfully I'm not that much of a music-head. Never have been."

John was doing really well lying, it was strange to hear him. There was silence for a moment, then Dagge said, "I see. It seems funny to me that these…papers would be all over town, and yet no one seems to know what they mean. Does that strike you as odd, John?"

"Well, sure. Why would someone go to all the trouble? Maybe it's a business, sir. Maybe some clever guy wanted to take advantage of all the…you know, intrigue…and get people humming his jingle before they even know what they're doing. It wouldn't surprise me."

"A business." Dagge laughed a short small burst. "Why didn't I think of that? That's got to be it, Treslo, leave it to you to figure it out." There was a brief, dangerous-sounding pause. "Except, everybody says it sounds familiar. Every last person has said that." His voice was very close, so Roberta knew he was standing right in front of John. "So I'm thinking it's actually something else."

When he said the next thing, his voice was farther away again. "How about you, Robert, have you ever heard that tune?"

Roberta had to listen close to catch what her son said. "I'm afraid, sir, that I can only say it sounds familiar, like everyone else."

"Really? How disappointing." Dagge's voice was falsely loud, almost a shout. The mother could imagine that her son was probably quaking, on the inside.

Roberta had never felt so helpless in her life. Anything could happen. They could be beaten, tortured, even killed, and she'd hear it, every blow, every scream, because she could not tear herself away.

"I like you, Robert. You remind me of me at your age." Dagge's voice was too bright. "I tell you what, how about I hum it for you? Maybe that will jog your memory."

The tune started, normal at first, then pounding out of him like he'd swallowed a big bass drum. He was so loud, he made the microphone buzz, and Roberta had to put a finger over the receiver to mute it. That was what she was doing when David came in.

"There you are," he said pleasantly, "what are you doing?"

"Go away." She looked right at him to let him know she was serious.

A dark cloud passed over his face. He was tired of this. She completely knew how he felt but it couldn't be helped. "Go. Away," she said again. Then the buzzing noise stopped under her finger, and she had to lift it up so she wouldn't miss anything. She held the receiver to her ear.

"Did that sound familiar? No? Well, maybe it's a lighter tune." He switched the way he sang it to some kind of vaudeville sound. When that didn't get a response, he switched to an orchestrated style. "Possibly it went more like this…" The changes in his voice told her he was moving around the room, dancing, probably. He got very close to John again, likely right up in his face, but John didn't say anything.

"Is that Dagge?" Crap, she forgot David was listening.

"David! What are you doing still here? I said go on, *go on*!" She shooed him out the door to the hall.

"Mom, you're acting weird. Have you bugged Dad?"

"David…" She stood in the doorway, he stood in the entry hall, and she told him the very thing John told her over a year ago. "I can't tell you what I'm doing, you're just going to have to trust me."

He looked at her for a slightly stretchy second, and she felt like her whole history with him was on trial. Then he shrugged and said, "Okay." Roberta's heart wrenched, and she had to go hug him. He was a good kid. A loud noise on the receiver shocked her back the way she came, and her last image of the hall was David waving to her as she closed the door.

Dagge was shouting into the microphone, and Roberta couldn't understand what he was saying. Did he find the bug? She stopped breathing. If Dagge found a bug on John, he wouldn't make it out of that room alive. Why didn't she think of that? Her palms got sweaty, and her throat was as dry as the desert. The shouting stopped, and words were coming through.

Dagge's voice was much lower, and right on top of the microphone. "I wonder if a little piece of your ear would jog your son's memory."

"Sir!" Robert shouted, stopping him, she guessed, because Dagge's voice turned away.

"Yes?"

"I think that last…way sounded a little familiar. More familiar." His voice sounded high and wavery. "Um, would you mind if I tried?"

"No, of course not," Dagge said pleasantly. The psychopath.

"Um…um…uh…" Robert never ummed so much in his life. "Let's see…" He took a breath, and a thin, uncertain hum carried the tune's correct hymn tempo to Roberta's ears. *It won't matter, Robert, it's all right,* she poured her strength to him. Gaining confidence as he went, Robert finished with *dum de dums* and said, "I think that's the way it goes, sir."

"What are the words?" Dagge sounded so angry Roberta wasn't sure what happened.

"I—"

"Don't tell me you don't know them!" he shouted again. "Wharton, kill the father!"

Roberta cried out, smacked her hand over her mouth and sank onto the floor.

Chapter W.6

Song lyrics seemed like a stupid thing to die for, at least compared to all the stuff he was really guilty of. Almost a shame, in fact, and John briefly fantasized getting up off his knees and shouting the little man down with a big dose of humiliation. But no. Not a productive plan.

John's hands were tied, literally. Wharton stood behind him with his knees in John's back, a knife at his throat and the other hand grasping his ponytail. Across the conference room, Dagge was in Robert's face, and Robert's eyes kept shifting from him to his father. John tried to send him calm energy.

Robert was singing. His voice shook, and John doubted he even knew the words. Hymns were never his thing.

"Voices rise,

The Host shall sing,"

He cleared his throat.

"The song of life

For you and me."

The notes faded and Dagge stared a hole in Robert for about fifteen seconds, then he turned and came John's direction. "How inspirational," he spat, then he grabbed John's ponytail from Wharton's grip and pulled John up to his feet with it. When John stood, though, he was about four inches taller than Dagge, and it was a small thing, but it felt good to look down at him.

"Does that sound familiar to you too, Mr. Treslo?"

"Yes, that sounds about right, sir."

It was a long five seconds. "That's the stupidest thing I've ever heard," Dagge said, trying to stare the bigger man down. John plastered an open, honest look on his face, he hoped, but since it wouldn't be smart to play the staring game at the moment, he shifted his gaze to Robert, whose tied hands were up rubbing his eyes. Dagge followed his look, which made John regret doing it, but instead of playing with them anymore, he took out his big, shiny knife and cut John's hands free. Then he walked over to cut Robert free as well. "See, that wasn't so hard, was it?"

Robert rubbed his wrists then, and didn't say anything. Dagge clapped him on the shoulder and acted like they were best buddies. "No hard feelings, right?" He put his arm around his shoulders and guided him over to John. "We all have to go through it. The discipline, the fear, huh? HUH?" He nudged Robert in the side and guffawed, then he walked perkily over to John and held his hand out. "You're coming to the banquet on Saturday, then. Is your wife coming?"

John avoided Robert's eyes and said, "No, sir, she has a prior commitment, but she said I should thank you for the invitation."

A ghost of a shadow passed over Dagge's face, constricting John's throat for a second. He really didn't want to do this anymore. But after a bare few seconds while it hung in the balance, Dagge let it go and smiled like their best friend. "Well, that's too bad. Maybe next time."

Over my dead body, John thought.

****

Roberta still sat on the floor in her office, leaning against the desk, listening through the noise of rustling fabric to John and Robert whisper at each other angrily.

"There has to be a reason he brought us in there." Robert had accused John of doing something that would "raise ire." Yes, he said that. His mother guessed he meant something on the job site, because the good news was that he didn't seem to know anything about what his father was really doing.

"Robert, Dagge doesn't need an excuse to kill us. Or harass us. He took us in there because he knew he could make one of us talk by threatening the other." John was angry, Roberta could tell, but he kept his voice low. "Don't you defend him."

Robert made a little choking noise, and there was quiet for a few moments, until: "All I'm saying is that I hope you're being careful, because you don't want to make him angry."

The rustling of John's coat stopped, and Roberta pictured them standing, perhaps just inside the big main door, facing each other.

"Son, I know that. I appreciate your concern, I really do. I know you love me. You proved that today when you saved my ear." John laughed lightly. "Thank you for that." No sound from Robert. After a few seconds, John said very quietly, "I hope one day you realize that some things are worth risking everything for."

Rasping and a couple of thuds sounded like John may have hugged their eldest son, which would be remarkable because Robert didn't especially like to be touched. Roberta waited breathlessly to see who would speak first.

Robert did. "I love you because you're my father, and because I love you, I'm going to pretend I didn't hear that, since it sounded an awful lot like treason." After that, it was all silence, and the movement of John's clothing had him going out the door and into the cold.

Chapter W.7

Disguised as Junika, Hellen walked timidly up to one of the workers at John's job site and asked where the "man boss" was. Mixing mortar, the worker looked up and told her that General Wharton had come and taken John away. Hellen's heart had dropped to her shoes, and all brain function had stopped until John surprised her with his hand on her shoulder.

Minus her brain, she almost said "John!" but she managed to disguise it as…something unintelligible. It came out like "Jaha!" which could be construed as surprise, she told herself, and she laughed her way through it and said, "You scare me!"

"I'm sorry, miss," John said kindly. "I'm in charge here, can I help you with something?" He pulled her by the arm and led her away to the edge of the work area where he made her face away from everyone.

Hellen felt like she'd been run over by a team of horses. Still, she had to look like she was Just Junika, here with some question or whatever. She smiled up at the big man next to her and waved her hands around while she talked. "Wharton took you? Are you okay?"

"I'm okay." He nodded. "They got Robert, too. We're both okay. Dagge wanted to know about the song. Apparently, no one knew what it was." Leaning in a little, he added, "But that's not true because Rack sang it to me this morning." He pulled back with a sly little smile on his face, careful to keep it facing out.

If people were singing the song, but denying they knew what it was, that meant—a spark ignited in her brain—that meant they were willing to resist. Her brain tripped forward about a mile. "We need weapons."

John looked flabbergasted, but kept up. "Yeah, I suppose we will." He thought for a few seconds, then said, "Remember the lightning weapon?"

"Of course I remember it, it's mine." Hellen hadn't even thought about the weapon since she and John exploded that fish on their trip to find the monastery.

"Right. Well, I never made any progress on duplicating it."

"Eighteen months, and nothing?"

"I got busy!" John waved his hand at the wall. "And as far as I can tell, the book doesn't cover it. I think the secret is the way the carapaz is cut, but I don't know for sure. All I know is that whatever I point it at, it takes over half a minute to load up a charge. Even if I could replicate it, they'd be useless in a fire fight, anyway."

One more disappointment to add to the list, which reminded her of why she came here in the first place. "Dagge's sending troops into the forest tomorrow, and to the Rocky where it borders Pulari, because he suspects Pulari is going to try and invade while he's here. That means soldiers will be in the forest for days, and I haven't told you, but the rock giants had to leave because the tear is getting too strong." Her voice had risen involuntarily, and she had to breathe a second and get herself back under control. "I talked to Browbone, he said they were going to pile their boulders up around it to try and keep it contained, but he wasn't sure if it would work."

"We have to get you and Adia out of the forest."

"Yes, I talked to Beau about that this morning and he said we could go there... but John, first I'm going to try to sneak into the palace tonight and kill Dagge."

"Hellen, that's suicide!"

"No, it isn't. There are secret passages, and I know where they are and how to use them, and Diit's going to help me."

John shifted his weight and put his hands on his hips, agitated. "It's not a good idea. You don't know how crazy he's gotten, there's no telling what he'd do if he caught you."

"He loved me," Hellen reminded him.

"That doesn't guarantee anything," John reminded her.

He had a point, but it wasn't going to change her mind. "John, if I have even a hair's chance of changing everything by this one act, then I have to try. Don't I? Think of what it could mean."

After a few moments, the resignation in his sigh and slump told Hellen she'd won the round. John said, "Let me give you your weapon back, at least. With it you wouldn't have to get so close to him. Wait until he's asleep, okay? Don't be honorable about it—he's not."

"Okay," she agreed. "Can I go to your house and get it now? I really want to get some sleep later."

"Yeah, it's downstairs in the cellar, look in the tool box on the shelves to the left of the desk."

Junika held out her hand to the boss man, but the look on her face was all hug. It felt a little weird, like this might be the last time she ever saw him, and it made her sad. All she could do was look into his eyes and say, "Thank you, so much, for everything. You're a great guy, John." When he took her hand he bowed over it a bit, and she knew he understood.

"I feel the same way about you," he said.

She walked off toward the town with another little piece of her heart floating away in her chest.

A brisk walk later, when Hellen rounded the last corner to their street, she saw Roberta standing on the front porch of the Treslo house. That was strange, why would she be out in the cold? Swirling snow made it hard to see, so she couldn't get a good look at her until she was halfway up the steps. When she finally got close enough, the woman looked scary. She grabbed Hellen's arm and pulled her inside.

"What did I do?" Hellen was nonplussed.

"Hellen Parker, you cannot go into the palace alone."

Hellen drew a deep breath and got ready to defend herself, but instead she said, "Hey, wait a minute, how do you know about that?" Roberta raised her eyebrows at her and after a quick look around, pulled Hellen into her office. There on the desk was a small brass speaker, and... it sounded like John's voice coming out of it. Once Hellen realized what it was, she was very admiring. "Have you got John bugged?"

"It was a whim," Roberta said. "Just this morning. But I'm glad I did it, even if it did give me the most harrowing thirty minutes of my life. I heard any number of things I'm sure I would not have otherwise." She stepped closer and lowered her voice to almost nothing. "Like your crazy plan. What are you thinking? He is a cold and ruthless killer, and he will not hesitate to make a gruesome example of you. Hellen, I'm serious, you didn't see most of what happened in the beginning, did you?

"No, I couldn't leave Adia."

"Right, so you don't know. He won't just kill you. He'll humiliate you by stripping you naked in public. He'll whip you, and burn you, and hammer stakes into your body in places that won't kill you right away. Then he'll wrap those parts in special cages of starving rats so everyone can see you eaten, screaming in agony. Maybe he'll do it for one day, maybe for several. But either way, he will let you die slowly, then hang you on a stake in the plaza. Please do not give him the opportunity."

Cages of starving rats? Honestly, she wished Roberta hadn't said all that; it didn't help and she didn't know how to counter it. She'd already said everything she could think of to John, and Roberta obviously heard that, so what more could she say? "I have a plan," was the lame thing that came out.

"So did Camberton, remember?"

"Not the same," Hellen argued.

"Okay, it's not," Roberta admitted, "but plans fail. 'I have a plan' is not a valid argument."

"There is no valid argument. I know what I'm going up against, Roberta, but maybe my knowledge of him will help me. Maybe I'm the only person who can do this, and there was a reason for me having an affair with him and getting to know him the way I did. I would be happy about that, because it kills me that I did that if there's no purpose for it."

That stopped her. The conflict on Roberta's face was interesting to watch, and for a few quiet moments, Hellen wasn't sure what she'd say. She didn't say anything, as it turned out. Simply put her arms around Hellen and squeezed, then said, "I've got some hot soup for you, and some to take home. Come to the kitchen when you're finished in the cellar."

Roberta led the way to the double door and peeked out. "The cellar door is across the foyer, on the other side of the stairs. If you see a teenager, tell him his mother's looking for him." She casually walked out the door and toward the kitchen.

Hellen slipped out the other direction, around the base of the stairs where she could hear boys' voices floating down:

"You're crazy if you think Thorn didn't make that sign."

"I didn't say I thought that."

"Who else would do it?"

"All I'm saying is, wouldn't it be great if it was someone else? Someone we knew, even."

"We don't know anybody that brave. All we know are nerds."

Hellen wanted to laugh.

Chapter W.8

Of all the reasons to love the weekly mine inspection, the ride out was Dagge's favorite. Even blowing snow and bitter cold couldn't spoil the feel of his horse under him, the pounding of hooves on the ground, or the freedom of being out on his own. So gratifying.

His contingent was somewhere behind him, of course. Not the best horsemen, but that wasn't really their purpose. Thuggery was their purpose, and they were very good at that.

Over the rise, he could see the charred rubble of the Camberton home. His first. He had a strong sentimental attachment to it because it marked the day he realized he was meant for greater things. It was like something larger than Tomius Dagge took control of his life that day and made things happen the way they were supposed to.

And he liked it. Oh, he missed having Hellen, and life wasn't as simple as it used to be, but these days whatever Overlord wanted, Overlord got, so what's not to like about that? Eventually he'd get Hellen, too, and then life would be perfect.

Ahhh, going to the mine made him happy. The little wagons of carapaz, the sound of pickaxes hitting stone, it all sang power to him. Even the choking hatred the workers directed his way—he just couldn't seem to beat it out of them, *haha*.

Dagge passed the place of his epiphany and kept riding north. He'd get to the shack a good bit before his entourage, but that would give him time to pull out his dish and listen some before the guards knew he was there.

Nearing the shack, he reigned in and slowed his mare to a walk. The tiny plank building looked very much the same as it had the day Lord Camberton first offered him a deal. It amused Dagge to keep it, a standing testament to how he got here, a monument to Camberton's colossal stupidity. The sight of it made him feel all warm and fuzzy inside.

Sliding quietly off his horse, he led her to the east side of the building out of the wind. There, he opened the saddlebag and pulled out the silver harkener, which he trained on the ground. Blips of voices faded in and out as he turned the device toward the north, but going west, where they should've been, there was nothing. Back east, where the mouth of the mine was, he found an argument.

"I'm telling you, we need more water."

"My gun says you need to shut up."

"There are a lot more of us than there are of you."

"Then there'll be a lot more of you dead."

A pause, then, "Someday you won't have that gun, and then we'll see what happens."

"Bring it on, Petunia."

The miner must have backed off, because all Dagge could hear was shuffling and grumbling and then the chink of metal on rock. That soldier needed a promotion. He left his device in the saddlebag and walked into the dim and drafty shack. The hatch in the floor was open so he didn't even slow down, he just leapt down the steps several at a time into the torture room.

As always, the trip brought the lovely memory of hanging by chains, on his knees, in this very place. And how fortunate he was to have met Far Left Man, and his fists. And the other guy, Puke, or whatever his name was. Truly, they changed his whole life, and weren't they sorry later?

He smiled as he passed through the door in the back and started down the long ex-drug-lab room. The only noise floating down from the other end was *chink chink chink*, but before he was halfway there the song started. *The* song. The one nobody knew. It grew rapidly, so by the time Dagge stormed down the ramp at the mouth of the tunnel, it sounded like every worker in there was humming those blasted bars.

"Silence!" he yelled, sending his echoes down the shaft to every last man. All noise cut off like a curtain of absolute deafness fell, like no one was even breathing or moving at all. Good.

He stood a few feet into the room and cut every man in half with his eyes. Even the guards, why not? Being the alpha and omega meant you could do what you wanted. The miners looked down or to the side, or the bolder ones glared right at him, but not for long. Dagge approached the nearest guard and said, "Which man was giving you a hard time?"

"I was." An older, rather soft-looking guy stepped forward.

"You?" Dagge eyed him up and down and stepped toward him, got right up in his face, trying to make the guy look at him, but he wouldn't. "Is your name Petunia?" Happy with himself, he laughed and looked at the guard for agreement. The guard laughed.

"My name is Boit. Sir." His voice graveled up on him and he had to clear his throat.

"How's your singing voice, Boit?"

"Lousy, sir."

"That's too bad, I was going to ask you to sing for me." Dagge started walking down the mine, center aisle, so he could look at all the men. "I have a theory, Boit." He threw the name back over his shoulder like a ball. "I think men with lousy singing voices ought to be shot. We can just end that genetic strain starting now." Dagge stopped and looked around at the men looking at him. Or not looking at him. The looking ones dropped their eyes.

"What do think of that theory?" he called up to Boit.

"It's not for me to say, sir," Boit called back.

"Why not? It directly involves you." Dagge resumed his walk down the mine, past the first guard at the exit where the wagon rails went to the train, past the cold wind that wormed its way in through the ramshackle doors, past the second guard, on the other side of the exit. Playing the waiting game.

Silence stretched out, and Dagge turned to face him. The air got thick, and thicker. Boit got agitated, no doubt remembering the blood and screams of the early days. He finally answered, "I have a... conflict of interest."

"Sir."

"Sir," he amended, choking a little.

Dagge was pleased, he'd broken him. That one tiny sound said it. Never underestimate the power of anticipation.

Satisfied, he started walking back toward the front quickly, and from behind him a single bar of that song dum de dummed its way to his ears. He stopped and whirled around, but all the men behind him just looked down at the floor, or at the wall, or at their hand or nowhere.

Fury combusted him like raging lava. He wanted to open his mouth and spew it all over them, drown them in it, flood the mine, vomit lava until it ate up the world. They were laughing at him now, with grotesque faces, writhing back and forth like snakes ready to strike, tongues lashing out at him.

Blindly, he went for the nearest guard's gun and opened fire down the tunnel, blowing the snakes apart, pieces of them flying, screams and yells coming from all around him until there weren't any snakes left, and he spun and faced the other way, pointing his rifle at the workers still standing.

It got very quiet. They looked at him, and not as many dropped their eyes right away, but the terror he saw told him he still had the upper hand. He let his gun drop slowly to one arm, usable at his side, and glanced back to make sure all threat was removed. It was.

Step forward slowly. Keep eye contact. This was the most fun he'd had in a while. Their fear pumped him like a drug, he could feel it clanging in the air and it fed him. His whole body was a taut wire, charged with electricity, strung out like a kite.

He made his way back to the front of the mine, followed a little nervously by the guard who wanted his gun back. When he reached the front, past the workers and no longer surrounded, he spun around suddenly and pointed his gun at them. A bunch of them hit the ground, covering their heads with their arms, and Dagge laughed. But Boit didn't duck, he was still standing there. Surprisingly courageous.

Dagge shot him in the chest. He fell to the ground and Dagge stepped over to him and shot him in the head. Then he shouted down the tunnel, "You will never sing that song again." He handed the rifle back to the guard and turned and left the mine in silence.

Chapter W.9

"John, I want to go with you."

"Roberta, I don't know what he'll do. I think he suspects me, at least of something. He's been treating me different, and not in a good way. I can't take you with me to the banquet."

"Maybe he'll be less likely to do anything if I'm there."

John's brows shot together. "Are you kidding?" He took her arms in his hands and stepped close to her, sandwiching her between his body and the kitchen counter. "I wish I could take you, I do, but you don't honestly want to risk it, do you?"

She looked like she was about to say yes, and John would be worse off than before, but she stopped herself and looked away from him, miserable. He put his arms around her and kissed her hair, and in a few seconds, he could hear her sniffles.

"Aw, Roberta, you can't cry about this."

"I can cry about anything I want, John Treslo! If I want to cry, I'm gonna cry, and you don't get a say in it."

"Okay then, I'm sorry," he soothed, putting his arms snug around her again. "Just don't bite my head off." Roberta sobbed and punched him on the chest, then she hid her face and really cried. "What?" he asked. Women were so indecipherable.

"What if something happens to you?" she wailed, muffled in his chest.

"There's always that chance, my love, every day I work for him. This isn't any different, except maybe not as dangerous. What's he going to do, kill me in front of all his guests? Take me prisoner there at the banquet table?" His voice lowered and he stroked her hair. "Maybe he really does want me there to make a good impression."

"Then you should let me go." She leaned back abruptly and looked up into his face. Her eyes were all red and her nose was running. She brought a sleeve up to wipe it. "Sorry," she said, laughing a bit.

"That's okay." John laughed with her. When she had dried her nose, and looked up at him with her heart all over her face, he felt again how much he loved her and said, "I don't want you to go."

It took a few moments, then her face crumpled like a piece of paper and she fell into him weeping. He held her, and comforted her as best he could, whispered that it would be okay, but he wasn't going to change his mind. She sobbed, and he walked her, still wrapped in his arms, over to the tissue box and pulled several tissues out and stuck them in the hollow between them. She took them and blew her nose without ever looking up, then she put her arms around him and they stood there like that until the visaphone chimed in the front room.

John disengaged himself and walked through the foyer to take a look in the front room. Dagge's head hung in the projection space, waiting for someone to project back. John turned back to Roberta, who lagged a few feet behind him.

"I don't want to talk to him," he complained.

"I'll answer it." She pushed past him, but he grabbed her arm.

"No, I don't want him to even lay eyes on you. Better that way." He nodded at her and urged her back out into the hall. "Don't even come close," he said to her scowling face as the door swung closed. Steeling himself, he hurried to the visaphone, sat in the seat and flipped it on.

"Overlord, sir." Ugh.

"Treslo," Dagge grumbled, "took you long enough."

"I'm sorry, sir, we're cooking dinner. I didn't expect you to call."

"Yes, yes." A hand popped up in the view area and waved his explanation away. "What I want is for you to find out all the words to that little song we discussed this morning, remember?"

"Of course, sir." How could he not remember?

"Great, I'll expect them tomorrow." And flick, his head was gone.

Who knew two little bars of music could be so much trouble? John turned the visaphone off and walked out to find Roberta. The brilliant code maker really was in the kitchen stirring dinner. John came in, leaned up against the counter and whispered, "He wants to know the rest of the words to that song." He edged closer until he was in bare whisper range. "We'll make them up. Tonight. We can do it."

Roberta stopped stirring, put the lid back on the pot and said, "John, if he finds out, ever, he'll kill you."

"Roberta, I can't stop doing everything because of that."

"What's for dinner?" flew across the room from the six hollow legs walking in from the hall. Okay, four hollow legs, Robert didn't eat so much anymore. David and Joey, on the other hand, needed to go into agriculture just to replenish the food supply.

"I hope you made a lot, 'cause I'm hungry," Joey announced.

"I did make a lot, and it's chicken soup," Roberta answered, still looking at John.

"Aw, who's sick?"

"No one's sick, and don't you dare complain about your food. It's good for you."

John could tell they were going to have to leave the song until later, when he could pull out the pad and pen and take no prisoners. "Be appreciative of what you get," John said, and shepherded the family into the serving line. "Your mother works hard to feed us well, and we need to be thankful." He bent down to kiss his passing wife.

"Thank you, husband," the passing wife said, just before she latched onto him, arms around his midsection, content to watch the hungry swarm of locusts devastate the food.

"Can we take the bread to the table?" David asked, holding up crusty loaf.

"Sure," the mom said, "take a cutting board."

"Can we take the cheese, too?" Joey added.

"Yeah, same deal."

"How about a plate?"

"Plate's fine."

"Does anyone want milk?"

"I want milk."

"Me, too."

"Pour us all milk," the dad said.

"Can we take it to the table?"

"Sure," the mom had such an amused twinkle in her eye, she looked sparkling. The dad was enchanted by her, and when she caught on that he was staring, she looked up and sparkled at him. "What are you doing?"

"You're enchanting," he said.

"Oh, stop!" she laughed up at him like a girl, and her dark blue eyes jolted his heart.

"Guys! What are you waiting for?" David reminded them, "it'll be gone if you don't get moving."

Good point. John was hungry himself, and he didn't intend to let the locusts get it all. He followed Roberta to the stove and they served up, and by the time they got to the table, the bread and cheese and milk were half gone. Life with boys.

For a few seconds all you could hear was blowing, until the Mom brought up Joey's birthday. "Joey, what kind of cake do you want for your birthday?"

"A giant cake," Joey squeezed out just before a big wad of bread went in.

"Can we have vanilla for once?" Robert groaned. "It's always some kind of wild fartberry cocoa pineapple nut thing. What are you, eleven?"

"Eat me, Robert," Joey retorted with his mouth full.

"Joey, chew first, would you please?" his mother chastised him.

"If I don't say anything, Robert'll think he won."

"Both of you, leave it," the Dad stepped in. "Joey gets whatever kind of cake he wants for his birthday. You don't have to eat it."

Joey threw his arms up and said, "I want a wild fartberry cocoa pineapple nut cake, yahoo!" and he laughed.

David laughed with him, getting the Mom all chuckly, and John was the only one who noticed that Robert wasn't even looking up. Something was coming.

When the hahas died down, between bites Robert said, "Mother, I'm sure Dad told you what happened with the Overlord today." That ground the good humor to a halt.

"What happened?" David asked, and Joey's head reared up from the depths of his bowl.

"Yes, Robert," she said, "but let's not discuss it at dinner." Too late.

"What happened?" David's voice was more insistent this time.

"It was just a ...chat," John intervened.

"Sure it was," David said.

"David…" Roberta's calm put a damper on him. "We'll tell you all about it after dinner, I promise."

"You're telling me, too, right?" Joey wasn't about to let that one go by.

"Yes, it's a whole family meeting." Roberta's stress was showing, and everyone shut their mouths for a minute.

"I was just going to say," Robert continued after a few quiet bites, "that I think I know why he didn't kill both of us."

"*What*?" David's glare flipped from parent to parent.

"Robert!" his mother snapped. "I told you I do not want to discuss this at the dinner table."

"I don't know why not. I was just going to tell you he likes me," Robert answered smugly. "He said I remind him of him when he was young." He took another bite of soup, and the silence around the table was akin to a black hole.

David had to put his bit in. "You remind me of him, too, Robert," he agreed pleasantly, "maybe you should ask him to adopt you." He shoveled a spoonful into his mouth.

"*Don't you see*?!" Robert stood up quickly, knocking his chair over backward, his spoon clattering into his bowl. He leaned over the table toward them all. "You should be glad he likes me! All of you!"

He leaned back and stood up straight, pride creeping into him, then he shook his head, and waved his arm in dismissal. "You can't fight him. You have to realize that."

"We can't not fight him, Robert!" David stood up too, and they faced each other across the table. "Are you stupid?"

"Okay, stop." the Dad said, laying his own spoon down and spreading his voice up like a shield between them. "I'm not going to listen to you two fight each other this entire meal. Or anyone else, either, do you hear that, Joey?"

Joey nodded, squeezed a "Yes" out of his full mouth, and got up for seconds.

"All right, then." Dad skewered the two older boys with a pointed look. "Agreed, fellas?"

"Yes." Robert was the first and sat down. David took a little longer, but soon they were all eating again.

"Boys," Roberta tried to soothe them, "people disagree, okay? NO one is going to feel exactly the way you do about anything. We..." she circled her finger to all of them, "are family, and we love each other no matter what."

"Let's play a game after dinner," Joey called over from the stove.

"Empire!" Robert held a hand up.

"Black and White!" David's hand shot up.

"Oh no, I have call privileges, I won last time." John smiled.

"You always win!" Joey complained loudly on his way back to the table.

"That way you know that when you beat me, you deserve it," he answered brightly, "and I choose Spin Around." The boys were quiet for a split second, surprised because he usually picked a brainier game.

"Sweet!" Joey enthused, his big mouth-open smile eating up his face.

"Dad, you suck at that," David observed astounded.

"I know. Never let it be said I am not merciful."

"Guys," Roberta said, laying her hands on the nearest arms, "I'm going to excuse myself, if you don't mind, in favor of a hot bath." She got up and took her bowl to the kitchen. "Will you clean the kitchen please?" Returning to her husband, she kissed his cheek. "I'll see you later," she told him, and connected with his eyes before she walked away toward their room.

"She okay?" David asked when she was gone.

"Yeah, it was a hard day," his father answered. "But not near as hard as yours is going to be when I whip your butt at Spin Around."

"Oh, right, like you could." David laughed.

"You're so old, you'll be lucky to Turn Around!" Joey catcalled.

"What about you, Robert? You think you can beat your old man?" John smiled at him, challenging.

"You are never gonna see me coming." Robert smiled back.

Chapter W.10

Hellen waited at the edge of the forest for Dagge's light to go out. The patrols around the perimeter were timed, she knew when she should run, and all she had to do was wait for him to go to sleep.

Happily, she'd slept all afternoon and evening. Glorious sleep, she never knew she could miss it so much. This resistance business was exhausting.

The light went out. She checked her watch, 11:52. She checked her equipment: knife, rope, bulb torch, weird old weapon, check. She checked her impatience, drew her hood closer around her head, waited and planned her route across the meadow.

Her gray cloak was white on the inside, and she'd reverse it just before she went out. The snow wasn't so deep that she'd sink in it, and there was still enough tall grass to hide her footprints pretty well, so she figured she could probably make it in without raising the alarm. Making it out would be the tricky part.

In fact, she didn't have a plan for afterward at all. Play it by ear was basically it. She knew the palace, could hide if she needed to, and she'd have Diit to help her. Probably any of the other servants, too, if they didn't die from the shock of seeing her. She didn't know what would happen if she killed Dagge, or what would happen if she didn't.

Midnight came and the patrol passed in front of her, great clouds of breath huffing out the horse's nose. Bundled and hooded, the soldier sat hunched in his saddle, motionless with cold and boredom. Excellent. Once he got far enough past, Hellen flipped her cloak and eased into a crouched run, anxious to get to the palace before the next patrol rounded the north corner.

It was farther than she thought. She'd made it only a little more than halfway when the next soldier rode into view. Diving to the ground, she lay in the snow under her cloak. Damn. Her soft knit clothes, while great for silence, were not so great for snow. Could she risk it? She lifted her head slightly to watch him. He was far away still, and the moon wasn't too bright, she could probably move along the ground and he wouldn't see her.

She tested that theory, scrambling on her hands and feet, which was awkward. Her hood fell forward on her head so when she glanced up to check the patrol, all she got was an eyeful of gray. Okay, this wasn't going to work. She shifted her weight back to her feet, glanced at the patrol and went for it at a bent-over run.

After about thirty strides, her quick look over found him stopped, staring straight at her, and when he pointed his horse in her direction it dropped her like a rock. Not much time. Under her cloak she made herself as flat as possible, hoping that if she stayed still, she'd be very hard to see.

Coming from the northeast corner of the property, by the time he reached Hellen's general vicinity his estimate of the distance had gotten off. He steered his horse around about forty strides short of where she lay, inching back the way he came when nothing turned up. Hellen peeked from under her cloak, heart pounding, and watched him pull something off his belt…a walk-n-talk.

"Baskin." He waited about five seconds. "*Baskin.*"

"Yeah," crackled a voice.

"Where are you located?"

"I'm on the west side, where are you located?"

"I'm east, I just got off my orbit a little. Thought I saw something. Are you at 270 yet?"

"No, but I'll let you know, be waiting."

"Roger that, over and out."

"You're such a dork, Toddo."

"And you're an idiot, man." Toddo pocketed his talkie and steered away from her. Could it get any better than that? With the hooves' rustle masking her movement, Hellen got up and ran like smoke to the trees at the southeast corner of the palace.

In the relative shade it was darker and less snow, so she swept her cloak off, flipped it over and wrapped herself up in it again in one smooth, quick motion. She had practiced that, even though Adia made fun of her, because sometimes a quick change was very important. Tree to tree, she sped to the shadows where the round atrium room at the corner met the flat east wall. A deeper shadow told her where the opening was, and she ducked quickly into the secret passage.

Diit was waiting for her. He pushed the door closed behind her before he lighted the bulb torch, then he shined it up onto his face with that young smile and said, "Hi."

"Thanks, Diit, that was perfect." Hellen threw her hood back; underneath, her head and face were wrapped in a thin black cloth so that only her eyes were showing. "Nifty, huh?" Her eyes crinkling with a smile, she pulled the cloth away from her mouth and tucked it under her chin. "I'm going to leave this here." She took off her cloak and piled it on the steps. "If we don't come back this way, take care of it for me, will you?"

"Certainly, miss." Diit bowed his head in a valet's yes and shone his flashlight down for them to see by. "Are you ready?"

"Yes…no. Wait." She pulled the energy weapon out of its strap on her utility belt and turned it in her hand until the button was close to her thumb. Her knife was in its sheath on her thigh, and she unfastened the safety strap on it. Then she pulled the cloth back up over her mouth. Now she was ready. "Okay," she said.

Diit led the way up the old stone steps to the second floor. It got so warm, even in this unheated passage, it felt like summer to Hellen, who was apparently used to the drafty old monastery more than she realized. Thirty-nine steps and two turns later, she and Diit were in the secret vault beside the King's sitting room.

The King's cloak hung on its stand, nearly stopping Hellen's heart for a moment. It had been so familiar to her on his strong back that when she saw it she forgot where and when she was and thought it was him. Her heart leaped, until she remembered.

The crown perched on the dummy head above it, too. It was a miracle that Dagge hadn't found them. He searched the palace over and over, Diit said, but Diit had locked the secret locks and all the secrets had stayed secret. Hellen was so glad Hilman made him stay here.

He walked past the cloak and released the hidden latch to the sitting room. "I have to leave you here," he said.

"Yes, absolutely," she whispered back, moving into his upturned torch light. "Is the furniture the same? In there?" She jerked her head toward the door.

"Almost entirely," Diit said, "the two easy chairs are in front of the fireplace now, and the two in front of the desk are gone. The rest is the same. Except, there's a new statue in front of the front pillar."

She nodded and turned to the door. On the other side of it waited the stolen, corrupted world in which Tomius Dagge lay sleeping. *Please One, let him be sleeping*. Murderer, torturer, …lover…could she do it? Could she point that weapon at him and watch him explode? *All the king's horses and all the king's men couldn't put Tomius back together again.* Hellen set her mouth; as grim as killing him would be, leaving him alive would be worse. "Any other last-minute anything?"

"Just be careful in there, Miss Hellen, please don't get caught. You remember where the hidden doors are?"

"I remember," Hellen assured him, moving her mind into gear for the task at hand. When Diit's light went out, she pushed open the wall panel and stepped into the inky blackness alone.

The Royal Bedchamber sat more or less adjacent to the sitting room, separated partly by a servants' hall, and partly by a hollow wall. The hollow wall served as a hiding place for mistresses, or eavesdroppers, or whoever—assassins, for example. Why not?

Unfortunately, the sitting room was profoundly dark. All Hellen could see was the rectangular outline of the balcony doors. Honestly, no shapes, no light and dark areas, no hand in front of her face. She really needed some night glasses.

Time enough to whine later. Best to take the shortest route across the room, which would be between the pillars. There'd be more cover that way, in case of an emergency. With any luck, she wouldn't crash over some piece of furniture or decoration Diit forgot about. Or she forgot about.

Hunched, with her hands out in front of her waving around, Hellen walked as lightly as she could in the direction she thought was right. Sound became everything: her softest footsteps, her knit clothes, the tiny popping of her big toe. Stupid thing.

Her face found the potted tree on the side of the front pillar, so she was able to use it, and the pillar, and the tree on the other side to keep a straight line. The hidden door should be pretty much straight ahead.

Hellen was standing right beside the servants' entrance when Dagge walked through it.

She nearly had a stroke, and froze, not even breathing. If he turned a light on, her black clothes were not going to blend well with the blue decor. Her weapon was in her hand, she turned her body, her feet, as quietly as she could, raised the pink cylinder and peered into the dark reaches of the alcove by the desk.

His voice surged through the space and over her like a wave, paralyzing every muscle for the span of a breath.

"I know you're here."

He said it quietly, calmly, even indulgently, which just pissed her off. How could he possibly know?

"I haven't survived this long in my business without having an extra-well-developed survival instinct, Hellen." He drew in a long audible sniff. "And I have a good nose."

He was quiet again then, and Hellen was just as quiet, both of them waiting for the other to make the next move. In the meantime, Hellen's brain was a churning, clanking furnace—she decided the only way to pinpoint her target was to get him talking again.

"I came here to make a deal with you." When she said it, she moved back to the nearest tree and spoke around the front of it, then when he answered, she moved behind.

"A deal, really?" He sounded genuinely amused. "Something that would benefit both of us?" He chuckled, paused, sat on the desk—she could hear it squeak. "Like, you're going to stop your terrorist activities, in exchange for what? Amnesty? Freedom? My resignation?" His laugh went up a few notches she noticed.

Quietly, while he was talking, she felt her way past the pillar and to the next tree.

"Oh, you may have wasted a trip if that's what you want, darling." His soft voice was coming toward her. Damn, she hadn't heard him get up; she stopped moving and waited. A rustle of clothing, a brush of a swinging arm. Quiet footsteps squeaked ever so slightly on the bare floor. As he walked past her into the faint light from the balcony, she could just make him out. She'd know that silhouette anywhere.

"But I have a better deal, if you're wanting to make a deal." He laughed from the edge of the window, casually looking out the glass panes like he didn't have a care in the world. Well, that was because he couldn't see the little red circle on his back.

"No one else knows you're here, so let's take this into the next room and we can discuss it like we used to."

Was he serious? *As if.*

He moved over a couple of steps, and the red circle flashed briefly on the glass then went out. *Damn.* What a stupid weapon. If only he'd been asleep, a formless lump in the bed where he had killed the King. That would've been better.

Better? If she couldn't see him, maybe. If he wasn't a moving, talking, obviously living human being. Could she really do this? Could she kill Tomius?

He's not Tomius, don't fool yourself. Whatever it is, it's something completely different, and it'll kill Adia the first chance it gets. Hellen adjusted her aim, fought back the image of the fish exploding in the river, and pushed the button again. "You know I could just turn the light on, and that would be the end of this."

No, I don't think so.

Pause.

"If you give up now, I promise I'll be lenient." His voice was so condescending, she wanted to kill him twice.

The ramp-up started with a crackle, and white lights flashed and sizzled in the air between them. Dagge turned around, confusion and surprise on his face as the lights joined into lightning arcs. For a split second they looked at each other, then those survival instincts kicked in, and he dropped to the floor, breaking the connection. The light flickered out, the crackling faded away, and all that was left behind was the smell of ozone.

Hellen felt her heart in her throat. He'd be angry now…very angry. She had to move, right this second, because when she saw him for that brief moment in the sparking light, he had a gun.

She shifted the weapon to her left hand, put her right on the tree behind her and spun around it to get to the back of the sofa.

His voice was four feet from her.

"You want to play cat and mouse?" he asked, his voice husky and low and loaded with anticipation. "That's fine, I like that game."

Hellen squatted immediately and ducked behind the end of the sofa. He lunged for her, but the dark was so much darker after the flashing death ray that his blind grope missed her, and hit the plush fabric instead. With a furious growl, he grabbed the back of the sofa and heaved it away.

She ran to where she thought the desk would be, but it wasn't there and she felt around for something, anything that would tell her where she was. Behind her, over the pounding of her heart, she heard Dagge load a round in his gun.

He came for her, footsteps slapping on the bare floor. Hunched over, she moved faster, hands waving wildly through the empty space until her fingers brushed smooth flat paneling and she knew where she was. Footfalls, gaining, soughing the carpet now—quick, purposeful strides only scant feet away. Down the wall she hurried, followed it tight, fingers light, into the corner and over toward the door. If she could make the door, she could get away. *Not far now, not far now*, but Dagge was on her, she could feel him, quiet as death.

"Hellen, you've gotten quite sneaky," his delighted voice whispered in her ear. "I always knew you had potential."

Instinctively she whirled around. His face was right there, his breath on her eyes; his body pinned her right arm against the wall. It was strange being so close to him again, it threw her off. Every inch of her body could feel him, feel his energy, so powerful. It fogged her brain for a second.

But only for a second. She swung her left arm up, energy weapon in hand, and slammed the pink stone into his jaw. It didn't hit just like she hoped, but enough to stagger him back a little so she could reach her knife.

Gunshot explosions blinded her eyes and tiny splinters of paneling rained down on her head. *Do you know why I like bullets, Hellen?* Dagge roared. Hellen ducked and ran, he grabbed at her, his hand skating down her back, almost catching her belt. *"More blood!"* he howled. She jerked forward frantically, groping the wall and finding the trim. Turning at full tilt, she slammed into the doorjamb loud enough to wake the dead.

Dagge's body grazed her as it dove past in the blackness. His hands scrabbled at her in desperation as he went to the floor, grasping at her hand, her leg, her pants, her ankle, and foot. She wrenched away, knife slashing at the invisible arms, making contact at least once, if his curses meant anything.

Out the door, down the hall, hand out for the wall. Thuds and scrambling from behind spurred her faster.

"Hellen! I'm not going to hurt you! I was playing! *We* were playing!"

Uh huh.

The stairwell opened up on her left. She felt her way down the steps, along the wall, Dagge's yells chasing her, raising holy hell. "Guards!" Feet were already running. "An intruder," he told them. "She went that way!" His voice faded as she disappeared. "Sound the alarm. I want her alive!" All of it became muffled as she rounded the corner to get to the secret passage.

Diit was there, in the barely open door. "Miss Hellen," he whispered quietly as she felt for the painting that covered it. He let her in quickly, and closed it after her. "Your cloak, Miss." He pressed the soft fabric at her and she shrugged it on.

"Do what you can to cover me, okay?" she asked hurriedly, putting her hood up and fastening the clasp.

"Of course, Miss," he said, opening the outer door. "I've tied two horses in back of the stable for you." His face looked concerned in the light from the bulb torch. "You'll need to get out of the forest tonight." Running feet pounded down the stairs, but Hellen was outside before they reached the bottom.

Thursday

Chapter Th.1

Pounding on the front door woke John Treslo from a deep sleep. He and Roberta both sat up in bed and looked at each other, panicked.

"Hellen," Roberta breathed.

But it wasn't Hellen at the door. Four soldiers were waiting there, with orders to take John back to the palace, now. Roberta, in her dressing gown, demanded to know why. "He's needed," was all the talker said, and wouldn't say any more than that, he just kept repeating "You are to come now." The whole family was there by the time John asked if he could get dressed. He closed the door in Talker's face and herded the fam into the den.

"Robert, if I don't come home, find out where I am and tell your mother. Do you understand?"

"Yes, Dad, I understand."

"David, Joey, help your mother. Do not be slobs and grumblers, is that clear?"

"Dad, you're coming back." David's voice and face brooked no disagreement.

"I am coming back, and I want this house to be spotless, got it?"

"Are you serious? Is he serious?" Joey wanted to know.

"I'm serious, Joey. I love you guys." He grabbed the three boys in his arms and hugged them. "Don't ever forget it. Roberta, will you come with me?"

"Of course, John." The parents hurried off to the bedroom and closed the door.

John undressed and dressed while they whispered. "I don't know what he wants me for, but he may have captured Hellen and made her talk. If you don't see me, or Hellen, go to Beau, or Taymer, as soon as you find out where I am. If Dagge knows I'm Thorn, he'll probably put me in the dungeon, and I might be able to escape from there."

Two shirts went on over his head, then he sat on the bed to pull on some socks. Pounding on the door said the soldiers were getting impatient. "I'm coming!" John shouted, and the pounding stopped. Whispering again, he said, "Don't try to come see me. I don't want Dagge to know what you look like. *You* don't want him to know what you look like, okay?"

He looked up at her, and she nodded, her face all tear-streaked misery. John stood up and went to her, put his arms around her and crushed her to his chest. "Robie, Robie…" He tried to comfort her. "I will always love you, no matter what happens."

Chapter Th.2

It felt good to be on a horse again— different without eyes, but the smells were the same, and the sounds, and to Adia it was a little like being home.

"Home" being a hard feeling to come by at the moment. Icy air blew down on them at the base of the mountains, the terrain was lurchingly uneven, and it was as far from home metaphorically as she could imagine. Hellen had said they couldn't even wait until morning. Most likely the soldiers would be in the forest early, and they had to make time while they could. They were taking the back way around the palace because it was safer.

Hellen told her the whole story of what happened with Dagge while they were packing. Adia was by turns furious, terrified, furious, and relieved. As much as she wanted to, it wouldn't do any good to scold Hellen; she should just be glad she made it home. Maybe now Hellen would realize she couldn't beat Dagge, and that would be the end of it.

In front of her, Hellen's horse clicked along a patch of rock, letting Adia know what was coming. It was hard not having the reins, but truthfully Adia was ecstatic just to be doing something. Anything was better than another long dull day by herself at the monastery.

Except... She hated to admit it, but she was dreading all those people seeing her— people she liked, and cared what they thought. It was going to be hard to stand in front of them now, changed as she was. Hard to face the shock of them seeing her for the first time. *But I won't see them, will I? I won't know what they're really thinking. "Remember the perfect princess? She was someone else entirely."*

She had asked Hellen more than once if they could just camp for a while. Hellen scoffed at that idea though, saying they may have toughened up some, but camping in the mountains in the winter was still beyond them. Adia suspected she was right.

Hence, the little white-bread princess bucked up and agreed to go to Beau Hodges' underground room. Hellen told her it was connected to a network of tunnels now, and that was pretty cool. Why hadn't these people just tunneled out of the kingdom and gotten away?

Would she? Hard to say, she had never thought about it before. At this point she imagined herself stuck at the monastery for the rest of her life, which would probably be unnaturally short with all the threats around all the time. But what if she had a chance to leave someday instead? Would she take it?

Her father would never leave this kingdom. Nothing could drag him away. Not even if he was armless and legless and tongueless, he would find a way to do what needed to be done. Hellen wouldn't leave either. Even if someone tried to force her, or threaten her, or beg her. Her loyalty would always win. How could Adia live up to that? She wasn't either one of them. Maybe Hellen should be queen.

A sudden rise brought the saddle horn up and it nearly hit her in the face. Was she slumping? Good thing Hellen was ahead of her, she'd be chewing her out if she saw that.

Did it always have to be something? You know, some correction, some admonishment, some thing she wasn't doing up to princess code? Oh, now it was queen code, right.

Too much thinking. Adia was so tired of her own brain she wanted to scream, and here she was stuck with it again. Forget the usual relief when Hellen came home, no relief for the weary today.

Okay, yes, it would be great to be around other people, even if she did dread the reveal. Maybe she could wear a mask, or a veil, or a scarf. She needed to ask Hellen again how bad the scars were. She had said they looked like fire, but Adia thought she was probably trying to make her feel better. Fire was at least cool, no ridiculous wordplay intended, and maybe it was better to have the hope of that, because a mask would be stupid.

Shut up, brain.

You shut up.

Yes, I am going to shut up, then you'll have to shut up.

Shut up, then.

Frustrated, Adia inadvertently sucked in a loud breath, squeaking Hellen around in her saddle to check on her. Hand up, she waved it back and forth to signal there wasn't a problem. Then she tried to pay more attention to her surroundings.

The forest loomed on their right, hushed with cold. No little animals were out foraging, no birds, no insects trilling or buzzing. Middle of the night, okay, but there should be something, shouldn't there? The only sounds were the soft shuffle of their horses' hooves in the sodden old leaves, and the deep huffs of their breathing. A smell of snow blew down the mountains.

At some point she started hearing taps, far away, and only sometimes, then as they got closer to the edge of the woods, distant shouts echoed back to them from something still going on at the palace.

Hellen's horse stopped and let Adia's catch up to her. Hellen's hand rested on her forearm, but her face turned away and back as she talked. "They're tearing the nursery apart. The lights are all on, there are huge chunks of rock on the lawn—probably thrown off the balcony—men are breaking it up and carting it away, over to the other side of the palace, it looks like. There are goons everywhere."

"Can we make it?" Adia asked. Hellen's plan was to get to Beau Hodges by daybreak, staying in the fringe of trees all the way around the cove that protected the palace. However, she probably didn't plan on being next to the Tomius Dagge Exploding Dwarf Star, with only a few trees between them and a horrible death. That might change everything. "Does this change everything?"

"No." Hellen patted her arm. "In fact, it's great. Nobody's going to be looking this way." Nevertheless, she led Adia's horse back more into the trees, so Adia knew she was worried. The fringe of trees at the base of the mountains tended to get thin in spots, especially over on the west side, and how fortunate that the sun would be shining right on them when it rose. A chance glance from the wrong person at the wrong moment could conceivably do them in.

But she guessed they'd just have to deal with that when they came to it.

155

Chapter Th.3

Dagge leaned a shoulder against the wall thirty feet away from the destruction, casually eating an orange, tucking the peel in his pocket by subtle force of habit. Leave no traces, right? The room was full of men and their traces, clearing, carrying, smashing, but he watched the ones with hammers and chisels punching test holes in the third wall of the morning. That was the one John Treslo suggested, and a lot was riding on it. Treslo's life, for example.

But it took a while to get through that rock. The stones were staggered inside, so you couldn't just go straight through, you had to make your hole bigger. Treslo was using his considerable knowledge of masonry to tell them where to chip, and what to chip, and what were the chances he'd delay them on purpose?

Probably pretty good, but it didn't matter. Hellen was long gone, and who could blame a man for delaying his own death? Not that he *knew* he would die, because Dagge didn't tell him, but he was a pretty smart guy and bound to have figured out the chances on his own.

A chunk of rock came loose and a couple of men pulled it out of the wall and walked it over to the balcony door. He should have done this the first time—found that secret passage. It was his own fault she got away.

He had other things on his mind then, though, so he put it off and of course now he was about to have a house full of guests, and the nursery would have to be "under renovation" or something so they couldn't go in.

What a troublemaker, he smiled.

Step by step, he went over the encounter with Hellen in his mind. The smell of her, soap and fresh air, almost forgotten in the last year and a half, so it took a minute to place it. The tingling when he heard her voice. He knew it was her, knew she was alive, knew she was trying to start some kind of rebellion. He was right about everything.

She'd mentioned wanting to make a deal, but never said what. If that was true, that she wanted to, then maybe they really could. What if she'd agree to be with him if he'd make some concessions? Then he would actually make some concessions. Maybe not everything exactly the way she wanted, but he wouldn't have to tell her that.

Sure, he could change a few things. It'd be worth it to have her back in his bed. And he could win her over, no doubt in his mind, he knew exactly what buttons to push. Yeah, the more he thought about it, the more he knew it was meant to happen.

For a lot of reasons. Having a queen would be the last step he'd need for real legitimacy in the King's Club. So far, he hadn't gotten a whole lot of respect from the nose-in-the-air crowd, but a queen like Hellen could change everything. She knew all the ins and outs, all the telling codes of behavior, all the sordid secrets, he hoped. Armed with information and the money from the carapaz mine, there'd be nothing stopping him becoming a world player, even from this dinky little kingdom.

What woman wouldn't want to be on the arm of that?

Chapter Th.4

Figuring out where the secret passage had to be only took John Treslo a few minutes. The real hurdle was deciding whether or not to tell. In the end, one secret passage wasn't worth his life. It was pretty much a given that if he screwed up or failed, he'd be shot. No, strike that. Shooting would be too quick and easy.

Dagge was cold as ice to him when he got there. No greetings, no pleasantries. From now on, John's game was going to have to step up a notch. Death was probably always going to be on the possibilities list. Torture, too.

He should've made himself a poison tooth or something. If he got out of this today, he was going to do that.

The last swing of the pickaxe chinked through the old mortar deep in the wall and pulled out a little black hole. John could see it; he waved his hand in front of it and could feel the cool air and he knew they'd broken through. "Sir," he called over to Dagge, "we've found it."

Dagge pushed off the wall and walked over to the crowd of men standing around the hole. They parted for him, and he leaned forward and put his eye up to it. Not much chance he could see anything, John thought, but the breeze should tell him what he needed to know.

"Mr. Treslo, it appears you've made a wise choice." Dagge leaned back out of the hole and fixed his eyes on John. "I congratulate you." He smiled that fake smile and clapped John on the back. "I knew I asked the right person."

To John, that sounded like a loaded statement, but he wasn't sure what Dagge meant. He was the Royal Architect, but he didn't build the palace, and he wasn't privy to all its secrets. It worried him some that Dagge might think he was.

"Just a good guess, sir." He tried to smile. "A matter of unused space."

"Then I hope your guesses continue to be so good." Dagge turned away from John and ordered the workers. "Take out this entire wall, find the entrances. Do NOT mess up anything downstairs, is that clear?"

A few "Yes, sirs" turned him back to John, and he said in a low voice, "I want you to find the other secret passages in this palace. If there's one, there's more than one." Dagge was so close to him, John could smell the orange.

"Would you like me to do that now, or should I finish the wall today?" John asked quietly.

Something kind of snapped in Dagge's eyes, and John felt a sudden stab, like he'd crossed the line somehow. But that wasn't rational. Not that Dagge was rational.

Whatever it was, it passed and Dagge smirked instead. "No need to rush here, man, they're not going anywhere. The wall is your first priority, understood?"

"Yes, sir, I should probably be going then. Is there anything else I can do for you before I go?" *Grease the skids, grease the skids....*

"Do you have the words to that song I asked you about?" Dagge's voice was quiet, and laced with threat.

"Oh, yes." John reached into his pants pocket and pulled out a folded piece of paper. "We didn't have a copy of it anywhere, so we asked around and different people thought it was different words, but we put it together the best we could." He held the little rectangle out to Dagge, who took it like it might bite him.

"Funny, no one I asked knew any words at all." His gaze lingered on John for just a few seconds, then he palmed the piece of paper and turned away. "Do plan to come see me when construction is finished," he said, walking toward the hall door. "Which is still slated for today, is it not?"

The nausea in John's stomach surprised him, he thought he was used to this idea. "Absolutely, sir, the wall will be finished today."

Chapter Th.5

Wharton stood on the field between the palace and the barracks and watched the cartloads of rock that were getting hauled from the east side. He wished the Overlord had waited to do this, there was already a lot of other stuff to do in the next two days. No explaining the whims of people in power, though.

Dawn was lightening the sky over the palace. Normally the troops would just be getting up, but they'd all been awake for hours now. Those who weren't hammering or hauling were packing up tents and policing the area.

Two-thirds of the troops would be going to the eastern border: some along the river, more into the forest since that was the likely point of entry. His source in Pulari's army still denied any threat, or at least he did before he was beheaded. With so much power in play— armies, foreign dignitaries—it seemed to Wharton like anything could happen.

Half of the remaining third of the soldiers would patrol the town and make sure everything was in order. No signs, no dead bodies. All roads led inside the wall now, and naturally the Overlord wanted to make a good impression on the visiting royalty. Therefore, the other half of the remaining consisted of the better-looking ones, and they would be scattered around the palace and campground, "keeping the peace" and "providing security."

Wharton chuckled. He had to hand it to Dagge, wasn't anything going to stand in the man's way.

Chapter Th.6

Hellen let her horse go before they left the relative cover of the barracks. She considered releasing Adia's, too, since they'd be a considerably smaller target without them, but decided that in this case it would be better to have the one who could see doing the walking.

Thusly, Hellen was on foot, leading the gray mare with the gray hooded figure on it, in front of the gray rock, trying her best to impress upon a horse the need to walk quietly. Talk about a lost cause. Dodging from cover to cover was a bit tricky, too, since the horse was a little high strung and the tense situation made it hard for her to be calm. Luckily, it was Adia's horse, and she knew how to soothe it.

To their advantage, the entire camp was occupied with other stuff at the moment, and the tree line here had a lot of cedar mixed in, so aside from the occasional gap, they had a fair share of good cover. All in all, Hellen felt pretty safe where they were, in the shadows outside the palace floodlights. It wouldn't be long though, before the sun came up and shined right under these trees, and they didn't want to be visible when that happened.

Thankfully they were very close to their destination now. Hellen's plan was to take Adia around the outcropping and hide her until she could get into town and make contact with Beau. John had told her there was a climb-over spot near the end of the rocks, but she'd have to find it, so it was a good thing she was wearing her soldier's uniform.

Suddenly, Adia pulled the rein in Hellen's hand, and Hellen looked back at her. She was lying over the horse's neck, reaching her hand to the rein, head turned ear up. Hellen got very quiet, looking up at the rock beside them, and put her hand over Adia's on the rein so Adia would know she was alert.

Hellen couldn't see or hear a thing. She wondered if Adia imagined it, or maybe it was a goat or something, there were supposed to be some in these mountains. She patted Adia's hand and pulled the rein again, urging the horse back into motion.

That was when the amused voice whispered in her ear. "In a hurry, ma'am?"

A disembodied head grinned down at her from its perch atop the rock.

"Cary!"

"Shhh," he shushed her, "follow me." He swung his body down to the ground in front of her and led her around the end of the rock and into the big irregular shadows on the other side. Ahead of them, the tree line petered out just short of the wall, and they could see the long west side of it fade into darkness across the farmland.

There was some protection over here against being heard, so they talked in whispers, Hellen the Impatient first:

"Cary, you scared the crap out of me."

"I will never tell. Anyone who can save a Queen from an assassin, an explosion, and a serious brush with death deserves to keep her reputation." He reached his hand up to Adia, mysterious in the shadow of her hood, to help her off her horse. "Your Majesty," he spoke up to her, "I'm Cary Roades. It's an unbelievable honor to finally meet you."

"Adia, ten o'clock," Hellen told her, and the young royal put her hand out at the ten position and found Cary's hand waiting for her. She grasped it and released it, and got herself off her own horse. Hellen thought that was pretty great.

"Cary, thank you for meeting us. How did you know we'd be here?" Adia stood on the ground, covered in gray cloak. She was very careful not to reveal herself, Hellen noticed, but didn't blame her. It would happen eventually; she was just going to have to do it at her own speed.

"We have people in the palace now," he answered proudly. "They knew you escaped, Miss Hellen, so it was only a matter of time, since you needed to get out of the forest."

"Call me Hellen, okay? Did you use the handholds?"

"What handholds?"

"In the wall. Didn't John tell you?"

"I don't have any idea what you're talking about."

Hellen was confused. "How did you get out here?"

"I used the tunnel," Cary said. "There are handholds?"

"There's a tunnel?"

"Last I checked," Cary bantered with her, in the meantime taking Adia by the arm and propelling her toward an alcove in the rock.

"Wait a minute!" Adia pulled away. "I want to get my things."

"I'm sorry," Cary apologized, "I wasn't thinking. Here." He offered his arm to her and led her back to her horse.

Hellen was already pulling crap off of it and piling it on the ground. She handed Adia her backsack and her bedroll, and hung the heavy saddlebags on Cary's broad shoulders. The horse they tied, with Cary's promise to take care of it.

Ready to pass into captivity now, Hellen stood beside Adia and waited for her to take her arm. On Adia's other side, Cary took her bedroll, and wrapped her hand under his arm protectively. Adia turned her face to Hellen and pulled her hood aside so Hellen could see her raised brows. Then she walked off with Cary into the gap.

Basically, the entrance to the tunnel was a crack in the mountain. Cary led them, squeezing between rock faces and down into the ground. Hellen held Adia's arm while she followed, scuffing down an incline, hand in front of her. Cary caught her hand, and momentum made her run into him. "Easy there!" he said. "There's a ladder right here. I'll go first." He spun around and started down the ladder, but forgot to show her exactly where it was.

Adia was waving her hand in front of her knees when Hellen said beside her, "Two o'clock," and led her hand to the top of the ladder. Once Adia established the uprights, she wasn't sure how to get on.

Hellen said, "Wait, give me your cloak and backsack, I'll toss them down."

"Good idea," Adia said, removing them. She could hear the thuds behind her, not too far down.

"I've got you. One foot at a time."

Holding her arms securely, Hellen guided Adia onto the ladder.

"Can I help?" Cary called up. "Want me to come stand behind you?"

"No," Hellen answered. "Just make sure you catch her if it goes bad."

"Goes bad?" Adia gripped the uprights like her life depended on it.

"It's not going to go bad. Cary just needs a job."

Adia filed that away with a tiny smile. Once her hands and feet were steady, she climbed down.

Turned out most of the tunnel was a fissure. According to Cary, Beau discovered it by accident while digging the tunnel to Vartile's. It was tight, and a bit treacherous, with narrow headspace and bumps of rock their guide forgot to warn her about. She held one hand in front of her face as a shield, and ran the other along the wall beside her.

Cary tried. He wanted to be thoughtful and considerate, and remember that she couldn't see, but he was more focused on all the innovations and accomplishments the merchant group had made in the last eighteen months.

And she had to admit their accomplishments were impressive. The network of tunnels they'd built connected downtown basements with the underground drainage system all over the west side. Once businesses started getting the axe, they'd put in line-phones and amassed enough supplies to break a siege. Some of the people, like him, did this full time—waiting for the pink summons which would call them to work in the mine, and not sure what they'd do when it came.

Obey or die. The thought gave Adia a sick feeling in her stomach.

Adia was actually glad Cary was talking, even if it did mean a few scrapes, because it kept her from obsessing about what she was going to do when it came time to pull back her hood. Of course they'd understand, they all knew what she'd been through, but would they also realize that the disfigured person she'd become on the outside was just as disfigured on the inside?

After a while, the fissure opened up and became a regular tunnel. Voices murmured not far away. Cary dropped back beside her and offered his arm.

"Um…" she said. Walking in on Cary's arm didn't seem quite right.

"Cary." Hellen came up from the rear. "You should go first. I'll take care of her." Adia's pack was removed from her shoulders, and Hellen said, "The way is clear. I'll be at your eight. Ready?"

Adia took a deep breath, trying to calm her heart. "As I'll ever be," she whispered.

She couldn't tell how many people were waiting in the HQ when Cary led her and Hellen in. Rustling and low voices told her there were more than a few. After a brief pause, the pitch in the room got higher and became excited whispers. Someone came up to her and put a strong hand on her arm. "Your Highness, it's Vartile Sha." Pause. "We met outside my shop after you came home from college. It's wonderful to see you. We all thought…" She inhaled, the hand on Adia's arm tightened and she couldn't speak, only squeaks between little gasps. Vartile patted her arm and stepped away.

Other sounds echoed around the room and she realized people were crying. It surprised her; she didn't expect tears. She thought happiness, probably, and certainly curiosity. She expected to take questions, and it would be excruciating, but she would soldier through.

None of that happened.

They were crying because she was alive. Would it be different when they got a good look at her? Would they gasp in horror and find reasons to leave? Terror grabbed her and squeezed as she pulled the hood off her head. Standing there, she felt naked and vulnerable, unable to breathe, wanting so badly to turn away, or run. But she didn't; she lifted her chin and let them see her, changed as she was.

The applause started spontaneously. Scattered claps at first, it grew until it filled the room from all sides. The noise seemed deafening. Hellen's arm snuck around her waist and as the applause died down, Adia could hear a rustling of feet and clothes, but she didn't know what it was until Hellen whispered, "They're kneeling."

A flood of emotion nearly knocked her down. Dismay flattened the air in her lungs and her knees got weak. She didn't want this, couldn't accept this. What did they expect from her? One of her feet stepped back and her hand reached behind her in an instinctive urge to flee. Did they expect her to lead them? To be their Queen?

"Adia." A voice broke through her panic attack, sounding very much like Chief Taymer. "We're just glad you're alive, that's all," he said. "We're going to look out for you now, so you don't have to worry, okay?"

His words poured over her heart like a salve. She could count on him, she knew. He was her father's Captain, his most trusted man, and he wasn't expecting her to be the boss, he just wanted to take care of her. Relief brought tears, and as much as she would have liked to break down and sob on Hellen's neck, she stood erect and let the tears flow down her cheeks unashamed.

Chapter Th.7

After locating the secret passage in the palace, John had enough time before work to go home and finish the little box he was making for David. The fake hinge pin was successfully in place, thanks to some banging on the table, and it looked as normally impenetrable as a little locked box could look. He tucked it in his shirt and headed for the stairs.

At this point he had to be practical about dying. Only so many secret passages were worth his life, and Dagge wouldn't be tolerant of delays. Looking ahead, the big item on his pre-death to-do list today was telling Roberta and David about the monk bloodline and the carapaz book. Robert was a big risk at this point, and Joey wouldn't mean to blab, but he had loose lips, as they say. Still, they both had a right to know. John wasn't sure yet what to do about them.

Feet shuffling, hand gripping the rail, it was a slow, tired trip up the stairs for so early in the morning. Too many secrets, too many burdens, and John knew that of all the people playing this game, he was skating on the thinnest ice. He topped the stairs and opened the door into the foyer. Robert sat on the bench pulling on his boots, getting ready to go to work early again.

"Robert!" John's surprise came out louder than he intended.

"Dad!" Robert looked surprised, too. "You're back."

"I am," John agreed. "Dagge summoned me to find a secret passage in the palace." He tiptoed through what to say. "Someone apparently got in and out last night."

Robert looked at him for a moment without speaking. He leaned down to tie his boot and asked, "Was it you?"

"No!" John knew his surprise sounded genuine, because it was. "I was here, remember? You saw me?"

Robert let that pass and stood up to face his father. "You don't fool me pretending to be the obedient royal architect. I know you're up to something that you think is going to make a difference for the people of Great Hand, but Dad, you're making a mistake." Robert's expression was a mixture of pity and exasperation. "He will crush you, and he'll crush Mom, and every last person in this kingdom is going to have to bow to him or die. Do you really want to die?"

John wasn't sure what to say to his eldest son. The parent in him wanted to teach the young man, to explain things in the hope that the light would go on, and he would suddenly understand and it would save him. Another part of John was too cautious to say much.

"Robert, every day, when I go to work and I see the fruits of my labors building a wall to keep all the good people inside this prison, a little part of me dies. Every day that happens. Then every day I remember what it was like when the King was alive. Every day I want it to be like that again, and a little piece of me stays alive. Life is all in how you live it, son."

Robert was quiet, gazing at his father, assessing what he said, then he replied, "For me, living is doing the best you can with the hand you're dealt." He reached for his coat and put it on. "I don't know what you think is going to happen, but don't expect any sympathy from me when you get caught." His hat went on his head, he smacked his gloves onto his palm and said, "I've got to go, see you later. Tell Mom I said bye."

"Bye, son. Have a good day." John held his hand up in a wave, and watched Robert walk out the front door.

He didn't know whether Roberta was up, so he went into the kitchen to start breakfast. The three, or maybe four, of them could sit at the table, and eat some something, and he'd tell the secrets. They might pelt him with rotten tomatoes for not telling them sooner, but there weren't any tomatoes, so John felt relatively safe. He was just taking the eggs out of the cooler when Roberta sailed into the kitchen in her flowing dressing gown.

"What are you doing, you big handsome man?"

John was glad he woke her up when he got home. She was happy to see him, and he could tell she thought she might not ever again. She cried, and he held her and loved her, and the joy was bittersweet. This resistance business left scars on all of them.

"I am making one-eyes for breakfast." He kissed her and reached the eggs to the counter, then he pulled her to him in a firm embrace, making her laugh that deep throaty way he loved. He looked down at her shining face and kissed her tenderly, on her cheeks, her eyes, her mouth. She buried her head in his neck and settled into him, arms tight around his middle. Did it get any better than this?

"Guys, what's up?" David brushed around them on his way to the fridge, where he pulled out the OJ and drank straight from the bottle.

"David," his mother groaned, "could you at least pretend you don't do that?"

"Why?" David asked.

"Because at least I can have my illusions if you aren't doing it right in front of me." Her voice was mock-annoyed when she looked up at John. "Would you make him stop?"

"David!" John scolded and held his hand out for the bottle. David turned it over to him grudgingly, with one of those "uh!" sounds more typical of teenage girls. John took the bottle, put it up to his mouth and finished it off with a big "Ah!" of satisfaction. "There, now you don't have to worry about it."

Amid the laughter from father and son, and the good-natured protests from the wife, Joey stumbled into the den rubbing his eyes. "What's going on down here?"

"At the moment, we're making one-eyes," John explained. "How about you do the buttering?"

"Okay, I love one-eyes," Joey mumbled, lurching his way into the kitchen and over to the butter.

David stood over the stove and heated the pan, eggs ready at his side. "What did Dagge want last night?"

"Some architectural advice," John hedged.

"In the middle of the night?"

Roberta took the reins. "Someone got in and out of the palace, so he wanted your dad to find the secret passage they used."

Joey was agog. "Someone got in and out? Did they do anything?"

"No." John shook his head. "Probably just someone showing off."

"Risking death to show off? Not smart," David observed. "Maybe it was Thorn, and he was really trying to kill Dagge."

"Thorn hasn't done anything violent," Roberta cut in. "Why would you think it was him?"

"He's the only one brave enough." David plopped the first slice of buttered bread into the pan.

Joey handed him an egg. "He's the leader!"

Roberta and John exchanged looks behind their sons, who were working away at the stove. Roberta's face was full of pride for him, because it meant everything to a man for his sons to admire him.

Chapter Th.8

Dagge watched the troop deployment from the large curved balcony over the front entrance of the palace. Groups of four or five passed below him in an endless parade, some mounted, most not, all with packs and gear and weapons. To his left he could hear Wharton, bellowing instructions to each group as they stepped up, echoed by an officer, belittled by a sergeant, and sent on their way.

In the distance, the wall was very near completion. A gap of probably four feet marked the last vestige of the concept of freedom for the stupid schmos inside the town. Served them right for so many of them trying to run in the early days. Quite of few families and small groups were caught, and then they had to be made examples of. A little flaying went a long way, as it turned out. What did they expect? If everybody ran, there'd be no one to work the mine.

Once the wall was completed, everything would be in order for the arrival of his guests tomorrow. Outside, the lawn was cleared of debris, the portable latrines would be carted in this afternoon, and the banners would be raised in the morning. Inside, the kitchen staff was already in high gear, and the palace looked beautiful. It seemed in spite of everything Thorn had thrown at him, plans for the banquet were going to come off without a hitch.

If Thorn knew what those plans were, she would have tried harder.

The more he thought about it, the more he was disappointed with Hellen. She barely acknowledged him. At their next encounter, he was going to have to insist on some respect.

Dagge spun away from the balcony and went inside.

Chapter Th.9

David turned the little box over and over in his hands. The wood was rough, barely sanded, and plain as plank. "It's a puzzle box," Dad had said. "See if you can open it."

He'd given it to him right after the big talk about how he and Robert and Joey were all monk-spawn. *Haha, crazy shit, man.* Like finding out you were actually royalty. Too bad Dad didn't tell them about it eight or ten years ago, it would've been great to lord it over the snotty kids in school.

Except they weren't supposed to tell anyone, of course. Joey got read the riot act before Dad would tell them anything, but David knew Joey could keep secrets, so he vouched for him. Robert wasn't at the meeting, and no matter how much David begged, Dad had refused to not tell him about it. Knowing Robert, it was only a matter of time before he "let it slip" to Dagge—no way could the brown-noser resist showing off that kind of pedigree.

Dad's call, though, so no point in stewing over it, his brain had better things to do. As cool as it was to be descended from a monk, it did raise the bar a bit. Leaning back in his squeaky, worn-out desk chair, David accepted the challenge with a grin. *Let's put this gene pool to the test, then, shall we?*

It looked like an ordinary box. Hinged lid, tiny hole, the words "Hope is never really lost" on the front in blocky writing. *Cute, Dad.* David held the box up to his ear and shook it gently. Nothing. A closer examination of the hole revealed…a hole. Could be a keyhole, but there was no key. That meant it was either a fake keyhole, or there had to be some kind of key.

Dad would never do something as obvious as allow any old long skinny thing that fit in the hole to work as a key. So of course David decided to try anyway, just to rule the obvious out. Glancing around, he realized his immediate vicinity was short on long skinny things. Pencil, *no*, pen, *no*, compass point, *not really*. Twist-tie on the stereo cable, *try that*. He loosed the tie, straightened the tip and stuck the wire in. A hard push crumpled the wire, but didn't do anything to the box.

Hm. From the desk drawer, David pulled out a magnifying glass and a bright little bulb torch and examined the hole again. Looked like there was something behind it, which meant it wasn't just a drilled decoy. It was either functional, or his dad spent way too much time on this.

No key. What did that mean? He examined the box again. It must be put together with glue, because there weren't any nails or screws, or plugs to hide them. David pushed on all the sides…nothing. Pulled on all the sides…ditto. He twisted, smashed, shook and slapped, but none of it made any difference. Blowing didn't work, singing didn't work, biting only left teeth marks (if Dad asked, he could say he was chewing on the problem outside the box. *Har har*).

What about the hinge? It ran the entire length of the back, which was unusual. A piano hinge, right? Jiggling the lid, he tested it for play—any looseness that might tell him something. But there wasn't any.

Hey, all he had to do was take out the hinge pin. Could it be that easy? He turned the box to find the head of the pin, and tried to wedge his fingernails under it to pull it out. Okay, that didn't work, he picked up the twist-tie and tried to force that under.

Uhhhh, yeah. After some effort, the wire separated the head enough for David to get his fingernails in, and he pulled the sucker out. The pin was a lot shorter than the hinge, which was weird. No head on the other end of the hinge, either, but with the magnifying glass, he could see that there were a few tiny soldering tacks.

Aha, fake hinge. So why was there a hinge pin at all? He looked at it, and it was just about the right size for the keyhole. Well, what do you know? He stuck the end of the pin into the keyhole, and it went in, then it went farther in, and the end of the box sprang open. Victory!

Inside the box was a collection of gears and springs and a folded piece of paper. David reached into the space and pulled out the note. It said:

"Dear David,

Congratulations, son, you did it! Excellent work. Sometimes the simplest assumptions, like the function of a hinge, can be the hardest to overcome. You are hereby awarded the "Don't Let Appearances Fool You" award, a rare and exalted honor.

Salute!

Dad"

Dad was so weird. Great, but weird.

Chapter Th.10

Early afternoon came round before Adia got a minute to herself. With traveling all night and meeting about a million people, in and out, all day, she was exhausted. As kind and respectful as they all were, some of the visitors were awkward about her scars. She could tell because their voices were slightly turned away from her, and their pitch was higher. Those people made her uncomfortable, too, and she had to admit she got to a point where she couldn't think of anything else to say. Hopefully she wasn't rude, definitely she was rusty.

And tired. And sore already. This was the longest she'd ever been without riding, and she was feeling it all over. It was hard to admit to herself she'd gotten that out of shape.

Gratefully, she sank down onto the couch in Vartile and Luhe's basement, her new home for however long. She'd given the room a quick once-over when they brought her in: measured off the steps, got sound bearings, learned the layout. A wall of shelves divided it into two rooms, not very big, but later today they were getting real twin beds from someone, and even a basement was warmer than the monastery. Pure bliss.

At the moment, the greatest upside was that the couch was soft and she had a real feather pillow. Adia stretched out and piled the fat blankets on top of her. Heaven. Hellen was gone for a little while, which lent an air of normalcy to the situation. Maybe she wouldn't wake her up when she came in.

The day replayed itself in her mind…mostly the part that had Cary Roades in it. Right after the whole "queen" thing in HQ, while she was still wiping the tears off her face, he came up to her again, and he must have looked right at her scars, but his voice sounded no different, the way he treated her was no different, and the fact that he hung around was interesting. Later she learned he worked as a rabbit, meaning he drew off the bad guys because he could jump and swing and run like most people could only dream.

His attention flattered her, but she wasn't sure what to think. No doubt all her blubbering made it abundantly clear that she wasn't queenly, nor up to planning a castle onslaught or anything of the sort. Therefore, without a throne dangling in front of her, weren't all the rules for princess expectations pretty much trashed? Not likely she would marry some prince or noble's son now, so maybe she could do what normal girls do. *What is that, exactly?*

Dating. She'd heard of it. The guy picks you up, takes you out to dinner, a movie, a picnic, or something. You see if you're compatible in an easy, no-stress environment. Hm, somehow she couldn't see that happening. Next topic.

Beau told them there was going to be a meeting tonight. Hellen had gone to get word to John, via Roberta, that she and Adia were officially in the system. Someone else was getting word about the meeting to Chief Taymer, who was busy with the new troops deploying in town today, and couldn't come by until later. Adia would be very glad to talk to him. She didn't get a chance before he left that morning, and he remained the most significant link to her father she had.

Adia exhaled and let the tension go out of her body. For a few minutes she lay quiet in her eternal dark and listened to all the sounds she could hear. Upstairs, someone walking around, barely audible voices, Vartile's laugh. Off to the side, clanging noises drifting down the tunnel from HQ.

Warmth and food and sounds of people were like heaven after the long hard months at the monastery. But how stupid was it to run *into* a prison?

Chapter Th.11

On the whole, moving through town went a lot easier when she wasn't being hunted. Truth was, she probably didn't even need the Junika disguise, but felt more comfortable with it on, just in case. There could still be a few people around who knew who Hellen Parker was.

But why worry? The streets were practically deserted, if you didn't count the steady stream of soldiers checking locked doors and pulling down flyers. A lot of flyers, in fact. Looked like the crew was busy last night.

Catcalls and whistles dogged her steps, but Junika strategically ignored them. Going solo made her an easy target. Once or twice some huge ego started toward her, but she moved away quickly and left them behind. Getting recognized wasn't her biggest threat, as it turned out, getting accosted was. Stupid jerks.

The snow had mostly melted and the wind was mild, so the afternoon was a lot more pleasant than some. Overhead, the cloudy sky had bare spots that promised occasional sun, and any amount of sun would be welcome. Might be worth trying to maneuver Adia out into it somehow. They hadn't even been in town a day yet, but living underground couldn't be all that good for a person. It seemed better to make fresh air a habit as soon as possible.

Hellen crossed the road that let her into the neighborhoods. John needed to be in on what they were doing, and as much as John resisted, the Resistance needed Roberta in on it. The flyer was proof of that. She might not have the physical skills some of them had, but that wasn't all people were good for. Everyone had their part to play.

How likely was it that Roberta had the bug on John today? After yesterday, not very. What with the near-death scene in the palace, she probably spilled the beans to him about the bug as soon as he got home.

She was in such a state she'd have had to. There's only so much stress a body could take. In a lot of ways, it was probably better not to know everything.

But on the other hand, people need to know some things. Like did the people in these houses have any idea they could fight? A few of them were outside, checking their mailboxes, walking the dogs. Some of them were in the mine, no doubt. All of them, every last one of them, could make a difference if they knew they could. They didn't have to be athletic, or super intelligent, or trained, or anything, they just had to be willing. Deep down inside they had to know that all the things that are good and right in the world are worth dying for.

Behind her, a faint whistling floated down the street to her ears. She tuned in for a few seconds, listening, and there it was, "We Are Free." Hellen's heart surged in her chest, and she turned around to see where it was coming from—a man in a black coat was walking his dog, his back to her. Just an ordinary man, in his sixties, probably, graying hair, doing an ordinary thing.

And it gave her hope.

David answered her knock. Holding the door open wide, he said, "It's you again."

"Hello!" She smiled, glad she had worked out her cover story.

"What are you doing here?"

"I am having something bring for you mother," Junika said.

David screwed his forehead up and said, "Do you need language lessons? Because I'm for hire."

"David, don't be rude." His mother appeared behind him. "Please," she said, and held her hand out to Hellen, "what was your name?"

"Junika." Hellen took Roberta's hand and got pulled into the house.

"Junika, that's right." Roberta put an arm around her shoulders as they walked through the foyer. "David, will you put some water on the stove for tea? You like tea, don't you?"

"Oh, yes," Junika answered, chilled enough to be really glad.

David closed the front door and loitered behind them, but his mother wasn't having any of that. "David, do you need something?"

"No." He shook his head. "Just listening."

"Go put some water on." Roberta glared at him until he surrendered.

"Okay! I didn't know it was time-sensitive," David complained, and went around them.

Roberta looked after him until he was almost gone. "Junika, why don't we step into my office?" She herded Hellen through the double door.

Inside, she sat Junika down on the little sofa and hurried to the other end of the room to check the door to the kitchen. David was apparently there, because Hellen heard the door open and Roberta said, "Do NOT eavesdrop at my office door. I don't care if you're nineteen, I wouldn't care if you were thirty, I will ground your ass for the next fifteen years. Is that understood?"

"Okay, okay. I was just…never mind."

The last part drifted away, to the stove, Hellen guessed. Roberta reappeared and came to sit on the sofa with her. Her voice was barely above a whisper. "I'm so glad you're okay. John was called to the palace last night to find the secret passage you used. Dagge's destroying it."

"Which one did he find?"

Roberta looked puzzled for a second. "The one in the nursery. Isn't that the one you used?"

"Not this time," Hellen said quickly. "But thanks for the update. You never know when I might need to know that. I'm actually here to tell you and John that…" *oh dear, Roberta doesn't know about Adia yet*. "Well, I'm here to tell you that Adia's alive. She survived the explosion, she's at HQ, and there's a meeting there tonight that you and John need to come to."

There was a moment of silence, and another, and another, and another, then, "Hellen Parker. I can't believe you didn't tell me this before." Roberta's whisper was shocked.

"No one knew, except me and John and her valet. We decided it was better that way— safer for her, and you. Please don't be angry." Into Roberta's silence, Hellen explained Adia's condition, then and now, and how much the clothes and blankets and supplies were appreciated.

Finally Roberta nodded, so much had been kept from her she must have been used to it. She said, "If I had known, I could have done more. I would have done more, I would have helped." She lay her face in her hands, overcome.

"I know you would have. So did John. He knew he wouldn't be able to stop you, and he couldn't risk your life like that. And I couldn't argue with him." Hellen shook her head and continued, "Unfortunately, everything's changed, it's not safe in the forest anymore." She shrugged. "Or maybe it's not so unfortunate, I don't know."

"What do you mean?" Roberta asked.

"Adia is…refusing to participate. 'Participate' isn't the right word, she's not on board with the whole idea of getting the kingdom back."

"Really?" Roberta frowned.

"She feels damaged now. Not just the scars and the blindness, although that's part of it. It's that, in her eyes, those things represent what's happened to her on the inside, in her spirit. Everything was ripped away from her that night, in the most violent way possible, and I think seeing her father murdered has made her afraid." Hellen shook her head sadly. "Who can blame her? He was everything to her, she saw him as invincible, and when he wasn't, the world became a terrifying place. And even before that she didn't feel ready, so she doesn't believe she can rule now. She doesn't want to, and I don't know how to convince her otherwise."

"Well, we'll have to put our heads together," Roberta said, over the noise of David entering with a loaded tray. She stood up and met him with a kiss on the cheek. "Thank you so much, honey." Taking the tray from him, she set it on the desk while David walked his mollified face back the way he came.

"You're the best," she called after him, "be sure and close the door on your way out." David laughed and threw his hands up, shaking his head all the way back out to the kitchen.

Roberta handed Hellen her teacup and they blew on the hot liquid. Hellen wrapped both hands around her cup to warm them. "I want you to come back with me. I know it's short notice, but it'll be easier before curfew, and you can get up to speed before the meeting."

Roberta met her gaze over her teacup. "All right," she agreed, then sipped petitely but the tea was still too hot, apparently, as she resumed blowing. "Should we take some food?"

"Food is always good." Hellen grinned.

Roberta chuckled. "Done," she said.

Chapter Th.12

Rubble gone and floor clean, the only evidence anything was different in the nursery was the gaping hole in the wall. At last the secret passage sat exposed, and sweet success beckoned him in from the doorway to have another look. Of course, downstairs in the Official Greeting Room the walls were still intact—he *was* hosting a party for goodness sake. However, at the opposite end of the passage, the door to the outside was locked and the lever removed. See Hellen use that. Wouldn't he love to catch her down there, trying to get out?

Dagge bent over and looked up inside the small rectangular room at stones that hadn't seen this much light in hundreds of years. No telling how many more secret passages cut through this palace. All afternoon he'd used his excess energy prowling the halls and rooms: examining, estimating, figuring. A few likely spots had occurred to him, but any excavation would have to wait until after the banquet, and who knew what would happen after that?

While he prowled, he'd considered the probability of Hellen taking advantage of the confusion this weekend to sneak back in. Instinct said high. Obviously she wanted something, maybe even to kill him, which was kind of thrilling.

Poor, deluded woman.

Chuckling to himself, he ducked through the hole, crossed the passage, and went into the princess's room beyond. A lot of the dead girl's things were still in there, on the shelves and in drawers, because he thought Hellen might appreciate that someday. See, he wasn't entirely without compassion.

If Hellen could just back off her vendetta long enough to look at that side of him, she'd feel differently. She'd know that none of the things he did were personal, they were all business. Like Camberton.

Okay, Camberton was personal, but his wife was business. Dagge didn't want to kill her, she turned out to be a pretty spunky package, and he admired that. But it had to be done, just like the girls, in order to get Camberton's property. Like he said, business.

Maybe if Hellen came back this weekend, she'd be doing it because she really did want to make a deal. Maybe she thought he'd be more lenient on her with so many people around he wanted to impress. It was true, he would be more lenient, so that was smart. Company would be a good excuse to have mercy.

Later, after the atonement, life would be so much better with her at his side. Something sparked between them, that was undeniable. She felt it too, no matter what she might say now. With Hellen he felt certain he could produce a son, or a daughter would be okay too. More than one, she was young enough.

He stopped at the edge of the curtained bed and let his eyes take the room in. Definitely this one had to be off-limits to guests. Every inch of space was a screaming reminder of the former occupant: photos of the King and princess, of the little princess and the Queen, cute girl toys and heart-covered things. Tiny shoes.

Dagge had to laugh, he completely understood the impulse to save crap. For example, a shred of broken balloon with dried white paint was even now in his desk drawer. It served as a reminder to ask Hellen how she got it up there. And then maybe he'd strangle her with it.

His brain shorted out for a second. He didn't mean that! He wouldn't strangle her…he didn't want to *strangle* her, he just wanted her to quit fighting him.

He shook his head clear and walked to the north windows to look out over the town. Wharton told him there were more flyers up this afternoon. Either Hellen never slept, or she had help.

Of course she had help; help got her away somehow that night in town. Help printed out all these flyers, because they weren't hand drawn. Help took her in and fed her and got her clothes, because she wasn't living on the street, and if she lived in the forest, help still had to get her clothes.

Ten to one the name of that help was John Treslo, even if he did find that secret passage. Instinct said kill him, but Dagge didn't want to do that yet, not while he remained useful. Once the secret passages were all found, and Hellen was his queen, then the big man could be killed. Oh, he looked forward to that day.

As he turned to go out the door, Dagge caught his reflection in the mirror over the vanity. The gray patch had spread down to his neck, and he stepped closer to examine it. The flesh looked dead; he reached up and ran his finger over it. It felt normal, so he pinched it. Normal. Weird. His eyes came up and met his eyes, and for a second they looked wrong, the pupils were purple. *What the hell is that?* Leaning into the mirror, he looked more closely, but the little round spot was as black as usual.

Trick of the light. He leaned back from the mirror and looked at his face again. If he put some makeup on the gray patch, no one would ever be able to tell. After all, the rest of him looked just fine.

Chapter Th.13

Warmth and the smell of dinner wrapped around John when he walked in the home door. He breathed deeply, shook off his coat, hung it up, lowered himself slowly to the bench, and pulled off his boots. Tired as he was, he wished the family would just bring him everything he needed, and he could stay right there and never have to move again. Except it wasn't all that comfortable. It took some determination to stand up again, but he did it, and shuffled into the kitchen.

Roberta wasn't there. David stood at the stove, Joey was setting the table, and Robert filled glasses with water. "Where's your Mom?" he asked.

"Hi, Dad!" Joey said, typically cheerful.

"She's gone with that lady who came here the other day." David answered without turning around. John walked over to the stove and leaned against the counter next to him.

"The maid?" John adjusted his mental path.

"She's no maid," David whispered. Like that was going to keep Robert from hearing him.

"Took you that long to figure it out?"

"Shut up, Robert," David shot back.

Robert snickered at him. "I thought you were supposed to be smart."

Joey entered the fray. "Robert, you wouldn't know smart if it bit you in the butt."

"Joey, when you get a brain, you can talk to me."

"Guys…" John had to call a halt to this. "How long has it been since you washed your hands, huh? Go wash up for dinner."

"I washed mine just a few minutes ago," Robert said.

"Do it again," John replied, allowing no room for disagreement. Robert tossed the cup towel on the counter in a small huff and followed Joey out of the room to the guest bath. John wanted a quick word with David, who was taking fried chicken up out of a skillet.

"I don't know who she is," David said, "but her accent was fake, I heard her talking in Mom's office."

"I'm not concerned about that," John said. "What I want is for you to come with me later tonight, and not say anything to your brothers."

David frowned up at him. "Okaay. Any clue what this is about?"

"No," John said, just before the other two boys came back into the room. "Did you actually turn on the water?"

"Yes," Robert assured him.

"And we even used soap," Joey announced triumphantly.

"What about David?" Robert asked.

"I would hope David washed his hands before he started touching the food," John answered. "You did, didn't you?"

"Yes, Dad, and I haven't petted the dog or anything."

"We don't have a dog," Joey objected.

"Precisely," David agreed, and carried the plate of chicken over to the table. "Let's eat!"

Without the mom to supervise, dinner was an entirely less civilized thing. The rolls, the mashed potatoes, the green beans all flew around the table like they were caught in a tornado. Plates were heaped to overflowing. Food was copiously spilled by the barbarian hordes. "It's not so bad being without the womenfolk once in a while," Joey concluded.

John wanted to laugh, but he resisted it. He would much rather Roberta were here, he had to admit. So much of what he was, what they all were, depended on her. David pretty much summed it up when he said, "Next time, you cook."

After dinner, Joey and Robert were in charge of cleaning up, over their grumbled objections. "Getting drinks and setting the table absolve no one from duty." John was firm. "When you cook, that is absolution." Their groans went unheeded as John dragged David into the foyer.

"Dad, I love it when you do this, you know I do, but how am I supposed to become a normal human being when you and Mom provide such a terrible example?"

"David," John stammered, "t-t-ts-stop talking for a minute. Did you figure out the box?"

"I did." David nodded, very proud of himself.

"Splendid!" John smiled proudly. "You did better than I did." He looked over his shoulder back toward the kitchen, and pulled David past the stairs. "Don't ever forget it. You never know when something like that could be useful."

"Now, you see, Dad, that's exactly the kind of stuff I'm talking about."

John shoved David's coat into his hand, and took his own off its hook. "Smart ass."

Outside, the night was cold, no moon yet, pretty much no snow, so cover was good. They went left, passed the lighted windows and porches to the outer edge of town, and stopped at an oak on the edge of the last neighbor's yard. Across Wagon Wheel Road it was open grass all the way to the stone-lined drainage ditch. Luckily, Thorn didn't need no whiner-baby light.

Normally there weren't any patrols over here, but John couldn't be sure with all the hoopla today, and even though it wasn't past curfew, if a group of soldiers saw them get in the drainage ditch, they'd be asking questions.

He listened. Scanned the area. Normally patrols weren't too careful, talking and lighting cigarettes, so they came with their own early warning system. Tonight, they were probably all busy looking for the reprobates who were putting up the flyers in town. Goody.

The two of them crossed the road and the crunchy grass on the other side at a brisk walk—not up to anything, not sneaking around, just an innocent trip to the drainage ditch. Wow, isn't it interesting? John dropped into a squat and let himself down the rocks.

David followed, not quite as gracefully. When he hit the bottom in a stumble, he looked up at John with a new admiration. "That was pretty slick, Dad, you made it look easy."

Dad's eyebrows shot up, and he felt quite lofty. "Thank you," he replied, "all that heavy lifting has really paid off."

"I'll say." David squeezed his bicep and nodded approvingly. John couldn't resist the impulse to flex. *Ah, manly at 60.*

"Let's go." He nodded and took off at quick half-crouch. David followed. They headed south to where the drainage ditch passed under the wall and became a creek bed again, a short distance from the big pipe ends he and Hellen used to go to HQ.

John stopped at the pipes, leaned against the wall, and motioned to David to do the same. Sight lines weren't so protected past this point, so he wanted to have another quick look and listen, just like Hellen had taught him.

Somewhere above, soldiers were talking in low voices, nearer than he wanted them to be. He focused and tried to hear what they were saying.

"I wouldn't want to be in that forest tonight."

"Me, neither. There are spooky things in there, man, I seen 'em."

"What do you mean, you've seen 'em?"

"I seen lights, man. I had night duty when they were building the wall over there, and crazy lights were in there, I'm telling you. Moving around, showing up and disappearing. And you could feel something watching you all the time. You could *feel* it, man. Creepy."

John wanted to laugh they were so right. The voices got closer, heading their way, circles of light skipping around the wall opposite.

"I wonder if they'll all be dead by morning. People don't come out of there, you know." John and David stepped quietly into the pipes, the conversation continuing right above their heads. A thud, and one light stilled on the rocks across from them. The other disappeared. There was a jingling sound, and a thin stream arced out and splashed down into the ditch a few feet ahead. "That's why Overlord stopped sending patrols. Guys started saying they wouldn't go, saying they'd leave first." The stream sputtered out and the soldier walked away jingling. "Guess you can't stop an entire army."

The voices faded as they went back to their patrol. "I'm hungry," the first guy said.

"You're always hungry," said the second guy.

"I have a high metabolism," the first guy replied, and they were gone.

John stepped out into the ditch and backed up far enough to look after them. Their backs were turned, and their voices were inaudible. Worth the risk. He gestured to David and they hurried to the grate under the wall.

Pressing his finger to David's lips for silence, John reached for David's hand and put it through the grate on the left side. Then he stuck his own hand through, guided David's finger into a groove, pushed a slide up and pulled the grate open.

"I'm not telling anyone else about this. This is your secret, and you will know the time and place to share it, but not now, and not with your brothers, do you understand?"

"Yeah, Dad, not even Joey?"

"Not yet, he's not responsible enough for this kind of secret. Before you tell him, be sure that he won't misuse it, or use it carelessly." He paused, hesitant to say this, but knowing that David would understand. "And don't ever tell Robert." He shook his head for emphasis.

"I won't," David answered, looking like he was getting the seriousness of it. "I'm glad you showed me, though." His voice was uncertain, so John wasn't sure if he meant that, but he continued, "But you're worrying me. You're acting like you don't think you're going to be around much longer."

John didn't know what to say. He pushed the grate closed and showed David how to pull the slide back down. "You know Dagge, son, there's always a danger that something could happen. But if it does..." He put his hands on David's shoulders. "I want you to know that I did what I could. And I want to tell you everything I can."

John pulled his son to him and stretched his arms around the broadening shoulders.

"I love you, Dad," David said from the depths of the hug.

"I love you too, David," John told him, and when they had enough, they ran back up the drainage ditch to home.

Chapter Th.14

Gloom gathered in silent pools beneath the trees around her, bare branches shivered in a chill wind above. Ahead of her stood a clearing, where she could see low clouds skimming in patches across the stars, and the last orange of the setting sun brushed their edges with fire.

In the center of the clearing, an enormous pile of boulders hunched like some ancient monument, towering over her, loose and formless, abandoned. But as she gazed at it, a white and magenta and blue light appeared inside, glowing in the spaces between the rocks, filling it, brighter and brighter. The light flickered, like something moved in it, and it grew until beams exploded through the cracks like searchlights in the dark.

The rocks must have begun disintegrating in the middle, because by the time she could see what was happening, the entire heart of the rock pile was a glowing, shifting light. She watched while the rocks on the outside dissolved into tiny pieces, shattered and sucked in by the force of whatever this was. One by one the huge boulders were eaten, until nothing was left of them, and all that remained was the hot light.

It flashed and boiled, big rolling colors that burst out in bright magenta rays, shooting into the air, out and back, like hungry lizards' tongues. Farther and farther they reached, almost to the trees, but not quite. One of them came toward her and time seemed to slow, because she got a good look at it, and it had eyes.

Suddenly the rays stopped, and soldiers were there, creeping up with their rifles. Hesitant, they seemed uncertain what to do, but irresistibly drawn to the dancing, shimmering light. Wide-eyed faces made a ring around the clearing, until a few of them got brave enough to move closer. Here and there, a man stepped forward slowly, gun raised, maybe followed by another, and another, all with weapons aimed at the roiling middle.

The first line stopped, just outside the reach of the rays. She wasn't sure who started firing, but laser pulses and bullets emptied into the light from all around the circle, only instead of damaging it, the light got brighter the more they fired into it, and when the rays started again, the people were well within reach.

Screams erupted around the circle as the rays hit their marks and disappeared. Men went down like they'd been shot, and no one was sure what happened, except that the rays got them. One man she could see near her arched his back and went down, landing on his side, where he cried and twitched horribly.

Everyone else tried to run, tripping over each other in their haste, stumbling, pushing, anything to get away. The magenta rays fired from the center, targeting every man in reach, knocking them down, leaving them to writhe in pain.

But they weren't dying. The first ones got up, shouldered their guns, and started firing, dropping the runners like game. Some of the men tried to shoot back, but it didn't matter—the laser pulses and bullets went into the first ones' bodies without killing them, or even slowing them down. Lasers charred the flesh, but fed the monsters inside; with every shot, magenta surged out of their bodies in flat and asymmetrical echoes of the human form. The magenta looked like sheets of paper cut into terrifying dolls protruding from the soldiers' bodies, and when the shots stopped, the angular fiends inside the men disappeared again.

Panic and horror swept over them. Many screamed and tried to run, but they couldn't get away, and more came who had missed what happened, and they were shot. Gunfire and laser pulses flew, until eventually only the first ones were left, and those were the soldiers who marched off into the woods.

The energy of the light in the clearing was low now, and the rays had stopped, and all that was left was a blinking, radiant hole, alone in the forest, surrounded by the dead.

Adia woke in a fog, not sure where she was, or why it was so loud in her room. Voices buzzed somewhere, not far away, Hellen was shaking her. "Adia. Adia, wake up. Wake up," she said.

"I'm awake," Adia grumbled. "Give me a minute, okay? I had a dream."

Chapter Th.15

Adia figured about twenty people, give or take, had gathered in Beau's underground room. Hard to believe it was the same room she remembered from her one self-defense class a lifetime ago—the space was different now, with four tunnel entrances, tables and shelves, and the big printing press. Still, the vibe was the same, except tonight she'd say cranked up a bit.

Chief Taymer was talking. It had been deeply wonderful to shake his hand again, but even better when he wouldn't take that for an answer and had to have a hug, too. Tall and deep-voiced, he reminded her so much of her father, it was excruciating. Somehow his history, having known her father since childhood, forged a link for her that brought her father back in a small way. She didn't want to let go of him, but she forced herself not to be pathetic.

"There's been some recruiting since the flyers started going up. Apparently interest is high across the board, and not just the people who seem the type. Do be careful if you get into a conversation with someone. If the person you're talking to truly isn't ready, or isn't in a position to guard that information, then it puts both of you, and the rest of us, in danger.

"The new troop deployments today are expected to last only through the weekend. During that time, more caution is the rule in town. However, the troops on the west side of the palace will be greatly reduced, and Hellen Parker has some ideas about that."

Adia didn't know Hellen was going to speak. She got up from beside her and went around behind the group to the front. "I think we should sneak into the palace this weekend and try to make contact with one, or more, of the visiting monarchs." A surprised buzz of commentary echoed the anxious knot that tightened in Adia's chest.

"I know it sounds really stupid, like kicking a hornet's nest, but I made it in and out two nights ago, and even though I nearly got caught, this time will be easier because we won't have to get close to Dagge. All we have to do is sneak into one of the guest rooms and let someone know that Adia is still alive."

Adia could feel all eyes turn to her. It was a good thing she had all those composure lessons, because she managed to sit there looking dignified when she really wanted to hide her face. She must have twitched because she felt Cary, who was next to her, take her hand in his and squeeze.

John Treslo spoke next, somewhere to her right. "I need to tell everyone that Dagge is going to have me find all the secret passages in the palace soon after the banquet. I can make it slow, but if I don't turn some up pretty regularly…" He stopped, loath to complete the sentence with his wife there.

"John, I will tell you where those secret passages are." Adia spoke up with firmness. "It isn't worth your life to keep them secret."

"Thank you, Highness. And I want you to know that I support Hellen's plan, to try and get into the palace this weekend, because if we can get some outside help, we're all ready to see you take back the throne."

Panic flared up in her again—giant, crushing hands she couldn't get away from because she couldn't run. What was her face doing? Yikes, she had a frown on, she wiped it away and put on a pleasantly royal expression.

"Thank you, but until I'm reinstated, let's not stand on formality. Please call me Adia, and that goes for everyone here, all right?" The response was surprisingly quiet, almost uncomfortable, but the hands backed off a bit and let her breathe.

Chief Taymer came to her rescue. "Thank you, Adia, I'm sure we can all get used to it, only hopefully you'll be on the throne before that happens." A low laugh bubbled around the room, and Chief continued, "Now, are there any comments or questions about Hellen's idea?"

"I'll go with you, Hellen." Cary's voice was strong beside her.

"So will I." That was the woodcarver, she thought, what was his name? Lan Something.

"I will, too," Zola the plant lady said, "if I can be of use." A number of voices she didn't recognize followed, volunteering to do "whatever" until Adia couldn't stand it anymore.

"Wait a minute!" she burst out. "Is there a plan, even? Are you all going to risk your lives? For what? What if none of the monarchs want to help? What if they're all afraid to stand up to Dagge, which they probably are? Do you really think that just the mention of my name is going to change anything? It's not!"

Having grown up a princess, she fully expected that no one would challenge her opinion, but it was Cary's voice next to her that shot that all to hell. "I disagree, Adia," he said calmly, after a quiet pause. "I think it would mean something to people, maybe especially to other royal families, because it could be them someday. It could be them fighting to keep their throne, and they'd be able to call on us."

Adia managed to get her mouth closed at some point during that, thank goodness, so now she could appear composed when she said, "But you don't know them like I do, do you Cary? You don't know that four out of the five of them are shaking in their boots when it comes to Dagge. They're going to suck up to him because they're afraid he's going to come after them next. And they're probably right. Personally, I can't believe they're all coming to the banquet this weekend, because he very well could kill them all. Right there. How can they have not thought of that? Well, maybe they have, and they'll bring their own tricks with them. But there is no way anyone is going to survive getting into one of their rooms. It'll be shoot first, don't bother with questions ever."

Silence descended. And it lasted for about ten uncomfortable seconds. She guessed everyone was waiting for her to say something else, but that was it. That was all she wanted to say.

"What about the fifth guy?" Cary asked. "You said four out of the five."

"Oh yes, Pulari. He might have the army and the stomach for it, if we can give him a better deal than he's getting with Dagge. After that, a lot would depend on whether he thinks we could win. And truthfully, we have twenty-odd people and a printing press, what are the chances?"

After another tense pause, Hellen spoke again. "You know, Adia, you're right. Our chances of success look nonexistent up against what he's got. But he's not infallible. If there had been one other person with me two nights ago, we could have killed him."

"Or gotten killed, because we both know he has a soft spot for you, but anyone else would be dead."

No argument. As the silence wore, Adia felt a little bad about beating them down like she did—she should be more supportive. "I'm sorry," she said, contrite, but the rest of her sentence was cut off by the breathless entrance of the older rabbit (*what was his name?*).

"Something's happening in the forest."

"What?" Chief Taymer asked.

"Gunshots, screaming, yelling—something terrible."

The sudden rush of movement kept Adia in her seat. People rushed away in all directions, down three tunnels, and up the stairs, to get outside. Cary was the first to jump up and go, which was a little disappointing, but Adia was also glad. Hellen would come for her, or Roberta maybe.

Truth be told, she wasn't in any hurry anyway; she knew what was happening in the forest.

Chapter Th.16

Urgent pounding woke Wharton from a doze, obliterating the endless drone of radio news with an explosion of sound. Adrenaline chased the fog from his brain as he jerked into a sitting position on the couch. "Yeah!"

"Sir," a voice called through the door, "there's trouble in the forest!"

Pulari. "All right, I'm coming!" Wharton got up, shoved his feet into worn-out boots, grabbed his coat and pistol and hurried out into the flat orange glow disappearing in the west, "Go find Reznick, tell him to raise the alarm. I want every available soldier. And bring me my rifle!"

Forward motion didn't stop until he reached the east side of the palace. There, the battle sounds became clearer. Gunfire popped through the quiet chill, and in the distance, beams of pink and blue light shifted and flashed out of the trees and into the night sky. *What the hell would make that kind of light?* Some trick of Pulari's probably. Too far to go on foot, he'd need a horse.

Then the screaming started. Not normal screams, either, but long terrified ones that lingered, so close on the frigid night air. In a space of seconds, the gunshots slowed to a trickle but the shrieks remained, echoing through the trees. Wharton ran for the stable, shouting instructions to the gathered soldiers. "Saddle up! Guns and grenades! Someone go tell Reznick!"

Farther down the castle wall, the Overlord was out on the War Room balcony, and Wharton stopped to give an impromptu report. "Overlord, sir, there's some kind of trouble in the forest. I'm taking every available man to engage the enemy."

Above, the backlight from the open balcony door threw Dagge's face into shadow, making it hard for Wharton to read his expression.

His voice, however, sounded…husky, tense, and with a shot of glee running through it. "I'm not sure this is the kind of thing that you can assist, Wharton. It's not a normal battle, wouldn't you agree?"

"We can always try, sir," Wharton said with the slightest pause, already bowing to make his exit, but Dagge stopped him.

"Has anyone come out?" he asked.

"Not that I know of, sir."

"I don't want you to go into the forest." Wharton started to object, but Dagge talked over him. "There isn't anything you can do in there, believe me." He smacked his hands on the cement balustrade and shifted into I'm-going-inside mode, but first he said, "In fact, I want you to wait and see what comes out. Don't clean them up, don't doctor them, don't do anything but hold them for me until morning." Instructions given, he turned and went in.

What the hell? Now Dagge wanted to let Pulari invade? Without shooting back? That was hugely fucked-up. Dagge may have been right about the invasion, but letting it take place had to be crazy. Unless he knew something Wharton didn't. It wouldn't be the first time that happened. Well, if Overlord wanted big fat bloodstains all over the lawn for his fancy party, that was his choice, wasn't it?

Wharton jogged off toward the stable because he'd sent everyone there anyway, and he could call off the dogs and give the new orders and make the whole snafu a lot more efficient. A lot of the men were in the stable when he got there, and more continued to arrive. Some of the early birds were saddled and ready for a fight. Those guys were gonna hate what he had to say.

He waved all the excitement down and talked to them in his General voice. "All right, all right. Our orders are to wait." Moans and groans and protests. "Never mind!" he shouted. "Our new orders are to apprehend anything that comes out of the forest. Do you know what I mean by 'apprehend'?" A scattering of "yeses" around. "Do you know what I mean by 'anything'?" *Yes, sirs* were a bit louder.

"Very good. I want Company A on forest watch for the next four hours, then Company B, and so on; the rest of you sleep with your boots on. Reznick!" he called to the Captain coming in with the first night watch, which had been sleeping. "Spread Company A between the forest and the palace, take anything that comes out of the trees alive and put it in the dungeon. Dismissed!" No more to say, he took his rifle from the soldier holding it and ran back up the hill toward the palace, intending to do some guard duty himself that night.

Chapter Th.17

Tension rang high; Hellen waited beside Adia against the wall, keeping her out of the agitated hubbub that crisscrossed HQ. The crowd was larger than it had been at the meeting: John and Roberta talked to an unfamiliar couple by the steps, Cary hung around at the front with Firio and three men she didn't know. Actually there were many faces she didn't know. Holy cow.

"Purda said she heard screaming," Vartile shouted over the buzz to Chief Taymer, who stood at the desk attempting to get some order.

Since the excitement in the forest had mostly played out by the time they all got up top, they had to get what stories they could from the people in the streets. Patrols came all too soon and broke up the little gossiping groups, so once they got back downstairs the meeting became about what none of them saw.

Except Adia. She had pulled Hellen aside on their way back through Vartile's basement and told her what happened in the dream. As much as Hellen didn't want to believe it was real, she knew in her gut Adia's dream had been true. Everything Browbone feared happened, and worse. Now some kind of crazy super-soldiers were walking around out there, and no telling what they would do.

One of them had to tell the group, but such a story would be tricky. Too unbelievable. Dreams, dimensional holes, talking rocks—how do you explain that?

No wonder Adia wasn't in the most optimistic mood. Still, maybe there was some way this could work to their advantage. Hellen hadn't thought of how yet, but she was determined to give it a chance.

"Grovet heard gunfire. Lots of gunfire, he said, that was why he went outside to begin with," Cary said from across the room, and the murmur level went up a few notches.

"I know what happened in the forest."

All gazes shifted around until the room was wall to wall expectant moon faces. Hellen was sure Adia could feel all eyes on her. *Big step, Adia, I hope you know what you're doing.*

"Since I was a child, I've had what I call true dreams. I had a dream this afternoon that a big ball of light in the forest…" She stopped for a moment, trying to find the words. "It grew and got more powerful from gunfire the soldiers were shooting into it. Then it reached out with these long magenta rays that…infected some of them, and those soldiers have some kind of…flat energy beings inside them now. It's a very, very bad thing."

Wow, it was an awkward silence, but Hellen jumped in to do ground support. "I know it sounds like science fiction, and this is going to sound even worse, but I swear to you it's true. I'd been told of a possibility this could happen by a forest elemental."

"What's that?" Zola asked.

"In this case, it was a rock person." Okay, this really didn't sound good. "You know, we've all heard stories about weird things in the forest, and I'm here to tell you, after living in it for a year and a half, it's weirder than any of the stories say. There's a dimensional tear, which is what Adia saw in her dream, and it has apparently broken free of its containment. Containing it is what the rock giants were doing." She waved her hand back and forth. "But that's another story."

Hellen felt so uncomfortable, she almost couldn't stand it.

"I know about this, too," John Treslo spoke up, saving her from an acute aneurysm. "About the tear. Hellen and I heard that together, from the monks."

This was getting weirder and weirder. Stunned faces, shifting eyes, mouths hanging open, it was like being an act in a sideshow tent. Hellen retook the stage. "John and I found the monastery, at the King's request, and the monks weren't, aren't, exactly gone. They're in a different dimension."

"Can they help us?" a candle maker named Dessara asked. "They were supposed to be really smart."

“No, they can’t help us,” John said. “They’re not allowed.”

“Says who?” she asked.

“They didn’t explain the entire cosmos to us. Only that we have to win this fight ourselves.” Hellen lifted one arm in a half shrug. “And regardless of what happens over the next 48 hours—” She looked at Adia. “Because I do plan to sneak in again and try to kill Dagge,” she told her. “It sounds like we might need to figure out a way to deal with what’s going on in the woods.” She paused, a little out of breath so she took a quick deep one. “Is anybody here really good at science?”

Friday

Chapter F.1

Dagge looked the line over carefully. Sixteen soldiers stood on the south lawn in the dawn light, many of them wounded pretty seriously, with no acknowledgement of pain. The looks on their faces were all the same: focused, intense, and humorless. Very interesting.

They had filtered out of the trees for hours, Wharton said. One by one, slowly, acting like they didn't know where they were, or who anybody was. By all accounts it was almost impossible to get them to stop walking toward the castle, and it took threatening to bring them to the Overlord that finally got them to cooperate. Wharton added he thought the only reason that worked was because it was exactly what they wanted.

Some of the soldiers were men he knew. Two of them had been with him since the beginning of this job, and six more were faces he recognized from palace guard duty. Strange to say, three of them were Pulari's men, but they didn't act any different from the others. Whatever the forest did to them was an equal-opportunity nightmare on steroids.

He spoke to one of the old-timers. "Soldier." No answer. "Were you in the forest with these other men?" Start with something simple.

The stomach convulsed, the throat spasmed, and the voice that fought its way out of the open mouth sounded like gravel on sheet metal. "Yes, sir."

Okay, that took him by surprise. Definitely not normal. He tried to keep his face neutral, and stepped back a half step so he could examine the man. "Are you wounded?" he asked, because the answer was obvious.

A bit of a pause before "Yes, sir," in that voice again.

"Do you need attention?"

A longer pause this time, but no change in expression. None. "No, sir."

Dagge examined him a moment longer, then moved down the line. He took slow, deliberate steps, studying each face until he came to one of Pulari's men. "You," he said, "what are you doing here?"

The mouth opened and shut repeatedly, like the effort to speak was too much for him, but by and by it worked. "To serve."

Defecting. Or lying, he could be here to spy. Not a very inconspicuous spy, but this sure would be a novel approach. Dagge reached down and grabbed the guy's gun. He checked it, then he brought it up to his eye and aimed it at the soldier's head. No change. He lowered it to his torso, nothing. He lowered it over the guy's package and didn't even get a flinch, so he shot that soldier in the leg. The guy barely moved. "Still want to serve?" He shouldered the rifle.

"Yes, sir," he said.

If he was a spy, he was incredible. Dagge brought the gun up again and put a bullet in the center of his chest. For ten seconds nothing happened. Everyone stood there, mesmerized, waiting for him to fall, or scream, or something. Nothing changed until he coughed and dark red blood splattered out of his mouth, down his chin and into the space between them.

Dagge backed away and watched. The knees began to buckle and he sank slowly down onto them, eventually resting his buttocks on his heels while the hole in his chest poured blood, covering his chest and stomach in crimson. Was he breathing? Dagge walked up to the soldier's side this time to avoid any more spattering, and he pulled the guy's head back by his hair. His mouth fell open and Dagge could see the blood inside.

Did it matter if he was breathing? He wouldn't be for long. Dagge looked closely at the man's eyes, unseeing and dull with death. It only took him a few seconds to notice what was strange about them— the pupils were tiny. Almost nonexistent.

A long, rasping breath rattled out of his mouth. Guess that answered that question, but it was the eyes that interested him now.

Those pupils, something happened in there, didn't it? Some movement. He bent down and looked closer, focusing into the pinprick of black, ignoring the choking and convulsing of the body.

And he saw it. The stuttering flash of purple he saw in his own eyes, only weak and small, and then gone. All life left the body then, and it relaxed and leaned over and fell to the ground.

"Take the rest of them, get them cleaned up and their wounds tended." Dagge walked up to Wharton and gave him the rifle. "They'll stay in the palace with me."

Wharton's face registered shock. "Sir, are you certain? Even Pulari's men?"

"I'm certain, Wharton," Dagge answered with exaggerated patience. "Do you think I would underestimate the risk?"

"No, sir, I just thought it was my duty to remind you."

Dagge brushed past him with a tiny smile and walked up to the palace for breakfast.

Chapter F.2

Amazing as it was, John had the entire day off today. The wall had gotten finished, the visitors would be arriving, and Dagge had nothing for him to do, so he could spend the whole day conspiring with like-minded people. What fun!

He rolled out of bed way earlier than he intended. Roberta lay sleeping, so he snuck out of the bedroom in his robe and slippers and traipsed the well-worn path into the kitchen. There, in his pajamas, stood David at the stove again.

"Are you cooking?"

"I'm boiling eggs," David said. "I thought I'd make some egg salad."

"That sounds good, wanna help me make some breakfast?"

"Sure." David turned around with his hands on his hips. "Because you know, a watched pot really doesn't boil. I'm sure if I look away for five seconds, it'll be boiling when I look back."

"Are you conducting an experiment?"

"I am. An experiment in frustration."

John chuckled and opened the cooler. Let's see, this morning they could have... "ham and cheese toasteds," he announced. He grabbed the cheese, and the ham, and the mustard, and took them all to the counter by the sink, then he turned the oven on to heat. "Has Robert gone?"

"Yeah, he left early again," David said, bringing the bread and the cutting board. "He made it clear that it's a big day today, and he didn't expect to be home for dinner."

"Do you know what he does up there?" John had tried many times to get Robert to talk about his day, but he seldom got more than a "just book work" response.

"I asked him once. He's basically an accountant."

"An accountant needs to go in early and stay late?"

"Well, you know Robert, he won't want to stay an accountant."

That made perfect sense to John. "Is Joey still asleep?"

"Yeah, we didn't get a lot of sleep last night. Didn't you hear the crazy stuff going on in the forest?" He paused and looked up at John. "Wherever you were?"

It hadn't even occurred to John that their children would've heard what happened in the forest. They were all early risers, so they went to bed before he left last night, and he just thought of them as asleep. He wondered if Roberta had thought of it. And did she come up with a story? Because he never even tried to explain that he was leaving. Better not to lie.

Of course the gunshots woke them up. Of course they wondered where their parents were. He heaved a big sigh; how was he going to get out of this one?

"David, what if I told you that architect isn't my only job?"

His son stopped slicing bread, leaned against the counter, and looked at him expectantly. "Okay, I'll bite. What's your other job?"

"I'm a cabaret dancer." John stuck his hip out, sashayed across the floor, stopped with a slap to his behind and a coy look over his shoulder.

"Dad!" David laughed, "that's just…scary." So John really turned it on, and the more he pranced, the more David laughed, until John started laughing, and the two of them giggled and guffawed until they had to shush each other to be quiet.

Eventually they resumed fixing breakfast. "You know, Dad, I don't think you and Mom are having problems, you guys act like a couple of teenagers, so whatever it is that keeps you out all night, I trust you." He shrugged and put the toasteds on the oven rack, then stood back up. "Even if you're a cabaret dancer."

John struck a quick pose and did a step and a spin, and another pose squinched at the knees, pointing his finger at David. "Someday you may find you've inherited a talent for it," he whispered breathily. That made them giggle again, which was why Joey showed up.

"Can you guys keep it down? Hey, where were you last night? You weren't in your room. Did you hear all the weird stuff out in the forest?" He scratched sleepily and yawned as he walked to the table. "What's for breakfast?"

"Ham and cheese toasteds, but they're not ready yet," David said, turning off the eggs and covering them. "See, I told you they'd boil."

"What did you guys hear out in the forest?" John asked.

"Gunshots. And screaming—these long, awful, high screams. Really gave us the willies, didn't they David?"

"Yeah. All over in ten minutes, though, so it couldn't have been an invasion, could it?"

"I guess we'll find out more today."

"Where were you guys, anyway?" Joey remembered to ask, because evidently somewhere under that comical hairdo, there *was* a brain.

"We had an errand, and it's none of your beeswax, so don't ask."

"Fine," Joey said, "but I want you to know I feel like I'm the last person in this house to know anything, if I ever know anything at all, and it's starting to irritate me."

"Ah, Joey…" The Dad tried to pacify him. "It's not you, son, you're just the last man on the totem pole. That's the luck of the draw for every youngest child."

"But in this case, you aren't the only one in the dark, so don't feel bad," David said, and changed the subject. "How are we going to find out what happened last night?"

"Robert'll know." John sat down at the table with Joey.

"If he'll tell us," Joey complained.

"Oh, he'll tell us." John sounded more confident than he felt, but what else was he going to say?

Chapter F.3

"I'm a transfer," Hellen said.

"I ain't heard about no transfer," the muscley one said. "What's your name?"

"Brucella." Hellen winced, on the inside. "Brucella TaSwinn."

"TaSwinn? What kinda name is that?" the short one mocked.

"It's my name, wanna make something of it?" Hellen advanced on him threateningly. She felt pretty sure she could take him, she had about two inches and ten pounds on the guy, plus some skills.

"Naw, man." He backed away and held up his hand. "it's your name, okay, don't get your privvies in a vise."

"I'm Guindo," Mr. Muscle made the introductions, "this is Vizo," the one who hadn't spoken, "and this is Tony," the short one.

"Nice to meetcha," Hellen nodded, hoping they wouldn't ask any more questions. She felt stretched to the believability limit already. There were a few women in the army, but not enough for her to feel like she blended in.

"Where'd you come from?" Vizo asked.

"Oh, I came from Ishop, but I lived in Baldan for a long time."

The three of them looked at her like she was a total idiot. "I mean what *Company*, you moron, I don't care what country."

Oops. "Oh, yeah, yeah, C Company." She wasn't even sure there was a C Company, but there must be because no one challenged it. *Whew*.

"Where are we, uh, headed?" She looked around at the familiar downtown buildings, appalled that she could see her hair out of the corner of her eye, and it looked like a nest. Vartile had spent twenty minutes on it, though, and it was Fabulous.

"Our patrol for the next three hours is Central 1," Guindo said, popping his knuckles. "You may or may not know, that means Victory Plaza, two blocks each way, and the road going out to the main south entrance. Everybody got that?"

"Yeah, we got it, Guindo, it's not science," Vizo said.

"We only been doin it for a week aready." Tony hitched his pants up.

Guindo ignored that and continued, "We're s'posed to also watch for anyone coming out of the woods. We see someone, we get 'em and take 'em to Wharton. Does everybody got that? Because that's new."

"Man, I don't want to do that," Tony said. "Those guys are messed up."

"Messed up how?" Hellen asked.

"You ain't seen 'em?" Guindo asked.

"Naw, I been up on the north side."

"They're not normal people," Tony said. "They don't say nothing, and their eyes don't look right. I think they're repossessed or something."

"Tony, shut up," Guindo said and stepped off the curb into the street. Overhead, the holo-ad droned on about the virtues of some serious-looking attorney, as Guindo led them into the bustle of customers and merchants set up around the well. People went their ways with bundles of produce and fabric and bags of popped corn, which smelled so good it made Hellen's mouth water. Small children ran through the spaces between them, shouting and chasing a ball in blissful ignorance.

Commerce wasn't as brisk in the plaza as it used to be, but some of the traveling booths were run by people Hellen recognized, and she kept her face turned away from them just in case. As she walked by, her eye was drawn to the black stone slab mounted on the well cover. The white paint from John's balloon was still evident in the creases of "Obey or die," and the sight of it made her appreciate him all over again.

The patrol idled across the plaza and on down the main road to the south gate. Hellen mulled over what Tony had said, and the irony of how close he was to being right. Adia had described her dream in detail, and Hellen knew something came from that dimensional tear— things with eyes, and they took those soldiers' bodies. What else was that but possession? If the difference in the soldiers was that obvious, Dagge had to know they weren't normal, but maybe he didn't know yet what they were.

That day at the monastery, when the monks whisked her and John into their dimension, they explained that the evil entity would leave his buddies at the dimensional tear to wait for him. The flat magenta things had to be the buddies, and apparently they got tired of waiting. What did Dagge do about them when they showed up? Did he have any idea they were on his side? And most importantly, how was she going to kill them all?

"Where are they now?" She sped up to Tony and asked him.

"I don't know," he said, "palace, I guess. I heard Overlord killed one of 'em, shot him dead, and he took a long time to die. Then he had 'em cleaned up. I guess he was gonna keep 'em." He laughed at his own cleverness.

Oh, that sounded bad. On a lot of levels.

When they got to the south gate, Guindo greeted the two guards. "Yo, Jozzy, Benk, this is Brucella...she's a transfer from Sector 12." Jozzy and Benk nodded her way, but otherwise remained motionless. The two big metal gates were open, and the patrol stood in the road and looked out at the trees. After a moment, Hellen walked forward a few steps. "I think I saw something."

"You're kidding." Tony grabbed his gun and took a ready stance.

"Where?" Guindo was more unflappable.

"Through the trees." Hellen pointed. "Past that big oak, see?" She lurched a half step for effect and said louder, "There it was again!"

"I didn't see nothing," Guindo scoffed.

"I thoughta mighta seen something." Vizo surprised her.

"I better go check it out." Brucella started off toward the trees, and looked back over her shoulder. "It's probly nothin', like you said, but it can't hurt to check. I'll catch up with you guys in a minute."

"Hey!" Guindo hollered after her.

"Yeah?" She turned around, but kept walking backwards.

"This how they do it in C?"

"Yeah, alla time!" She held her hand up in a wave and turned back toward the forest. No one stopped her, so she just kept going.

Chapter F.4

Adia lowered her butt onto the beat-up sofa in Vartile's basement, fury and fear battling it out in her chest like a tiny fireworks show. The first public fight with Hellen had gone pretty much like all the others, except Adia did try to keep her voice down out of consideration for Vartile and Purda. But even so, it was another strained argument which ended in Hellen leaving, just like always.

Because of course if there was any kind of bizarro danger, Hellen felt compelled to be in it. This time the big attraction was the deeply alarming hole in the fabric of space-time somewhere in the forest, and the fun new playthings coming out of it. And as if that wasn't enough, her recon included the ridiculous idea of talking to real soldiers. Like they were so stupid they wouldn't know she wasn't one of them? Okay, well maybe they were that stupid, but still.

Deep breaths...*shake it off, shake it off.* Her hands flapped in the air in front of her, tension flying out of her joints and off her fingertips. Dropping them both into her lap, she blew out a long exhale. Shaky breaths, and another exhale...and another...her head fell forward, and she tried to let it all go. Every nerve felt strung out, and it wasn't just because of Hellen. She hadn't had to deal with this many people in a long time. People wanted to see her, talk to her, and always the first hurdle was how they reacted to her scars and her blindness. Distress waves came off of them when they were uncomfortable, and it made her uncomfortable, but she had to pretend she was all right, and be gracious and charming. Dad wasn't kidding when he said she would deserve acting awards. It wasn't the people's fault, though, she wouldn't have done any better if it had been her doing the looking.

They were all really very kind; they wanted to do things for her, wanted to talk about how much they missed her father. Yeah, she knew how that felt. Every thought of him brought that night rushing back. Dagge and his obscene knife. Her own failure. She couldn't talk about her father yet without dissolving, so she tried not to, and usually changed the subject.

Fortunately, she had this little getaway hole. Vartile's basement only had one tunnel that connected to Beau's underground room, so once Vartile put up a curtain for them, they had as much privacy as possible in the warren. Even a little distance was better than being in the stew, but sometimes Adia wished her ears weren't so good. If she was awake, she heard everything.

Sooner or later the whole "Oh, my body clock is off," excuse wouldn't fly, and she wasn't going to be able to escape back here for hours. Maybe she could say she was writing a book, but then she'd have to actually write something or people would catch on. A book about surviving an explosion, perhaps, since so many people were interested.

She leaned her head back and rested it on the top of the cushion. Not the most relaxing position, but she'd deal with that in a minute. For the moment, she didn't have the energy to change anything.

Pieces of earlier conversations floated into her head:

"Was there a lot of pain?" *Yes, there was for a while....*

"Anything we can do for you?" *You're so kind to offer, if I think of something....*

"Would you like some books?" an awkward pause, "I'm sorry."

"It's okay," Adia had said, "if you know someone who can read Braille, though, I could use a teacher." She'd stretched her mouth into a smile.

"Well, really, if you need anything...."

"I'll certainly let you know, thank you." Then she'd realized she wasn't even sure who she was talking to. How many conversations had she had like that today?

Then there was this other one:

"Can I bring you some cake? I made a four-layer chocolate..." The voice faded out when Adia's brain was seized with the notion of chocolate cake.

"You made a cake?" she interrupted.

"Yes, would you like some?"

Oh, my One, would I. "Yes, please," she said, showing more teeth than she had in a while. She couldn't wait for that lady to come back.

Chief Taymer came by for a while, and Adia was able to get him off to the side for a few minutes so she could talk to him. He reminded her so much of her father, it was difficult and wonderful at the same time, and she couldn't help but put her arms around his waist and lay her head on his chest. Without hesitation, he put his arms around her shoulders and lay his head on top of hers, and she cried, silent tears dripping down her face. She was able to let her guard down, and unburden her heart just a little. "I miss Dad, every day. Every day I feel this hole, and I can't fill it."

"Adia, Adia. I'm so sorry this happened to you," he said softly. "I'm sorry about your father, and about your home, and about everything you lost. I wish desperately that I could go back and change it."

"So do I," she said, pulling back and wiping her face. "I constantly think to myself that I should have done something. I knew Dagge was bad news, and it was probably only a matter of time before he did something we'd all regret, but I never thought it would happen like that." Her voice trailed off into a hoarse whisper and tears streamed down her cheeks again.

Chief wrapped her in his arms. "You couldn't have done anything. Som knew Dagge was a risk, but it was a risk he felt like he had to take, and all the responsibility for it lies with him. Do you understand?"

He held her back away from him so he could look into her face. She hadn't stopped crying, so she nodded, mostly because she knew that was what he wanted her to do. Truthfully, she wasn't at all sure it wasn't her fault, but nothing could be done about that now.

"Hey, why don't you help us figure out what to put on the next flyer? The elephant in the room," he gestured in the direction of the idle press, "needs to be put to work." Regretfully, she let him lead her back into the fray.

Hellen was still there with Vartile and Roberta then, and all the talk eventually got around to what to put on the next flyer. People came and went, including Chief, and everyone had a comment but no one had a solution. It needed to be some kind of code, but what? By the time Hellen was getting ready to go, Adia hadn't had anything to offer on the subject. Nor had she wanted to.

Her tired head cranked erect, and summoned up the will to flatten her body into a full lie-down on the couch. Her feet came up beside her and ran into something on their way to the armrest. Surprised, she stopped and felt the cushion with her hand. There was a headset there, the music kind, with the box above the earcup that held the library and the controls. Who put this here?

She turned it in her hands and felt all the parts to make sure it didn't have any surprises, then she put it on her head. Her fingers found the familiar buttons and turned it on, blasting her ears with a drum riff she hadn't heard since college. Once she got the volume turned down to a less-than-deafening level, she laid herself back and listened. After a few minutes, she found herself singing (very quietly, of course), and ch-ch'ing, and tapping along.

Which was why she didn't hear the knock. In the middle of a wailing high note on a guitar, a warm hand on her arm scared the crap out of her. She jerked up and back, her hands fumbling at the headset, her back up against the corner of the couch as far as she could go. "Who is it?" she demanded, out of breath and her voice unnaturally high.

"Adia, it's me, Cary," he said in a soothing voice. "I knocked, but you didn't hear me. I see you found my present." She could hear his smile.

"Yes," she said, trying to gather her wits. "Did you leave this?"

"I did." He sat down beside her, which made her a little uncomfortable. Unfortunately, she couldn't back up any more, so she held the headset between them. *Not much of a fence.*

"Thank you." She tried to smile, because she truly was grateful, but the whole fight-or-flight thing hadn't dissipated yet, so it was probably a lame effort. She wondered if she could ask whether the light was on without sounding... what? Blind? "Is the light on? Would you like me to turn it on?"

"It's on," he said, "and you look fine. Beautiful, in fact. Is your hair always perfect?"

Adia wasn't sure how to respond. Hellen was constantly trying to get a comb through her hair, and so far Adia had managed to slap her hands away pretty successfully. So was he teasing, or b.s.-ing? She reached her hand up to feel it. Hard to tell.

"I wanted to see, number one, how you liked your present." Cary shifted on the couch, more to face her, she thought. "And secondly, to apologize for challenging you in front of everyone last night. I should have saved it until we were alone."

Hm. At the same time, a more and less comfortable topic than how beautiful she looked. "Cary—"

"Adia, I know you know the other kings and queens and presidents better than I do, and I deeply respect that, but..." He paused, and Adia couldn't tell whether he was looking at her, so she kept her face neutral. "I've been out here." His voice got quiet and turned to her. "I've been seeing what's been going on, and hearing what people are saying, and I think I have a point of view that could be very useful to you."

What was he trying to say? Maybe she should keep quiet so she could find out.

"I know it's been hard for you to lose everything, to be so injured and alone, and to have to learn all over again how to deal with the world. You've done an amazing thing, just to survive, and I'm really glad you moved here into town, because I want to help you with the rest of it. I want to be someone you can count on. I want to earn your trust so I can be by your side."

Her little safety boat was on the verge of tipping. Time to shift into Royal Gear.

"Thank you, Cary." She sat up a little straighter and put her queen smile on (did she even have one? She could fake it.). "I understand you've been a valuable asset to this group, and no doubt you honor my father's memory." (Yeah, throw in the Dad thing, that'll cool him off if he needs it.) "I'm inclined to trust you already, and if you have special knowledge that applies to a situation, I want you to put it on the table." A pause to listen, but she heard nothing. "However, passion and patriotism aren't the same as knowledge, and for many things, you will have to trust me."

He was still quiet, and quietly still. Had she offended his pride? That would be tiresome, but instead when he spoke, he sounded like he thought she didn't quite get it.

"I do trust you, I absolutely trust you, I just think maybe your experiences have clouded your—"

"Judgment?"

He laughed lightly. "I was going to say 'assessment.' Which is the same thing, I guess." He sounded a little embarrassed. "But I don't mean that in a bad way."

Well how else could he mean it? As in it's a good thing her "assessment" is screwed up? Adia tried to tamp down her annoyance, and waited for him to fumble through his explanation.

"I don't doubt your knowledge, Adia, and I don't question your intelligence. What I'm trying to say is that maybe the pain you've experienced has made you cautious. Too cautious. I wonder if you're just afraid of getting back up on the horse."

She couldn't say why this infuriated her as much as it did. Maybe it was the horse analogy, because the one time she was thrown, she was afraid. Her riding instructor made her climb back up in the saddle, and she hated him for it. Like she hated Cary in this moment: she wanted to explode all over him, or maybe scratch his face and gouge his eyes out. Okay, that was probably a little too strong, but either way, she swallowed all that fury into a stone cold lump in her stomach, and just said, "I think you'd better go." Then she put the headphones on her ears, laid her head back on the cushion and ignored him until he left.

Chapter F.5

Hellen could see the dimensional tear from a good distance away, which was just how she wanted it. With the giant rocks gone, it was hard to recognize the place. The clearing was bigger. Large and small branches were shorter, raw ends tattered and broken. Leaf detritus and topsoil were gone, exposing bare rocks and the severed ends of tree roots. The creek where she and John had exploded the fish had no sides anymore, just a smear of water in the bottom of the pit the shimmering hole had carved for itself.

Stood to reason that if she stayed in the trees, she'd be okay walking a perimeter. It seemed important to get a 360-degree picture of what she was dealing with. Hanging in the air about six feet above ground level, the tear was somewhere between a triangle and a diamond shape, with an irregular rim. The edges looked like charred and glowing embers, the center was a constantly shifting blue and white and magenta light.

Although it maintained a constant shape as Hellen went around, the farther she went to one side, the more she could see it was flat, like a hole in a piece of paper. From the side, she almost couldn't see it at all, just some edge and some radiating light. Then around to the back, she could see it again.

Did the monks ever say what dimension this came from?

"It's the second dimension." A rough voice startled her from behind.

She jumped and whirled around, at the same time backing to the nearest tree and holding her useless gun up in front of her. Whoever said that didn't know it was useless.

"What are you doing? Are you going to shoot a tree?"

Where the hell did that come from? No one was there! *Stay calm, Hellen, it's probably just some friendly, other-dimensional…whatever.* "Who the hell is that?" was her not-so-friendly question.

"Let's see, I'll give you a hint." It obviously enjoyed toying with her. "I'm tall, better-looking than I used to be, and you're looking right at me."

Hellen peeled her eyes and examined the tree in front of her. After a bit, she could see the enormous face made up by the branches, and the unibrow that told her who it was. "Browbone!" she exclaimed. "You're a tree!"

"I'm a tree," he agreed pleasantly. "Well spotted." He stretched, waved his branches, and soughed like the wind. "Not bad, huh?"

"You look great," Hellen said. "I didn't know you could be anything but a rock."

"Oh, we can borrow anything, really, but if a form has life of its own, it has to agree to share first. And the more complex the life forms get, the harder it is on them, so we like to stick to rocks. Which brings me to what I'm here to tell you."

"Oh, good. Are you coming back? As rocks? You know, like before?"

"Yes, actually, the dimensional tear is back to a low enough energy level to do that, and unless you can figure out a way to seal it up, which would be the best solution, we'll come and guard it like we did before."

"Seal it up? Can that be done?"

"Sure, but it'll take something like lightning, and I don't know how you could get lightning to strike it without getting close enough to risk trouble. So the guys will find new rocks and format them, and that will take some time, but we should be able to get it all together pretty soon. Anyway, that's not really what I'm here to tell you."

"What are you here to tell me?"

"Second-dimensional entities came out of the tear last night. They took over some of the soldiers who were here—the ones who were the first to approach the tear after the rocks were gone. Those soldiers didn't give permission to be used that way; the possession was hostile, and a violation of cosmic law.

"All the 2-Ders are negative-energy dark beings—evil, the only kind who will take a life form by force. The good news, bad for the soldiers, is that their vibrations aren't compatible, so the bodies they took won't be able to last long. Two or three days, tops. The bad news is that they can move from body to body, over a short distance and with enough time."

Wow. That was bad news. Stunning, in fact. "Do they know that?"

"Excellent question. Not necessarily. And if the body dies while they're in it, they die. Unfortunately, anything short of heart-stopping death doesn't affect them, they can hold a body up with their energy, even if it's very injured."

Sheesh, this was some relevant information. "Where did they go?"

"To the palace. They've been waiting for this very opportunity. There was an agreement made more than a century ago, in your time, before the leader was incarnated here. They're here to help him."

Better and better.

"All right," she said, "we'll have to take as many of them out as quickly as we can. What's the best way to do that?"

"Stop the heart. Bullets, knives, spears…any material weapon, really. Beheading might work, but no guarantees on that. Just don't try to kill them with energy, unless it's extremely powerful. Energy feeds them, and you don't want that."

"Right." Her hair was going to be white before this was all over. She paused, looking up at him. "What about you?"

"What about me?"

"Are you going to stay like that?" Her hand made a vague circle in his direction. "Because it would be nice to know you're here."

"I will be here for a while," he said. "At the moment it's my job; I'm the watchtower while everyone else finds their rocks. If something happens, I radio."

Radio. Probably meant something different in the twelfth. "Good. I guess I'll leave you to it then, and keep, uh…" she jerked her thumb over her shoulder, "making the circle, if you don't have any more for me."

"No, that about does it. But I will give your love to everybody."

"You do that," she smiled wryly. "And thanks for the heads up."

"You're welcome, Miss Hellen. For what it's worth, try not to let the grimness get you down. You guys can do this." Hellen eyed him skeptically, but he insisted. "I know winning looks impossible from here, but take it one day at a time. Do what you can do in that day and you'll get there."

Getting a pep talk from a tree was so…sweet. "Thanks," she said as she left. Was that the right response? Maybe "Are you crazy?" would have been better.

Because he was right, winning did look impossible.

Chapter F.6

Pulari's angry, floating head barked at him from the confines of the visaphone projector pad. "What the hell happened over there, Dagge? One of my patrols is missing, and you're telling me you don't know why? I suppose you didn't hear the guns last night, either!"

One of his patrols? *Lying asswipe, try ten or fifteen.* "Two of your men are over here, Pulari, in the palace. Would they be here if my men attacked them? Or if they were fighting at all?"

Pulari's stunned mouth hung open, which made him look ridiculous, and he said, "What are they doing there? Dammit, Dagge, what happened!?"

"Like I said, I don't know."

"Send them back to me, then, so I can question them."

"You can see them this afternoon," Dagge said, flashing a bright smile. "After you arrive."

"You don't seriously think we're still coming to the banquet."

"Of course I think you're coming. You want to see your soldiers, don't you? You want to know what happened. So do I. Perhaps we could go into the forest together."

The floating head frowned. "There's no way I'm going into your part of the forest. Mine's bad enough, but yours is death."

"All right, then, we won't go. I'll have my general Wharton do it. If anyone can survive, he can. Maybe you could send someone of your own, since your men are also missing." Dagge was in a generous mood, swiveled sideways in his chair, gazing at his fifteen eerie personal bodyguards, lined up in two rows beside him.

"You'd like that, wouldn't you?" Pulari sneered. "What the devil are you looking at? I'm over here!" The angry head turned and muttered to someone else in his room, "Can you believe this? I've never been treated so rudely in my life."

"Please, accept my apology." Dagge turned to face the visaphone again. "I was distracted by a minor emergency. Lots of company coming, you know." He smiled really big and friendly. "I look forward to seeing you and meeting the Queen, Your Majesty. You can see your men, we'll get to the bottom of what happened in the forest, then we'll have a nice dinner. It should be a wonderful weekend."

Pulari wanted to yell some more, Dagge could tell, but something was stopping him. Dagge could see the debate he was having with himself; to go or not to go, that was the question. Or from a military perspective, was his objective bigger than the risk?

He must have decided the chance of owning a carapaz mine was worth showing up, because he said, "Fine, Dagge, we'll see you later this afternoon," and he disappeared.

Fine, Dagge thought to himself, smiling as he switched off the machine. Now he could do what he really wanted—he pushed up out of the chair and strode to the front of the group. When he could see all of them, he put his hands on his hips and looked them over one by one.

They all had that same deadly look. "Sit down," he ordered, and they all sat, right in their place, on the floor, no hesitation. "Stand up," he said, and they did that, too. Time to try something a little more complicated. "Hold up your left hand."

Some hesitation, some wrong hands, some hands switched. Okay, that was normal, so they still had the same level of intelligence. Too bad.

He held up his left pinky finger. "Put the end of your little finger in your mouth and bite it off."

They did it. All of them. He could hear the crunching of bone and see blood spurting out the sides of some mouths. "Take your finger out and hold it up," he commanded. The ends of the fingers turned from red to black while he watched, like they were burned, much the way the wounds from the gunfire looked when he first saw them.

"Swallow," he ordered, more to dispose of the fingertips than anything. Then with his finger to his lips, he turned and paced around the room for a minute. Entire new vistas opened in his mind. These soldiers would make him the most uniquely terrifying leader the world had ever seen. How exciting!

He'd have to be sure and tell them not to kill Hellen. Chances were good she'd come back and try again. He could even leave that hidden outer door unlocked, just in case she hadn't heard the secret passage was found. One guard hiding there in the dark should be enough, with explicit instructions to capture the little sneak and bring her to him.

Dagge turned back and walked over to stand in front of them again. After cleanup they looked a bit better—less blood, fewer visible holes—but the flat stares and sallow purple complexions weren't going to pass for normal. Safe to say, his guests weren't likely to feel comfortable with them around. Of course, they could be put away during the day, and no one would be the wiser. Pull them out at night, put them on guard duty, and who knows how many assassins might be caught? Smiling, he went to pull the bell rope that summoned the valet.

The old nursery suite would be a perfect hiding place. Put a "closed for remodeling" sign up, a normal guard outside the door to redirect the misguided or curious, and voila! Oh, that all problems were so easy to solve.

He turned to yank the pull rope again, and ran over the valet, who was standing to his immediate back left. "What the...?" Dagge griped, grabbing the thin young man by the shoulders, and setting them both back on their footing.

"I'm sorry, sir," the valet said, catching his wig and settling it firmly. "I thought you knew I was there."

"You're like a ghost, dumbass, how would I know you were there?" Dagge's irritation was mostly at himself, because why didn't he know the kid was there? His supersense almost never failed, except with him. And Hilman. Must be a valet thing.

He pushed the kid away from him and gestured at his soldiers. "I want you to take the new guards upstairs and put them in the nursery. They are to stay there until everyone retires for the night. Once the guests start arriving," he turned back to the valet to emphasize the importance of what he said, "I want you to stand outside the door and make sure no one goes in. Or comes out."

"Certainly, sir," the boy said, always so agreeable it was irritating.

Dagge turned back to the soldiers and gave his orders. "You will follow this servant and stay in the rooms where he puts you. You will not come out until I tell you. You may be at ease, but you will remain absolutely quiet, is that clear?" Silence. Did he really expect a response? "Dismissed!"

The valet hesitated, but only for a second before he turned and led the way out into the hall. The soldiers followed him single-file, front line first, all in step. Beautiful.

Dagge smiled as he watched them go. What the hell could've happened in the forest?

Maybe that smart guy John Treslo would know.

Chapter F.7

By the time Roberta got up, it was early afternoon. She hadn't slept like that since before her first child. It felt great.

Robe, slippers and a toothbrush later, she walked out to the kitchen and found David at the table by himself. All the chairs were pushed in, counters were bare, dishwasher hummed and everything was clean.

"Wow, who did this?"

"We all did." David turned around in his chair to look at her, a half-grin on his face. "We thought we'd surprise you by not making you tell us to do it."

Roberta laughed, her face alight. "Years of training, paying off," she exulted, opening her arms and giving David a hug. He chuckled and hugged her back, rolling his eyes when she sat down across from him. She took his hand and held it. "Where's your Dad?"

"Downstairs." David tossed his head in the direction of the cellar door. "Inventing, I guess."

They were all on strict orders not to bother him when he was downstairs. If there was an emergency, such as imminent death, they were supposed to crack the door and yell. Roberta was never comfortable with that, since in her mind there were many degrees of lesser emergencies that would need his engagement, but fortunately, the system had never been tested, so it stood as it stood.

"Where's Joey?" She jumped to the next mental lily pad.

"At Barto's, as usual," David answered. "He's been practically living over there."

"Yeah, we should probably buy them some food," she said.

"I sent them a pie. Not much I know, but at least it was something."

"A pie?" Roberta was very interested. David's cooking skills were really blossoming.

"Yeah, I made two." He nodded toward the stove. "Coconut cream, Dad's favorite."

Roberta's eyebrows went up and she went to the stove to see David's handiwork for herself. The crust wasn't burned, the meringue was peaked and lightly browned, it looked perfect. "I can't wait to eat it," she said, coming back to the table. "You did a terrific job, it looks perfect."

"Let's hope it tastes good," David said with genuine modesty.

"Oh, I have no doubt." Roberta patted his hand and got up to make some coffee (who cared if it was really the afternoon?). "So, what are you doing over there with that piece of paper you were trying to hide from me?"

David didn't answer right away, so she looked over at him while she was counting scoops. He gazed down at the table, shaking his head, and the half of his face she could see was smiling. "You never miss a thing, do you?" he asked.

"Not after thirty years of teaching," she acknowledged. Once she filled the water pitcher, and poured the water into the tank on the coffee maker, she went back to sit at the table. "Boy, you must really not want to tell me."

"What if I said it was better if you didn't know?"

"As your mother, I'd be skeptical."

"What if I asked you to trust me for it?"

Roberta looked at her nineteen-year-old son differently for a minute. So many things were happening now, so many secrets, so many threats. She hated to lose that sense that she could protect her child, and she wasn't ready for him to make that move away from her.

But she knew she could trust him. He'd proved that over and over, making good choices, doing what needed to be done even when it rankled. How could she not let him be the man he was becoming? "All right, then," she nodded. "I trust you. But if you need something, you'll ask, won't you?"

The look on his face was hard to read, she thought maybe it was…pride? He said, "Yeah, Mom, you'll be the first or second person I'll ask if I need anything."

"Dad being the other option, I hope."

"Yes, Dad is the other option."

"Okay." She gave his hand a squeeze. "I'm going to go get dressed, will you mind the store?"

"Sure," he answered, and she got up to go hop in the shower.

David pulled out the paper he'd been working on when his mom came in. It was crumpled from being shoved in his shirt, but he smoothed it out on the table and looked over his work again. He was trying to come up with an emblem for the Resistance. A signature, like Thorn's thorn, only a group of them. A bunch of thorns. *Hell yeah.*

The paper was covered with different designs: thorns stacked on top of each other; thorns in a row all facing the same way; thorns facing different ways; thorns in a circle; long thorns, fat thorns, straight thorns, curved thorns. Some of them looked like explosions, which was cool. Or maybe like sea urchins, which wasn't so great. The circle one looked too much like a sun. His favorite was a group of three thorns, overlapping, a taller one in back. It looked like a fire, and that seemed perfect.

How could he get this to Thorn?

A knock at the front door brought him back to planet home. Was anyone expecting anyone? He wasn't, but with Mom in the shower and Dad downstairs, he was who they were going to get. His paper got folded and stuffed into his back pocket on the way through the den and into the foyer. Yikes, the tile floor was cold on his bare feet, why hadn't he put socks on?

Another loud banging said it was Mr. Impatient out there. "I'm coming!" David called. "Keep your pants on," he added under his breath, and opened the door to two soldiers on the front porch.

"John Treslo," the nearest one, probably the knocker, said.

"No, I'm afraid he's not here," David answered, as per centuries-old instructions.

They glanced at each other, apparently not briefed on what to do if this happened. "We have orders to bring John Treslo to the palace, to see the Overlord," Mr. Impatient insisted.

"I can give him the message when he returns, but other than that I can't help you."

"You could tell us where he is," the other guy said.

"I don't know where he is, he had errands to run or something."

They mumbled to each other for a second, then the first guy turned back to David and said, "Tell him the Overlord wants to see him, right now."

"I'll do that," David assured him, wondering if the man even knew how ridiculous that sounded. What if Dad didn't come home for hours? He watched the two soldiers turn and start off the porch, then he closed the door.

The real question was, did this qualify as an emergency?

Chapter F.8

Handholds in a stone wall were a lot harder to navigate with five extra uniforms and four rifles. Hellen's breath puffed out in clouds, muscles straining to lift her bulk and compensate for the swinging guns on her back. Trudging through the forest with all this stuff had been bad enough, she fell down twice and was damn lucky she didn't shoot a leg or something.

Caught by an ammo belt on a jagged edge of rock, she jerked to a stop. *Crap!* she pushed herself away from the wall and yanked herself free. The rifles swung out, pulling her so far she almost lost her grip.

All three rifles were bullet guns because of what she learned from Browbone. Risky, too, because she dumped her useless laser dud, and a bullet rifle wasn't going to be very convincing for walking around as Brucella. At first she'd tried to take five guns, one laser, but she just couldn't manage it. Pity, too, there was so much there for the taking. If she'd had time, she'd have hiked some of it to the monastery, but there wasn't any telling when Dagge would show up and put an end to the ransacking, and they needed this stuff in town.

The real prize were the two pairs of night glasses. That would even the playing field some. Two rabbits already had night glasses, but they were the only ones. Now there would be four, and Hellen was claiming one of them as her own.

She grabbed the top handhold and pulled her body into a lying position on top of the wall, hoisting her legs up to join her. Rolling over was not an option because of the guns, so she lifted and scooted her way to the other side to look out.

No sign of the patrol. If she hurried, she could probably make it down and over to the ditch without any trouble. She took the guns off and dropped them to the ground, then she swung her legs over, found the first foothold and lowered herself as quickly as she could.

On the ground, she squatted and looped the gun straps over her head and shoulders. Luckily, the sun was out today, so the tree branches dappled the area with shade and made her harder to see. Crazy how this stuff went through her head when there wasn't even anyone around.

Still crouching, she ran to the edge of the drainage ditch and half-slid, half-jumped down into it. Only slightly bent now, she made her way down to the stone-lined tunnels, into the maw and the dimness beyond.

Safe in the tunnel, her brain drifted to the new friends she'd made today: Guindo, Vizo and Tony. "Brucella" had worked out pretty well, and could be useful. Hellen had to grin to herself, she didn't know if she was that good, or if they just weren't the brightest bulbs in the pack. Either way, she was happy with it.

The long trip to the warren made her realize how tired she was. Tired and hungry. Maybe there'd be some food when she got back. She had no idea what time it was, but as helpful as everyone wanted to be, she was sure someone would rustle up something. Thinking of that made her ravenous, and she stepped up the pace.

Every so often she'd pass a spot where a storm drain opened to the street, and sunlight streamed into the gloom through the long rectangle. She slowed down and hunkered over at these spots because you never knew who might be close enough to hear or be facing the right direction to see into it. At one of these places, about mid-town, a raised voice caught her ear so she stopped and tuned in to listen.

"I'm tellin' ya, ya don' know whatcher talkin' about. I heard, straight from a guy who was there, that one a our guys walked in there today and never came out. I'm tellin' ya, ya need ta listen to me."

Too funny, they were talking about her. When she left the patrol that morning, she never went back, so they thought she disappeared in the forest. How perfect! Except how was she going to explain it when she saw them again? Aah, she'd think of something. She kept listening.

"Yeah, yeah, sure he was there. Some guy's always there. Hey, did ya see the new guys? They're fucked up." General agreement to that, then the first guy started talking again.

"I heard the Overlord's keepin' 'em in the palace. He must like 'em, but I don't think I'd want 'em around me."

"I dunno." Another voice floated down, and a cigarette butt bounced through the drain, ricocheted off the wall and fell at her feet. "I hear they'll do anything he says, and that'd be worth 'em being creepy."

"Yeah," the second voice agreed. "One of the palace detail said he saw 'em after they were in with the Overlord for a while, and they all had the ends of their pinky fingers missin'. I bet he cut 'em off." General agreement again.

"We need ta get movin'," the first guy said, followed by another cigarette butt and a candy wrapper. The sound of shuffling drifted down and the voices faded off.

"I heard one a Wharton's guys said Overlord was gonna take Pulari into the forest to see what happened in there. Man, that asshole's gonna shit his pants." They all thought that was riotously funny, so she missed anything else that was said. Figured.

Pulari in the forest, would Dagge really do that? Could he? According to the King, Pulari hated the forest, thought it was haunted, which wasn't too far off truth, as it turned out. Sounded like a tense situation to her, but rife with possibility.

By the time she made it past the first warren tunnel to the left, and into the warren tunnel on the right, nearly home, she knew what she was going to do.

Chapter F.9

Wharton checked his compass to make sure he still headed in the right direction. Not that he was a bad navigator, but something about this forest tended to turn people around. To be safe, he took a careful compass reading before he went in, and he kept the thing tied to his wrist to remind him to check it often.

After riding for an hour, he hadn't found anything, and he didn't think it was that far to the location of last night's incident. His direction must be off some, but which way? He stopped his mount and swiveled around, looking for any clue, listening for any odd sound. Closing his eyes, he let his ears reach out farther.

There, inside the soughing wind, a crackle, or a spit, like the lightning scientists make with those balls. Brief, and barely audible, but there over and over, same volume, same place. He turned his horse to the south at a fast walk.

The sound got louder. Part of him wasn't too surprised to see the flickering, burning tear. Had to be something crazy like that, didn't it? Considering?

Careful to stay outside the death radius, he made the perimeter, forcing his jumpy horse close to the corpses. The anomaly looked to be about six feet tall, three feet wide, and…flat. The ring of dead bodies was pretty far away from it—scattered where they fell, possibly from shooting each other.

Or the new guys were shooting them. Who were those guys? Because they sure as hell weren't the men he sent in here.

Wharton got down and examined some wounds, reins in hand, careful not to touch.

Mounted again, the trip sped up when the view kept being the same. Even on Pulari's side, it was just dead bodies all around. Until on the north side, near the border with Pulari, he saw that a few of the soldiers had been stripped.

Off his horse again, he tied the reins to a tree before kneeling to examine the first body —one of his own men, missing jacket and shirt and pants. Boots, knife, and gun were right there. At closer inspection, the guy before him, Pulari's man, had everything but his ammo belt and gun. Two guys farther on were his own, and they were missing everything but boots and guns. A couple more a few feet away were missing uniforms, too.

This near the border, his first thought was to blame Pulari. Uniforms would be very useful in an invasion. But why not take the guns, too? Why not take all the guns? The ammo belts were useless with the laser rifles, but *why not take the guns*?

He couldn't figure it. Maybe it wasn't Pulari's men…maybe it was someone else. Who would want a soldier's uniform? A spy, but a spy would want the guns, too.

Unless it was one spy. But why would one spy want five uniforms?

To make other spies. Or decoys.

Hm. Thorn might do that. As an answer it felt very right. He mounted up, and clucked his horse toward the palace.

Chapter F.10

John flipped the crystal pages of the pink book lying open on his worktable. How many nights had he slept with it under his pillow? Five hundred something? And he could still only read a little. Where were those monk genes when you needed them?

Gee, maybe four or five hours of sleep a night wasn't enough. Well, amen to that, not enough on so many levels. He closed the book and rubbed his tired eyes, then he swept his hands back on his head and gave his scalp a good scratching. Nothing like tingles to wake the brain.

Running his fingers over his head, he pulled the little elastic off his hair, reached for his water bottle and doused his upturned face. *Ha-ah!* He put the bottle down and rubbed his face and hair with his open hands, rumbling like an old bear. Refreshed, he smoothed the ever-whitening locks back into a ponytail and secured it with the band.

Roberta was no doubt wondering where he was. *Oh, I'm just trying to find something that will help me stay alive, honey.*

Dread hung like a black cloud in his chest. If something happened to him at the banquet tomorrow, if any tiny thing he did flipped Dagge's switch and he got taken or killed, who could do this job? So many things hung in the balance, and at the very least he needed to find a place or a person to hide the book, just in case.

As far as guardians went, Hellen would probably be the best choice, except she might not survive the night, either. David would be the next choice, but that was a big responsibility to dump on a kid's shoulders. John didn't think he would have wanted it at nineteen. Hell, he didn't want it now. But maybe Roberta could hold it for David…until he was ready. David was a monk, after all. There was always a chance he could sleep on it and get more out of it than his father had.

Decision made, he tucked the book in his jacket pocket and made plans to hoof a quick run into town. He tidied up his worktable a bit and got ready to go upstairs. A knock at the cellar door surprised him.

A slow squeak of hinges told him someone opened the door. "Dad?" David's cautious voice called from above.

"Yeah, David, what is it?" John walked to the bottom of the stairs and looked up.

"Soldiers were here asking for you." His face was worried.

"What did they say?"

"They said the Overlord wanted to see you right now, but that was actually about two hours ago. I told them you'd gone out, running errands, to give you some time, but I wasn't sure when you planned on coming up, and I know things have been a little…strained lately with Dagge, so I thought maybe I should you know, knock."

"You did exactly the right thing." John took the stairs two at a time. At the top he turned out the lights and pushed past David to get his coat.

"I want to come with you."

"Not a chance," John said.

"He might go easier on you if you have your son."

"It wouldn't make any difference, you'd just have to suffer, too." John didn't stop, he rounded the end of the stairs and went straight for the coat hooks.

"Then don't go. Pretend I didn't tell you."

John shook his head. "It's probably nothing. He's got company coming very soon and he won't want any last-second mess." He grabbed his coat and slid his arms into it. "I haven't done anything so obviously mutinous that he'd want to put me in the dungeon, either." *A few covertly mutinous things, yeah, but Dagge doesn't know about those. Does he?*

David was looking a little mutinous himself. "Dad, I know you're trying to protect me, but I feel like you don't trust me. I want you to trust me."

It was a hard spot the boy put him in. John knew his son felt anxious, that he hated being a prisoner in this town and wanted desperately to do something to change it, but unfortunately for him, his parents weren't ready for the idea that they should let him put his life on the line. He put his hands on David's shoulders. "I've told you as many secrets as I can right now. You know I trust you, or you wouldn't have the responsibility for those." The disappointed expression told him his volley was good. He did trust David, it was Dagge he didn't trust. Which was why he planned to hit the drain pipe and run by HQ before he went to the palace. It'd be quicker if he could go overland through the streets, but he didn't know how many soldiers might be on the lookout for him.

Maybe a disguise would do the trick. Turning to the storage chest, he flipped open the lid to reveal a rainbow of hats, scarves, gloves and the like. A quick pawing through the assortment yielded a couple of unlikely candidates, then he yanked a pair of sunglasses from the bottom and closed the lid. Hat on, sunglasses on, scarf up over his nose, he was ready.

"I've gotta go," he told his forlorn son. "Where's your Mom?"

"She left, too, about an hour ago, said she had some errands to run."

"Did you tell her about the summons?"

"Yes, she said I shouldn't bother you with it."

"Well, can't blame her for that. When she comes back, tell her I went."

"She's gonna hit the roof," David grumbled.

"Yeah," John admitted. "Be sure and say you tried to stop me."

Chapter F.11

Adia's laugh muscles were evidently way out of shape. Her sides were hurting, and she was out of breath, and her face was wet with hysteria. Purely sublime.

Roberta had come to see her at the perfect time. With no one else around, they had a chance to get to know each other minus interference. Adia couldn't believe she'd been deprived of such a phenomenal woman all these years. Well, not anymore. Was kidnapping still illegal? Because they sure could use some funny down here in the hole. All the conversation was so *serious*. *Seriously* serious. *Excitedly* seriously serious. It drove her crazy.

But thank One, the John/David/Joey stories worked pretty well to keep her mind off Hellen's latest dangerous mission. Not that Adia didn't have her ears peeled every time she stopped laughing, but at least she didn't have to sit there and stew in it. Truth was, she was deathly afraid Hellen wouldn't come back, though Hellen assured her she could keep safe. "Don't worry," *yeah right*, "I'm surprisingly good at this," she'd said. "I wish I'd known a long time ago that my parents were spies, I would've…" She paused while she searched for the right word. "…acquired some skills."

Well, she must have some skills, because they'd know by now if the soldier disguise didn't work. However, they wouldn't know if she got sucked into the demon hole. Or worse, if she was even now at the palace with some kind of magenta creepazoid slice sticking out of her head.

Okay, time to change thought tracks. What was Roberta saying?

"…I'm so glad she showed up that night, John would never have told me about all this." She paused and took Adia's hand. "Hellen will be back."

Adia dropped her face, feeling like she had revealed too much. Talk about needing to acquire some skills. Hers were way out of practice. For a second, she had to think about what was the best expression, because royals and politicians seldom just let their random feelings show.

But then she blew that with an avalanche of random feelings. "I'm terrified every time she leaves, Roberta. Hellen always has to go do these life-threatening things, why can't she be normal, and go to the store or something?" She rubbed her forehead with her fingertips. "This is so incredibly stressful, I thought it would be better here, but I'm not used to so many people, and they all want to talk to me, and I have no idea whether they're looking at my scars."

Okay, she opened her baggage right up, didn't she? All the insecurity and vanity and victimhood that she pretended not to feel tore out of her heart and fell into Roberta's lap, letting all her messy, squishy insides come pouring out the hole. She sighed, suddenly very tired.

"Let me see." Roberta stuck a finger under her chin and pulled her reluctant face up. "Come on, let me see you, I'm going to tell you exactly how you look."

Doubtful, Adia let her face get drawn up, her hair tucked back behind her ears, brushed off her forehead, and her head turned to the light more. A few moments passed while she sat there in silence and let Roberta examine her.

"Okay, here's the deal. From a distance you look half and half, the left side more red and darker than the right. It's almost like theater makeup—you know, dramatic the way it sweeps up your neck and across your face. The dark hair is a good color around it, too, frames it well.

"Close, the skin is uneven. It is a scar, there's no getting around that. You have interesting points, though, that must have been from the straw, or the way the fuel from that barrel ran." She traced her finger along Adia's cheek, as Adia had done so many times. "They're like the tips of flames that just miss your eye.

Roberta took her hands in her own warm ones. "The best news is that your eyes and your mouth are just as beautiful as they always were, and from the right side, you can barely see the scar." She leaned in closer and squeezed her hands. "On the left, you look like you've been painted with stylized fire."

Like the fire is still on you, that's what Hellen said. At least fire had a little awesomeness factor, and she supposed she could live with that. She let the burden drop a tiny bit. As scars went, it could be worse. And as a price she paid for surviving, she had to accept it.

Hellen's voice surprised her. "Hey, look who's here!" was the cheery greeting from the curtained doorway. Roberta got up and walked over, explaining that she'd come here to visit the girl because she'd had enough of boys at home. Adia paid close attention to Hellen's voice as they chatted the normal nothings: she sounded tired, and there seemed to be a new undercurrent of stress. Oh boy.

"There's some soup," Adia said loudly enough to be heard. "Vartile saved you some."

"Thank One, I am so hungry." Hellen walked over, and Adia stood up for the familiar warmth that a hug from her always meant. "It's good to be back," sounded loud as Hellen leaned in to put her arms around her. Adia wrapped her up and held her and made her stay until she had her fill. Hellen laughed and squeezed her.

"I brought five uniforms," she told the two of them when Adia finally let her go. "And four guns. It was pretty much a massacre in the forest, maybe a hundred dead. I saw the tear."

Adia sat down again. It could so easily have been Hellen dead. "I'm okay."

"I'm not scolding you," Adia replied, harsher than she meant to. Holding her breath for a second, she backed off. "I'm relieved, that's all." A silent pause prompted her to add, "I can't not worry."

"Of course not." Hellen put her hand on Adia's shoulder and squeezed. "My overreaction." She patted the shoulder and said, "I'll tell you guys all about it after I go get a bowl of soup." Adia could hear her taking off her soldier equipment; she must have left the other stuff somewhere, because it was just her usual noise.

"Bring it back down here, and I'll set you up a table." Roberta moved around now, too. "Do you need any help?"

"Probably not." Hellen's voice faded away toward the stairs. "I'll call down if I change my mind."

"Hello?" John Treslo's voice snuck in from behind the heavy curtain.

"John!" Roberta was surprised and stopped what she was doing. Her voice turned to Adia and she asked, "Should I let him in?"

"Definitely," Adia answered, always happy to see the big man. How funny that she still thought in terms of "see."

Roberta crossed to the doorway and opened the curtain for John, saying, "Come in, honey," which Adia thought wonderfully sweet. She hadn't had a lot of experience being around married people. "Hi!" Roberta and John said at the same time to each other, and they sounded so happy, like it had been a week. How interesting.

"Hello, Adia," John said as he came into the room, thoughtfully remembering she had dispensed with formalities.

"Hi, John," she greeted him cheerfully. "I can't believe I get three of my favorite people in one room, all to myself."

"Three?" John asked, confused. "Do I count as two? Because I wouldn't be surprised."

"No, Hellen just went upstairs, but she'll be back in a minute," Roberta answered, rustling like she was helping him with his coat.

"Your timing is perfect, too, she's going to tell us what she saw in the forest," Adia said, and for the first time ever regarding Hellen's apparent death wish, she felt a twinge of jealousy. Because even with dreams, which were seldom like reality, she was never going to be able to see these things for herself, and it kind of pissed her off.

Well, whatever. She got up out of the chair she'd been sitting in and asked Roberta, "What can I do to help?"

"Let's move your chair over a little, and we can use…" her voice swiveled behind her, "that chair, John would you grab that?" John went to fetch and Adia pulled her chair over, and soon they had a nice little grouping in front of the couch, just in time for Hellen.

"Hey, this is great!" Hellen greeted John, put her soup on the table, and sat down to eat while she told them what she saw in the forest. Her long story finished with, "I've got five uniforms we can use now, which means we can make a better plan for tomorrow. There's got to be some way we can create a diversion, or cause some confusion so I can get in and out unnoticed."

"Aren't you going to use the secret passage?" Adia asked.

"I haven't contacted Diit, so he won't be there to let me in. Everything happened so fast, he doesn't even know where we are." Hellen shook her head. "So, I thought I might go in through the kitchen, as Junika. Cookie won't turn me in, so it seems like my best bet."

"Are you really going to try and kill him again?" Adia could hear the whine at the edge of her voice.

"It's a perfect opportunity." Hellen was being patient, but firm. "He won't expect me to try again so soon, and with all the people there, I have to do it."

Adia's heart sank. She hoped after the visit to the forest this afternoon that Hellen would say it was too dangerous and they should wait. Fat chance.

"She won't be alone, Adia," John tried to soothe her. "I'll be there, at the banquet, and I can run some interference if I need to. And Chief and Cary and Zola—a bunch of people all said they'd volunteer."

So she remembered, but it was minimal help. Dagge could kill five of them as easily as one. "Then all five of you are likely to die," she said. "How do you know Hellen's luck hasn't run out? Or yours, John?"

Frankly, she couldn't believe that came out of her mouth. It sounded so hurtful when she said it. The three others were quiet, and Hellen finally said, "We have to try, Adia. Would you really rather we just live with it?"

Adia opened her mouth several times to say something, but nothing came out. She had no answer because either way was bad.

"Then help us," Hellen said. "Be the queen you were born to be."

Fury surged up out of the pit of her stomach and exploded in her chest. She wanted to scream at them, blow them backwards in their chairs with the force of her rage, flatten them, especially Hellen, until they stopped pushing her. If the monks wanted Hellen to kill Dagge, let them tell her how to do it, because Adia's world had been lost to her. Her destiny and responsibility had been stolen by a madman she couldn't beat, whose power and advantage were too great. Whatever future she'd hoped for died in her father's bed, then went up in flames in the stable. Why did Hellen refuse to accept that?

The answer knocked at her brain, but she didn't want to open the door. Instead, she stood up and started toward the curtain, but the furniture had been moved, and in her upset state she wasn't sure how far away the exit was. So she had to go more slowly than she wanted, and with her arms out in front of her like a blind person, which she hated, but it was worth it to get away.

Chapter F.12

No one said anything until Adia was gone. In the silence, Roberta fidgeted with Adia's headphones, her husband sat staring at the table, patting the front of his coat with one hand, and Hellen sighed, pushing her bowl across the table so she could lay her head on her arms. Roberta understood the agony, frustration, and general neural overload of being a parent. "She'll come around, Hellen," she reassured the dejected head on the table. "She will. You can't make it happen any faster than it's going to, but it will happen. I can feel the conflict in her."

"I'm not sure the conflict you feel is the one between *yes* and *no*. It's more like *yell at Hellen* or *run*." Hellen held up her hands one at a time like a scale, leaving her face to brave the table alone. She waggled her head back and forth. "This time I'm glad it was run."

John shifted gears for her. "We are intelligent, capable people, we'll figure out our own plan." He dropped his voice like he was sharing a secret. "I have some experience in espionage, you know." That made Hellen laugh a little and she sat up with a wry smile on her face, making Roberta thankful again for her husband's charm. He scooted his chair exaggeratedly close to the table, acting like a kid at a tea party. "Let's conspire!" he exclaimed.

"Okay, well I have no experience in espionage," Roberta started, "but when I want to tackle a big project, I find it useful to make an outline."

John's forehead got all wadded up. "What are you, a language teacher?"

"Oh, funny!" she said.

"Hey, I'm all for whatever helps. Let's write stuff down." Hellen got up, retrieved a pen and paper out of a box and handed them to Roberta.

In her element now, she wrote: *Objectives and Goals:*

"Okay, what are we trying to do?" She sat poised with pen.

"Kill Dagge." Hellen flipped her chair around backward and straddled it, then resumed her soup.

Roberta looked at her intently before writing. "You're sure you want to do that? Kill someone?"

Hellen nodded. "I'm certain, Roberta," she said. "He isn't going to stop hurting people. It's only going to get worse, he's young." She shrugged. "He'll spread like cancer, especially with those undead super-soldiers he's got now. We will save countless lives by separating him from his body. Will that make me a murderer? I suppose it will. But all the pieces of my life come down to this: I am the only one who can do it. My skills, my position as protector, my knowledge, even my past relationship with him makes me uniquely qualified. So it's *my* job, my burden."

Her voice got stronger. "And I take it. Almost my only misgiving is that I didn't do it before. How many good lives could have been saved?"

Roberta nodded, and wrote down *1.) Kill Dagge.* "Anything else?" she asked.

"I want to make contact with Queen Eladora," John said out of the blue.

"Why?" Roberta frowned at him. "She probably wouldn't even understand what you're talking about." Honestly, she was beautiful, but kind of a poof-head.

"Oh, I don't want to tell her anything, I just want to make contact," he teased, and Roberta slapped his arm with her paper.

"She'd be telling you to take a hike," the Wife gave it back to him, "and don't you come crying to me when her boot makes contact with your rear end."

John laughed and hugged his sweetheart. "Are you jealous?" he jibed.

"As if," Roberta scoffed. "If she wants you, she can have you," she said. "Get your silly butt off my 'to do' list."

"You would never." He smiled, and she had to admit he was right.

"Okay, you two, you are seriously off topic," Hellen reminded them. "We're trying to make a plan."

"Right," John agreed, leaning back and thumping his hand on the table. He looked right at Hellen and asked, "Have you given any thought to what if Dagge's expecting you?"

Hellen paused for a second. "I don't think he will. Logically, who would attempt an assassination with so many people around?"

"He would. And I think he might think any assassin worth his salt would do the same thing."

"Maybe we should put it off," Roberta said.

"No," Hellen came back fast. "It needs to be done now, before he figures out what to do with his scary new toys. That's another objective, to take out as many of them as we can. And they have to be solidly dead, injured won't do it."

"And energy weapons won't do it. How many bullet guns do we have?" John asked.

"I got four today," Hellen told him. "But we might be able to get more if we hurry."

"Can anyone throw knives?" Roberta asked.

"I'm not bad," Hellen said, "but I'd hate for my life to depend on it."

"Well, you know I'm highly skilled," John joked. He was in a weird mood, Roberta thought.

"Yes, John, you are highly skilled." Hellen was very patient. "Just maybe not in knives."

"John, focus," Roberta chided him and turned to Hellen. "What is the last thing you need to have accomplished before you can kill him?"

"I need to get to him, either within shooting distance, if I'm in uniform, or within knife distance."

"People around or not?" Roberta busily made notes.

"As a soldier, that would be okay, although in any situation where there are other people around, my chances of escape go way down. So optimally, no crowd is better."

"Okay, you need a situation where you can catch him alone, which probably means in a private place, like maybe a bathroom. How do you feel about that?"

Hellen thought for a moment. "I feel pretty good about it. If I can get to his bathroom, which I almost certainly can, I can hide there and wait until he comes in, which he undoubtedly will, since he'll have to eventually. And he's not likely to take anyone else in with him." Hellen's face lighted up with relief. "It's a perfect plan. I can get out the same way I came in, or if I have to, I can use the secret passage that lets out by the atrium."

She leaned in over the table and whispered, "No one will even find him until morning. We can all be long gone by then. In fact, I won't really even need anyone else, so we don't have to run the risk of losing anyone or being discovered."

"Except the more people we have to eliminate the freak contingent, the better," John argued. "Don't try to do all this alone, Hellen. There's not much chance you could kill them all without getting caught or killed yourself, and you have people who can help you."

His switch must have flipped into serious mode, finally, and Roberta wished it hadn't. He was right, she knew, but she didn't want him to be one of those helpers. Assassination wasn't really in his skill set. "John, you won't even have a weapon. I hope you're not planning to try and do this." She looked at him, sternly imploring.

"I have to do what I can do, Roberta." He met her gaze with an intensity of his own, taking her by surprise. "Dagge already doesn't trust me, and I think he invited me to the banquet for reasons he didn't mention." He shook his head and smiled wanly at her. Roberta's brain went into a spin; was he thinking he was going to die?

Hellen steered the debate into safer territory. "John, you don't have to risk anything. We can take Chief, and Cary and Zola, and we can put them in uniforms, and I have no doubt that between the three of them they can do plenty of damage. Okay?" she pressed.

"Yes, okay." He held up his hand like he was taking a pledge. "I promise I won't try to take out any of the dimensional weirdos unless some miracle falls in my lap and I have a perfect opportunity. I mean, I couldn't turn that down, could I?"

Hellen grinned her acknowledgement. "Yes, all right, if a miracle falls in your lap that's different."

"See what I've been living with?" Roberta complained. "And there are three more at home."

"We have to get more guns." Hellen stood up and scooped her bowl off the table to take upstairs to Vartile's kitchen.

"Is that the extent of our plan?" Roberta asked, incredulous. "Wait for Dagge in the bathroom, and try to kill as many of the 2Ders as possible? That's not a plan, that's a shortlist of goals."

"We don't have time for anything else," Hellen said. "There's no telling when body recovery will start, so we need to get to the forest and take what we can."

"Adia's going to have a fit," Roberta called after the retreating back.

"Yeah, I know." Hellen's voice floated back to her from the stairs, and that was it. Roberta turned to John, who was putting on his coat and scarf again.

"David told me about the soldiers at the house today, when I came upstairs," he said. "I was on my way to the palace when I came here, but now I won't be going, and you know Dagge." He left his scarf draped around his neck and stepped close to her, his hands on her upper arms. "I brought something to give to you." He pulled a wrapped bundle out of his coat pocket and held it up to her. "Would you please give this to David, when it's time. Tell him to sleep on it, and maybe he'll have better luck than I did."

Roberta looked down at it and said, taking it. "But why don't you just give it to him later?" She looked up at him, willing his answer to be light and innocuous, not the dreadful thing she thought it might be.

He gazed gently down at her, love shining in his face. His fingers reached up and ran softly over the laugh lines at the corner of her eye. Oh no, this was bad.

"Just a precaution." He smiled. "I'm trying to be as smart as my wife."

Roberta was seized with a sudden, powerful urge to pull John home, to not let him go with Hellen, and especially not let him go to the palace tomorrow night. She needed her family intact. She couldn't do it all without him, couldn't be a role model for two teenage boys, feed them without a job, and protect them from this strange, scary new world.

But she also knew this situation was bigger than she was, bigger than all of them. Somebody had to fight, somebody had to stand up and do the right thing and if that meant dying, then thank One for the people who were willing to die.

As long as it wasn't her husband.

"John, you'll be okay. Dagge won't do anything in front of all those people, even if he does suspect you. He can't afford to show himself like that."

"Of course. You're right," he agreed earnestly. "I'm not going to do anything foolish, I promise."

Hellen's footsteps hurried down the stairs and toward the table. "We can get some more uniforms, too," she said. "Whoever collects the bodies will know they're missing, but it'll still be hard to tell who's who when we've got them on."

"Aye aye, cap'n." John picked up the ends of his scarf and wrapped his neck, stopping briefly for a kiss before turning to the curtain.

"John," she said quickly, and he turned to look at her again. "I'll see you at home," she finished, suddenly on the verge of panic. Swallowing the lump in her throat, she turned away and started pushing the furniture back into place.

****

Fifteen minutes of alone time worked wonders for Adia. Her rage drained away, and she had time to kick herself for reacting like such a spoiled brat. Thank One, Hellen came out and got a hug before she and John headed upstairs to take the faster overland route to the forest. Hellen's plan was to act like she was escorting John to the palace, and let the confusion of the royal arrivals mask their detour.

They had to hurry, so Adia didn't get much more than a quick squeeze, and she went back to loading the printer with paper. Five steps to the shelves, paper at shoulder height on the right, five steps back. It was a small job, and not necessary at the moment, but it kept her from being pathetic, and gave her something constructive to do.

She kept hoping Cary would show up. Yeah, she felt bad about shutting him down like she did, he was only trying to help, but she was so frustrated with these people who thought they knew what her life should be. She sure didn't. Like every day for the past eighteen months, she wished her father was here—he could help her straighten everything out.

Anyway, she wanted to…apologize or something. Okay, apologize. That's what good people did, right? Not to mention the fact that he might be the only guy who would ever pay attention to her. No matter what Hellen and Roberta said, scars weren't a big attraction.

But power is. The thought jumped into her mind from nowhere. She stood up and snapped her mouth closed, surprised. *There may be another reason he's courting you.*

You know, why do you have to come along and spoil things?

You know I'm right. He's been coming on pretty strong, hasn't he?

What does that mean?

He doesn't even know you.

I'm a celebrity. Weird stuff like that happens.

All I'm saying is that you might like to give it some thought.

Sure, I'll add it to my list.

Great.

Fine. (Stupid voice.)

"Hello!" Roberta's greeting made her jump. "I put all the furniture back as close as I could remember, so if you stub your toe, I'm sorry, you may have to recount or something."

"Thanks for the heads up." Adia managed to get her company face on. "I'll be careful. Hey, are you in a hurry? Do you have time to talk about something?"

"Sure." Roberta came closer and put her bag down. "What's on your mind, young lady?"

"Is there a chair?" Adia waved her hand around vaguely. They kept the middle of the room clear for her, but she didn't venture around the edges much because people were always bringing stuff in and moving things, and it just didn't seem worth the knee and toe trauma.

Roberta got a chair and they sat by the printer, which smelled lightly of ink and dust. Adia's hands found Roberta's and she leaned in to her to speak. "Do you know anything about Cary Roades?"

"He was the print manager at the Books 'n' All. Made it pretty fast, too. I've heard he's a hard worker and not afraid to let his ambitions show." She paused and asked, "Shall I describe him to you?"

"No, Hellen's done that, she says he's cute. Do you think he's cute?"

"Yes." Roberta sounded like she thought he was very cute. "He's definitely cute, but—" an awkward pause, and Adia could tell she didn't know how to say what she wanted to say. Finally, she creaked out, "I don't know if I should be giving you man advice, but I think if you're not careful, he could try to push you into something you're not ready for. Not that I think he would succeed, or that he's a bad guy," she added, "but how many battles do you really want to fight right now?"

Adia deflated like a balloon. Her air went out, and her body relaxed, and she stopped flailing at everything that was wrong in her life for a minute. It felt good for someone to understand that she had too many battles, for every last blasted thing in the world, and she was tired.

"Thank you, Roberta." Her voice was small, just like her wrinkled little balloon self.

Roberta squeezed her hands and released them so she could pull Adia into a hug. It was too far, though, so she let go, scooted her chair up beside Adia's and put her arms all the way around her. Adia relaxed into her, and tears stung her eyes, and it was almost like having her own mother there. Part of her wanted to stay like that forever.

But it only lasted a little while before Cary's excited voice burst in from the main tunnel. "Pulari's caravan just came through town," he rushed. "Hellen and John got away fine, Mieko and I made a little diversion for them." The laughter in his voice carried over to them and they sat up to listen.

"What did you do?" Roberta asked.

"Faked a fight. Got out in the road a little, right in front of Pulari. He was so mad, he yelled out the window at us, and shook his fist! It was hilarious!" His joy was contagious, and Adia had to smile. The man did have his good points. "I'm going to go find Mieko, he cut north 'cause the guards were watching us. If you see Beau, tell him!" And the roomful of energy was gone.

"I gotta say," Roberta commented when the air returned, "we're lucky to have him." She paused slightly. "Is this organization organized yet?"

"I'd say no, but it's trying," Adia quipped. "You're right about Cary." She searched for Roberta's hand, which Roberta handed to her. "Maybe somewhere down the road, but not now. Thanks for understanding about the battles, and about ... having too much to deal with."

"I do understand," Roberta told her. "More of us do than you realize. The others just want you to be on the throne. They want it to be like it was when your father was alive."

Adia sighed and nodded. She really did understand that. The problem was she didn't think it was possible.

Chapter F.13

Pulari was the first to arrive. When the valet informed Dagge that guests had reached the south gate of the town, Dagge hurried through the palace and out the main entrance to wait on the steps. As arranged, a multitude of guards and servants descended outward from him in a grand "V" shape, ready to welcome and serve.

The magnificent caravan trundled up the main road between the village and the palace: three carriages, a mounted royal guard, four wagons of servants, plus a wagon for baggage. Dagge had to laugh at four wagons of servants. He guessed the man didn't want to risk having to wipe his own ass or something.

The mounted guards lined up facing the lead carriage when it stopped in front of the palace. Footmen raced to open doors and offer hands. Dagge was a little disappointed none of them got down on all fours to be stepped on; that would have been perfect.

The few pictures Dagge had seen of the Royal Couple Next Door didn't prepare him for the reality. In the visaphone, King Pulari was just a scowl on a granite face, but he unfolded a tall, lean frame as he stepped out of the carriage, looking much younger than his 70+ years. Queen What's-her-name, by contrast, was a little butterball of a woman, who looked like she might have had a twinkle once, but years of sleeping with granite had pretty much worn it away. Dagge smiled inwardly, maybe he'd see if he could coax it out.

"Your Majesties!" He gushed down the steps toward them. "It's so good of you to come. I'm Overlord Tomius Dagge." He held his hand out to the Queen, who placed hers hesitantly in his, and he bent over to kiss it. "But you may call me Tomius," he said, radiating the charm full on her. "Your husband and I have met already. Your Highness!"

Turning, he shook the King's hand and bowed slightly. "You are most welcome."

"Yes, Dagge, dispense with the formalities and get us inside, it's cold," Pulari grumbled, moving toward the door. Dagge let him go, took the Queen's hand, and tucked it in his arm. "What may I call you?" He smiled down at her.

She laughed nervously and said, "Most people call me Queen Nylah."

"Then I shall call you Nylah," he purred, patting her imprisoned hand gently.

Guards and a handful of lesser guests—a general, two ladies of the court, a foreign minister or somewho—piled out of the other carriages and flowed toward the big doors. Their valets and footmen and ladies' maids and butt-wipers all piled out as well and the portico got full of people. Good grief.

Dagge let the butler sort all the servants out, and he escorted the guests into the cavernous foyer. "My footmen will show you to your rooms, since I'm sure you'd like to freshen up after your trip," he announced cordially. "We're expecting other guests tonight as well, so there will be a light supper after everyone arrives."

"Dagge, we have business to discuss," Pulari interrupted, "and it can't wait."

Irritation flickered purple across Dagge's vision, and Pulari must have seen it because he frowned a little more. Then it was gone, and King Royal Pants must have thought he imagined it, because he assumed top dog again.

"Get your butler to attend to these people, and take me someplace we can talk," he insisted. Dagge just smiled and nodded, and a few gestures later, he and Pulari and two members of Pulari's guard were on their way to the conference room. He couldn't resist a quick glance up toward the nursery door.

Behind closed conference room doors, Pulari stayed as far away from Dagge as subtly possible. It was funny, really, Dagge would walk toward him and Pulari would stroll away on his next sentence. Naturally, Dagge couldn't resist a little play time.

"I'm guessing you want to discuss what happened in the forest." He advanced.

"Oh, do you think?" Pulari's sarcasm stayed behind the desk until Dagge got close.

"I sent my man Wharton into the forest to see what happened." Dagge sat on the desk facing his opponent. "He saw something very interesting."

Pulari moved to the oversized globe in the corner and pretended to look at it. "Did he? And he came back alive? Not a typical experience, I understand."

Dagge stood and walked over to the globe and pretended to look at it, too. "Well, he's a very capable soldier, and knows how to take care of himself. But the important thing is that there's something in the forest that you should see."

Pulari squinted at him. "I don't think so, Dagge." He shook his head and walked to the settee, but he didn't make the mistake of sitting, he leaned on the back of it. "I think I can find out everything I need to know from my men you're holding prisoner."

"I'm not holding them prisoner." Dagge drifted toward the settee. "One of them died of his wounds, and the others are recuperating in the med ward. We did what we could for them, and they'll be fine."

Pulari puffed up and looked like he was going to explode. "You didn't mention they were injured! How did it happen?"

"Do you think I ordered it?" Dagge asked, stepping closer, his voice all careful innocence.

Pulari stood straight, unwilling to look weak by moving away. "I know you could have, but you wouldn't have let them live to talk about it. I'll find out from them what happened. I demand to see them immediately."

Dagge did his best to control his smirk. He loved it when things went his way.

A short while later, he stood to the side while Wharton brought Pulari's soldiers into the room. There were two of them, back in their old bloody uniforms, minus their weapons and with the added bonus of that freaky shark expression.

Pulari's mouth hung open. He stood in front of them, leaning way back and not saying anything. Possibly he was put off by their dead eyes and forehead-first posture. Possibly the blood and rot smell. Dagge suppressed a smile. The poor man looked like he wanted to flee, but was far too kingly to do it, so instead he pulled himself together and barked at them. "Highest ranking man step forward!"

Nothing happened. Not even blinking. Pulari copped a royal swagger and shifted to the soldier on the left. "What's your name, soldier?" Nothing. Pulari stepped closer to him, like he was going to dominate the guy. "I said, what's your name?"

The soldier looked at him, and opened his mouth, and a screeching hiss came out. Pulari stepped back, horrified.

"They can't talk, really," Dagge threw in conversationally, joining Pulari in front of the men. The guy on the left went back to attention.

"What the devil happened to them, Dagge? Did you do something to them?"

"No, they were like this. My men, too. I've got no explanation for it except to say that there's something in the woods, close to our mutual border, and we probably need to do something about it before it gets bigger."

"How do I know this isn't some ruse you cooked up to lure me into a trap?"

"Well, I guess you don't, Your Majesty. But honestly, if I wanted to kill you, I could have done it already."

That shut him up. Royal Asshole. Dagge took advantage of the pause to tell Wharton to take the men back, but Pulari found his indignation and said, "Hold it, these are my men and I want them to report to my master sergeant."

Dagge said, "Sure, fine, you tell them wherever you want them to go."

Pulari turned to the soldiers and ordered, "Report to the Master Sergeant, who will be supervising the setup of the tents on the field west of the palace. Dismissed." They stood there, no change in posture or expression. Pulari twitched, like he wanted to hit the nearest guy, but he was afraid to.

"It's not your fault." Dagge patronized him, just for fun.

"Of course it's not my fault," Pulari snapped. "Take them wherever you want to, they're useless."

Dagge was happy to do that, because the jerk couldn't be more wrong. "Wharton, when they've been returned, notify the stable that we'll need several horses. You do ride, don't you, Your Majesty?" He put just enough spin on the last two words to rankle him.

"Yes, Dagge, I ride." The King could barely hide his irritation. Well, he wasn't really hiding it at all, was he? Such a pleasant person. They'd see how much starch he had left after a quick trip into the woods.

The old guy might need a nap later, so they should get going.

Chapter F.14

John couldn't believe he actually wished he had a horse. After their adventure to the monastery, he swore he'd walk for the rest of his life, but trying to keep up with Hellen's breakneck pace made him reconsider. How he'd love to gallop past her and look back and smile.

If they could fly, it wouldn't be far, she said, and now he could see why she put it that way. In this part of the forest there was no such thing as a straight shot anywhere. Always bushes or ravines or rocks in front of you, no matter which way you turned. What a pain in the feet.

Ho ho ho, at least he could still laugh. *Stay tuned for the second half of the show!* As he waved to the crowd, his foot slipped off a rock, into a crevice by a tree root, jolting his heart and throwing him off balance. His hand shot out to the trunk to catch his weight, and he managed not to fall. A shaky laugh sent breath clouds into the air as he worked his foot out of the hole. *And I thought running around town after curfew dodging patrols was bad.*

Hellen's arm gesticulated back and forth in front of him, so he switched to focus mode. About twenty strides on, she smacked the air in his direction, which he guessed meant slow down or back up or something, so he compromised and stopped. Her face turned to the side so he could see her profile, and the intensity of her expression told him she was listening.

His focus moved to his ears. Quiet, then a faint popping. Hellen turned to him and signaled him in.

"The outer perimeter is right in front of us," she whispered, pointing ahead. "We're on the side, so you can't see the tear very well, but once you get ninety degrees around from here either way, that's straight on. One of us should go for uniforms on the palace side, and the other should go for guns on the Pulari side. Which do you want?"

"I'll get the uniforms," he said. "How far away should I stay from the tear?"

"Far. Let the dead bodies be your guide. They'd be gone if the hole could suck them in."

Somehow that wasn't comforting.

"Do you want me to get guns, too?"

She hesitated. "Can't hurt. If we can't carry them, we'll leave them somewhere. They're already going to know someone's been here, so there's no point in being subtle."

"All right, then," he said, and took off toward the right.

The first dead soldier he came to had a black hole in his chest, rendering the uniform unusable. Bent over the body, John studied the soldier's face for a moment; his eyes were open and his jaw hung slack. "Not looking too good, there, buddy," John whispered, and slid the rifle strap out from under the arm. "One of a hundred people to witness history, and you can't tell the story." He stood up and shouldered the rifle. Adia had said it looked like the creatures sliced their victims in half, top to bottom, but she also said the dreams weren't always literal. Still, if it was even close, he pitied even more the ones who had walked away.

Farther on, the next two guys were shot in the head and neck—their uniforms were perfect. Being too big to wear them, John stacked the clothes, intending to pick them up on the way back. Two laser rifles went beside the stack.

John picked over the wide swath of corpses, leaving a trail of clothes and guns in hurried piles. However, once he was far enough around to really see the tear, the scientist in him, or the monk maybe, became completely absorbed. All the flashing, shifting mystery of it drew him like a hooked fish, and he forgot where he was until he tripped over some poor guy's very dead head.

That brought him back some, but he still couldn't drag his eyes off the thing. He stood there and stared at the moving and burning, and he *desired* to his very core to know what was on the other side. It killed him not to be able to find out, to know that this singular occurrence would expand the discussion of the nature of reality so far beyond what presently existed that it would make his era seem like the dark ages. What a discovery! What huge strides toward truth!

His heart pounded, and he couldn't get enough air through his nose. He bent over and tried to calm down, but it didn't do any good. Was he having a heart attack? That freaked him out, and his breathing got more frantic. No chest pain, no left arm pain, just gasping. *Maybe an anxiety attack...people do have those.* John stood up with his hand on his chest and paced back and forth a few steps to try and shake it off. Interestingly, once he stopped looking at the hole, he felt better. Standing there, facing away, he felt fine. Weird.

Should he? Yes, he should. He turned back and looked at it again, and after a few moments he started gasping, so he turned away, walked to the nearest tree, and leaned on his hand while he caught his breath.

All right, his first non-scientific experiment, based as it was on anecdotal evidence. *Object produces anxiety, at least in me.* Why? Monk blood maybe? Or basic cowardice? Could be the pull of energy. He'd have to ask Hellen if it happened to her. John recommenced his search for usable uniforms.

But that didn't stop him thinking. *Two dimensions...what would that be? Not inherently physical, 3D is physical, so...mental and emotional? Yet there are beings, and they have... finite forms of some sort. Which can inhabit people, but only for a short while, Hellen says. They support the body, but they also kill the body. Interesting.*

This is what his brain was doing when the laser pulse zipped past his head. He was bent over taking a shirt off a guy, and the ground blew up in front of him. He jumped like crazy, and Dagge's voice skewered him right through the gut.

"Treslo!" He jumped off his horse and catapulted in John's direction. "What the hell are you doing?"

A voice started coming out of John's mouth, but he had no idea what it was going to say. "I decided to come out here and see what happened." The voice was so calm, John wondered at it. "And since I'm sure you noticed our…visitor, or whatever it is, I'm sure you can understand I wanted to examine these bodies."

Dagge's face wore a mask of polite skepticism, but it didn't cover the danger of his eyes. "Did you find anything?" Superficially, he was very courteous.

John jerked his head a bit from side to side. "Not really."

"Guns, perhaps." Dagge pressed.

"Yes, I didn't think they should be lying out here. I was going to bring them to you before Pulari's men got them." That was when he noticed King Pulari on one of the other horses. "Your Majesty." He bowed. *Unbelievable.* And there was Wharton, and a couple of Pulari's guards, he guessed. How did he not hear them?

"How thoughtful of you, John." Dagge whacked him on the back and hung his arm from John's shoulder. "We wouldn't want so many guns falling into the wrong hands, would we?" He stretched his mouth into an imitation smile.

John got the message, but kept his expression innocent. "Absolutely not, sir."

Dagge continued loud enough for the visiting king to hear. "Although I'm sure Pulari's men would never come take our guns." He faked a hearty laugh. "I'm sure those of his men who were over here were simply drawn by the noise to help in whatever way they could, right Your Majesty?"

"My soldiers are all trained in emergency protocols, Dagge," Pulari answered in a bored tone. "Naturally they're instructed to render aid whenever needed."

"Naturally," Dagge echoed, then turned back toward John. "Since you mentioned our 'visitor.'" He strong-armed John around to face the tear. "What do you think it is?"

John took a breath and turned toward Dagge—he couldn't risk having an anxiety attack in this particular situation. "I think it's some kind of a… Some kind of a… I don't know what it is, sir. I've never seen anything like it."

Now he stood at the mercy of the court. He'd started out so well, it depressed him to end that lamely. The look on Dagge's face, though, wasn't skepticism, or outrage, or evil, he simply looked like he might believe him. John crossed his mental fingers.

"I appreciate your honesty, Treslo." He turned to Pulari and called over, "Pulari, I want you to meet John Treslo, noted architect and resident genius."

That sounded like a bad setup to John. "Oh, sir, I wouldn't say that." He tried to laugh it off.

"Oh, I would." Dagge whirled on him abruptly, and whispered, "And I'm not the man to argue with, am I?" His hand held tight on John's neck and his eyes glittered. It was so threatening, John's heart flipped.

Nevertheless, he smiled and replied, "Then I change my response to 'thank you,' sir, and please forgive my manners. I don't get much call to have them."

"Then I hope you brush up before tomorrow night!" Dagge said louder, and strong-armed John over to the mounted men. "Mr. Treslo here is going to join us at the banquet tomorrow, Your Majesty."

"Yes, fine, what is that thing, Dagge?" Pulari said.

"John was just telling me that he has no idea what this is, and if John doesn't know, I would say nobody knows." They all turned to look at the gleaming, flashing hole. Wharton got down off his horse, but the other three stayed mounted. John looked everywhere but at the hole, and that was how he saw Hellen, who was watching through a fork in a tree on the other side. She saw him see her, and she jerked her head to the left, her left, which John figured meant "head that way." Okay.

Idly, he moved away from the group, pretending to investigate from all angles. What was Hellen going to do? A glance back at the tree told him she had already gone.

As he walked, he kept his eyes on the bodies and the spans of ground between, and Dagge's voice jumped him from right at his elbow. "Too bad we came along and spoiled your fun, isn't it?"

Strange thing to say. How to respond? "I noticed that all the injuries were actually from guns. It doesn't look like whatever that is can hurt people. Suck them in, maybe, but beyond that radius I think we're safe."

"Yes, Wharton already determined that, although the sucking thing is new, why do you think that?"

"Because there isn't anything around it—no plants, or bodies, or decayed matter. Even the organic detritus of the forest floor is missing. In other cases, that could indicate that they were blown away, but remnants aren't anywhere to be seen. Consequently, they were sucked in, which is the only option left."

"Mm hm." Dagge's gaze scanned the bare circle and stopped. His hand flew to his dagger, his body went all tense, and he shouted to Wharton, "Get over there! That way! If you get to her first, take her alive and unharmed!" And he rushed off before John could do anything.

"Sir!" he yelled, not wanting to appear too anxious. "It was a deer!"

"Shut up, Treslo," Dagge shouted back to him, "I know what it was."

Oh, shit. What could he do? John grabbed his gun and ran.

****

Lousy timing. Too close to the clearing, between trees, and when Dagge saw her, the best choice seemed to be to keep running. Maybe it was a bad idea to draw John off. He seemed to be doing pretty well on his own, and she didn't know what she could do to help anyway. But she couldn't leave John to his fate, not with him skating thin ice already, and now her good intentions had gotten them both in trouble.

Hellen moved back into the shadows, away from the hole. Fewer rocks right here meant easier going, and she darted from tree to tree in the gloom. Even with the advancing twilight, she knew this area plenty well, and her night glasses stayed hooked to her belt.

Dagge had disappeared amongst the trees, which worried her, but he was probably slowed down by more treacherous terrain. Wharton had been sent around the long way, behind her. He'd probably ride up on his horse, so she'd have good warning.

She dashed to the next tree and peeked through the fork in the trunk. Still no Dagge, but across the clearing she could see John Treslo hopping awkwardly over a hollow in some tree roots, carrying a gun. He swore and clattered and made way more noise than necessary, and when he fell, Hellen had the sneaking suspicion he did it on purpose.

As he went down his gun went off, repeat-firing in a wide arc, shooting branches and sweeping across the tear, which gobbled up every pulse that came at it with a flash of light and a loud sucking sizzle. *Did it stay brighter?*

From the other side of the tree she'd stopped at, she could see Dagge across the clearing, back a bit in the dimness at the edge of the death zone. Mouth open slightly, he stood there mesmerized, smiling, eyes glued to the dimensional hole like he was seeing it for the first time. Hellen watched him, fascinated, and wondered what ran through his head—probably all the fun ways he could use a handy dimensional tear to his advantage.

Well, good thing Dagge was so distracted, because John fell nearly beside him, and if Dagge happened to decide he wanted to feed his sparkly new friend, John's flesh would sure be convenient. She willed John to move away, far away, while he could.

As she watched, John got up and moved behind Dagge, who didn't seem to notice in the least. Careful and quiet, he raised his rifle to shoot.

His left arm blasted open with a laser shot. Hellen's head jerked around to see where it came from—Wharton, of course. On foot and in the open, he never stopped walking, crossing the clearing at the other end of the tear, eating up the distance to John, who had dropped the rifle and clutched his bloody tatters with his other hand.

"John Treslo, you are under arrest for treason!"

****

Dagge heard Wharton's voice, but he couldn't understand what he said. It sounded to Dagge like he was under several feet of water, and Wharton called from the bank, and it didn't matter what Wharton said because down here he was floating, and the light pulled him and pulled him with its shimmering beauty.

Blue and pink and white light, dancing. He wanted to get closer, he wanted to go in it and feel it around him, caressing his skin, penetrating his eyes.

What was that? He stopped and came out of it some. No, he didn't think he wanted the light to penetrate his eyes. Not after what happened to the last guys who got penetrated. Dagge shook himself, and made himself turn to see what Wharton was yelling about.

He had John Treslo at gunpoint. John held his arm, all black and bloody, and a gun lay at his feet. *John Treslo, you bad boy you.*

Glee surged in him. "Bring him to me," he said to Wharton. The General tapped John with the muzzle of his gun and the big man picked his way through roots and rocks and bodies to get to where Dagge stood. Dagge watched the traitor come reluctantly toward him, reading the pain, the dread, the way-out pulse. The fear before death was always the best. A person could never be more real than when they were shitting in their pants.

"Dagge, what the hell is going on over here?" Pulari's unwelcome voice grated into his pleasant imaginings. He forgot the fool was here. How disappointing, now he had to make this civilized.

"Pulari, how good of you to come in my emergency," he oozed. "I was just telling Mr. Treslo—" *no, not the truth* "—that we needed to get him back to the palace and have that arm looked at. It seems he shot himself while running." He finished with a slightly amused eyebrow lift.

"Let's get on with it, then." Pulari urged his horse around and called back over his shoulder. "I hope you have a good dinner planned, Dagge, this was a waste of time."

Dagge watched Pulari ride off with one eye on the tear. It hung there in space, beautiful, flashing like a jewel in bright light, flaming a little at the edges, ever burning a bigger hole. Confronted with all that magnificence, the coward edged his horse away, and contempt flooded through Dagge. *Weak. Let him go his own way, maybe he'll get lost.*

He brought his gaze back to the face in front of him, pale with pain, and he stood there expectantly, waiting for John's eyes to come up and meet his. After a few moments, he had to prompt him a little to get him to do it. "Hello-o. Jo-ohn?" John lifted his head and looked at him, and was that hatred on his face? Dagge laughed.

"Wharton, take him to the dungeon," he said, and whistled for his horse.

Chapter F.15

When the song ended, Adia pulled the headset off her ears and mimicked the fading guitar for the benefit of the empty basement. With the chorus still playing in her head, her left hand tapped the air and the right hit her thigh on the down beat. One last wailing line in a whispery falsetto, and he spoke.

"Uhh, I'm here."

She must have jumped three feet off the couch, heart in her throat, face flaming and spit sucking down her windpipe. Spasmodic coughing ensued, lasting at least half a minute before she finally regained some normalcy. Mr. Clueless was not winning any points doing this.

"Cary, you have got to find some way to let me know you want to see me."

"I'm sorry! I didn't know what to do! I knocked, you couldn't hear me, and I knew you were in here because you—" He paused. Took a breath. "Were singing."

"I was not singing."

"You were singing."

Of course she was, but she didn't want to admit it, so she changed the subject. "Throw something at me, or fan me or something. Just don't come in here and watch me, that's creepy."

"I haven't been here long," he assured her, voice coming closer. "If you want me to throw something at you next time, I will. But I get to pick what it is."

"Keep in mind I can have you beheaded." She leaned forward, but backed up surprised when his energy bulled in close and collided with hers. He had to be…like less than a foot away. It made her draw her breath. Okay, so it was going to be a proximity visit. Connection and all. About what? she wondered.

"I'm reaching my right hand up to shake yours," he said in front of her, and bumped his knuckle against her shoulder.

That had to be so she'd know where his hand was, right? Hesitant, she raised her right hand across her body, in a careful no-touch slide up to meet his. "What are we shaking for?" she asked.

"It's a truce. You and me. No more me telling you what you should do, and no more you shutting me out when the conversation doesn't go your way."

People were usually much more careful with her. Cary acted more like the boys she met at college, who didn't know she was a princess—the difference being that she never considered any of them beyond that setting. The possibilities now, with Cary, gave her conflictions. "Well, if you're not telling me what I should do, then I won't have to shut you out." She smirked.

"Fine." He sounded a little amused. "At least we can agree on something."

"Fine," she said. "Do you always talk to girls this way?"

"Only when I'm hoping to alienate and anger them. How'm I doing?"

"You're losing your touch, I'm happy to say."

"Darn, and I was so looking forward to another night of kicking myself."

Adia laughed unexpectedly, to her real pleasure. Too bad it was spoiled by the desperate hope she didn't have anything stuck in her teeth.

"I would tell you if you had something stuck in your teeth," he said.

Was he reading her mind? Oh, she had her hand up over her mouth, when did she do that? "You would?"

"Sure, that's what friends do. You'd tell me, wouldn't you?"

"I would definitely tell you." She suppressed a smile. "Would you like to sit down?"

"Actually, I thought I might take you for a walk." Her concern must have shown because he added quickly, "I've learned a lot since that first time. I promise there won't be a barked shin or stubbed toe involved."

A pretty big promise, considering the terrain. If only she could see his face so she could get a read on him. The words felt sincere, sounded sincere…maybe he was sincere. She shelved her skepticism. "Okay, I'd love to get out and get around," she agreed, and as she readied herself (toss the headphones, slip on the shoes) she became eager for it. Her body felt oh-so-tired of doing nothing.

The warren buzzed with activity—quick steps coming and going, questions and instructions flying through the air: "Does anyone have any tape?"; "Check the left drawer in the desk."; "Has anyone been to the train station yet?"; "Zola went with the palace kitchen wagon, and took about 25 flyers."

End Tyranny. Adia appreciated the sentiment, but honestly, it was a waste of time, and would mean an instant death sentence for anyone who got caught. And of course "instant death sentence" also included any number of creative tortures, handed down special from Head Sicko himself.

Fat lot of good the message would do even if they weren't caught. All these guests were only coming to Dagge's party to try and stay on his "nice" list. Carapaz did that to people, made them suck-ups, sycophants. But it wasn't her call. She made her speech and what they did was up to them. For those who were really good at the old sleight-of-hand, she guessed putting up flyers seemed worth the risk.

It must've been the end of the workday, because Beau was there.

"Adia!" Beau called to her from beside the press and came over. "Do you know where Hellen is?"

"She and John went back out to the forest to collect guns and uniforms."

Cary added, "Mieko and I saw they got away safe."

Beau was always a high energy-output guy, but he seemed especially jumpy and restless this evening. "What's going on?" she asked.

"I don't know," he answered, "I think something's wrong." Then he chuckled a little sadly at himself. "Pick anything, I suppose." He shifted his weight from foot to foot, shoes rasping the packed dirt as he turned on his toes. "I'm going up," he declared. "Cary, you should come with me." He didn't leave room for a no.

Cary took Adia's hand from his arm and squeezed it. "I'll be back as soon as we're done doing whatever we're doing," he said, and followed Beau's exit up the stairs.

Sounded like a lot of people were in the streets, watching the royal caravans come through town. Crowd noises floated down the tunnels—cheers and aahs and applause. Her whole life she'd taken such things for granted, and now…well, not much point in self-pity. No doubt the pomp and grandeur the royals brought with them were pretty great eye candy.

Dagge was such a clever man. *Give them spectacle*, didn't someone say that? Some other tyrant? She shut that mental train down and reached out with her ears.

Vartile was over by the press, talking to herself, and it sounded like there was a problem. Adia used her echolocation superpower to navigate the ten feet of clear space over to it. "Okay, I was the last one to load paper, did I mess something up?" she (mostly) joked.

"No, it's the ink," Vartile reassured her. "These headline letters use a lot, and we're running low on black."

"What about red?" Adia suggested.

"Too light, I tried that."

"Mix a little black in it."

A pause. "I like it," Vartile agreed, "let's do that." A bit of shuffling on shelves and in drawers and she came up with what she needed.

"How many more of these are you going to make?" Adia asked while Vartile mixed a little black into the red.

"I don't know, the patrols are pulling them down almost as fast as we put them up. We're having to pace ourselves and limit the posting time to just before the caravan passes. At this rate, we'd run out of paper in a week."

"We have some smaller paper, book size, maybe you could use that."

"Maybe, but it can't be too small, it has to be seen from a distance."

Adia's brain, however, was already thinking about something else. "Vartile," she said, "would there be any way we could make books? You know, print them, and bind them together?"

"We could print them easy." Vartile shook the ink mixture in its bottle. "Binding them might be a little more difficult, but I'm sure someone in this crew could figure it out. Why? You planning to write a book?" Adia could hear the smile.

"I'm sure I need to," the Royal Refugee said, "but, no, I was thinking we could make books and give them out. Books could have instructions, and code keys, and maps. The guards aren't going to examine books. Put a nondescript cover on it, and it would be a perfect way to hide the information you want to spread."

Vartile stopped moving and the pause told Adia she was thinking. "You're right, the guards aren't likely to think twice about books. How many of them can even read?" She set the ink bottle on the press. "We could pass around instructions for linephones, we could make multiple codes and—" She stopped and took a breath and said quietly to Adia, "We could make a hell of a book."

Behind Adia, Hellen's urgent yells echoed in from the main tunnel. "Emergency! Emergency!" she shouted, and her running footsteps barreled into the room. Adia held her hands out and stepped in her direction, and Hellen came over to her. "John's been taken," she said breathlessly. She let go of Adia's hands, and her next words came from the level of her knees. "Dagge's got him! I should never have let him come with me," she said, and her voice trailed up into a wail. "It's all my fault. Oh my One, he's going to be killed!"

Her voice broke into a cry then, only she couldn't breathe well enough yet, so she ended up gasping harshly, and Adia lowered herself to the floor to steady her. "Hellen. Hellen," she said, trying to slow her down. "Breathe. Just breathe for a minute. You can't do anything if you can't breathe."

"Give me this stuff," Vartile said, and Hellen's arms waved through the air in front of her as her equipment came off.

After half a minute of forcing air through her constricted throat, she slowed down some. Panic eased, and the gasping quieted. Once she found her breath, though, she cried. Great looping sobs. Adia stayed with her. She had no idea where Vartile went.

"I brought chairs over." Vartile's voice came from behind. "Adia, yours is behind you at five o'clock. I'm putting Hellen's at two o'clock." Hellen got helped up into her chair, so Adia found her chair and got up into it, too. Steps faded off to the right and Vartile's voice went away and came back, saying, "I'm getting a chair, and I'll put it at nine o'clock." The chair scraped and squeaked and by the time they were ready, Hellen could talk again.

"Dagge and Wharton and Pulari showed up while we were there. They got to John first—he was on the palace side—and he did really well. I don't know what he was telling Dagge, but he calmed down, and it probably would've been okay, except Dagge saw me, and they came after me." She shook her head and struggled. "And John had my back, you know? He tried to take the heat off me, but Dagge wasn't stopping. Then John got the idea that he had the perfect shot." She paused, made a swallowing noise. "He was going to take it. He was going to shoot Tomius Dagge." She sounded like she couldn't believe it. "But Wharton saw him, and shot him in the arm, and they arrested him for treason."

Adia's mind was awhirl. They'd torture him, wouldn't they? Just like her dream. Oh, dear One.

Horrified, she reached her fingers up to her forehead and rubbed, trying to put out the little flashpots going off in her brain. Her mouth hung open and she had to consciously close it, making her breath whistle in and out of her nose. Coherence evaded her. What to do? *What to do?*

"We have to get him back," Vartile said, her voice calm and strong.

"Yes," Hellen spoke immediately. "Will you get on the line and contact everyone? I'll go upstairs and talk to Beau."

"Beau's gone," Adia interrupted. "He took Cary up to town to look around. He had a bad feeling, he said."

"Really? Well, he was right," Hellen said, getting up. "I'll go to town then, and find them." Her voice walked off toward the stairs as she added, "Get in touch with everyone! Call a meeting immediately!" She paused when she saw her foot on the stair. "Crap, I need to change clothes!" and her bootsteps faded down the tunnel to Vartile's.

Vartile got up and took her chair back to wherever it had been, then she got Hellen's and put it back, and she didn't say anything to Adia until that was done. "What do you want to do, honey? Do you want to come with me? Shop's closed, no one will see you."

Adia thought for a second. "No, I think I'd rather be alone for a little while."

"All right," Vartile said. "The press is about ten feet back to the eight, using the same clock as before."

"Thanks," Adia said, deeply grateful for Vartile's thoughtfulness.

"You're welcome," the good woman answered, and she patted Adia on the shoulder and walked away toward her basement tunnel.

In front of her, down the main tunnel, through the stone-lined plumbing system into the center of town, cheers and fanfare for the last royal caravan were drifting down through the storm drains like snow. Faint, but she could hear it pretty well, considering. Between the oohs and aahs fireworks were popping, so it must be Mapo and Ming, who were a funny little couple to be the emperor and empress of a country. Adia liked them, hated to imagine them having to deal with Dagge.

None of them should have to deal with Dagge. The image of John hanging in the air by his wrists flashed into her mind, smoke rising from his blackened body, the echoes of his screams consumed by the roar of the fire. The fire. The dragon. The Black Dragon with magenta stripes…

No, she couldn't think about that right now. Adia forced her mind to switch gears to Roberta, who didn't know yet.

Someone needed to tell her. What would she do? Would Dagge go after her next? And her boys? He liked to kill the whole family, the sick freak. Someone should get them out of there.

No one should have to die, or be tortured, or lose everything. No one should have to be afraid just leaving their house.

For the first time she got it. She got why Hellen was so determined to run these missions. Why she was willing to risk death, and why it didn't stop her when Adia begged or yelled or cried.

Someone had to stop him.

For the first time, Adia wanted Hellen to fight.

Chapter F.16

Dagge sat at the head of the long table and listened to his guests bicker. It was fun. They discussed the pros and cons of democracy, and almost everyone had an opinion. A handful stayed silent, and most of the opinionated ones were ridiculous, but a couple of people at the dinner were actually pretty interesting.

Aside from the various servants and food-tasters that lined the walls, each ruler brought with them two or three other people they wanted to have at the table. Backup, he supposed, although some opted to have their suppers in their rooms this evening, since the gathering was informal. The missing amounted to two cabinet ministers and a noble—all old—plus Queen Eladora's whole party, which wouldn't arrive until tomorrow.

Tonight's get-together in the dining room included the five leaders, two generals, a senator, a professor, and two purely decorative females courtesy of His Royal Randy Majesty. Dagge wondered what Mrs. Majesty thought of that.

The two generals, dour as hell, belonged to His Majesty of Pulari and Arburash, of Valdia. Prime Minister Arburash was younger than the other leaders, but nearly as humorless as Pulari. Tall and handsome, elected by popular vote, he seemed as fond of his own voice as any politician. Not one of the interesting ones.

He did, however, bring one of the interesting people. A woman senator of a certain age (isn't that the polite way to say it?), Gladius Bunch, who might've been the only person in the world who could survive a trip with Arburash and General Weeks. She had a way of nailing people with humor that Dagge really appreciated; after a few spot-on remarks, she put herself on his "good" list.

Professor Wan was the other interesting person—he had brown, leathery skin, and a wild white hairdo that Dagge couldn't get enough of. His chin hair was white, too, and he must have been old, but he was vigorous and very sharp, and Dagge admired him almost immediately.

The Professor was brought by Mapo and Ming, lifelong leaders of Shindao. Emperor Mapo and Empress Ming were tiny, gentle people—almost like puppies. They had round, twinkly faces that smiled a lot, and they acted like they were two halves of the same person. Which, maybe they were.

All in all, he was most thankful for the decorative females. They looked nice, laughed when they were supposed to, and never burdened the company with their opinions. More people should be like that.

The discussion about democracy was entertaining, though. It had only been going on for a few minutes, but already collars were a little hot. Pulari, of course, was a scoundrel after his own heart and said, "Screw democracy. The common man knows nothing, why should he have a say? I wouldn't want my life to depend on a bunch of stupid people."

To which Mrs. Bunch replied, "One stupid person is enough, isn't it?" But she said it so innocently, it confused him, and he couldn't be sure if he only imagined an insult. Dagge wanted to laugh out loud, it was a stellar attack on her part. Mrs. Bunch no doubt had utter disdain for a man afraid to educate the "commoners."

Arburash the Elected naturally had to stand up for his country's policies, in spite of the definite feeling Dagge got that he would love to be a tyrant just like him. *Oh, give me power* his suit said, *and I will wield it*. With a big fat smile he would, Dagge was sure.

Emperor Mapo and his wife supported democracy. They had, for the first time in their country's history, created an elected council intended to represent the will of the citizens. Enter bribery and corruption, undoubtedly causing them all kinds of trouble, but Mapo believed it was important to give the people some sense of control. *Even if they didn't really have it*, Dagge finished the sentence in his head. Mrs. Mapo agreed with everything her husband said.

Professor Wan changed the tilt of the conversation by saying, "Democracy is a necessary evil. It is true that it is inefficient and hard to maintain, but as we in our country believe that we are spirit beings, first and most importantly, we feel it is essential that we learn to work together for the benefit of all."

Very noble. Hugely naive. It was more often a mistake to believe in the best in people, Dagge thought; most of them will give in to temptation in a heartbeat.

"I agree completely." Arburash graced the table with his opinion again.

His general, Weeks, spoke for the first time. "I'm glad you said that, Professor Wan, I do believe we are spirit beings. I've seen some things on the battlefield that make it impossible to believe otherwise." He forked a bite and ran his eyes up the table. "Once I saw a dead man get up, walk two steps and disappear, but his body was still on the ground behind him."

"Precisely, General." Wan held his fork up at him. "What if we are eternal? What if it matters how we treat our fellow man?"

"I think when you die, you die." Pulari took his stand. "I've never seen anything that would make me think there's a life after this one, and I suspect anyone who has is an hysteric."

"I'm no hysteric, I assure you, Your Majesty," General Weeks said.

"No General, I'm certain you're not," Dagge surprised everyone by saying. "I've been with many dying soldiers who saw angels, or people who died before them." He turned his attention to Professor Wan. "I agree with you, Professor, we are spirit beings. I'm just not sure the life outside the body is any different from the life inside it, aside from the obvious. Nice people are nice, mean people are mean, and most of them aren't very good at working together."

"That is an interesting way to look at the world," Mapo said, "but it leaves out one very important element."

"What's that?" Arburash asked, intensely interested, Dagge observed.

"Hope."

"Excellent point, Your Eminence." Professor Wan laughed heartily. "There has to be the hope of improvement, or the species is doomed." He stabbed his fish gleefully.

"What if the species *is* doomed?" Dagge wiped his mouth and sat back in his chair.

"Then we'd be a waste of a good design." General Hatch, who came with Pulari, didn't speak much, but when he did it came out with authority.

"I agree, General," Mrs. Bunch said earnestly. "Personally, I can't imagine life without a greater purpose."

"I cannot as well," Wan chimed in.

"My greater purpose at the moment is to find the washroom." Pulari stood and spoke in Dagge's general direction. "Since I missed the tour."

"I shall take you around myself tomorrow, Your Majesty, first thing in the morning. In the meantime, one of the servants can show you the way."

"I don't need to be escorted like a child, Dagge, just tell me." Pulari's insistence on being alone sent up a red flag; not normal for the royal set, was it? Who was going to wipe?

But he couldn't make a big deal about it. They were all friends, right? He made eye contact briefly with one of the soldiers he had disguised in kitchen livery, and the soldier faded out the door into the hall while Pulari was looking the other way. Namely at him, waiting for instructions. He told Pulari, "Down the hall to the right, through the big double doors and it's on your immediate right. You can't miss it."

"Splendid," was drily sarcastic. "Please excuse me." He bowed to the table and they all watched while he walked out.

"Politics and religion," Mrs. Bunch said, amused. "Don't you know, Overlord Dagge, that those are the forbidden subjects in polite society?" She smiled coyly, but didn't meet his eyes, busying herself instead with drinking water.

"Who ever said I was polite?" Dagge grinned in return.

"I think you're very polite," Nylah said matter-of-factly in her soft voice.

That took him by surprise, being the first thing she'd said all evening. Pulari must really keep a muzzle on her, but she didn't waste any time after he was gone. She sat just to Dagge's right too, her own choice, since this informal meal was general admission. That must have pissed Pulari off. It delighted Dagge.

"Thank you, Queen Nylah." He put his hand over her hand on the table. "You are the picture of graciousness and good breeding." She blushed, gave him a shy smile, and didn't pull away. One in his pocket.

Arburash was on his left and missed none of that. "Yes, our host has a remarkable gentility," he said loudly enough for the table. "Not at all like his reputation. Wouldn't you agree, Professor?"

"Yes, I would agree." Wan nodded, and looked toward Dagge. "This is a most pleasant evening." He chose a glass from several in front of him and raised it. "To our host," he said, "with many thanks for this opportunity to work together."

His joke got a laugh from Mrs. Bunch, but only from her; everyone else said "hear hear" and picked up their glasses. The moment felt a little surreal, like a dream. The room got a sparkly quality and the light went golden as his guests all thrust their glasses forward and toasted him.

Who would ever have thought?

As the fish course was cleared, conversation ran idly around about nothing: the recent weather, the Winter Festival holiday, the coming weather... dull small talk. They were at least very careful to color between the lines this time, no forbidden topics, and there was only one patch of thin ice when General Hatch observed that the town hadn't decorated for the Winter Festival like it used to. The implication being that the people were too oppressed, or depressed, or DEAD to do it anymore.

It was Arburash, of all people, who helped save that one. "People don't decorate in Valdia like they used to, either. For a long time it seemed like the stuff stayed up half the year, but eventually everyone got tired of it and now they hardly do it at all."

"That's true," Mrs. Bunch agreed. "For years the whole thing was entirely overboard. Perhaps even the Prime Minister can't remember this, but when I was a young parent, we used to spend twice our monthly income on gifts and parties. The season lasted for weeks, and burdened several months with bills. I'm sure someday there will be a resurgence in celebration, but for now the drunks probably need to dry out a while."

Dagge kept his eye on the door, waiting for the soldier who followed Pulari, but Pulari showed first. He walked in and moved quickly to his seat at the table.

"I hope you have some interesting entertainment planned for us tomorrow night," he said as he sat down, just in time for the main course.

"Oh, yes!" Dagge took up the subject with relish. "I don't want to tell you what the lineup is, but we have several different performances in store."

"Performances, huh?" Pulari stuffed a bite in his mouth and talked around it. "Not magic, I hope."

"No, not magic. Something much more visceral."

Suddenly the old royal had a fit, coughing and trying to draw breath, but unable to. They all watched him struggle for a few moments until, a panicked look on his face, he shoved his chair back and bent over the floor. Voices rose around the table, people stood, calling for assistance and Dagge leaped up and ran around to Pulari. He jerked Pulari up out of his chair put both arms around him, gave him an eye-popping squeeze and Pulari cacked out his half-chewed bite.

A long, harsh breath and he was still among the living. He coughed and hacked and people rushed over, but Dagge sauntered back to his chair, feeling pretty smug. The post-trauma drama played out while he ate his veal: lots of sympathy, eventual control over the spasms, drinks of water, then they all sat down again, or drifted back to the wall, and Pulari rejoined the party.

"I'm afraid my entertainment tomorrow won't be that exciting," Dagge joked pleasantly, eliciting a polite laugh from the others.

"Hopefully it won't be any more 'visceral' either," Pulari rasped.

"Your Majesty, was that a joke?" Dagge teased. "I've never heard you make one before."

"It wasn't a joke," he croaked. "I'm serious. 'Visceral' doesn't sound good for the digestion. I'm sure everyone agrees with me."

"Perhaps 'visceral' was a poor choice of words. Let's say…thrilling. How about that?"

"Hardly better." Pulari picked up his fork and knife. "But if it's too dyspeptic, I daresay you won't blame us if we have to leave." A jab and a look from his wife and he grudgingly offered, "Thank you, for doing that for me, Dagge."

"Certainly, Highness," Dagge said graciously. "After all, I can't have my guests dying at my table, can I?" He laughed, but no one else seemed to think that was funny.

Chapter F.17

The big room was filling up. Adia could feel the closeness of people, the density of heretofore empty space. Truthfully, it made her a little nervous, or maybe the word was anxious because a lot of anxiety and anger crowded the room, too. She could hear the restlessness, the shuffling of clothes and feet, quiet murmuring. Somberly quiet. Hushed conversations passed the time until the meeting could get started.

Chief Taymer's voice ramped up from behind the desk to speak to the crowd. "Everyone," he began, then waited for the whispers to die down. "We've called this meeting because John Treslo has been captured." A few gasps and quick voices from those who didn't already know, and he continued, "We all know what Dagge does to people." He paused, giving them time to remember. "And we don't want that to happen to John."

Adia was glad Roberta hadn't come. Chief sent Purda to tell her about John, but she went under strict orders to discourage Roberta from attending the meeting. Which meant, of course, that Roberta was bound to show up at some point.

Hellen was sitting beside her on one of the tables in the back, a good thirty feet or so away from Taymer, but all the people were so quiet, his normal voice could be heard by everyone. He said, "We're going to mount a rescue. Before I ask for volunteers, you should know that there's almost no way we can succeed. Most or all of us will likely be killed, and it won't be pretty."

He stopped, let people shift and whisper for a few seconds. "What I will say is that if we don't try to save John, if we just let him stay in there, knowing what will happen, in my opinion we're no better than Dagge is. *I'm* no better. I have to fight for Thorn, for John, because we need him, because he's my friend, and because it's the right thing. I have to stand up and do anything I can do, because I can't let him get taken and do nothing. I can't let life be like this and do nothing.

"Thorn risked his life for all of us. He showed this whole town that we don't have to take this horror lying down. We have brains, we have abilities. We have to reclaim this kingdom. And we need John Treslo to help us do it."

Murmurs, assent, one voice raised, "Yes!" The energy in the room had quickened, less about anxiety now, more about determination. Amazing what a few simple words and some good leadership could do.

"All right, then," he said, "now I'm asking for volunteers." Some hands must have gone up, because he quickly added, "But let me tell you first what we need. We need at least one to go into the palace with Hellen and me, and there, some fighting skills will be necessary. Then we need a handful to create a distraction. Maybe more than one distraction. Inside and/or outside."

Is there a plan? Adia wanted to ask, but she was afraid that if she did, and there wasn't, they'd ask her to make one. She couldn't have their deaths on her hands. She couldn't.

"What kind of distraction?" sounded like Grovet, Purda's husband, who Adia remembered was a lamp maker with a small, round face that fit on his small, round body.

"We're open to suggestions," Taymer replied.

Cary, standing on her other side, said, "Mieko and I faked a fight as a distraction today, and it worked really well. Maybe we could do that."

"That wouldn't last very long," someone said, "we need a big long distraction that isn't easily stopped."

Hellen raised her voice and spoke to the room. "All we need is something big enough to disrupt everyone's attention for eight to ten minutes. That should give us enough time to get in and get John out."

Adia couldn't let that one pass by. "How are you going to do that? Say you can get into the palace, even though that's saying a lot, do you know how many guards they're going to have on him? Down the halls, at the doorways, in the dungeon itself? It's not likely to be that easy." She worked to keep the irritation out of her voice.

"I didn't say it would be easy." Hellen was working at the same thing. "I'm prepared to kill the enemy, and anyone who volunteers will also need to be prepared for that." She said that to the room, then she turned back to Adia. "But we'll have the element of surprise, especially since we'll be in uniforms."

"Why do you think they won't expect you? Dagge will be expecting you."

"Then what do you suggest?" Cary jumped right in. *Damn.*

Adia thought for a moment, really wishing she could punch him. Her brain scrambled for a plan. After a moment, she said, "There's a dumbwaiter that goes from the kitchen to the dungeon. One person could take it down. The opening is down the passage from the guard room, not very visible, and someone might even be able to get John out that way."

"That's a great idea, I didn't think of the dumbwaiter," Hellen said, all irritation gone. She turned to the room. "There's something else we have to do as well—we have to kill the soldiers that came back from the woods last night. Adia's dream was right, some kind of super-soldiers came out of a hole, and they're here to help Dagge."

The excitement levered up a notch, concerned murmurs filled the room until Taymer had to raise his voice over them. "It won't do any good to panic." He let his words be heard, waited the few moments it took for people to settle down again, and spoke to Hellen. "Do we know anything about how to find them?"

"No," Hellen said, "but it occurred to me that if I kill Dagge, they won't have any reason to stick around, will they? They'll die in a couple of days, kill their hosts, and we'd be rid of them."

Roberta's voice speared in from the stairway. "Didn't you say they could move from body to body?"

The silence made the sound of her feet coming down the last few steps really loud.

"Is that true?" Zola asked.

"Yes, I was told that, but *they* don't necessarily know that."

"Then we still need to kill them, because they could figure it out," Cary said.

"Or isolate them, but I'm sure complete removal would be best," Hellen agreed.

"Hellen!" Roberta's voice and feet crossed the room to them, accompanied by the gentle scraping of all the other feet moving aside.

"You can't let Dagge live anymore." Her voice sounded quiet and reasonable. Her energy was calm and steady. Warrior mode. "We can't let this continue. We have to fight Dagge, whatever it takes, and we have to stop this." She stood in front of them, and for a second Adia thought she could hear her heartbeat. It was fast. "We have to do it now."

"I agree," Hellen said. "I'm going to do it. Later that night." She raised her voice and included everyone. "I'm going to hide in the palace, catch Dagge alone, and kill him. No matter what happens with everything else."

"Roberta," Chief Taymer called to her, "we're going to try and get John free."

"I know," Roberta answered. "I knew you would try. And I hate to say this, but John would agree with me, and he would want me to tell you: the most important thing is to stop Dagge."

"We still need a distraction," Cary said quickly. "So we can get in, and get John out."

"And so you can find as many of those soldiers as possible and kill them," Roberta added.

"Yes, that's right," Hellen said. "They're bound to be hidden while the guests are there." Adia could feel her shift on the desk, and the next question was aimed right at her ear. "Where would he hide something like that?"

She wasn't going to give up, was she? Adia kept a careful face. If Hellen was going to put her on the spot like that, in front of all these people, she had to say something. "I don't know, his old quarters maybe? They're not likely to be on the visitors' tour."

"Stable or barracks, either," Cary's voice came to her rescue. "And with so many of the soldiers deployed to the border, the barracks would be ideal."

"You know," Hellen said, "it doesn't matter, we'll find out when we get there." Adia felt her get up off the desk. "I need two volunteers to go into the palace with me."

She reached out and found Hellen's arm. Adia knew she was disappointed in her, and as much as she felt conflicted about what to do, the ex-princess-turned-royal-jerk knew one thing. "There will be fireworks in the stable," she said loudly enough for everyone to hear.

No one said anything, so she kept talking. "Remember how Mapo and Ming always bring them? It's their thing. They'll be in a wagon, under guard, but they'll be big, long, spectacular explosions…exactly the kind of distraction you're looking for."

Chapter F.18

Dagge toyed with the harkener in his lap, pointing it by degrees up the line of fancy guest rooms so he could hear what his fancy guests were saying. Juicy stuff, he hoped, in spite of the low wine consumption at dinner.

Arburash's room came first, but it was General Weeks' voice that picked up. "Sir, our economy is in the tonker, our military is underfunded, and unemployment is at an all-time high. The best way to solve the problem, and stay in Dagge's good graces, is to sign a trade treaty."

"Don't you think I know that?" Arburash snapped back, and the clink of glass on glass told Dagge he was drinking. "With elections next year, if I don't do something I'll be out on my ass, it won't even matter who runs against me."

"Prime Minister…" So Bunch was there, too, sounding very controlled. "Dagge is dangerous and unpredictable. There's no telling what he'll want in return. We cannot make a deal with him. It will go badly for us, and we'll never get out of it."

"Then why did we come?" the stuffy, self-serving general wanted to know.

"Because we're neighbors, and we couldn't refuse—"

"Because his invitation was a veiled threat," Bunch talked over Arburash. "Do we want Dagge as our friend? No, not particularly, but we sure don't want him as our enemy."

Now wasn't that interesting? Bunch had the backbone…and the brain, he smiled to himself.

"I'm tired," Arburash said. "I've got to get some sleep. We can finish this in the morning."

"Good night, sir." Bunch's voice faded away. "Sleep well."

"Think about what I said," Weeks said softly. "We've got two production plants sitting idle, it wouldn't take much capital to get them up and running. If we can get Dagge to buy weapons from us, it would solve all our cash flow problems."

"The senator has a point, General."

"Bunch is a crybaby liberal. She has no idea how the world really works!"

"Fine, Weeks, just give it a rest, will you? Go to bed!"

Dagge chuckled upstairs in his sitting room as he listened to Arburash's door close. Tomorrow he'd find out who won this little debate—the cautious senator or the gnashing general. Not that it would matter in the long run, of course.

Dagge shifted the dish and tuned in to Mapo and Ming, who were speaking Shindaoan, so that was useless. He shifted a little more.

"I don't care what you want, Nylah," King Top Dog was saying. "I'm going."

"Arvos Pulari, if you embarrass me here, I will never forgive you." Nylah sounded like she had some bite herself.

"Then don't be embarrassed," he replied dimly, and Dagge adjusted his dish. "There's no reason for you to be embarrassed anyway, I come from a long line of virile kings."

"Virile? Is that what you call it?" She goaded him, "Ha!" and there was a clatter like something got tossed onto a hard surface. "Not so virile, believe me," she spat. "I wish I had a copper coin for every disappointment." A long pause. Dagge waited to hear if Pulari would hit her or say something.

In a few moments he answered. "This is why I get away, Nylah—the snide comments, the shocking ingratitude. It's always something with you. You're a spoiled, selfish, useless little bitch." A pause, a pause, Dagge could imagine Nylah's gaping face.

"It's never anything with you!" she shouted back, the high pitch buzzing his device. After that, in the background, Dagge could barely hear some distant mumbling with the guard, and the closing of the door as Pulari left. Two faint thwacks followed, accompanied by rustling, grunts, and a thin wail that dissolved into tears.

So the old guy's been a disappointment in the bedroom. Apparently not all of him was made of granite. Dagge smiled.

Now would be an excellent time to visit the Queen.

Saturday

Chapter S.1

Queen Eladora's caravan arrived midmorning and brought everything by train: big elaborate carriages, fine horses, splendidly dressed people. Watching them all disembark was like watching a circus come to town. Hundreds of people crowded the ends of the station platform and trailed along the tracks to each side, buzzing excitedly in the clear morning air. Laughter and applause greeted each grand new thing that appeared from the depths of the unloading cars. David and Joey stood packed in the throng to the side of the platform and craned their necks to see.

David didn't want to bring Joey, but his mom said he had to. After the bad news about Dad last night, and being all brave and strong when she told him and Joey, she probably needed a boy-free zone for a while so she could cry, or throw things. Women had to do stuff like that sometimes, according to his dad.

As bad as he felt for her, David had a different way of handling it, and it worked for him to get out of the choking-thick black cloud and do something. However, Joey put a real damper on his plan, and now David had to figure out a way to ditch him. Without divulging, of course, that the reason for coming to the train station was to sneak in with the caravan, go to the palace and find his father.

With any luck, getting into the caravan wouldn't be a terrible problem. He'd ease in at the end, toss some bags, do some heavy lifting, and act like he was supposed to be there. In all the hubbub, maybe no one would notice him. Seemed to work at school, so why not here?

Once he got to the palace, though, he'd be winging it. If he could make it into the kitchen, he could find that cook Dad said he liked, and maybe she'd help him. Hopefully she was still there.

He wished he had a better plan. Spent lots of time in the middle of the night thinking about it, but truth be told he didn't know anything he needed to know to make a better plan. Like how many guards he'd have to get past, and would anybody help him? What he *did* have amounted to some childhood martial arts training and a fairly good brain. The rest had to go on One's good graces.

Only how was he going to get rid of Joey? "Hey, I'm going to go around to the other side of the train and see if I can look in the windows."

"I'll come with you," Joey said, smacking his first attempt.

David huffed his air out the teeniest bit. "Come on, then." They threaded through the crowd and aimed for a space between railroad cars to climb over.

A soldier stepped in front of them and blocked their way. He had a big gun across his chest and a smirk on his face. "Where do you think you're going?"

Yowza. David held his hands up and backed away slowly. "Never mind, just wanted to see from the other side, but I take it that's not allowed."

"You take it right." The guard meandered forward. "And if you don't back up a little faster, I might have to motivate you."

"No need, no need. I am motivated on my own." David pulled Joey, turned away and moved off quickly. Back through the gawkers, up onto the platform behind the crowd, they didn't stop until they got close to the entrance of the depot.

"That was creepy." Joey gave a little spasm.

"Listen, Joey," David whispered in his face, "can I trust you?"

Joey looked blank for a few seconds, then he frowned. "What are you going to do? Are you going to get us in trouble again?"

"Me get us in trouble? You're the one who has all the crazy ideas."

"Oh yeah? Who thought of trying to jump from the house to the tree when we were kids?"

David sighed. "We could've made it if you didn't hesitate at the last second."

"I was *four*."

"Fine." David ate that one. "But it wasn't me who thought it would be fun to sled down the ice-coated drainage ditch, and we couldn't stop, and we crashed into the rock wall and I broke my arm."

"You thought it was a great idea! And at least you didn't get work detail for it, digging a stupid grave for Dad's stupid coat."

"Hey, I was not the one who had the idea to shave Dad's coat. That was also you."

Joey's mouth dropped open. "It was you who thought of filling the flour container with plaster of paris."

"Okay, okay, this isn't helping." David put the brakes on. Queen Eladora had just appeared, a cheer rose from the crowd, and he needed to hurry. "Look, the Queeen," he cooed, and as soon as Joey turned around to see her, David ducked into the building.

Just inside the door, a stack of overnight valises nearly sent him sprawling. "Watch out!" an irritated voice boomed in his ear.

David looked up at the porter setting more bags beside the neat pile. "I'm supposed to pick up some luggage to take to the wagon?"

"Are you blind or just stupid?" The young man scowled at him. "You're standing on top of 'em, get a move on!"

Bags went over David's shoulders, across his back, under arms, on his head and in both hands. Smiling, he exited the side door toward the tail end of the train.

Several wagons stood in the field east of the depot, surrounded by servants and workers who hitched horses and loaded boxes and climbed aboard for the trip to the palace. A stout man in a hat shouted orders, pointed, and hurried all over putting out fires. David decided it would be best to avoid him, and heaved a bag to his shoulder to block his face.

Behind the rest, the baggage wagon had two men working—a young man up in it, and an older man on the ground. David approached with the luggage, and the older man eyed him warily. "Whatcha doin with them bags, boy?"

"I was hired help you," David said. "As a courtesy from Overlord Dagge. I'm to ride with you all the way to the palace, so I can help you there, too."

"Is that a fact?" The man squinted.

"Yes, sir." David set his baggage down and nodded at the large trunk sitting just to the guy's left. "Where would you like it?" Before the man could answer, he walked over, hefted the trunk onto the wagon, jumped on board beside it and whisked it to the front center. "How's that?"

Eyebrows up and a smile teasing his mouth, the man said, "Looks fine to me."

For the first time ever, David was happy he'd chopped all that wood.

Chapter S.2

By lunchtime, Adia and Hellen had gone over every secret passage, every servants' corridor, and every hidden door in the palace. They'd been at it all morning, sitting and talking on Adia's bed in Vartile's basement, and to Adia it felt almost like old times. The planning an invasion thing was new.

"If Cary and Chief are going in with you, we should get them both over here and tell them about all the secret passages." Adia's voice dropped, and she shook her head slowly. "I hate to tell anyone outside the family, but we have to. We can't let anyone get caught in there just because they didn't know. Vartile!" she hollered up the stairs.

"Yeah?" The familiar voice floated down from the kitchen.

"Did Chief or Cary say what time they were coming?"

"Midafternoon!"

Adia turned back to Hellen. "That'll be enough time. It might help if you draw them a quick map to look at. Does everyone else know what they're doing?" As much as she was determined not to plan, she couldn't help herself.

"Yes, Zola and Lan are in charge of securing the fireworks. Grovet, Elzbieta and Luhe are under their command. Von, Donas, and Dessara are staying close to the kitchen."

"What weapons will there be?"

"I'll have my knife, and Chief and Cary will have knives and bullet rifles, plus they'll carry a bullet rifle for me. But Lan and Zola will be in uniform, too, and they'll have Beau's laser rifles. For the others it's best to appear innocent."

"You're only taking a knife?"

"Junika can't carry a gun, and I haven't made up my mind whether I'm going to risk the energy weapon. Wouldn't want Dagge to get hold of it."

"Right. Probably best not to take it."

"Lunch is ready!" Vartile's voice was closer this time, and she stepped down onto the stairs sort of clanky and hesitant.

"Holy cow, Vartile, let me help you with that!" Hellen bounced off the bed and ran up the stairs, her feet scraping on the woody steps all the way up. They stopped at the top, there was some difficulty, and Hellen said, "I can't turn around while I'm holding it. Here, pass it over my head." A couple of steps creaked.

Adia listened to the jangle of dishes, and a few "waits" and one or two "watchits" and she called up. "Put it *on* your head."

A hair of a pause and Hellen said, "Put it on my head."

"Are you sure?" Vartile asked.

"Yeah, I'm sure." There was a rattle of dishes, and a loud clang, and the third time Adia thought it was a goner, but after that, Hellen's feet started stepping down.

Vartile mumbled, "Here, let me take that...and that." She lightened Hellen's load, Adia supposed, and they came carefully down the stairs. Adia smoothed the bed blankets, scooting herself back to the pillow.

"How about right here on the bed?" she asked.

"We haven't had a picnic on the bed in ages." Hellen reached the bottom of the stairs and started toward her.

"Vartile, I hope you plan to join us," Adia said. "It would be good to have your brain."

Their scuffling footsteps stopped by the bed. "Ordinarily, ladies, I would love to join you." The tray tinkled and clinked down off Hellen's head, and made a four-hand landing on the mattress. "But Luhe is upstairs waiting for me, life is short, and love calls." A strong hand squeezed Adia's shoulder, and Vartile turned and made her way back to the stairs.

"Thanks for the lunch, Vartile."

"You're the best!" Hellen called.

As she listened to the fading footfalls, Adia wished she could have someone who loved her like that, and whom she loved. Even if it meant heartbreak, like her Dad felt, or like Roberta was feeling now. The good years would be worth it, wouldn't they?

Hellen sat on the other end of the bed with the tray between them. "Let's see," she said, "we've got deviled eggs at nine, bleu cheese and cabbage salads from six to twelve, and canned pears at three. Your napkin is on the right, silverware inside, and we have hey! vegetable juice to drink. I love that stuff."

"Me, too," Adia agreed. She found her silverware and unrolled it: a fork, a spoon, a knife. Adia put them carefully by her bowl, and her napkin across as much lap as it could cover. She'd learned her lesson about picnics on the bed.

"Tell me," Hellen said, fork clinking, "Do you think you might like Cary?"

Funny she would mention that. Adia chuckled into her salad, which she stirred under her chin. "He has his charms."

"Cary's a good guy." Hellen picked up her bowl, and squeezed out her next comment before taking her bite. "He'd love to be king."

Adia wasn't sure how to take that. "Do you think that's the only reason he's…flirting or whatever?"

"No," Hellen assured her quickly. "Heavens no. You've got everything—brains, humor, capability. It wouldn't matter what your name was. All I'm saying is that if you want a man who will make decisions and take action on his own accord, ruling your kingdom, then he's a good one."

Adia set her bowl down, suddenly not hungry. The bite in her mouth felt dry and way too big. She chewed slowly, and finally swallowed.

"Adia…" Hellen's voice was soft, and she set her bowl down, too. "I don't mean to upset you." Her hand lay warm on Adia's arm. "I guess I feel the need to…tell you what I can before I leave. It's a little silly," she continued, "because you will make the right decision. Your instinct for this kingdom is remarkable, and I know you'll make the right choice when it comes time."

Said the being Adia trusted the most in the entire world. In a flash of silent-movie clips, Adia saw the Hellen of her past: dark blond hair pulled back, angular face bending close to her. Hellen had always been strong and capable and reliable. She had defined Adia's world with dignity and grace after her mother died.

Now that person was drastically reconfigured—a lethal Hellen she would never see. Did she look different? Adia had never thought to ask.

"Do you look different?"

"Not really, except I'm thinner, and meaner, and I have dark hair."

"Same length?"

"Yeah, I keep butchering it myself." They laughed and Hellen continued a bit slyly. "What about you? Do you look different?"

"I look very different," Adia confirmed, nodding slowly. "I'm a lot older, and some thinner, and I'm pretty sure my hair is crazy."

Hellen laughed, so good to hear, and Adia realized again what she'd lose if her mother person didn't come back. She reached for Hellen's arm, ran her fingers down and took Hellen's hand into both of hers. "I know you're thinking it's likely that you won't come back," she said, "but you have to know that I'm not through with my training. You've got to come back, that's all there is to it."

Hellen's hand squeezed hers and let go. Adia could hear the bowl scrape as it was picked up, and sounds of chewing soon trickled into the space between them. "Really? You're not going to say anything?"

"What should I say?" Hellen's voice was guarded. "I have every intention of coming back, but I can't make any promises."

"I know that," Adia said. This wasn't the reaction she intended, why couldn't she do this right? "I didn't mean that. I don't mean to pressure you." She tried to explain herself. "What I'm trying to say is that I love you."

Hellen's bowl went down again and the end of the bed went up as she stood. Adia could hear the slide of the tray over the blanket to make a place in front of her, and Hellen sat close enough so their knees touched. Adia folded into Hellen's warm strong arms and rested her head on Hellen's shoulder, just like she had since she was five.

They sat like that a long time before Hellen spoke again. "You understand why I have to do this, don't you?" she asked softly.

"Yes, I do, finally. I'm even glad you're doing it." Adia nodded. She turned so her forehead was against Hellen's hard collarbone, then she sat up. "I believe you have a good idea of what you'll do to free John, then hide and wait for Dagge, but you haven't said anything about how you're going to kill those soldiers."

"Other than bullets, I don't know how. I'm going to have to figure that out as I go."

"It will almost undoubtedly turn into a fire fight. Find Diit, ask Cookie where he is when you go in. She may not know, but she might, or she might know someone who does. Diit will know where the soldiers are, and he'll be able to help you get away."

She sighed a little, didn't really want to bring this up but, "I know I don't have to tell you I'll be devastated if something happens to you. But I want you to know that I'll be okay. Eventually, I'll be okay. I understand that you have to do this. I would do it, too, if I could." She stopped and waited for Hellen's response, but there was only silence.

"I'm sorry I've been so difficult. I know I have. All of this," she spread her hands to include the world in general, "has been hard on me, and I've made it harder on you, and now I feel terribly guilty." Her hands dropped to her lap. "I so wish none of this had happened. I'd give my life to change it. And I guess that's what it comes down to, being willing to die for something important."

"Adia," Hellen said softly, "there are no apologies needed. I can take some yelling and crying, and even some whining and moaning," she teased. "I mean it when I say *do not feel guilty*. You have endured the worst kind of stress a human being can endure, and you're still walking. I don't know very many people who could've done so well after losing so much." Her hands grasped Adia's where they lay in her lap. "You know what that says about you?"

Adia had no idea. "What?"

"You have character. You have strength inside you that refuses to be broken. Remember that when the path in front of you seems impossible. If you need to walk it, you need to walk it even when you feel like you don't have a clue what you're doing. A choice doesn't have to be life-threatening to be a risk, you know."

She patted Adia's hands and said more lightly. "Let's not talk about that anymore." She turned on the bed and made some scraping noises in the vicinity of the tray. "Let's eat. I may not get anything else for a while." Adia felt the edge of her bowl prod her arm.

Without a word she took it, found her fork and thought about what Hellen said.

Chapter S.3

Joey came home alone. Roberta listened to his story of waiting woes, how his big brother abandoned him and needed to get in trouble. Maybe so. She should have guessed David was up to something, asking to go to the train station by himself, and she almost let him. It wasn't an unreasonable request, all things considered, sometimes people need to be alone to deal with difficulties in their own way. Herself included, which was why she insisted David take Joey. Now she wished she had kept them home or gone with them.

The news of their father's capture made David quiet, unlike Joey, who ranted and railed. She had to stop them from going to the palace immediately, like they thought they could shame Dagge into releasing him. "Boys, he could very easily kill you both right there." She raised her voice at them, "He's not going to let you have your father!"

"Maybe Robert could get him out," Joey insisted. "He knows Dagge, he works for him. Why couldn't he get Dad out?"

"Joey, listen to what you're saying," David said. "No one crosses Dagge. You want Robert to die, too? For all we know, he already has."

"David!" she'd snapped, but didn't go any further than that. Robert had not come home last night, and since John's capture, the stubborn picture in her head was of her husband and son, bruised and bloody in the dungeon. She refused to let the image get worse than that. Dagge had no reason to kill Robert, though there wasn't much chance he'd let him walk free, either.

Last night, after Purda left and she broke the news to them about their father, she'd pulled her two younger boys into her arms for whatever comfort they could give each other. Holding them up, being the mom, Roberta stood firm even when she wanted to scream and cry and rage. For that moment, it was more important to be there for them, and they all stood that way for a longer time than they had in years, then the boys went to bed early.

Before curfew, thank goodness. Purda told her Chief said she shouldn't come to the meeting, but why? Too upsetting? Could she be any more upset than she already was? Grief and fear were tearing her heart apart. Her stomach sickened to think what might be happening to her husband.

She didn't say that to the boys, of course. To them, she imagined Dagge would wait until his company was gone before he'd do anything to their father. It could be true, and that was about as far as she'd let her brain go with that.

Now, if she surmised correctly, David was walking into the cobra pit alone. Hellen needed to know. Or Chief. Or Vartile.

"Come on, Joey," she said, standing up from her desk where he'd found her. "Let's go buy some soap."

Chapter S.4

Eladora's caravan arrived at the palace just before lunch. Convenient timing, because the need to get inside put everyone in a hurry, and David was able to scurry off with the rest of the servants without any inspection.

He'd never been this close to Dagge before. After unloading the baggage, he slipped in with the group of servants going to the kitchen, and had to walk by the grinning freak on the way to the west side. The guy stood fifteen feet away, radiating. David had to beat back the urge to fly at him, throw him down and wring his bloody neck.

Once they got around the corner, he barely had time to be relieved before a bunch of the group split off to find the assigned barracks. His cover instantly dwindled to almost nothing; the handful of servants that remained were all women, and he didn't exactly blend in. Still, he could make it to the kitchen as long as he acted like he knew what he was doing, right? "Who are you?" a loud voice demanded over his left shoulder.

David's heart jumped in his throat, he quick-checked behind, and yeah, the guy was talking to him. "Hired by Dagge" wouldn't help him at this point, so he had one line ready, and hoped it would hold. "I'm with the baggage," he tossed over his shoulder as casually as he could.

"Hang on." The voice was joined by a hand, which came down on David's shoulder and turned him around. They were still on the west side, closer to the back than the front, and David's mind was rapidly calculating exit options while it scrambled for viable excuses. In front of him, David recognized the man who'd been shouting orders at the train station. In the shade of his wide-brimmed leather hat, intelligent eyes squinted up at David over a slightly open mouth. "You don't look familiar to me."

David nodded agreeably, a trick he learned from Joey. "I'm new, I was just hired for this trip."

"Who hired you?"

Crap. David knew only that Queen Eladora had a lot of women on her staff and in her Cabinet. "The lady who came to the market, I didn't catch her name."

The guy frowned, eyes still squinty, mouth open. "Mem Doran?"

"No, I don't think that was it." Just in case the guy was testing him.

"Why aren't you with the wagon?"

"Jayco told me to go on ahead." *Thank One I got their names.*

"Get on to the stables, then, you won't be coming inside." He brushed past David on his way with the others to the kitchen. "You can sleep in the wagon!" His voice faded off as he hurried.

Inside would be better, but he'd have to wait until the boss cleared out. Until then, the stables it was. Who knew, maybe he could find something useful in there.

Chapter 5.5

Adia listened to the sounds of rustling clothing, clanking metal and scraping feet. Chief Taymer, Cary and Hellen were getting themselves ready, and at the moment there wasn't a lot of talking. The vibe was tense; they'd had to pick and choose who could go, and some of the skilled who weren't chosen put up arguments. Beau was one of those who had a hard time with it. He kept saying "You need me," but Chief was finally able to convince him that he needed to stay and be the anchor for everyone else if the mission went bad.

A number of the chosen had gone on before: kitchen crashers, decoys and escape markers (more ideas she couldn't keep to herself). They'd trickled out a few at a time so they could make the trip through the fringe of trees, then walk out through the barracks or stables to get in position. With so many people in play, there was no backing out of this now.

Down here in the hole, time was running out. Several feet away, a restless Cary whispered to himself, listed his equipment, double checked, triple checked. He was driving her crazy. She had to tune him out.

Chief Taymer was calm, but intense. Experience sat on him like armor, made him steady and impenetrable. Adia's heart lurched at the thought of something happening to him, so she didn't think it.

Hellen seemed like a mixture of the two. Part of her was fluttery, and part was extremely steady; they battled back and forth, but Adia didn't doubt what would win in the end.

"I'd like to talk to you all before you go," she said aloud, and the slight pause in noise told her they'd heard.

"Certainly," Chief said, his voice straining a little as he shrugged on the heavy ammo belt.

"I'm about on my way," Cary said. "I'm ready, I just…have to…," he paused, "take this off," and he shifted around some before his footsteps carried over to her. "Okay," he said breathlessly right in front of her.

"I'll be there in a sec," Hellen called over, from down low, so she was probably putting shoes on or something.

"Adia," Cary whispered, and moved to lean against the table beside where she was sitting. Her scar side, which made her uncomfortable. Once he got there, he hesitated, like it was awkward, then he took a quick deep breath and whispered, "I wish I could hold your hand."

That was a shocker. Adia's heart pounded. *Tell me he's not going to declare something.* Subconsciously, she picked her hands up and put them in her lap. (Easier to reach, or harder? She wasn't sure.) Did he notice?

"Don't worry." He laughed in that quiet voice. "I'm not going to grab you."

Okay, so he noticed. She tried to shake her mind clear without shaking her head. Is that even possible? She squeezed her eyes shut instead, and pressed them with her fingers to cover it.

"I'm sorry." He turned his body so it faced the room instead of her. "I just don't have a better time. I wanted you to know how I felt."

Adia lowered her hands back down to the desk, leaning on them with straight arms so he wouldn't change his mind and grab her after all. "Cary, I want you to be careful," she said, not really knowing what else to say. "Don't take any unnecessary risks, okay? Do what Hellen tells you, and don't go off on your own."

"Adia," he whispered amused, "I know how to take care of myself."

"Right, I know you do," she acknowledged, a bit grudgingly because she couldn't help being a smidge irritated. "But you have to be a team player. You can't run off and leave them, do you understand?"

All right, she must have offended him because he didn't say anything until Hellen and Chief were almost in their space. Hellen's footsteps scuffed up first, and she started saying something, but Cary's voice slipped in under her, "I can't believe you'd think that of me." It wasn't his happy voice, either.

"Are we about ready?" Hellen asked the two men.

"Ready as I'll ever be," Chief answered, clipping something somewhere.

Adia could feel Hellen looking at her, then at Cary. Maybe their faces gave them away, or maybe it was the awkward tension, because she said, "Did we miss something?"

"No," Adia hurried to answer. "I was just saying you guys need to take care of each other." Now was not the time for any more than that, so she moved on. "I'm sorry we didn't have more time to go over the secret passages. I should have thought of it sooner." She shook her head at herself. "Stick with Hellen, and if something happens…" She couldn't say *to her*, couldn't think it. "Get out however you can."

"I think we should try to complete the mission." Cary's voice was quiet, resolute.

It felt like Adia had the rug pulled out from under her. Was he determined to die? "You have to evaluate the situation," she said with exaggerated patience. "Chances are, if something has happened to Hellen, you won't be in a position to finish the mission."

"Maybe, maybe not," he said stubbornly. "But that'll be our call to make, won't it?"

"All right already," Hellen interrupted, annoyed. "Could we please not argue over what to do if I die?"

Chief's hand landed on her upper arm. "Adia, we'll take care of her, and we'll make good choices, I promise. Please try not to worry yourself an ulcer."

Her head dropped; she didn't want them to see the tears that came up so suddenly. It was unbearable, saying goodbye again, like she had countless times at the monastery. Only it was tripled now, more people, that much more to lose. She felt sorry she'd made Cary angry, she didn't mean to, she only meant that running was what he usually did. And now she wouldn't have a chance to explain.

And having Chief around was like having a part of her dad, and she wanted to throw her arms around his waist and not let him go. Would he stay if she asked him to? She wouldn't ask, of course, but it made her feel a little better to think he might stay. It made her feel like she had some choice.

All she could think about Hellen was that she better come back.

Hellen must have read her mind, because she came close and put her arms around her. She always knew when Adia was suffering. Chief or Hellen must have signaled to Cary somehow because he got up and the two men moved away to give the two women a moment. Hellen sat down beside her, never taking her arms away, and Adia reached around her and pulled her close.

What could she say? What could she say that she hadn't said a thousand times before, that wouldn't start a fight, or wouldn't sound lame? Nothing, and that's exactly what she said.

Too soon, Hellen whispered, "It's time for us to go."

"I know," Adia said and squeezed her tighter. "It's just really hard."

"I know," Hellen squeezed her back and released her. "I'm sorry I've given you gray hair."

"What?"

"I'm kidding!" She tweaked her chin and patted her shoulder. "A little mood lightener for you."

"It wasn't very lightening," Adia groused, stroking her hair, which felt tangled.

"Time to go," Chief's voice approached, Cary's footsteps like an echo behind his. The older man stopped close in front of her, taking Hellen's place. "Give me hug, girlie," he said tenderly, and leaned down to put his head beside hers, his arms around her. "Give Cary a hug, too, you'll feel better," he whispered in her ear.

She nodded on his shoulder and he gave her a kiss on the head as he stood. He knew what he meant to her, she could tell, and he took up the post like the honorable man he was. A little piece of her tore and dangled.

"Cary," she spoke to the general vicinity, since she'd lost track of him for the moment.

"Yeah?" Cary's voice was guarded.

She held out her hand and it was a long moment before he took it. Firmly in her grasp, she pulled him close to her. "I'm sorry," she said quietly, and tried to imagine he was one of the boys she'd known in college, fun and unimportant, so she could give him a hug. They managed it, it was awkward, but not too terribly, and she thought they both felt a little better afterward.

The linephone on the desk interrupted them as Cary moved away. Chief answered it with a terse "Yes?" and after a minute he said "Roger," and hung up. "Roberta came by Vartile's, she thinks her son David has gone to the palace."

Chapter S.6

It had been a long day. Dagge was glad when the big royal babies wanted to retire to their rooms for a while before dinner. He needed the down time.

Not to mention a little eavesdropping! The thought energized him and he practically ran up the back staircase and into the sitting room (*war room*) to fish his favorite toy out of the desk drawer. Sitting in the posture-friendly chair, feet up on the desk, he trained the dish onto the row of fancy guest rooms again. First, Arburash.

The preening Prime Minister was complaining about him. *What nerve!* Dagge smiled. If prissy-man only knew who was listening.

"I did try! He kept putting me off with that ridiculous fake smile of his. What was I supposed to do?"

General Weeks was apparently his grouch-buddy, because his voice answered. "He's wily, Arburash, that can't possibly surprise you. He knows you want something, and he's going to make you work for it."

"What if Bunch is right? What if we make a deal to sell him weapons and he uses them on us?"

The general pulled out his most convincing voice. "As long as we're providing him something he wants, he won't attack. Any deal is better than no deal. You have to get him alone tomorrow, and don't take no for an answer."

"Fine," Arburash grumped, clinking glass on glass again. Dagge almost felt sorry for them; the poor saps didn't realize they were playing entirely the wrong game.

Eladora came next. She and her companion, Rabinette, were sharing a room, and it sounded like only the two of them were in there.

Rabinette had a flat, loud voice. "We should lie down, darling, I'll help you relax."

"I don't want to lie down, Rabi, it's been such a fun day—the spa, and the games, and the movies! I want to explore the castle some more. Great Hand is legendary, you know. My nanny told me stories about the forest and the old royal family that are fantastically mysterious!"

"I don't think the Overlord would appreciate us poking around, my dove. And I definitely wouldn't bring up the old royal family to him." Dagge chuckled in his chair. Rabinette continued, "Let's ask for an in-depth tour tomorrow, all right? Come on now." She patted something, presumably the bed. "You'll need some rest to look your best at the banquet."

"All right," the young queen agreed. "Tomorrow? You promise?"

"I promise," Rabinette assured her, and the conversation dipped into muted whisperings and giggles. Too bad he didn't have a spyhole.

In the next room, Mapo and Ming spoke Shindaoan, as usual. Their voices sounded quiet and subdued. From exhaustion, Dagge guessed. The two of them were very active in the servants' field games, much to everyone's surprise. It had been comical to watch them take part in the three-legged race, but their tiny short legs moved in such unison they got an early lead and almost won. Dagge had to hand it to them, he hadn't expected any of the muckety-mucks to rub elbows with the common folk.

Moving on, Pulari wasn't in his room. Only the sound of gentle female snoring. Dagge scanned the palace until he located Graniteface's voice in the block of lesser guest rooms on the second floor. The King was with General Hatch, and his Foreign Minister, Somebody Terlaine.

Pulari was saying: "Hatch, the man is crazy. He can't be reasoned with; it doesn't matter what proof you give him."

"I want to know who the spy is," Foreign Minimal said.

"There is no spy!" Pulari's voice got louder and higher. "I sent those soldiers into the forest to find the old tunnels. Pull your head out of your ass, Terlaine. Dagge made the whole attack story up as an excuse for his own invasion."

Arvos Pulari, you old liar, you. Why are you keeping secrets from your own team?

And old tunnels, well, well, well. Why would Pulari be interested in old tunnels in Great Hand?

What's down there?

Chapter S.7

Hustle and bustle kept the stable hopping: servants from five countries tended horses, oiled gear, mucked stalls, pitched hay and either loitered or came and went. They talked in loud voices or didn't talk at all, some laughing, some grousing, some trash-talking about their masters in the palace. A person could learn a lot by listening to the servants, David realized.

David sat on the wood-plank platform that lined the back west corner, in the same spot he'd been occupying for the last bit of forever. Next to him, stacked three high, were the boxes he'd unloaded from the baggage cart. They were reportedly "the most exquisite fabric," a gift from Queen Eladora and her country, Rofland, to Overlord Dagge. David was told to "guard it with his life." Why it was worth his life was not in David's know-zone. Still, they had to be guarded until she saw fit to call for them. Hence his tired butt.

At least there was a steady stream of entertainment. He caught bits and pieces of news, arguments, stories, and orders. For instance, he learned that it wasn't supposed to snow tonight, that Arburash sat on an extra carriage cushion that had to be fluffed, that Pulari rode with his general most of the way here, and three of Eladora's housemaids were hot for one of her stable boys.

Whenever traffic slowed down, David turned his attention to a couple of men who sat on the back of a wagon that had a tarp over it. They were from Shindao, and he couldn't understand a word they said. They were laughing, and joking around, and it was fun to try to figure out what was so riotous.

Probably not the steady supply of people coming in the back door next to him. All the cold air was really spoiling his spot, and David wished they'd cut it out. He looked up complainingly when the next person slid the wooden door to the side, but she didn't see him because her head was down, and she was covered in an old brown cloak.

In fact, that cloak looked familiar. David swung his legs around and peered up under the hood. Two brown hands reached up and pushed the hood back until it fell to her shoulders. It was that cleaning woman, Junika.

"Hey…" David stood up and walked over to her. "What are you doing here? Are you working at the palace?"

She grabbed his arm, freaking him out a little, and pushed him backwards behind her while she made a quick scan of the area. Then she turned around and bulldozed him over to the hay bin by the back stalls. Once there were no witnesses, she said choppily, "You must go home now, you mother very worried."

"I don't think so, whoever you are," David jabbed back at her. "What kind of accent is that, anyway? Sounds like Malarkey to me."

"I am is not speak you language."

"Boy, no kidding, give it up sister. Are you working here or not? Do you know how to get to the dungeon?"

With a frustrated sigh, she waggled her head. "You do not stay. You go!" She pulled him to the back door and gestured for him to go out.

"Forget it." David shook her off. "I'm going inside, to the dungeon, and if you can't help me, I'll find someone who will."

Junika pulled the back door open and shoved him out. She was surprisingly strong. Outside, she closed the door behind them and bullied him over to the paddock fence. David would have resisted, but it didn't quite seem like an option.

"David," she said completely without an accent, "your mother sent me here to get you. You have to go home."

"I can't go home," he said. "I've got to try and find Dad."

"There are other people working on that. We're not gonna…just…leave him in there."

"Gosh, you inspire confidence," David snarked. "But forget it, I have a way into the palace and I'm not going home. I'm going to do something. I don't know what yet."

"It's the *I don't know what* that's going to kill you."

"Oh yeah? What's your plan? Are you the official dungeon-cleaning lady? The licensed chamber pot-emptier?"

Junika paused, her eyes got wide and a happy thought dawned on her face. "That's a great idea," she said.

"Oh, come on, you can't be serious." David threw his hands up. "You really don't have a plan. What kind of rescue squad are you on?"

"Be quiet!" she snapped, glancing around. Hands on her hips, she looked him over, and a grin spread on her face that he didn't like the looks of one bit. "But since you won't leave, I happen to need a distraction just like you."

****

A distressing chunk of time later, David watched Junika walk up the hill toward the kitchen patio. He was supposed to let her get about fifty feet ahead, and then follow, but the strings from his makeshift apron-skirt were tangled around the dangling part of his voluminous, pilfered headscarf, and she was about a hundred feet away by the time he got his arm free enough to carry the hammered brass pot the way he needed to.

Chamber Pot Emptier. How sorry he was that he said that. But it was a brilliant way to get him down into the dungeon. He just hoped he could pull off the whole I'm-a-girl thing.

"They won't look twice at a guy," she'd said, "I need you to *distract* them. And don't worry, if you get in trouble, I'll save you."

"What if they get fresh?" he demanded.

"Slap their hands and tell them you're not that kind of girl."

"Is that going to work?"

"Who knows? It's worth a try. Welcome to a woman's world."

David snugged the scarf over his face so just his eyes showed, and hustled up the hill after her. She'd been stopped by two guards standing at the edge of the porch, just under the cover of the roof. Were they the two she said came with her? He watched anxiously: ah there it was, the hand to the forehead sign for yes.

Junika headed toward the kitchen door, and the two men took up guard position again. David was on his own getting into the kitchen, since the chamber-pot disguise wouldn't be a valid passkey. Maybe he could say…he was supposed to get some carrots for Queen Eladora's horses. Perfect. Now that he had a plan, he felt better.

As he got closer, he could see that one of the soldiers was Chief Taymer. The white hair totally gave him away. "I'm instructed to get carrots for Queen Eladora's horses," David said in a high breathy voice when he reached them. The girl in him was a little phlegmy, and he cleared his throat.

"Really?" The younger guy challenged him.

"Yyyeess..." David replied, unprepared.

"By whose order?"

"By…Queen Eladora's order." David shifted into a different gear: *I am woman, hear me roar.*

Both guards stepped really close and examined him, saying nothing. The younger one fingered the silky, pale pink fabric draped in front of his face. David got a little uncomfortable, and gripped the drape tightly. He slapped the guy's hand away and said, "I'm not that kind of girl!" As he pushed past them, he could hear them laughing.

Two more guards stood at the door, but they didn't even ask him anything, just looked at him and let him on through. He could have had a bomb in the pot for all they knew. Not that he was complaining.

Inside, the kitchen was a madhouse. A zillion people were rushing around, carrying food and utensils. The ovens and stoves cranked out the heat, and there was an overwhelming amount of shouting. David tried to stay out of the way, pretending to pick through the piled-up produce on a counter by the door, all the while looking frantically around for Junika.

When he spotted her, she was talking to a short older woman on the left-hand side by a huge stove. They talked quickly, privately, and at the end the woman hugged her, so she knew her. Interesting.

Junika threaded her way through the bustle to join him at the produce. "Come stand in front of the dumbwaiter and block me while I get in, then go out and tell the white-haired guy I'm ready."

David followed, munching on a carrot, amazed that no one paid them any mind. Junika slid the dumbwaiter door open, glanced around quickly, and climbed inside, leaving a gap when she pulled the door closed behind her. Slick.

Both guards hurried in when he delivered the message. Taymer pulled an extra gun off his back and went in holding it. He barely paused at the dumbwaiter, where he slipped the gun into waiting hands. The other guy walked past him at just the right time to distract from what he was doing, and once the door was closed, Taymer followed him down a narrow hall.

These guys were too good at this, no way was this a first mission. Maybe Taymer was Thorn. In that case, David felt like he was certainly in the right place. He suppressed a smile, adjusted his chamber-pot, and took off after.

Chapter S.8

Cold had seeped into every part of him, sucking the warmth out of his flesh like a siphon, leaving his hands and feet bloodless and aching. How long had he been like this now? Arms dead by his head, hips and legs screaming. An eternity. John had never felt so old in his life. What he wouldn't give to get up off this hard, freezing floor.

After listening to them talk for endless hours, he'd come to the conclusion that the guards were mostly stupid. Every shift playing cards, arguing about nothing, gossiping, making inane comments, and weaving these insanely twisted, violent threats that were becoming incredibly creative. Almost savant.

John leaned his head back against the stone wall and gazed at the current installment of three, sitting around the table across the room at the bottom of the stairs: one leaned his chair back against the wall, one hunched over the table with his back to him, shuffling a deck, and the other had his legs stretched out, hands behind his neck, and his beady little eyes fixed on John.

Ignoring him, John flexed his fingers and rolled his head from side to side. Both hands were numb, shackled to the wall all night, and all morning, and for the rest of his life maybe. Figured he'd be stuck out here in the guard room, instead of in a cell where he could try one of the hidden hinge keys. Tricky business, though, getting out. If he did, Dagge would know there was an escape route; he'd tear the dungeon up to get at it and that would blow it for the Resistance. He'd find the tunnels, find the monastery, and John was not going to have that.

His friends would try to free him, probably. It scared him to death, put him constantly on edge so he couldn't sleep all night if you didn't count a couple of light dozes.

The trip back from the forest was bad yesterday…pulled behind a horse, how many times did he fall? It was a constant obstacle course of rocks and roots and gullys—they must have picked the worst path just to see him slam his knee or shoulder or face into the ground. Wharton and Dagge talked about whether they should hang all the rifles on him to get them back to the palace, but they decided against it because he was so old he might not make it. John was never so happy to be old in his life.

Which might not be all that long now.

Time to think about something else.

Flex the fingers, keep the blood going. John stretched his legs out in front of him on the floor and rotated his ankles.

"Hey!" the pig-eyed guard hollered at him. "Get yer feet back in, you'll be trippin sumbuddy up."

"Who am I going to trip up?" John gave it back. "All the supermodels coming through here?"

The hunched-over guy exploded with laughter. "Aw haw, he gotchu there! Supermodels! I wish! Aw ha-aw!" he brayed like a donkey.

The third guard, the one with his chair leaning back against the wall, didn't laugh. Didn't even look up. John studied him. He'd be the one to watch out for. He had a cold, efficient style to him, and seemed sharp where the others were thuggish. They could all kill, though, so in this tiny room, John supposed it was a pointless distinction. Not a lot of strategy going to happen down here.

A lot of something else, most like. John looked up at the heavy chain dangling from the ceiling thirty feet or so up. It teased him for a long time, lost in darkness the way it was. When one of the doors upstairs opened, just enough light came in to glimpse it, and he'd stared and stared until he finally figured out what was up there. Once he got that, he could follow the rope attached to it, across the ceiling, down the wall to the cleat, and then to the floor.

All the better to hang you with, my dear.

While his eyes were focused upwards, the inside door opened. Warm, dim light from the kitchen barely glinted off the chain's knobby lengths. Whoever entered wasn't Wharton then, or the changing of the guard, which always used the outside door. From inside it had to be a servant, or Dagge, and he hoped it wasn't Dagge—his breath stopped involuntarily.

No, not Dagge. The bigshot never came alone, and this person did. A servant then, no talking, just invisible feet scraping down the stone steps. The ghostly echo reminded John again of that first trip down here with Hilman and the King.

The first thing he saw was the bottom of a dress, swaying. Step by step the rest of her came into view, up her odd narrow skirt to a slim middle that disappeared under a filmy cloth, which draped around and around her head and shoulders, and made her look like a walking ice cream cone. A Devotee of the faith, then. He could see that she was carrying something, but couldn't tell what it was.

The girl stopped at the bottom of the stairs and addressed the guards in a breathy voice. "I'm here to empty the chamber pot." Chair legs screeched on the floor and the three stooges got up and ambled over to her to have a better look.

"Chamber pots, you mean, there's one here and one in the back," the squinter said, pointing at John and hitching up his pants. The woman glanced in John's direction, but he couldn't see her face because of the scarf.

Hunch-over guy swaggered the five steps it took to get to her and tried his charm. "You can bribe me, sweetness, and I'll let you in." He held his hand out to help her down the last two steps, but she ignored it.

"How about I give this pot to you, and you can empty the stink."

Hunch-over scowled. "That ain't my job, baby."

"That's right, it's mine, and I'm sure the Captain would love to hear how you kept me from doing my job."

The soldier backed away with his hands up. "I was just trying to be friendly," he said sourly. "You women are all the same."

"Maybe it's your technique," she huffed, descending the last two steps, and blowing by him on her way to John's pot.

Then John got a good look at her, and there was no mistaking those eyes. She was David.

****

Dad. His father's eyes went ever so slightly wide when he recognized him. David wanted to run over, but that would look suspicious, wouldn't it? So he satisfied himself with mouthing, "It's okay, we're coming to help you." The confused look on his father's face said his lip reading failed him, but oh well, he'd figure it out.

Luckily, they hadn't moved the pot since John used it so David was able to walk right over to him and kneel, blocking the guards' view. Dad looked terrible, all bruised and dried blood everywhere, some kind of mess on one arm, and a bloody spot on the wall behind his head. Nice.

"What are you doing here?" his father demanded in a tiny whisper.

"Getting you out," David answered, just as tiny. He busied himself with his headscarf, making a show of pushing the bulk of it behind him, so he wouldn't get it in the stink, right?

"Too dangerous, go home."

"What kind of thanks is that?" David leaned in to pick up the real pot so he could dump the contents into his big brass disguise. "It's not just me, you know." At the same time, he managed a close-up view of the shackles. They latched on one side, hinged on the other, and there weren't any locks, just clips. Simple.

"I'm surprised you haven't gotten out of this," he whispered.

"I didn't think the guards would appreciate that too much."

"Good point," David agreed. Setting the empty pot back down, he faked losing his balance and put his hand on the wall to catch himself. "Oh, my goodness!" he exclaimed, "I don't want to fall in that!" He giggled around at the guards, turned back, and held the shackle clip up for his dad to see, then palmed it. "Be ready," he said.

David stood and announced to the room, "I should go take care of this." Then he nodded and started for the stairs, hoping that would work.

"You got one more, missy." A guard stopped him in a bored voice, pulled out a ring of keys and walked over to the gate. The other two sat down again.

David peered into the dark hall. The dumbwaiter should be down there, and if Junika was out of it, she better find a place to hide. The guard turned the key in the lock and pushed the squeaky gate open.

A few strides down the hall, David spied a square of wood embedded in the right-hand wall. Had to be the dumbwaiter. The door was closed, except for a tiny slice of blacker black at the bottom. *Junika, if you're listening...* "So, it's only the three of you down here all the time?"

"Not all the time." The guard turned around and walked backwards a few steps so he could look at him. "Why? You wanna know when I get off?"

"Sure." David played the card.

"My shift ends at midnight, sweetness," he said, slowing down so he could walk beside him. "Whaddaya say you take off that scarf and lemme get a look at you."

His hand reached up and David slapped it. "Oh, no." He waggled his finger. "Unless you want this pot on your head."

The guard smirked at him. "I got a gun here says you won't do it."

Let's change the subject. "Do you like guard duty?" David glanced back towards the little door in the wall as he rounded the corner, tuning out the soldier's rambling reply.

Prisoner number two sat in the last cell on the left. David couldn't get a good look at him until he raised his head as they walked up. It was Robert. Of course Dagge would put him down here once their father was captured. Keys jangled and the guard opened the door to let

David in. He avoided his brother's gaze and aimed straight for the chamber pot, keeping his back to Robert while he did the job.

"Wait a minute…" Robert's voice stopped him before he could go. "Do I know you?"

"No chitchat, asshole." The guard grabbed David's arm to pull him out of the cell, but looked surprised at the size of it. "Wait a minute..." he said. David tried to circle around him and get out the door, but the dingo wasn't going to let him by. "I don't think you're a real toss dumper, and I don't think you're even a woman." He reached up to David's scarf and yanked on it, but it was too wound around David's head and it jerked him forward instead. That sent the contents of the pot onto the guard's chest and horrified him for a second—long enough for David to push him down and shoot past him.

"Help! Help!" he screamed in his girl voice, running around the corner, past the dumbwaiter, through the gate and into the arms of another guard. "He attacked me!" he exclaimed breathlessly.

Unfortunately, the loudmouth behind was yelling "Stop her! Stop her!" and the guard who caught him turned him around and hung on. David elbowed him in the ribs, slipped his hands inside the guy's arms and broke his grip, then he turned around and punched him in the face. *Owww.*

Lame punch, too. Barely even fazed the guy—pretty much just pissed him off. He came at David with both fists, and that was the last thing David remembered of that.

Chapter 5.9

Hellen slid the dumbwaiter door all the way open and waited for the guard to come around the corner. As he passed, wiping at the front of his uniform, she slid out behind him and buried her knife up to the hilt under his jaw, just like Beau had taught her. Limp, he went down in her arms without a sound, and left only two more to deal with in the guard room. *Thanks for the recon, David.* Hellen wiped her knife on the dead soldier's pants and eased closer to the bars to see what she could see.

One of the guards was putting David in shackles next to John, slapping his face and telling him he was a girl after all. The other guard was standing at the foot of the stairs, gun aimed at David, watching. It wouldn't be long before they'd wonder where the dead guy was, so she went back to the body, lay down behind it and propped his rifle up, ready.

In a few seconds, the guard who shackled David came to the gate and called, "Moritz! Where the hell are you?" This span of hallway was pretty dark, so it took him a moment to see the body on the ground. "Moritz?" He came through the gate and Hellen let him have it. Two down. She jumped up, took the rifle, and rushed the gate.

Gunfire had already brought Chief running. He came down a few steps, shooting bullets at the guard, but the guard fired laser pulses back. Black holes tore Chief up, forcing him back toward the door, tripping and jerking until his legs gave out and he went down. Half of him hung down the steps, and the other half lay on the landing in front of the door.

Chief! Chief! she wanted to scream, but the guard turned on her, and she had to duck back out of range. Where was Cary? Please One, not coming down the stairs. She couldn't stand it. But she couldn't stand not knowing, either, and, gun ready, she crouched to look out between the bars.

Cary stood at the top of the stairs, pointing his rifle at the guard's back. He saw Hellen, who was in his target zone, and he moved down the stairs quietly to get a different angle. The guard had his gun raised, walking slowly toward the gate, and waiting for Hellen to appear. When he saw her his aim was too high, and Hellen had already stuck her gun through the bars and fired a laser pulse into the guard's chest.

He didn't even flinch. Hot magenta shards flashed out around him, all sharp angles and glowing bizarro-ness. *Damn it to hell*, he was one of the freaking uglies. Cary started shooting, but he wasn't a great marksman, and didn't get a killing shot. The guard ducked under the steps where Cary couldn't see him.

"Cary! Guard the door!" Hellen ran back to the dumbwaiter to get her bullet gun, pulled it out and switched to semi-automatic on her way back to the bars. Peeking through, back against the wall, she could see John looking at her and his head gestured to the darkest part under the stairs, about fifteen feet to his right.

Hellen opened fire, blindly emptying her mag where she thought the monster's heart and head would be, then aimed lower in case he was crouching. Casings flew up around her, bouncing off the bars and going in all directions, raining down in a puddle. Finally, when there was no movement or sound or purple and she started to feel guilty about wasting bullets, she stopped. After a few moments, an uneasy quiet settled the ringing air.

"You missed me." The weirdly harmonic voice teased its way out of the shadows. She fired again. He laughed, a high giggle that broke and rejoined, alternating with flashes of magenta that jumped out of him, flickering like static. Her stunned brain got stuck in neutral for a second, looking at John, splattered with blood and shackled to the wall, mouth hanging open in terror. Next to him, David was in shock.

Hellen got the whole picture in one horrible moment. Desperate, she fired, and fired, and fired at it; reducing the guard's head to a pulp, his body to tatters, but she couldn't stop the magenta shard, stuttering and blinking itself free from the lifeless body as it stretched the short distance to John.

****

Horrified, David watched the soldier's head disintegrate under the barrage of gunfire. The body staggered (*It should be dead, why isn't it dead?)*—a man made out of bloody hamburger. A ray or a beam or something (*What the hell is that thing?)* came out of it and reached toward his father. When it touched him, it jumped over, slicing into his head, shooting down his body, and as the ray snapped into him, two purple eyes glared down at David from the flat, glowing magenta sticking up out of his Dad's gray hair. *What the hell IS THAT?!* His Dad's face had frozen, mouth open and eyes bulging, his body lifted and strained away from the wall while the magenta cut through, but there was no blood, no severing of parts, just purple points and edges that stuck out around him, glowing and flickering, changing shape as it shrank and shifted into the flesh.

David fought his shackles, frantically grasping at the clips, needing his hands free to grab his father away from that thing, to run, to leave it to Junika or anyone else. As he struggled, his father's body relaxed, lowered itself back to the ground, all the flat glowing edges disappeared and the head slowly turned and looked at him. Purple flashed and faded in his pupils, leaving him really quite normal-looking except for the gut-freezing malevolence David could see now. How strange to look at his father's face and not see his father looking back.

David dragged his brain back to functionality when Junika came through the gate, her gun leveled at the Dad thing. "I can kill you with this," she told it.

"Then you should do it," it said in a surprisingly normal voice. It was so much like Dad, David felt confused. He looked over at it again—it was smiling and calm.

"Don't kill him!" David blurted out. He didn't think he could stand it, watching his father shot right beside him.

Junika came to him instead, and unclipped the shackles on David's wrists. "Cary!" she yelled up the stairs. Nothing. "Cary!" No answer, so she turned back to David. "David, tell Cary to wait for me at the south doors, got that?" She helped him up, giving him instructions and pointing him toward the stairs. "Go to the stable, tell the others to wait on my signal. I'm going to find out where the rest of them are hiding, and we'll need the fireworks then."

David rubbed his wrists while Junika pulled him away from his father. He looked back at Dad, still sitting there. This was so messed up. He searched his brain for a solution, but none came. How could he walk away? How could he just leave him here? No goodbye, no hug, no nothing? What happened to Dad in there? Was he dead already? Or was he still alive somehow?

"David, it isn't him," Junika said. "Don't be fooled, it isn't your father."

But how did she know that? He looked down at the gun in her hands and had a wild urge to snatch it. She was going to use it as soon as he left. She was going to kill him without a trial, without a jury, without a chance to prove anything.

How did she know?

She didn't. That was why he started up the steps, and didn't tell her about the missing clip. If his Dad was still in there, he would know, and maybe he could get away. Maybe he could be saved.

****

Hellen was relieved to hear Cary's voice when David opened the door at the top of the stairs. No one had come running. No one killed him or took him prisoner. Even with all the shooting, the heavy oak door and ancient stone kept the dungeon secrets like it always had. Who knew she would ever be glad of that?

Once David was gone, Hellen turned her attention to the travesty still shackled to the wall. Truth was, she didn't know whether John survived or not. All she knew was that they couldn't afford the risk to find out. If that thing had access to John's knowledge base, they were screwed.

Raising the gun again, she aimed it at John's heart. It pained her to look at him, preparing to kill him, even with that scary look on his face. She considered closing her eyes, but didn't want to miss. One shot was all she needed. It would be done, they'd all be better off, and John would want her to do it. Still…agonizingly difficult to squeeze the trigger.

"*Hey!*" The voice echoed up the hallway from the cells. Hellen looked around at the gate. *Who the hell was that?*

"*HEY!*" it said louder.

Glad for the excuse, Hellen lowered the rifle and backed away.

She had to go check on whoever it was. If Dagge put him in the dungeon, he was probably a good guy. Snatching up the guard's laser rifle, she veered off through the gate and made her way into the bowels of the dungeon.

Before she rounded the corner, she leaned the guns against the wall for safekeeping. No need for the mystery prisoner to pin the gunfire on her just yet. When she turned into the cell block, a few cells down a young man stood at his gate, surly eyes directed her way. She recognized him when she got close. Robert, John's eldest, was squinting at her like she'd cheated him at poker. Of course he would be in here, she should have thought of that. Could this get any worse?

"You're that cleaning lady who was at my house. What are you doing here?" he said.

Riiiight. She took a moment to switch gears; maybe she could get out of here without him being any the wiser. "I am heard the sound, of the bang bang?" Honestly, if she survived this, she should get an award.

"What's going on out there? Who was shooting? Is everyone dead?"

"Um…" Hellen had no clue what she should do. She couldn't leave him. She couldn't take him. Only one other choice. "You want…"

She made a turning motion with her hand, like she couldn't think of the word for "key."

"Key? Yes! Get a key! Let me out of here!"

Hellen went back for the keyring—around the corner and up the hall to the first dead soldier. She squatted by the body and pulled it over to look.

And her eyes came up just enough to see that John was gone.

Chapter S.10

Dagge leaned back in his splendid chair and surveyed his domain. The tables looked beautiful, the food never failed to be exquisite, and his smiling guests appeared duly impressed. All in all, he was feeling pretty great about the whole evening.

At the moment, a portly limerick poet walked around inside the "U" of the table making up limericks starring the guests. Everyone wanted one, with the exception of His Majesty Graniteface. Which was of course why the poet picked him.

"There once was a King of Pulari,

Whose reign looked increasingly starry,

His coffers were big," he cupped his hands low in front of him,

"His scepter, a twig," he held up his little finger,

"But the court ladies weren't ever sorry," he stroked his fingers around the base of his neck, and then waggled them like he was showing off jewelry.

No wonder Graniteface didn't want a poem. The crowd broke up, and the two arm-candies Pulari brought looked like they wanted to melt into their shoes. Only Pulari's bare social graces kept him in his seat; he had to satisfy himself with picking up his cup and glowering over the rim. Dagge dared a glance over at Nylah, who kept her face carefully neutral.

Dagge laughed, and not just because it was fun to skewer Old Graniteface. He'd taken a risk with the quirky entertainment, and it paid off. The poet was a big hit. Even the generals were enjoying it, he thought, though you couldn't call their enthusiasm obvious.

Decked in their glittering attire, his guests cascaded down the side tables away from him according to a system that made very much sense to Dagge, although it seemed to confuse his company. To his right, the table was full of people whose heads were bigger than their brains. On his left, that table was full of people whose brains were bigger than their heads. Interestingly, the smart bunch didn't figure it out either. Maybe he'd been wrong about them.

Bridging the gap, the head table was reserved for only the leaders of countries. Like him. Dagge beamed, and took a satisfied sip out of his goblet. He did like cranberry juice.

Doors opened and servants brought in the palate-cleansing course (yes, there was such a thing), and Queen Nylah's turn on the roasting fork was coming to a close.

"When she saw what she'd done,

It was too late to run,

And she just had to lie back and fake it."

The room exploded in guffaws, with the exception of Pulari, who looked like he was ready to kill the guy. Nylah had a secret little smile on her face, which she covered by picking up her goblet and taking a drink. When she saw Dagge watching her, she toasted him with her cup.

Yeah, it was turning out to be a good party. No doubt all the snooty-heads were surprised to actually be having fun. Didn't they say a single party could make or break a reputation? Dagge smiled into his cup and sipped his juice. Only one more thing he had to wait for, and then the real fun could begin.

Chapter S.11

Hellen found the keys and unhooked them from the dead guard's pants as quietly as she could. In front of her, the gate was maybe eight feet away and wide open. If she could close it, and lock it, she and Robert might be safe long enough to get out of the dungeon through the dumbwaiter.

No noise, no movement, no sign of John in the guard room. Maybe he went upstairs. Good for her, bad for everyone else. Not very likely, anyway, leaving her alive.

Hellen stepped quickly over the body, grabbed the edge of the gate and swung it forward. A faint scraping sound across the guard room, and she looked up, fear stabbing her heart. John barreled out of the darkness under the stairs and came at her, eyes flashing that weird purple, a sinister smile electrifying his face.

His long legs gobbled up the distance between them. Slamming the gate closed, she fumbled the keys, got the biggest one, stuffed it in the keyhole, but it wouldn't turn. She tried the next one. Hand shaking, it scraped and bumped at the edge, slipped, wouldn't go in. Her panicked eyes ticked back and forth between John, the key, John, the key—*go in, damn you!* He bore down on her, the key slipped in the lock and turned, and Hellen jumped back away from the bars just in time to avoid the long, grasping arms.

"You're not going to get away from me," he said with that terrible smile.

She turned and ran back to Robert.

"Who was that?" he asked when he saw her. "A guard? Why doesn't he come?"

"Not worry," Junika replied, "I get you out." She picked out the last of the three keys, fit it in the keyhole and opened the lock. Simple dimple, now that she wasn't almost having a seizure.

Robert wasn't finished yet. "What the hell's going on here?" he demanded. "First the weird chamber-pot woman, then all the shooting, and now you?" Hands on hips, he stepped toward her, eyes narrowed. "What do you have to do with this?"

Punk kid. She didn't have time to baby him through. Junika smiled and patted his arm, then pulled him around the corner to the dumbwaiter. "You go," she told him, gesturing to the little empty box.

"What?! Why can't we go out the normal way?" Before she could stop him, he walked over to the bars and looked out. Her heart flipped. The boy couldn't handle Killer Dad, so she launched herself across the space and grabbed him, pulling him back to safety. This brat was going to be the death of her. "Not out there," she tried to explain awkwardly. "Out here." She indicated the box again.

He squinted at her for way too long. She was this close to shoving him in and cranking him up herself when he said, "I'm not going."

What? Now she really wanted to throttle him. "Go!" she said louder, jabbing her finger at the hole.

"I'm not going," he flatly refused, and turned to go back to his cell.

Trailing behind him, Hellen considered her options. She couldn't carry him, and she couldn't shoot him.

What choice did she have? She handed him the keys and left.

Chapter S.12

Dagge watched his guests enjoy their main course—knives flashing, forks spearing the bloody prime rib with relish. Talking not required. His own plate sat largely untouched; he had no appetite for such heavy meat, it would only weigh him down. More fun to observe the others anyway, it amused him to reduce the prissies to barbarians.

Out of the blue, a substantial knock at the main door surprised everyone. *Finally.* Dagge felt the sweet rush of adrenaline perk him into overdrive.

All eyes found the butler and watched him walk over to the door, open it slightly and stand there, presumably listening. He spoke through the crack for a couple of moments, closed the door again, and tried to look unhurried as he made the long journey around the table to the back, where Dagge was waiting.

"Sir, a gentleman is outside who insists on speaking with you." He leaned in and whispered in a voice so quiet, Dagge could barely hear him. "He says there's been an incident in the dungeon."

Dagge leaned back. Was he smiling? A quick check of his expression said no, not exactly. But he sure felt like he was smiling. All over. "Show him in," he said.

The butler bowed and hurried away, practically running across the floor, and when he neared the door, Dagge stood up. All eyes in the room were playing ping pong, between the door and the Overlord, and only a few quiet whispers disturbed the air. For a second the butler stopped at the door, then swept it open like visiting royalty stood on the other side.

There stood John Treslo, in all his long-gray-haired, dirty smelly glory. Dagge signaled for the guards outside to raise their guns and let the man pass. When he walked into the room, the buzz that erupted was like a horde of angry bees. Dagge heard himself laugh. *Oops, gotta watch that.* Only Pulari was looking at him.

"Mr. Treslo," Dagge greeted him cheerily, "do let me introduce you to my guests." The visitor stopped walking and stood expectantly, eyes studying the room.

Ever the showman, Dagge walked around the table and gestured largely while he talked. Being a grand occasion, it deserved something memorable. "Mr. Treslo here," he said in a booming voice, "is the royal architect, and our resident genius." Murmurs skittered around the tables. "He has come to us—" Dagge paused dramatically. "—by a wonderfully fortunate twist of fate." He meant that so completely, it was easy to say.

"Mr. Treslo…" Dagge got to the end of the table of smart people and stopped, leaning his hand casually on the last chair. "Would you be so kind as to tell the group…" He indicated the assembled with a wave of his hand. "What you are doing here?"

"Whatever you say, Overlord." The answer was immediate, decisive, and almost enthusiastic. Wasn't that nice? The voice sounded better than it used to, the eyes looked better, everything was better. Very nearly human. Oh, he couldn't be more pleased.

Nodding benignly to the guards lining the walls, he waved his finger in the signal for lockdown.

Chapter S.13

Hellen shucked her Junika costume and stuffed it in a storage cabinet on her way down the back hall from the kitchen. Underneath, she wore her soft blacks, which were better for fighting and sneaking. Out of her pocket she pulled a stocking mask, which she yanked over her head, and a tie for her hair.

Almost certainly John had headed for the dining room, or rather the thing inside John did. Pets find their masters, don't they? She considered following him there, but it seemed like a better idea to try for the bulk of the scary undead while she had opportunity and ammunition. Chances were most of them at least would be together now, hiding from the guests, and if she waited until after she killed Dagge, they may be spread to kingdom come in the aftermath. No way did she want to hunt them all down when they could look like anyone.

Cary was supposed to be waiting for her at the south doors. She would need his help eliminating the monsters, even if he wasn't a great shot. Having to do this without Chief made it a lot harder. Almost as hard as stepping over his dead body, but she couldn't think about that right now.

The back hallway from the kitchen ended in a hidden doorway that opened at the south entrance. A tapestry hung over it on the other side, so with any luck the guards didn't even know it existed. Unfortunately, luck had turned out to be a mixed bag tonight.

She pulled the door open gently and peeked through the thin spots woven into the tapestry. Two guards stood against the doors, facing the main hallway, guns up and ready. It struck Hellen that they looked more like they were keeping people in than keeping people out. What was Dagge expecting?

The tapestry hung less than fifteen feet from the nearest guard, who had three weapons: laser rifle in his right arm, knife strapped to right leg, pistol in a left underarm holster. Hellen took a deep breath. Light from the overhead fixtures made shadows under his muscles—he looked big, strong, and very pissed off.

Slow and careful, she set the guns down, loosened her knife, and considered her options. A firefight would bring other soldiers running, so that was out. No matter how many moves she'd learned from Beau, she doubted she could take both guards by herself with just her knife. On the other hand, if they weren't looking, she probably could.

Where was a distraction when you needed it? Oh yeah, Cary should be standing right outside the door. He had a walk n talk, she had a walk n talk. She closed the door, unclipped hers from her belt, faced away from the end of the hall, and whispered into it. "Cary!"

After a few seconds, he answered. "Yeah!"

"Knock."

"Knock?"

"Yeah, on the door, right now." She clipped her radio back onto her belt and hurried to open the door. Knife in her left hand, she readied herself.

A knock on the door turned the guards' heads away. Another one brought their backs around, which was perfect. Hellen darted out from behind the tapestry, jumped on the big guy's back, wrapped her left arm around his neck and plunged her knife into his jugular. Then she pulled his rifle over with her right hand and shot the other guard point blank. Yanking the rifle up hard, she whacked the first guy in the face with his own gun, and both guards went down without a fight.

The heavy door, blocked by hundreds of pounds of flesh, shoved open a few inches, then a few more inches, and Cary's head stuck part way in. One look at the devastation and he said, "Here I thought you needed me."

"I do." She smiled. "Help me get these guys into the atrium." They dragged the bodies, took the guns, and hurried up the stairs.

Hellen stopped at the top and peeked down the big hallway that ran by the sitting room and the royal bedchambers. Clear. Her mind clicked along like an oiled machine. Cookie told her Diit was standing guard at the nursery. Dagge's creepy pets were in there, she said, and it was Diit's job to make sure no one found them. No one but her, she hoped.

Down the long hall she set a quick pace, Cary clunking and rustling behind her. He seemed loud, but she was probably oversensitive. Too much time alone.

The doors of the royal rooms drifted past on their right—all of them closed, like tombs. The emptiness was more profound than she remembered it. Spooky, as if all the ghosts of all the kings and queens and people who lived here were helplessly watching them.

It stressed her out.

What seemed like miles later, she saw Diit, standing calmly in the hallway like he didn't have a care in the world. He was so weird. She knew he heard them, but he continued to stare straight ahead like a statue. Must be a valet thing, Hilman was like that, too.

He looked at her when she walked into his range of vision. "Miss Hellen!" he said enthusiastically, "how nice to see you!"

She had to wonder about his brain for a second. "Diit, we don't have much time, we need to get in there and get rid of those ...whatever-they-ares."

He leaned forward conspiratorially and answered, "They're not in here. I'm a decoy."

A decoy? This could be nothing but bad. "Where are they?" she dreaded to know.

"The General took them outside," he told her. "To 'eliminate the threat of retaliation.'"

"What does that mean?" Cary asked anxiously.

"It means none of the foreign soldiers will survive."

Hellen quietly freaked. Zola and Lan were out there, in Dagge's uniforms, but if Wharton was looking, he could easily know they weren't his men. She plucked her walk n talk off her belt and put it up to her mouth. "Zola!" she hissed. No answer. "Zola!" she called more urgently.

Nothing. "I'll go," Cary said, turning to run back down the hall.

"Cary, wait!" He stopped, and Hellen stepped back up to Diit, searching his face, hoping, wanting to know if he had that ...*thing* Hilman had. That ability to know.

"Miss Hellen, you should go to the dining room," he told her softly.

Chapter S.14

Once the guards blockaded the doors, heads started whipping back and forth, there was a lot of shifting and scooting of chairs, many of the snooties stood up, and he heard quite a few demands to know what was going on. He didn't answer, of course.

Personal bodyguards had to be removed first, and with a flick of his hand all the elite soldiers dressed as servants moved to disarm their targets and take them prisoner. Having them outnumbered two to one, Dagge's plan had been to get them all outside to be disposed of, but some of them insisted on dying right there in the dining room, and there just wasn't anything he could do about that. In the melee, a few of the guests tried to push their way past the guards, and then other attendants got involved, and quite a few bruises and a fair amount of blood occurred before Dagge intervened magnanimously. "Come now, no one wants to be hurt," he said, and gestured more guards into the dining room to sort them all out.

Less than five minutes later, calm had been fairly restored. Well, make that controlled hysteria, but at least it was controlled. The screaming had stopped, and the ladies who cried were doing it silently in their chairs. A few go-for-broke men had returned to their seats a bit worse off, and the seriously wounded were left where they were.

"Now." Dagge gave a nod from his position at the end of the smart table. "There's no need to be afraid of our friend Mr. Treslo. He will only do what I say, and why would I want him to hurt any of you?" They didn't look convinced. "Let me demonstrate." He borrowed a knife from the table and walked smoothly over to his toy. "Mr. Treslo, please cut your finger off with this."

"Which finger?" The better-but-as-yet-imperfect voice wheezed like an accordion.

"Oh…" Dagge put his hands behind his back and moved away, to give his audience a feel for the big picture. "What do you think, Nylah? His pinky? Let's say his pinky—your pinky!" he shouted in his enthusiasm.

John stepped quickly and decidedly over to the end of the table, and smacked his hand down. Then he took the knife in his other hand like a dagger and brought it down with such force that it stuck in the table and pinned his pinky to it.

Screams erupted all around the room again, and it wasn't just the women. The table on the big-brain side cleared in a blink, and all the smart people backed away to the wall where they got pushed along by men with guns and ended up in a huddle behind Mapo and Ming, who had not moved. They sat there staring at the severed stub dripping blood on the floor.

"Dagge, what's the purpose of this?" Pulari finally hitched his balls up and said something. What took him so long?

"That's Overlord to you, Pulari," Dagge said, all traces of his earlier good humor scraped away. Pulari's eyes narrowed at him, which meant His Dickless was not as afraid as he should be. But the evening wasn't over yet.

Once the frenzy died down, Dagge resumed his company face and walked up the center of the "U" with a bounce in his step. "Please, please, this anxiety is really unnecessary." He smiled, showing his dazzling white teeth. "What say we all resume our seats." He gestured to the servants to clear the tables. "And we'll enjoy the evening's last entertainment." With that, he vaulted the center table effortlessly, feet flying between the candelabras, and took his seat.

Nylah burst into tears. "Aw," he crooned, reaching his arms around her, and pulling her head to his shoulder. "It's okay, Nylah, this won't last forever." Shushing, he patted her back until she stopped crying and leaned away to look at him.

"What does that mean?" Her voice rose as she spoke, and got a little panicky. "What do you mean by that?" She looked around frantically for support. "What does he mean by that?"

"I just mean that someday you'll look back on this night, and it will be the best story of your entire pathetic life."

Her face looked like he had just knifed her. The shock and horror were clownish, and he realized she must have honestly believed he was interested in her. How funny! He laughed, genuinely amused, and watched the others get forced back to their seats at gunpoint.

"All right then," he said as seats were taken, "shall we have a game?" No one answered, so he answered himself, in a breathy falsetto voice. "Why yes, Your Eminence, a game sounds like a wonderful idea!" He clapped his hands together in glee. "Let's play Simon Says!"

"No, let's not." Pulari stood up, threw his napkin down and confronted him. Dagge had to give the guy points. "I'm not playing Simon Says, or Hangman, or whatever sick thing you have dreamed up. If you want to kill me, do it now like a man."

Dagge cocked his head to the side and debated himself. He could kill him, right now, but that would definitely induce a panic, and he wouldn't be able to show the others what he wanted to show them. There would be blood all over the dining room, and he just didn't think the carpets could ever be the same.

Or, he could say: "If I wanted to kill you, I'd have done it already."

Pulari lost his temper. "Then what the hell are you playing at!? You've taken us prisoner, Dagge. Do you think we'll all have a good laugh about it someday? I don't think it's funny! And I bet none of the rest of you think it's funny, either!" He checked the other tables and mostly they all just wanted to stay out of it. "I insist that you release us, and I for one will never be coming back!"

His obtuseness was jaw-dropping. Some people were entirely too used to getting their own way. Did Old Graniteface honestly think a kidnapper could simply let his hostages go? "Sit down, Pulari," he said, "or I'll have someone shoot your kneecap out and make you."

Chapter S.15

The secret passage to the dining room came from the music room above it. Hellen tried the walk n talk again when she and Cary made it to the library. "Zola," she said in a low voice, and "Zola!" more urgently.

No reply. This was bad, not just if something happened to them, but she desperately needed some commotion if she was going to fire. Otherwise, one shot would send everyone running for cover, and she'd be lucky to kill anything before Dagge's soldiers swarmed through the wall like termites. "We need those fireworks, Cary." She turned and stood in front of him, hating to send him out, but she didn't know what else to do.

"I'll go, I can do it," he agreed immediately.

Talk about earning a gold star. She suddenly felt so grateful for him. "Don't wait," she told him. "Pull the wagon around to the greenhouse and set them off, all of them. I'll wait for you, okay?"

"Trust me," he said, and stole back through the door to the hall.

Hellen went the other way, into the music room. Hellen unclipped her night glasses from her belt and put them on. Excellent. She navigated the furniture, went around the bookcase and located the lever release for the concealed door. It swung open silently, and she stepped into the dark hole.

Around the corner, the staircase down to the dining room was long, narrow, and straight—easy going in her soft black shoes. At the bottom, a hidden space about three feet wide lined the entire back wall of the dining room. Tiny beams of light streamed into it from mesh-covered spyholes built into the fat king painting that graced the other side. Those clever monks.

A unified scream/gasp/groan stopped Hellen's heart for a moment. She pushed her night glasses up on her head and put her eye to a spyhole. Less than twenty feet in front of her, she saw a portly woman in yellow lean to the side of her chair, and heave the entirety of her dinner onto the floor.

It was Queen Nylah, next to Dagge, who must be in the middle, blocked by two soldiers who stood behind him. At the left end of their table, Mapo had Ming clasped to him, and she was crying. *What the...?* Hellen's eye scanned the room until she found the problem. At the far end of the left table, John Treslo was tearing a strip of skin from his own chest.

Hellen jerked away from the spyhole and felt her own gorge block her throat. She clenched her teeth and swallowed determinedly several times. It passed. Shaking her head, she reminded her stomach that it wasn't John, even if it did look like him. She didn't know where John was, but hopefully he wasn't still in there.

Chief's rifle had nearly a full mag, so she set down her rifle, checked to make sure his had stayed on single-shot, and peeked through the hole again. The screams and protests had died down, and only some scattered crying remained. Many guests, in their fine clothes, were spattered with blood and vomit. Guards stood at intervals around the table, guns ready, and Hellen could see quite a few bodies of servants sprawled on the floor between the tables and the walls.

Dagge's voice rang out, clear and strong and horridly gleeful. "Nicely done, Mr. Treslo! You see, there isn't anything he wouldn't do for me. Anything at all!"

Yeah, she was going to have to kill John. The sooner the better, and he would agree with her. Hellen moved down the wall to see if she could get a better bead on him. Something that didn't involve possibly shooting Mapo or Ming.

She also kept an eye on Dagge, to the extent she could see him. He sat in his chair and waved his hands in the air like he was giving a performance. Well, he was, wasn't he? If only she could shoot him now...but the soldiers and his chair blocked her shot, and if she tried anyway, she might not be able to shoot John. She needed to shoot John, for all their sakes. His included.

As she walked down the wall, she got a clearer view of John's mutilated body. He had cuts down his arms, and on his face, and the missing skin on his chest, and she didn't want to think about how bad it could get.

"Would anyone like to give it a try?" Dagge asked. *Unbelievable.*

"I've had enough of this." A woman in blue, down the table toward John, stood up and pushed her chair back. Older, hair graying, she had more gonads than most of them, apparently. "Overlord Dagge," she continued, ignoring the soldiers that moved toward her, "shoot me if you must, but I can't be a party to this any longer." The lady turned and stepped daintily over what was probably her puke, just catching the edge of it with her heel, because Hellen noticed she dragged it over the carpet as she walked toward the main door.

John stepped in front of her as she rounded the end of the table. She looked up at him for a moment, gauging him, then she tried to go around him. He blocked her again. She tried the other way, he blocked her again, and she gave up and turned to Dagge. "Is there any end to this game you're playing?"

"Oh, there's an end," Dagge snapped abruptly. "There's quite an end." A long pause hung heavy in the air, and Hellen could feel the tension rise even higher, if that was possible.

Pulari stood up, pulled Nylah up by the arm and announced to everyone, "I say let's all leave. What's he going to do, kill every one of us? He'd have four wars on his hands. Even he can't want that." He hauled his red-faced queen up out of her chair and away from the table. Everyone else watched.

When the guards closed around them, Pulari made to swipe them away with one arm, but one of the soldiers grabbed the arm and swung it behind his back, trapping him in a mercy hold. Nylah squealed, clapped a hand over her mouth and looked back at Dagge, terrified.

Dagge got to his feet, leaned forward on the table, and watched like a frustrated parent. Once the monarch was painfully detained, he left the table, sauntered over to the two of them, and put his arm around the blubbering queen. "Nylah," he said gently, "I thought we had an understanding." He tucked a stray lock of hair behind her ear and wiped the tears from her cheek. "You betray your husband, and I get his crown."

Pulari renewed his fight with a passion. "You sick, evil…! Let me go!" he shouted hoarsely at the guy breaking his arm. "*Let me go!*" The soldier wrenched his arm higher and Pulari cried out in pain. His struggle went down several notches and his breathing was heavy, and he looked at Nylah like she was a vile thing.

"Oh, it's true." Dagge grinned, looking back and forth between them perkily. "Isn't it, cupcake?" He tweaked Nylah's cheek and set off a fresh flow of tears. "I'll be cleaning house in Pulari tomorrow!" He laughed and slapped Nylah on the back, and in a surprise move, she attacked him, fingernails first.

Unprepared, he got a bloody scratch before he caught her hands and pried them away from his face. Several guards came running and pulled her away, but she gave them some hell first. She ducked out of their reach, stomped on several insteps, and pulled some hair before they got her under control.

Dagge put his fingers gingerly to his face. "I wish you hadn't done that, Nylah," he scolded, "and you're going to wish that, too."

"Overlord!" Queen Eladora interjected, her voice a convincing blend of isn't-this-fun and you're-one-of-us. "Surely you can forgive a woman's passion." She looked around the company for support. "We all know you hold the cards here, is there really any need for further demonstration? I daresay you've made your point already."

He smiled dangerously at Nylah and walked back toward the end table. "Well, my dear," he said as he bowed with a flourish, "if you think I've made my point, why don't you tell me what it is?"

Eladora stuttered a smile and looked confused. "Isn't it just that? That we are at your mercy? What could be more important than that?"

Dagge chuckled lightly and strolled down the table in her direction. "That is so typical of you spoiled, self-centered, self-important bigshot rulers. Everything has to be about you. Have you, any of you, stopped to think what this might mean for your countries?"

"Of course we've thought about it, you idiot," one of the military types finally spoke up.

"Gosh, General Weakling, I don't think I was speaking to you." Dagge rounded on him. "Unless you think you run your country, which you might, now that I think of it."

"What's your point, then, sir?" Wan tossed in neutrally. "If you think we are all so stupid that we don't get it?"

"What do you think it is, Professor?" Dagge tossed the ball back.

Wan gazed steadily at Dagge for a few seconds, and then he replied, "I think you are waiting for something."

Chapter S.16

David watched the two soldiers, on their knees and gun barrels in their faces, try to answer questions to the satisfaction of the hard-ass officer standing in front of them. They were failing epically. He wished he could do something, but he was herded over to the side of the stable with the rest of the servants, and had several guns to contend with himself.

"I've never seen you before." The officer took several steps toward them and bent down to their eye level. "You must be spies." The man opened his mouth to speak, but the officer stopped him. "Do you know what happens to spies in this army?" Neither of them said or did anything then, they just knelt there, eyes ahead.

Beyond them, David had seen another soldier run into the stable through the wide-open doorway and stop when he realized what was happening. That soldier ducked off to the left, and showed up again between a couple of the wagons. David recognized him, he was Junika's friend at the dungeon door, Cary. As he made his way down the aisle, hidden from the soldiers by the load, he watched the drama for a few seconds and raised his gun. What was he going to do, shoot the officer? Bad plan, unless he wanted all the furies of hell on his ass.

In a quick glance around, Cary's eyes met David's, and David shook his head minutely at him.

"In this army," the officer said, "spies get executed. Unless they can make a deal."

Cary studied David for a moment, pointed at him, pointed at the load in the wagon, then over his shoulder toward the palace.

"Unfortunately for you, we don't have time for deals." The officer nodded at the soldiers flanking him and they unceremoniously shot the two dead.

Screams and confusion surrounded David as the servants scrambled, trying to flee with nowhere to go, shoved back by men with guns, pressing themselves against the tack, getting as far away as they could from the execution. In the chaos, David lost sight of Cary for a few seconds, and when he could see where Cary had been, he was gone.

Seconds later, gunfire outside stopped everything. The surprised officer rushed the troops out the doors, and seconds after that the stable became civilian again. Not normal, mind you, but not the inquisition either. Several servants stepped forward and surrounded the bodies of the two soldiers. Putting hands under arms and legs and torsos, they carried them out the back. David would have helped them, but he had something else to do.

Obviously, Cary wanted him to take the wagon out, which sucked because that was how the other two got caught. Still, it must be important, and since they weren't killing servants (yet), maybe he could fake his way through it. David walked over to the wagon and climbed up to the bench behind the team like it was his job.

No one tried to stop him. He didn't know what happened to the laughing guys who sat in the back of the wagon earlier, but he didn't really want to know. All he wanted was to figure out how to drive this thing, and get it where it needed to go.

David picked up the reins and clucked his tongue, and the wagon started moving forward just like it was supposed to. Maybe he could survive this.

Chapter S.17

Many of the guests were bordering on hysteria. All right, past bordering. Some of them had gotten all the way there.

Dagge leaned back in his fancy chair and sipped his tea. His table sat empty now except for him. How insulting. But it did give him a better view of the many little dramas playing out around the room. No theater could be better. He grinned and blew.

Professor Wan and Culture Minister Tsing sat with Mapo and Ming, all of them whispering like little mice. Ming got a bit panicky once, but Mapo said something that straightened her right up, and they'd been "handling it" ever since. Recently, they were joined by the other couple they brought, the Chaos, of whom Madame Chao was at the smart table, and she had to wave at her unfortunately stupid husband to get him to come over there. At first it was fun to see how often the man's eyes flitted over to look at the evil, scary Overlord, but it got old and Dagge had to put the quell on that.

Both arm candies were relentlessly hysterical, over on the dumb side of the room. Bloodstone, Eladora's advisor, got tired of trying to comfort them and having no luck, so he sat and watched his Queen and her companion huddle behind Senator Bunch. General Weeks, on the arm candies' other side, sat next to Arburash and they both tried very hard to ignore the wails and sobs.

Senator Bunch remained in her smart chair and eavesdropped on Wan and the others. Whatever use she had for her own Prime Minister, or his general, had dropped to zero. Proof she really was smart. She could probably speak Shindoan, too, and if that group was any kind of threat, he might think he should keep an eye on them. But they weren't.

Pulari and Nylah hung out on the dumb side of the room without even realizing it. So perfect. Nylah shot him dirty looks periodically, and that was far more fun than having her next to him. General Hatch, and their Foreign Minister, Terlaine, joined them, accompanied by several extra guards, thank you very much. Couldn't let that group get any big ideas.

The valets, tasters, boot lickers and what not had all been removed to the stable. Some ballsy ones wanted to resist and had to be removed permanently. Hence the hysteria.

Dagge set his cup down, pushed his chair back and stood up. Free time was over. "Ladies and gentlemen," he said in his best host voice, "you're all probably wondering why I've kept you here."

Pulari couldn't resist. "Dagge!" He advanced toward the table and proceeded to shout. "I demand you release us immediately! There will be no mercy for you otherwise, and only a fool would put himself in that position."

Dagge smiled languidly and faced him. "I assure you I'm not a fool," he responded calmly, "and I'm equally certain you are."

Pulari picked up a goblet and threw it at him. Nearly hit him, too. Dagge laughed as he straightened up from a duck. "Whoa-ho, Your Majesty! Who knew you had an arm?" He waved his guards away, tugged his clothes back into place and slowly made his way around the table toward Pulari. The arm candy screamed and fled to the sidelines, and the assorted men tried to look casual while they edged toward the door.

"I know you don't appreciate the gravity of your situation, sir. You couldn't possibly, because you don't know what it is." Pulari picked up a wine glass and threw it at him. Dagge ducked again, but this time he didn't think it was funny. "You're trying my patience," he said.

Another wine glass came flying at him. "You sick..." then a plate, "vicious..." and a goblet, "cheap..." and a salt cellar or something, and Dagge was knocking things out of the air with his arm while he rushed the bellowing idiot, fully intending to wring the life out of his flabby neck. *Cheap?*

But Nylah surprised him again. She *roared*—a massive, gutteral, bloodcurdling war cry— and ran at him, jumping on his back, hooking her left arm around his neck, pulling his hair, and clawing at his eyes with her other hand. Stunned, he grasped her hands and threw her over his shoulder onto her back at his feet. By that time, his guards had contained her husband, and Dagge was able to look down on the heaving woman at his leisure.

"Nylah, Nylah." He tsked, shaking his head slowly, still holding her hands. "All that feistiness! Did Old Graniteface love that about you? Huh? Or did he get tired of it? Is that why you don't talk anymore?" He pinched her cheek, too hard, and she cried and struggled, and Pulari struggled, too.

"Dagge!" He strained to speak through the grip around his neck. "Just get it over! Whatever you're going to do, just get it over!"

Dagge released Nylah's hands, stood up, smoothed his hair, and nodded to a guard to take her. He turned away from Pulari and addressed the room. "You forget, Your Majesty, I'm waiting for something. Right, Professor Wan?" The professor didn't answer. "But what am I waiting for?" Dagge teased them. "No one ever guessed."

Queen Eladora said with a strained little laugh, "You're not catching us at our best, Overlord Dagge. If you want to play games, your party planning leaves something to be desired."

"Ah, Eladora, ever the diplomat. It's so easy to see why your people love you." He bowed graciously to her, easing his way around the bottom of the table, enjoying the invisible wave that seemed to push everyone slightly more away from him as he went. "Perhaps you're right," he allowed. "Perhaps I haven't created the best environment for a game." He sauntered up the middle of the "U," pursing his lips, pretending to think.

A knock at the door stopped him, and he turned around to watch one of the guards open it. In a moment, the soldier turned toward Dagge and said, "They're here."

"Let them in." Dagge smiled, and the soldier stepped back and swung the door wide.

****

From behind the painting, Hellen watched fourteen ragged, bloody, gray-tinged soldiers file into the dining room to absolute silence from the spectators. They lined up in two rows facing the tables, and stood there quietly with their guns in their arms. She brought Chief's gun up and sighted: head wounds…neck wounds…this had to be them. Elbow to the wall, she braced herself and prayed she'd be a good enough shot.

"I'd like to introduce you all to my new army," Dagge said, like a bragging parent, parading back and forth in front of the soldiers, waving his arm grandly. "Aren't they wonderful? I'm so proud!" he gushed.

"What's wrong with them?" one of the military-types demanded.

"General Hatch…" Dagge stopped parading and reprimanded him. "Is that any way to greet your new personality?" Hellen's breath caught. *Holy cow, he can't be serious.*

Hatch paused and looked confused for a second. "What are you talking about?" he barked. "These soldiers have nothing to do with me."

"Oh, General…" Dagge smiled indulgently. "Don't be so sure. General Wharton!"

"Yes, sir!" Wharton stepped forward from his position by the door.

"You have performed your duties admirably, and I'd like to honor you with first choice."

"Wait a minute, Dagge!" Arburash blustered. "What… what… what are you doing? These soldiers don't belong in here. This is a party!"

"It *is* a party," Dagge agreed, "and these are my special guests, very much like Mr. Treslo here." He walked over to John and put his arm around him. "You don't want to offend my special guests, do you?"

"Overlord," Eladora said with all the indulgence of speaking to a child. "Perhaps you could explain to us what you want."

"What I want?" Dagge looked surprised, like that thought had never occurred to him.

"You must want something." Eladora stepped toward him conversationally. "You have us all hostage for a reason, right?"

Dagge cocked his head to the side and looked at her. "I would think an intelligent woman would be able to figure that out. Senator Bunch, perhaps you would do the honors."

The gray-haired lady hadn't taken her eyes off the soldiers since they came in. Until now. She looked up at Dagge from her place at the table and said, "If I had to guess, I'd say these soldiers are here to do the same thing to us that they did to that unfortunate man." She gestured to John.

"Bravo, Senator! You are truly a credit to your country." He bowed to her with a flourish, stood and turned to include all the guests with his wide-open arms. "The only question is, which ten of you shall I choose?"

Chapter 5.18

Happily, there were no dead bodies or trigger-happy soldiers between the stable and the kitchen. Only a crowd of rubberneckers milled around outside the patio, peering up at the roof. When David pulled up, a lady who seemed to be in charge was shooing everyone back inside like a worried mother hen. Possibly she could be Cookie. In the dark it was hard to be sure, but she looked like the woman he met a few times when he was a kid.

Only one way to find out. "Cookie!" he said loudly.

The lady turned around, took one look at the wagon, and said, "What are you doing with those fireworks here? They don't belong here, take them around to the front and set them off there."

So that was why they wanted this wagon—the fireworks. A distraction, perhaps, so not very likely they'd want them inside the palace. Although that might be more effective.

Two legs dropped down from the patio roof onto the seat beside him, interrupting his train of thought. David looked up and saw the rest of Cary, head at the top frowning down. "Come on, kid," the head said, "around to the greenhouse." He jumped down into the back of the wagon and pointed. "That way."

"I know where the greenhouse is," David grumbled under his breath, but he clucked the horses forward and drove them toward the west side.

"Are you a grandmother? Get a move on!"

David snapped the reins and urged the horses faster. Standing, he drove them around the corner, pulled up and looped the reins before he hopped out.

Cary stood in the back, throwing the tarp off the party explosives. "You've got to be David. Can you run? Fast?"

"Yeah, I think so," David answered. "Fast enough."

"Then head for the kitchen when I say." Cary located a flame in his pocket, and handed one to David, too. "Or the stable might be better, if you can make it. Come around to the back and you can light them from that end."

The guy was a little bossy, but seemed to know what he was doing. Fortunately, David had taken enough orders from his mom and dad, he could handle bossy, and he hurried around to the back of the wagon. All the fuses were bundled, which was smart. David only had to light five and half the wagon would go up. Cary worked the other half, still standing in the wagon, and already one of his bundles sparked and hissed with fire.

Flashes of blue streaked past David before he could finish. Laser gunfire coming from the north side. Cary turned and glanced over his shoulder. "Damn! Run!" he ordered. "Go NOW!" In one fluid move, he swung around, pulled the rifle off his back, and started firing.

David couldn't see how close the soldiers were, but he had one more fuse to light, and he couldn't just leave it. He ignored the flashes, and the shouting, and the screaming rearing horses jerking the wagon around, and he put the fire to that final fuse just in time to look up and see Cary get hit.

Knocked backward, he landed with his shoulders in David's reach. David pushed the fireworks aside and leaned in to grab Cary by his collar. The fuses were nearly gone, and he didn't know if it was adrenaline or wood chopping, but Cary came sliding out of that wagon like he was greased with butter.

Once David had him in his arms, there was only one thing he had time to do. He dove them under the wagon.

Chapter S.19

No other dinner party in the history of the world could compare with this one, he was sure. Dagge took a moment to revel in the historical significance of it. How many people could say they changed the world while they were alive? Only the great ones.

Feeling magnanimous, he allowed the guests to flee and shout and scream all they wanted. It wouldn't help them, but it wouldn't hurt, either. Nothing they did could make any difference now.

Eladora was fighting like a wildcat, though. It took three guards to hold her. Her companion, Rabinette, lay unconscious on the floor. She'd tried to save the queen, he had to give her props for that. Ballsy woman.

Once the guards got Eladora's hands and feet immobilized, it made her struggles more manageable and they were able to carry her to the front of the room. She did start trying to bite, but one of them held her under the chin, too, and all she could do then was screech in a most unladylike way. "You're crazy! You're crazy! You're crazy…" She tapered off, then started whimpering and thrashing again as the guards set her on her feet by the first soldier.

"SOMEBODY HELP ME!" she screamed, but no one moved. It struck Dagge as peculiar, almost like they were paralyzed. No screaming or crying, no sound at all came from the guests. They all stood or sat motionless, watching in horrified fascination.

Five or so feet away from Eladora, the soldier turned slowly toward his target. Something flickered in his eyes, flashes of purple light that grew stronger as he focused his attention on her. In a moment, sharp stabs of magenta began to jump out of him at odd angles, one after the other: reaching, pulling back, reaching, pulling back. All three guards holding Eladora cringed and tried to hide behind her. Eladora herself stalled in gape-mouthed terror. Moaning, eyes wide and rolling, her entire body strained to be anywhere but there.

After an agony of suspense, the creature thrusting toward the helpless woman finally touched her. It stretched and crackled across the space between them, searing the air and slicing into the soft flesh. Eladora screamed, her body went rigid as the thing impaled her. She gasped and gurgled as it filled her up, and its old host body fell down dead.

All eyes were on Eladora. The magenta light stuck out in points around her, twitching with static, adapting and adjusting, changing its shape until it fit smoothly within the new parameters. When it was done, it relaxed, held its head up and Eladora stood, a passable imitation of herself.

Dagge watched it, mesmerized. So simple, really. He clapped his hands together in satisfaction. "Wonderful! Who's next?"

The resulting melee grew into high entertainment. People in fancy clothes running away from guards, running into guards, falling on the floor apoplectic. Oodles of screaming and panic. It reminded him of something. What did they call it? A pig scramble? Dagge had to laugh out loud, especially when Madame Chao came running at him with a fork. He stopped her, caught her hand, and wrenched the fork out of it. The woman was surprisingly strong, and fought like crazy. She probably *was* crazy. Fear could do that.

Pops of gunfire erupted outside and brought him up short. All the foreign entourage soldiers should be dead by now, so gunfire meant trouble. He clipped Madame Chao in the temple and sent her to the floor. No time for that. Around the table, through the captured guests, he ran to the main dining room door, which he flung open. Louder here. Not gunfire, though. Explosions.

He was going to have to talk to Hellen about her timing.

Then behind him, a bullet gun did fire. Dagge ducked reflexively. *Damn!* He dashed back to the line of soldiers. Crouched behind them, he roved his eyes over the room, examining faces and weapons. Where was she? Seeing nothing, he steered left and aimed toward Wharton, keeping his body blocked by his indestructible army.

Another shot. At the end of the row, he shoved the last two soldiers ahead of him, using them as a shield. He refused to die today.

Screams and shouts started around the room again, loud and strident, driving into his brain so he couldn't think, pissing him off so that he wished he could just open fire on all of them. In the uproar, another shot. He pushed his inhuman shield past the end of the table toward where Wharton had Pulari in a mercy hold, but when he saw them, they weren't looking at him, their eyes were on the front of the room.

Another shot. Dagge glanced back at the soldiers, still lined up obediently, surrounded by empty space. Magenta flashes jumped around several of them, but it was Eladora who crumpled to the floor, a red stain spreading across her chest.

And then he got it. Hellen wasn't aiming at him at all.

"TEAR THIS ROOM APART!"

****

Sighting the next one, Hellen was just about to squeeze the trigger when something blocked her. Around the scope, through the jagged little hole made by the bullets, she could see John Treslo's face, long gray hair swinging down his bloody cheeks, eyes boring into the hole with malice.

She couldn't fire. As much as she needed to, her hand could not do it. Even when his fingers jammed into the hole, and started tearing the painting away, she still could not shoot him. Instead, she backed away, tripped over the other gun, and scrambled to the stairs.

John ripped a long flap out of the painting, then another one, and another, and his tall body squeezed through the hole, eyes sparking, looking for her in the dimness. Forcing her eyes away from John and up the stairs, Hellen begged her legs to move her. Every step seemed heavy, dragging her upward, ears straining to hear over the blood pounding in her head. Had he seen her? Was he behind her?

She had to look. John climbed calmly behind her, watching her, eating the distance two stairs at a time. If she threw the gun at him, it would free her arm, slow him down, but she needed the gun, needed to shoot him, what was she going to tell Roberta? *I had to, Roberta, I had to.*

His hand grazed her ankle. Panic shot through her and she tripped over the next step, falling onto her hands and knees, gun clattering against the stone. That moment was all it took and he had her; his big hand closed around her ankle in a crushing grip.

Hellen turned onto her hip and put the gun up between them. John's head was right there, face striped with cuts, eyes flashing purple fire. Still, she hesitated. *It's John it's John how can this be happening?*

Fear and grief squeezed her. She tried to jerk her ankle free, but he wouldn't release it, so she kicked the other foot at his face. It smacked into his hand, caught before she even saw him move. His fingers closed around the tiny bones like a vise, until it hurt even through her shoe. And he smiled…a dreadful cold smile that pierced her heart and felt like ice.

Suddenly it didn't look like John anymore. Hellen saw the thing it was, and it sickened her.

She brought the gun up and fired.

Chapter S.20

The horses bolted as soon as the fireworks started going off. Luckily, they ran north, right into the soldiers, so that gave David a little time to drag Cary into the flower bed and hide behind a bush.

Stopped for second, he checked to see where the crazy idiot was hit and found a gut wound, mostly over to the side, which thanks to the laser wasn't bleeding too bad. "Why didn't you duck?"

"I couldn't run," Cary said.

It didn't answer his question, but David went with it. "Can you run now?"

Cary looked up at him. "Yeah, I can run," he said, "but not too fast."

"Crybaby," David jabbed, and hauled him to his feet.

With Cary's arm hanging on to David's shoulders, they dodged and wove through the plants and statues, and made it almost to the palace wall before the soldiers got too close for them to keep from being seen. David let Cary down behind a big juniper and peeked over the top to watch the torch lights play over the beds they had just left.

Squatting, he peered through the surrounding darkness for an escape route. The greenhouse door was roughly twenty feet away. If they timed it right, they could make a run for it when the guards' view would be blocked by the water-toting nymph. If the door was locked, they could try for the kitchen, but David really hoped they wouldn't have to.

He checked the soldiers' progress…it was time. "Can you walk on your own?" he whispered.

"Yeah. Where are we going?"

"To the greenhouse," David said.

"Are you kidding? *Into* the palace?"

"Don't argue," David scolded. "It's that or more pretty holes in your uniform." Hunched over, he led the way, keeping as much stuff between them and the guards as possible until they only had five uncovered feet to the greenhouse door. Leaving Cary behind a big rock, David crawled over to test the knob. Unlocked. He gestured to Cary and the two of them hastened inside unseen.

Chapter S.21

Magenta shards began to flash around John's body, so Hellen had scant seconds to get far away from the secret passage unless she wanted to be the next tasty treat.

He still held her feet. When she twisted them free of his grasp, the motion set him off balance and knocked him over against the stone wall, but he didn't fall back down the steps, which was too damn bad.

Flipping to her stomach, she scurried up the narrow stairs, willing herself to make it into the music room before the monster could get her. After the gunshot, the soldiers who were about to come through that hole in the painting wouldn't be so lucky. She almost felt sorry for them.

Almost. Truthfully, she needed all the time she could get, and better one of them than her. By the time she reached the top of the stairs and rounded the corner, shouts were echoing up the staircase. As she felt along the wall for the lever, there were cries, and finally screams before she passed through the bookcase door.

Safe for the moment (*thank you, One*), she jammed the lever with a handy tambourine. It wouldn't stop them for long, but it should buy her a few minutes to get away. Which way? Obviously, she had to go back to the dining room. She couldn't let Dagge kill all those people, and take control of their countries with his scary undead. That had to be his plan, of course...to control the world. Didn't the monks say that?

Unfortunately, there weren't any vantage points as good as the one she'd just left, and Dagge would have soldiers combing the palace as well. Fortunately, she knew some things they didn't. The music room had another secret passage, down to the throne room. She could use the servants' hall from the back of the throne room to get to the subkitchen. The subkitchen had swinging doors that opened into the dining room, and the last time she saw Dagge's pet freaks, they were lined up right in front of them.

At least it was a plan. She crossed the room, opened the other bookcase, and passed through, closing the door behind her. About halfway down the steps, lights came on in the throne room: several spyholes lighted up like mini-searchlights shining across the narrow passage. It made her wonder if maybe the monks weren't a teensy bit paranoid…but in a good way.

She put her eye in one of the beams and looked down into the nearly empty room. Two soldiers walked through the middle of it, heads swiveling, looking at nothing but a few skinny tables set against the walls.

"I'm going to look back here," one said, and disappeared in the direction of the throne.

"A'right," the other one said. "I'll wait for ya, right here in this chair."

"Don't be an idiot," the first guy called back, but the second guy only giggled idiotically.

Hellen flew silently down the remainder of the steps and cracked open the door to the King's backstage prep room. The soldier appeared, walked directly to the camouflaged servants' door and felt around the moulding for the latch. When he found it, he opened the door and turned to check behind him before he exited.

It was David.

Fifteen questions popped like firecrackers in Hellen's mind, but she didn't have time for any of them. She left the secret passage and zipped through the room in hot pursuit, until she tripped on the rug, stumbled over a chair, and nearly hit the wall. Thankfully, she salvaged it. The throne-sitter's voice whined around the corner. "Hey, hurry up!" She ignored him and made it out the door.

The servants' hall was dark, but the subkitchen lights were on, so she could see David creeping down the hall, framed by the glowing doorway. Loud voices and banging sounds were reaching her, so she had cover to whisper David's name when she got close.

"David!"

He turned, surprised. She gestured him into the adjoining hall between the throne room and the dining room. At the other end of that hall there was a door to the ballroom, but all the doors were camouflaged, so she felt pretty safe.

"What are you doing here?" she demanded, as soon as he joined her.

"I'm going to find Dagge."

"Where's Cary? Why are you wearing his uniform?"

"I left him in the greenhouse. He got shot. A bunch of soldiers came running at us from the front."

"How many?" she asked.

"I don't know," he answered testily. "I was a little busy ducking."

She shelved it. "What are you going to do with that?" She pointed to his gun.

"I'm going to kill him."

"No." She tried to take the gun from him, but he wouldn't let her have it. "Give me the gun."

"I don't think so."

"I'm trying to help you." She gritted her teeth.

"Then help me get a bead on him." He gritted back.

Hellen closed her eyes for a moment, shaking her head to herself. Roberta would never forgive her if she let David kill Dagge. She pulled her patience card out. "You don't want that kind of blood on your hands, David. Not as young as you are, and not if you don't have to."

"We have to," he said, his voice low and angry. His eyes held hers and wouldn't let them go. "We have to save this kingdom."

"*I* have to, David. This is *my* job."

"This *job*, Junika, is big enough for both of us."

She wanted to argue, truly, but she couldn't find a single thought in the three spare seconds she had to give it. "Fine, but you do what I tell you. Are you a good shot?"

"Not bad."

Kind of vague, as answers went, but what was she going to do? She jerked her head toward the dining room. "I need you to help me shoot as many of Dagge's pet soldiers as we can. He's using them to seize control of the neighboring countries, and we have to try and save those people, for all our sakes."

David was quiet for several seconds. The big lead weight of his father hung between them, but he didn't ask. Instead, he said, "So what do we do? I saw you shoot that thing in the dungeon a hundred times, and that didn't kill it."

"You have to get it right in the heart." She peered around the corner to the now-quiet kitchen. "I don't think it works to chop its head off."

"Fantastic," David muttered.

"The last time I saw them," she pulled back and faced David again, checking the rounds in Chief's mag (there were plenty), "they were lined up in the front of the room, close to the main doors and the kitchen doors. I was going to shoot from the kitchen because of the cover, but really that angle sucks, and now the lights are blazing, too."

"The main doors would be better."

"Oh yes, and I'm sure I could just say 'excuse me' to the guards and they'd let me through."

"They wouldn't have to know. I can cut the power. It'll be dark, and they aren't carrying their night glasses."

"You can do that?"

"Dad taught me everything about this place," he answered. "He has like fifteen blueprints." He pulled Cary's night glasses off his belt and mounted them on his head. "See you in a minute," he said, and jogged off around the corner toward the dark end of the hall.

Chapter S.22

Of course the shooter had to be Hellen, who else would have that kind of information? Secret passageways and hidden rooms and cleverly disguised peepholes. Dagge shoved another grape in his mouth.

Elbows on knees, he chewed. The sharp edge of the chair-back dug into his flanks, but he didn't care. A little pain seemed like good penance for getting sloppy.

His new position at the front of the room helped him keep an eye on everything: the distraught guests, the destruction of the fat king painting, and all the doors except the main doors. The main doors, at his back, were blocked by the only people he knew he could trust. If you could call them people.

Eladora and the three others lay where they fell. He couldn't get replacements to them fast enough, and the three soldiers had died quicker than she did. It upset him. Losing Treslo was bad, too—that brain would have been highly useful. *Hellen, Hellen.*

Another grape went in and he bit through the skin, feeling and tasting the sweet juice explode in his mouth. She'd be back, too, they wouldn't find her. He should have kept all his soldiers around the palace instead of sending so many to the border. Bad tactical move on his part; he *knew* better. Damned hard to think clearly when she pissed him off so much.

But he was thinking clearly now. He dropped the rest of the grapes into the seat of the chair and climbed down. "May I have everyone's attention?" His voice rose easily over the subdued noise. His guests were re-seated in their places at the tables, minus Mr. Chao, who stubbornly tried to protect his wife and had to be shot.

All eyes turned to him, except the soldiers' aiming their guns, who were under strict orders to keep their eyes on the guests, and shoot anyone else who gave them trouble.

"I'm afraid we're in a bit of a hurry now." It pleased him to be polite.

"You can't be serious about this, Dagge," Pulari spoke up *again*. Didn't he know it was rude to interrupt?

"Your Majesty," Dagge's patience was less than thin, but he was about to solve the problem. "You can be first."

Nylah startled, pushed her chair back, and grabbed the edge of the table with her hands. The soldier in front of her put the barrel of his gun right in her face. She looked at her husband next to her, her face crumpled, and a high slow whine escaped her, making her sound like a leaking balloon.

"Nylah, please." Dagge would have thought this was funny if he wasn't so upset. "You're not helping."

"I don't want to help you!" she shouted, turning on him over the table, looking like she'd leap over it if there wasn't a gun in her way. "You are the most horrible, evil…" she floundered for words, "WORST possible human being I've ever met!"

Well, that was disappointing. She had a terrible vocabulary. Dagge walked up between the tables, took the gun from the soldier, aimed, and fired twice. The arm candies behind him screamed hysterically until he turned around and pointed the gun at them. One of them fell out of her chair, and the other clamped her hands over her mouth and muzzled herself.

Dagge looked back at his handiwork. Both of Nylah's eyes were wide, blackened holes, the skin around them charred and smoking, and still she sat there, mouth hanging open in shock. He handed the rifle back to the soldier, who trained it on the old, frozen monarch next to her.

Nylah's body slumped and fell sideways onto him. He recoiled, but caught her and laid her head in his lap. "Nylah?" he said.

"She's dead, Pulari, and you're next." He gestured to the soldier standing behind the table, who moved forward to take the old man's arm.

Abruptly, the palace went black.

Chapter S.23

Night glasses on, Hellen ran easily in the dark, through the subkitchen and into the servants' hub on the other side. From there, she could hear Cookie trying to calm the servants gathered in the kitchen. "It's all right! It's just the lights, they'll get them back on in a minute!" Hopefully it would be longer than that.

Hurrying through the hidden door into the main hall, she saw the guards were still at their posts outside the dining room. Possibly she could sneak past them, but when she opened the door they'd get her from behind, so they had to go. She unsheathed her knife.

Neither one heard her run up the hall toward them. Quick and silent, she thrust her blade up under the jaw and into the brain, first one and then the other. Both of them fell with hardly a sound, which was good because the dining room doors were open.

A line of backs was all she could see. That was fine with her, she sheathed her knife, stepped up close, and sighted.

Before she could fire, a hand reached over from beside the doorway, grabbed the barrel of the gun and jerked it out of her hands. The strap was around her neck, so she stumbled and fell into a waiting arm. It closed around her, and she looked up into Dagge's grinning face.

"I've been expecting you," he said.

Her left arm was still free. She took a swing at his head, but he blocked it with the gun, pulled the strap down around her arm and trapped it. He jammed the gun into the tight space between them and whisked the mask and night glasses off her head so she was as blind as the rest of them.

Then he wrapped her in both his arms, the gun sticking up between them like some obscene male fantasy. Effectively imprisoned, she remained motionless as he pressed her to him, his breath on her face.

"Hellen, I've missed you," he said softly.

Was he serious? Her fingers searched for the sheath strapped to her leg.

"I feel you looking for your knife."

"Just an itch."

"I know that itch." His voice got seductive. Holy cow.

"If you let me go, I can scratch mine, and then you won't have to worry about yours anymore."

He laughed quietly, in his throat, and shifted his weight a little so he rubbed up against her. It pissed her off that her body still responded to him. Cheap traitor.

"You know, I could kill you right here, right now, if I wanted to," he said.

"But then you wouldn't have the pleasure of my company." She matched the same soft tone he was using. "And we wouldn't be able to play these little games."

Squeezing her a little, he said, "You're such a worthy opponent." His voice practically glowed, like he felt responsible for her skill—which in a perverse way he was. He pressed her to him tighter, making it hard for her to breathe. "But I don't want to fight you." An earnestness crept into his voice that sounded to her like a turn for the worse.

"Then don't," she forced lightness. "Let me go, and I'll disappear and you'll never see me again."

Wrong thing to say. He got quiet for a few moments. "You're lying anyway," he answered. "You can't stop coming here. You can't quit trying to kill me."

"No, I can't," she agreed. Her fingers had found the knife, but she was having a hard time getting it out of the sheath. His arms squeezed her tighter.

"Don't make me hurt you," he said, caressing the words.

Loud and jarring, a harsh metallic crash shredded the air and whipped Dagge's face around toward the subkitchen, putting a tiny bit of space between them. As he turned, there was a solid *thunk* and something must have hit his head from the other side, because it knocked back into hers and loosened his grip. His arms still held her, but he staggered. She forced her knee up and slammed it into his groin, making him let her go.

A strong hand grabbed her arm and pulled her away from the row of burning purple eyes that started appearing on her other side.

****

Pain exploded in Dagge's groin, shot up to his reeling, throbbing head and out every nerve in his body. His knees buckled and he collapsed to the floor, where he lay unable to breathe, think, speak, or move, knowing she was getting away, but powerless to stop her.

****

David clutched the fabric of Junika's sleeve, and pulled her along down the hall, forcing her to run in absolute dark with nothing but trust to go by. At the hidden door he had to manhandle her a little to get her through. Her eyes were crazy wide, and she was taking tiny steps with her arms squeezed to her sides, trying to protect herself. All things considered, she coped pretty well.

The big guy and the woman and the short guy were in the servants' hub. "We blocked the door," the big guy said.

"It should slow them down a little." The woman looked like somebody's grandmother. How awesome.

"Luhe? Dessara?" Junika came in close, her hands reaching until she touched them.

Shouts and clangs started echoing in the subkitchen. No time for pleasantries. "Guys, we gotta get Cary." He herded them toward the greenhouse door. "This way, get low," he whispered, and opened the door to let them through.

Chapter S.24

Dagge pushed his voice through his closed throat. "Get the lights on!" it screaked. Pitiful. He tried again. "Get the lights on!" Better. He rolled over and raised his head. "Wharton!"

"Over here, sir," Wharton called, presumably from his post behind Pulari.

Dagge let his head drop back to the floor. The pounding in it was deafening. Sweat beaded on his upper lip, and his forehead, and his gut hurt. Rage shook inside him like an earthquake.

He took a few deep breaths and tried to dial it back some. Then he rolled over to his knees and swayed there with his head down.

"Help me up," he said in a hoarse whisper. He waved his arm in the air, latched onto an arm, and heaved himself off the floor.

The first thing he saw when he got up was a line of flashing purple eyes. They floated in front of him, looking at him, attached to nothing, getting smaller and smaller as the line receded away to the side. They were beautiful and eerie at the same time. It was mesmerizing.

He felt better already. "How many of the inside guard have returned from searching for the sniper?" he asked Wharton in a mostly normal voice.

"Most of them, sir."

"Surround this room with them." He stepped forward gingerly, testing. "I'll tear up the palace later."

The guests were restless, he could hear movement and murmuring, and he didn't like the way it sounded. It made him cranky. "Quiet!" he said in a passable imitation of a yell. "Everyone!" came out better, and he took a few hesitant steps toward the tables.

The hubbub died. "The next person to make a noise will be shot!" Kind of an outrageous claim in the dark, but they didn't know that. "Bring me a gun!" he tacked on for good measure.

Chapter S.25

Inside the greenhouse, David was able to take off the night glasses, and the warm glow of light made him wonder if it could already be dawn. Cary lay unconscious where David left him, under a raised planting bed by the door. Luhe pulled him out and tossed him over his big shoulders in a fireman's carry. "Which way?" he said.

"This way." A quiet voice carried over to them from the outside door. "I brought the wagon." David turned around and saw the silhouette of a slender young man who appeared to have a glowing orange orb on the top of his head.

Junika went to him immediately, prompting the others to follow. Craning her neck around his orb, she said, "The barracks are on fire, Diit! Did you do that?"

"Why yes!" he said brightly, and smiled at them all like it was the best thing ever. "No one said I couldn't, and the fireworks were just going to waste otherwise."

Junika moved him out of the way a bit so she could get by, and David followed. Outside, soldiers ran back and forth with buckets, dragged hoses across dead grass and through flaming tents, beat at the spreading flames with wet blankets, and in every way tried to contain the roaring fire. No one looked their way, or seemed to be curious about the two soldiers with the handful of servants who climbed into the waiting wagon and drove away.

"What about Dad?" David asked Junika as he settled himself on the sidewall across from her and gazed at the darkened castle.

Junika didn't answer, and David didn't ask again.

Chapter S.26

He found the chair he was sitting on earlier, leaned over the back of it for a minute and listened to Wharton giving orders. When it sounded like he was done Dagge called him. "Wharton!"

"Ready, sir."

"When the lights come on, flood the grounds. Notify the outdoor platoons, look for a woman and a man." Probably too late already, but he wouldn't assume. Hellen could get away, but would she?

No point in coming back, he got her gun and her night glasses. Of course, the man had them too. Another man. He wondered if he had anything to be jealous about.

The pain in his groin had finally faded. His head still hurt like a bitch—the guy nailed him pretty good with his gunstock. Dagge reached up and felt the bloody spot above his ear; he was going to have to get that asshole. Someday very soon.

Dagge turned around and gazed at the line of eyes radiating behind him. They hung there in the dark, blinking occasionally, all of them waiting patiently for his will. The beauty of it gave him chills.

Hellen could come back. And if she did, he wasn't going to screw up again. No more waiting, no more fun, the stakes were too high.

"Bring me Pulari!" he shouted.

Chapter S.27

Adia stood by herself against the wall of HQ, away from the crowd around Hellen, Luhe, John's son David and the others. Too many people there. The story had been long, with many chapters, and the grief around them all was thick. By the time the telling was over, every cell in her body shook.

Sick with it, she had to get away and breathe for a minute. Her hands kept running over her head, grabbing fistfuls of hair, and cupping her skull like she could keep the sanity inside that way. Was it working?

Guilt flayed her, exposed her as a fraud for all to see. How could she let them go in like that? Oh, she knew what they'd be up against, that Dagge wasn't just throwing a party, *and I tried to tell them, I did!* she argued in her own defense.

But she didn't try hard enough.

Adia leaned against the worktable, dropped her arms, and let her shoulders sag. Her mind stumbled, morose. How could this happen? Cary shot, Zola and Lan executed. And how could John be dead? They went in to save him, didn't they? *Didn't they?*

The grisly irony was that Hellen did save him, in the end. Whatever was left of him…the good man they all knew. Adia could hear Roberta clamping off her sobs while Hellen was talking. Other sobs around the room, too. Grievous for everyone.

And Chief…she couldn't believe it. Couldn't. Losing Chief was like losing her father all over again—brought all that pain right back in an agonizing implosion, heart turning to ash, falling onto her stomach and intestines and burning them.

She would never be whole again, would she? That's the way it is when you lose people you love. And still, even after everything else that had happened, these deaths, on her watch, would always be the thing that made her see the Resistance differently.

Now she had a job to do, and self-pity wasn't getting it done. Since she knew a thing or two about loss, it fell to her to carry the torch for these grieving people, to get them through the desperate darkness. This profane decimation would always be a part of them, would always be the thing that changed their fight. The Resistance had to move forward, but it had to have absolution first. A deep, shaky breath sucked into her lungs and raised her shoulders again. Her head came up and settled itself on her spine.

Adia walked back to the group. "I take full responsibility for what happened tonight."

"Adia, it wasn't your fault." Hellen's tired voice echoed in the depths of her lap.

"It *is* my fault," Adia rolled over her. "There were things I should have done that I didn't do. I sat here and let everyone else do the work because I was afraid. Afraid of failing, afraid of losing people. Afraid of being in the front, and leading." All the doubt and hardship of the last year and a half raised its ugly head as she confessed. "Because I'm blind." She paused. "And disfigured…and honestly, I couldn't see myself being Queen.

"It was selfish, staggeringly selfish, and I'm sorry." She turned to the person she had hurt the most. "Hellen, I owe you better than that." Guilt and grief and regret poured out of her, right into Hellen's arms, who got up out of the chair and embraced her. Her friend—her mother, really—Adia felt so grateful she was still alive.

When she could finally let Hellen go, she stood beside her, holding her hand, the other hand wiping away tears while she continued, "Hellen, you *do not* bear responsibility for John's death. Dagge does. John would have begged you to do exactly what you did, if he could have. We all know that."

Agreement hummed through the group. Hellen squeezed her hand.

"We're going to lose people," Adia said. "It's…devastating, I know." Her throat had to work a second to get the lump down. "But in this fight, it's a certainty." She hated to say that, hated the way it sounded, but it was true.

Adia pictured the people around her. Her tiny army. Her ragtag, misfit army. Any ordinary Joe you could meet on the street, all of them willing to die for what they loved.

They were amazing.

"We can't let this defeat us. We have to reach out, like John did. We have to find people who can bring their talents to this Resistance…and we have to win."

****

David watched the young woman on the other side of the circle, her dark hair wild, her face like some crazy painting. Even with all the grief and misery of the moment, in spite of loss that changed his life beyond recognition, he listened to what she said, and he couldn't tear his eyes away.

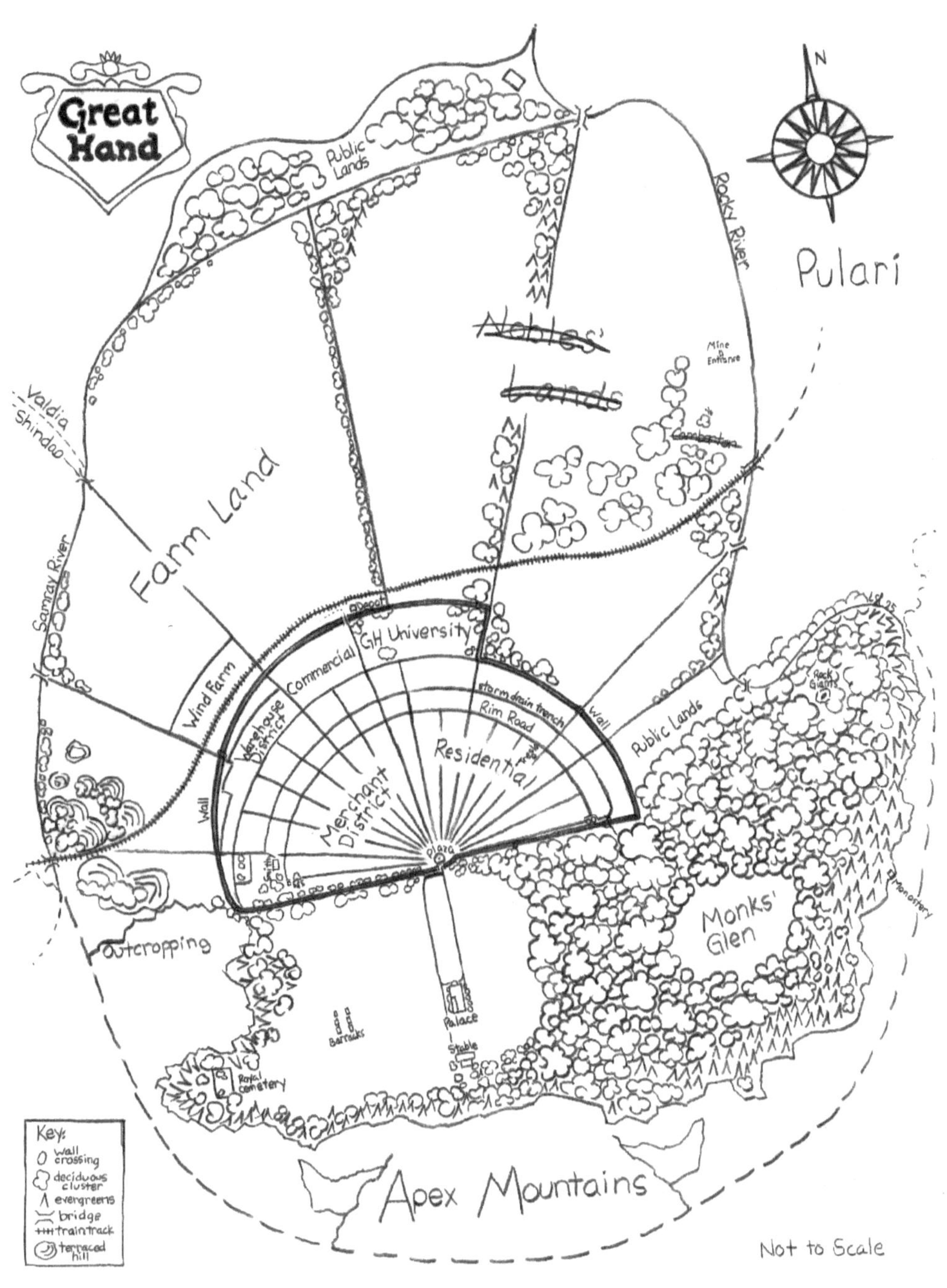

Great Hand
Pulari
N
Public Lands
Rocky River
Nobles' Lands
Mine Entrance
Cannbanton
Valdia
Shindoo
Farm Land
Samay River
Wind Farm
Warehouse District
Commercial
GH University
storm drain trench
Rim Road
Residential
Wall
Wall
Public Lands
Rock Giant
Monastery
Merchant District
plaza
Monks' Glen
Outcropping
Barracks
Palace
Stable
Royal Cemetery
Apex Mountains
Not to Scale
Key:
O wall crossing
deciduous cluster
evergreens
bridge
train track
terraced hill

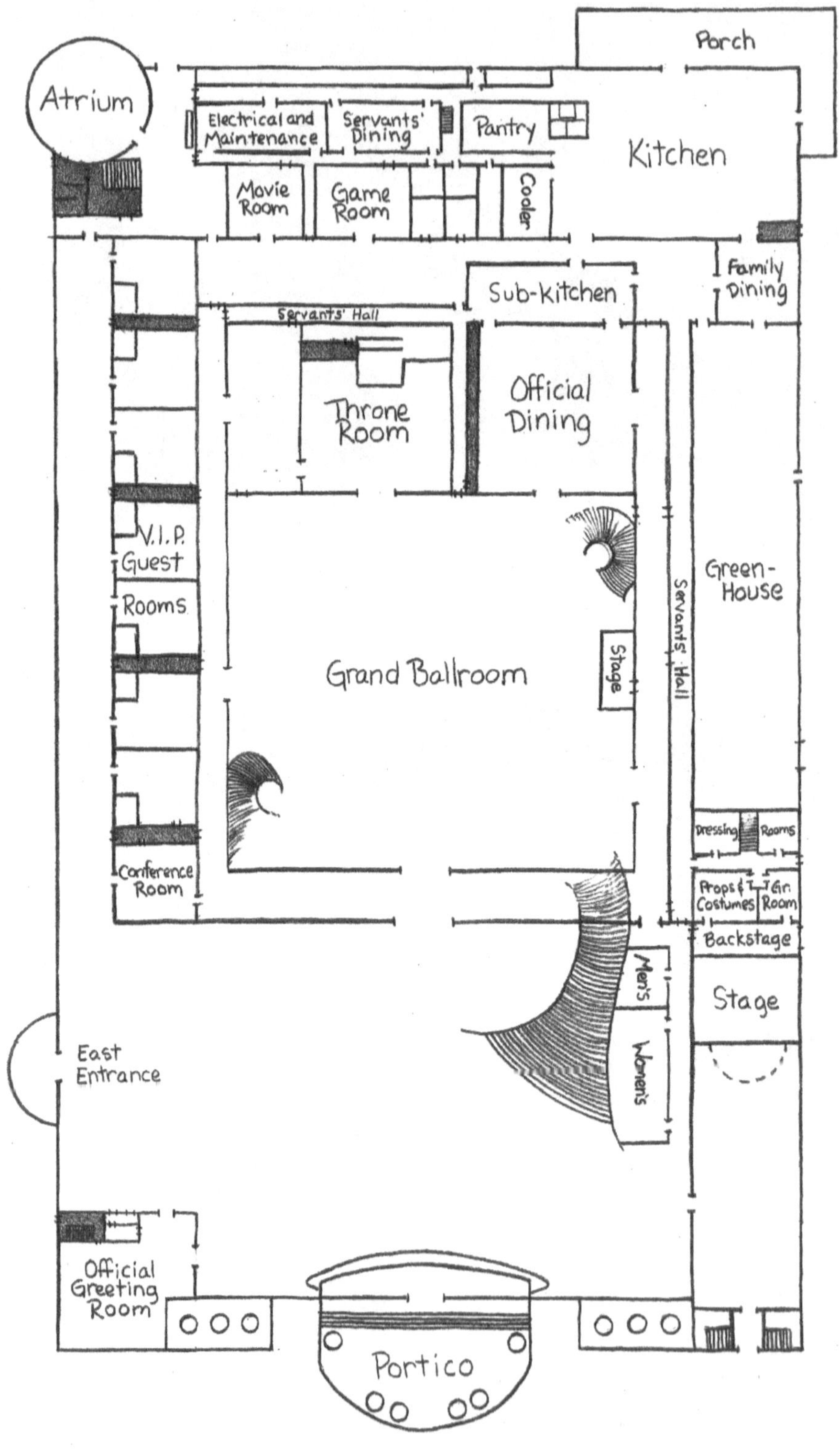

Atrium
Porch
Electrical and Maintenance
Servants' Dining
Pantry
Kitchen
Movie Room
Game Room
Cooler
Family Dining
Sub-kitchen
Servants' Hall
Throne Room
Official Dining
Green-House
V.I.P. Guest Rooms
Grand Ballroom
Stage
Servants' Hall
Dressing Rooms
Props & Costumes
Gir. Room
Backstage
Conference Room
Men's
Women's
Stage
East Entrance
Official Greeting Room
Portico

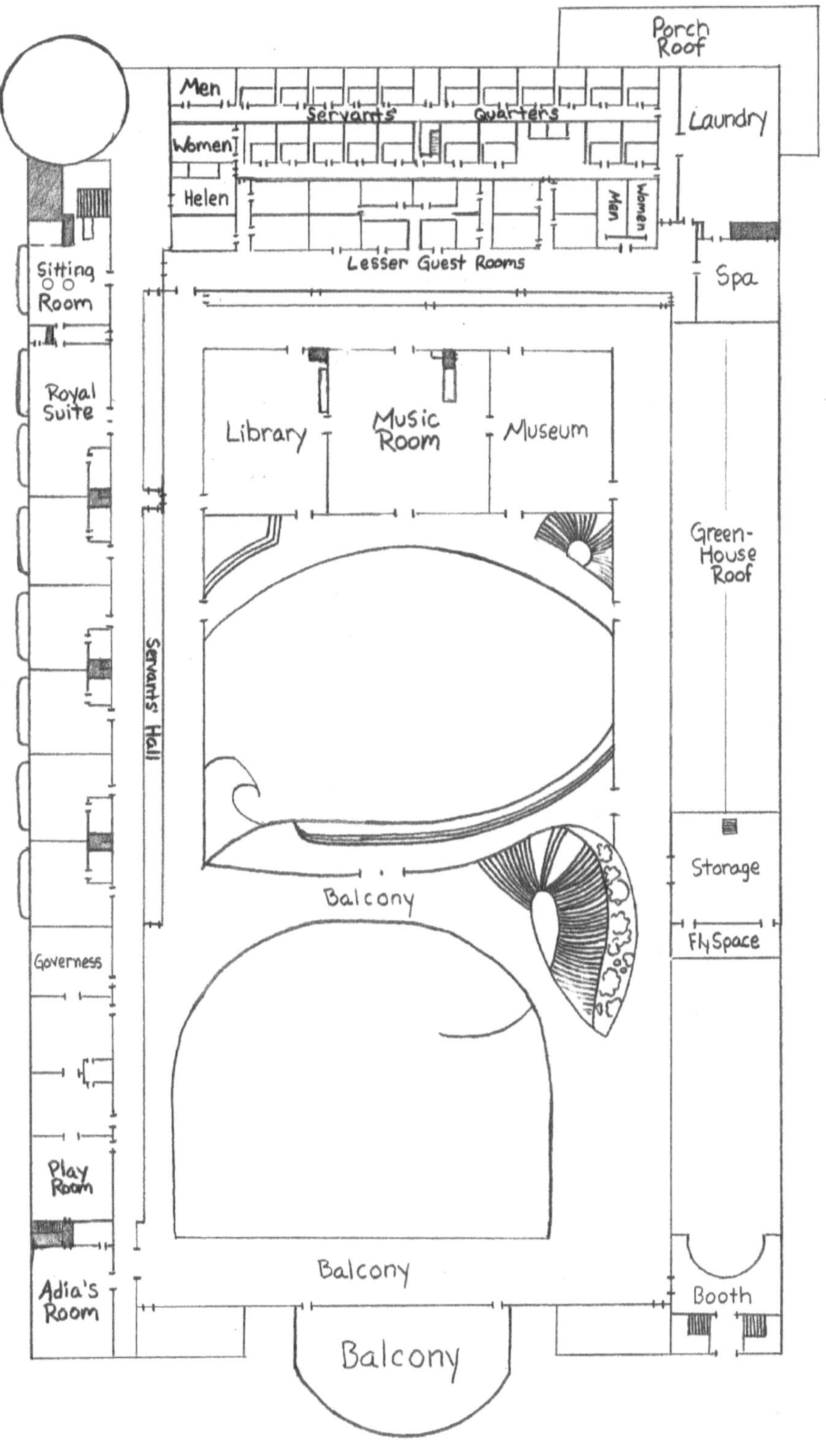

Porch Roof
Men
Servants' Quarters
Laundry
Women
Helen
Men
Women
Lesser Guest Rooms
Spa
Sitting Room
Royal Suite
Library
Music Room
Museum
Green-House Roof
Servants' Hall
Governess
Storage
Fly Space
Balcony
Play Room
Adia's Room
Balcony
Booth
Balcony

Acknowledgements

So much happened in this book, I had to turn to several people who have more expertise about certain things than I do. And let me just say that anything wrong or mistaken is because I didn't ask. I do sometimes think I know more than I actually know.

First, for the fighting (and I should have thanked him in Book 1 as well) I consulted John Barrett, an excellent martial arts and self-defense teacher whom I admire greatly. Thanks for all the help, John, I hope I didn't wear you out.

For miscellaneous rifle-related information, I asked my nephew Patrick Rothrock, who knows more about such matters than I could ever hope to. Similarly, I texted my niece Dr. Ashley Rothrock, DVM, about horses, probably less than I should have. Again, guys, if I got stuff wrong, it's on me.

Finally, I'd like to thank my encouragers. Jumping into writing a trilogy when you've never written a novel before is sheer lunacy. I quit more than once. My heartfelt gratitude to Deborah Colasanti, Kathy Lerich, and Dr. Cherri Randall for telling me the story was good and worth finishing.

About the Author

LP Rothrock is an artist and writer living in the middle of a cow pasture in east Texas. Her painting signature is either "Lea" or an unreadable loopy squiggle that starts with an "L" (she put one of those in the map of Great Hand). She's pretty sure her days as a theatre student are what gave her a flair for drama, though that was a very long time ago, and she really should stop blaming her youth.